Ancient F

By Paul H Rowney

Also by Paul H Rowney:

The Crown Post

French Creek

A Return to the 21st Century?

S.O.S. The Storm of all Storms

Praise for Book 1:
The Crown Post

Loved it!

'*An exciting look into the history and lives of the people who lived in this 500 yr old house. A good read, very well written*'.

Crown Post

'*A brilliant read and I thoroughly recommend it to anyone living in and around Bury St Edmunds or anyone with an interest in history. This book brings history to life.*'

Brilliant

'*I absolutely loved this book. It's very well written and the text flows effortlessly. I'm looking forward to the next one. Highly recommended*'.

Fascinating history

'*Simple characters being alive in a beautiful old house and it's past - ideal for anyone who ever wishes old houses could share their secrets*'.

A walk through lives lived.

'*Almost finished, please tell me you will write more about this house? please, please. I love old houses. Walking through the lives lived there was wonderful*'.

Within Its Walls

'*A fascinating tale of a house and its occupants . A home to some. A house of wickedness and evil to others. Yet, it survived to this day*'.

History As It Ought To Be

'*Well written, believable stories. Swallowed in one afternoon. Looking forward to more by this author. I highly recommend this delightful book*'.

The author has done a fantastic job of spinning history and fiction together to create an incredible read. Hope we see a sequel!'

Fascinating book for history lovers

'*A must read for anyone who loves history! Really enjoyed how the story progressed and am looking forward to the next one*'.

ANCIENT HALLWAYS

Ancient Hallways: One house's journey through history and the people who made it their home.

By Paul H Rowney.

Published by: PHR Media LLC, 197 Thompson Lane, Nashville TN 37211, USA.

For information on all my books, to order signed copies and receive advance notice (and maybe free copies!) of future books go to www.paulhrowney.com

For permissions contact: paul@phrmedia.com
ISBN: Paperback: 979-8-9869861-8-0
Cover design by Yeonwoo Baik

Thanks to:

All those who read The Crown Post, and left such kind, thoughtful and supportive reviews. Encouragement enough for me to write this sequel.

To David Addy (again) for being the source of inspiration for some of the stories in this book, courtesy of his mammoth on line history of Bury St Edmunds: The St Edmundsbury Chronicles.

To Sherry Elkins and Christopher Austin for their willingness to be characters in the book, I hope you are happy with your lives in the 17th and 18th centuries!

To, as always, my family for their help and support.

And to the (unknown) builders of the house in Whiting St for their ability to construct a home that not only has stood resolute for 450 years, but also provided such a gratifying canvas for my imagination.

Paul H Rowney
November 2024

Contents

Manchester

Birmingham

Bury St Edmunds

Bristol

London

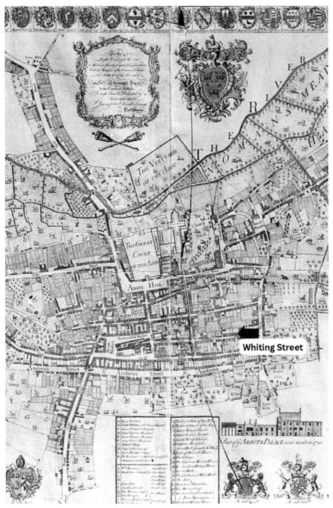

Whiting Street

Thomas Warren's map of
Bury St Edmunds in 1746

Previously in book 1,
The Crown Post:

The old house in 1485 was probably the second built on Whiting St, part of the original 'grid' designed by Abbot Anselm back in 1080. However, by the late fifteenth century, inhabited by an old lady known as Spinster Wordsworth, it was in poor repair.

Now in the dusk of her life, she cared little for the condition of her crumbling home. The spinster had lived alone, a hermit's existence, for fifty years, with her cats and one very well kept secret. She was a witch, one of extraordinary skill, and, it turned out, vindictiveness. Now as her death approached, the sweating sickness draining her life force away, she planned one deadly act of revenge. One so malevolent, so evil, its spell would last for 250 years.

Her retribution was for a life made miserable by children, and their parents, who for decades plagued her with insults, violence and contempt. The more she ignored them, the more they tormented her, making her life a misery, tortured by their endless cruelty and persecution. Her stunted figure made her easy prey for her young tormentors, who never ceased to poke fun at her disfigurement.

She read somewhere that the tree of bitterness grows stronger with age. It must be true, she concluded, for now she felt the power of her black magic like never before. An urge to complete one final display of her awesome, ungodly powers.

1

Spinster Wordsworth was a witch of unparalleled strength and knowledge; after a lifetime spent studying Satan's evil powers she was now focussed on this final task, creating a spell of immeasurable strength. In the waning years of her life, wracked with pain and seeking revenge, the spell would remain lurking, unseen, deep within the fabric of the house. A legacy that would make future generations suffer terrible pain, retribution repaid a thousand times over.

The spell, along with other hexes and runes she would conjure up, took her weeks to complete. Complex and dangerous, the foundations of it were written in cat's blood on a wooden tablet, or in a grimoire. These, along with other black magic artefacts, some of a truly detestable nature, she buried deep within the foundations of her ancient, ramshackled house.

Elsewhere the witch secretly carved the timeworn oak beams with yet more runes and symbols, further enhancing the power and longevity of the spell. As she'd hoped, ignorant of their meaning, many were re-used in the construction of the new house.

Which meant, even as her home was demolished in late 1485 to make way for a grand new house, her spell's evil influence would remain undimmed. The malignant effects of it would befall future generations of children conceived in the house.

Thus written for those who eventually would discover the wooden tablet, the spell read:

In this house where a child is born,
A deadly witch's curse was sworn.
Beware, young souls, its cruel root,

2

Their journey, a soundless one, a bitter mute.
Never to utter a spoken word,
Their voices will be forever unheard.
Others never to see or hear,
Living their lives in pain and fear.
For ten generations, this curse will last,
A payment for all the evil children past.

Chapter 1
(1666)

'The doctor says there is no cure for the twins' maladies.' Diane was crestfallen, close to tears, as she repeated the news to her husband. Their two beautiful girls, Danielle and Margaret, now six years old, were born, one with no sight and the other with no hearing. Diane had tried every doctor and apothecary's remedy since their birth to cure them, but to no avail.

Joan, Diane's elderly step-grandmother was in her usual chair close to a roaring fire in the great hall at their house in Whiting St. Despite going deaf, she somehow managed to hear Diane's tale of woe.

'I hate to say this to you again Diane, but there is something in this house that causes children born here to be without one of their senses. Remember I told you about my mother's friend, Grace? She was born here and could not speak a word. Her two daughters were equally impaired too. Grace became a successful business women_despite her problems, so you should not pander to your children's troubles too much. Raise them to make the best of their other abilities.' She added as an ominous afterthought, 'However, I would counsel you against having any more children while living here.'

Dominic put his arm around his wife's shoulder, trying, yet again, to offer consolation and convince her she was not to blame for their children's plight. He felt helpless, his efforts to dispel his poor wife's belief it was all her fault was unsuccessful. He'd long ago accepted the hand of fate God had dealt them. In contrast, his wife's stubbornness, as he saw it, led to these regular outbursts of disappointment.

'I know you want to keep trying to find a cure, but maybe Joan is right, we have to accept God's will and bring up the children as best we can with their afflictions.' He pulled her to him in a gentle embrace. 'Diane, my dear, I can tell you are weary after all this upset, why don't you lie down for a while? Remember, later today are the celebrations in town for the new King after his victory over the Roundheads. I have heard there will be much to see, including a play. If you feel well enough we should all go, it will cheer you up.'

Diane nodded, drying the tears from her eyes. 'Yes, you are right, let us all go out and put aside our worries. You are a good husband, Dominic, I don't know what I would do without you. I shall see you in an hour or two.' She pecked him on the cheek, his beard tickling her chin, a sensation that never failed to pleasure her.

Relieved his wife was getting over her moment of despair, he sat down opposite Joan, who'd dozed off, the heat of the fire having a soothing effect on her ageing, aching body. He poured himself a tankard of ale and stretched his legs out, luxuriating in the warmth from the burning logs in the huge inglenook fireplace.

Despite his young children's problems, Dominic was optimistic for the future. With the depressing yolk of the puritanical Cromwell lifted from the populace, money was now flowing again among the rich. As a builder, the rush of new building and renovations across the town was proving good for his business.

After the Civil War lands were hastily redistributed by the King to his supporters and wrenched from the unwilling grasp of those who had profited under Cromwell. Upon them, the newly minted gentry wanted to create grand homes, each one better than their neighbour's. The future looked bright for his business and not before time, he thought. They had spent, admittedly with help from Joan, large sums buying, renovating and improving their house over the last six years. Now he needed to start generating a more substantial income for his growing family and allow him to maintain one of the largest homes in the street. He knew that many of his neighbours regarded the presence of a 'lowly builder' not wholly appropriate for Whiting St. But Dominic was determined to move up the social ladder with ambitions to become a property developer and put the naysayers' snobbish comments to rest.

He was proud of the improvements they had made to the house. New oak flooring, glass in all the 'sash' windows, ones that now slid up and down to open. A new tiled roof after the old one caught fire, nearly destroying the house just after they moved in. New rugs and wall hangings were everywhere, giving a warm cosy feeling to the large house. Now almost 200 years old, he believed it was in good enough condition to last another 200. As he pointed out to visitors, 'They don't build them like this anymore, just look at the size of those beams, and how close they are together. The man who built this was wealthy and wanted everyone to know it. Nowadays the beams are half the size, it's just too expensive to build them like they did years ago.'

Twin gabled with a great hall joining the two, the house was big enough for the seven of them, and two maidservants who helped with the children, cooking and housework. Each gable had two large downstairs rooms, the southern one for cooking and household stores. Upstairs were the servants' quarters and storage. In the north wing were the private rooms for his family, and the second floor of the great hall, kept warm by the huge fireplace's chimney breast, were Joan's own quarters.

It was a fine, but cool, September afternoon when the family, minus Joan, who could no longer walk any distance, left the house to make their way to Angel Hill, opposite the gates of the old abbey. The traditional site of all the big celebrations in the town.

The reason for the town's celebrations: King Charles II's recent ascendancy to the throne had been widely welcomed by most of the country. Past grievances between Royalists and Roundheads – and the cause of the Civil War – were, in the main, forgotten. Helped by His Majesty graciously allowing Catholics to continue practising their religion, albeit in private. However, this move only partially solved the longstanding problem of how and where the country's various religions should be allowed to worship. Despite every effort it continued to vex the King and his government. In reality, the Civil War solved none of these questions, but tragically saw 200,000 people lose their lives because of them. Today, though, these lofty problems troubled few of the populace. After years of depressing Puritanism (including the banning of Christmas) people were out to enjoy their newfound freedom.

The fair took up the whole of the large sloping area of Angel Hill which ran down to the old, but still intact gates of the abbey, once one of the biggest and richest in England. The Dissolution ordered by Henry VIII in 1536 saw the magnificent abbey stripped of its immense riches, and its extensive buildings ransacked by the local people, taking their revenge for centuries of excessive taxes by the Catholic abbey, and control over every aspect of their lives. Within a few years, in places, nothing but stumps remained of the huge structure. Cleverly, though, some people had built homes into parts of the remaining walls that once stood thirty feet high and several feet deep.

Angel Hill was packed with stalls selling food, trinkets and household knick-knacks. Entertainers were everywhere, including one with a large brown bear who was making a valiant, or was it reluctant, attempt to dance while his master played a tune on his flute. The poor cumbersome beast seemed bemused by all the people and noise. For a few minutes the two older boys, Matthew and Oliver, stood amazed at seeing such a dangerous animal close up, and seemingly harmless. They stood mouths agape as the bear hopped gamely from one leg to the next in an attempt to dance. Now aged eleven, they were soon bored and wanted to roam the fair on their own. They ran ahead mingling with the crowds, darting from one stallholder to the next, occasionally running back and begging their parents for money to spend. Dominic gave them each a few farthings and some of the tokens that local businesses had minted as a form of coinage due to so little official coinage being in circulation. Dominic added the wasted advice to his impatient sons to "spend it wisely", before they rushed off into the melee of revellers. They agreed to meet up in front of the stage where a play was due to start later in the afternoon.

Suddenly above the commotion of the crowd a bell rang and the town crier stood on the stage where the play would take place later that day. He bellowed for everyone's attention. Those within hearing distance obligingly stopped talking and looked up expectantly. Now with everyone listening, he pretentiously unrolled a length of parchment and read its contents.

Composing himself, at the top of his voice he declared, 'Hear ye, hear ye, the people of Bury St Edmunds, on behalf of His Majesty King Charles II, I bring sad news from our capital, London.' He paused dramatically to heighten the expectation.

'With a heavy heart the King wishes it known that the capital suffered an egregious, ferocious and devastating fire during the first week of September. Such conflagration destroyed over the course of four days some 13,200 houses and 87 churches, including the magnificent St Paul's Cathedral. Be it known the King was unharmed and his palaces were not affected by the fire.....'

A gasp went up from the large crowd on hearing such terrible news. Many heard stories from their parents of the great fire that caused extensive damage to Bury in 1606, but this was nothing compared to the scale of the devastation in London.

The town crier went on to detail the extent of the damage and the 'magnificent contribution' the King was making to help those whose homes and businesses had been destroyed.

Turning away from the litany of bad news, Diane clutched Dominic's arm. 'Oh, those poor people! I remember my grandmother Grace telling me about the great fire in Bury. Maud's house was burnt down and she came to stay with our family. It is how they met...and thereafter never separated. I suppose good can come from bad occasionally,' she added thoughtfully.

Dominic agreed: 'It was a fortuitous meeting indeed. They had a long and happy life together! Anyway, let not this sad news about London ruin our day. It is good to know the King is helping those poor unfortunate people.' As an afterthought he said, 'Maybe one day we should go there?' Coaches leave from Bury every two days and the trip takes three, so I'm told. I would love to see such a big city.'

Diane's eyes lit up at the prospect of visiting London. 'Oh, yes please, Dominic, that would be such an adventure. Let us find out what it costs and maybe plan a trip there next year? We can save up enough, I'm sure.'

Dominic paused for a moment; it would be a lot of money, but then again business was picking up. If they didn't take a trip soon, then maybe they'd never get the chance. 'Yes, my dear, I agree with you. It would be an adventure. I will make some enquiries with the coach company and find out what it costs.'

Bubbling with excitement, they continued to walk around the fair, their two daughters never leaving their sides. Danielle, who could not see, was anxiously clutching the hand of her sister Margaret who was gazing in awe at the sights, which sadly she could not explain to her sister. She had yet to master the art of lip reading and speech, though she could utter the occasional word. Danielle, her head moving from side to side as a multitude of strange sounds reached her ears, continually asked her parents what they were, which animals were making them, in an effort to understand the confusing dark world around her.

The fair was an invasion of all the senses as musicians, jugglers, acrobats and entertainers strolled noisily through the crowds shouting for attention, all seeking pennies from anyone who would stop to watch them. Stalls offered every kind of mouth-watering hot and cold food, drink and treats. Dominic stopped and bought some small rabbit pies for the family, and they happily munched on them as they walked back towards the small stage set up at the top of Angel Hill, allowing the audience a clearer view of the actors. Under Cromwell's puritanical rule, all plays were banned, so the chance to see one was a novel form of entertainment to many townsfolk.

'What are we going to see?' asked a breathless Matthew as he and his brother came rushing up to meet them as planned. 'Will it be funny? I never seen one of these plays before.' Dominic read from a poster at the side of the stage. 'Well, apparently it is a comedy called *The Comical Revenge* by someone called George Etherege. Oh, and look! A woman is actually one of the actresses!' he exclaimed. 'That is different. How things are changing with our new King in charge. Normally men played all the roles. This indeed should be fun, children!'

It was, but only for a short while.

Unfortunately, Dominic and Diane only saw the first act. The boys soon grew tired and restless at sitting still for so long. Danielle and Margaret too became bored as they failed to understand what was going on. Accepting the inevitable, young children and watching plays did not mix, they decided to go home. Pushing their way through the crowd towards Churchgate St, they turned past the Norman Tower, one of the original gates to the abbey. Dominic pointed across St Mary's churchyard. 'Look! They are building houses into the remains of the old abbey walls. I heard told as much, I didn't know they had started doing so. I must come here tomorrow and offer my services, it looks like a large project. Who would have thought after all this time they would be put to such use?'

Diane and the children were too tired to care about Dominic's architectural discovery, and trudged up Churchgate St, thence into Whiting St and home. The street was lined with some of the biggest houses in the old grid layout. It was an area of wealth and prestige. Not for the first time, Diane inwardly glowed with pride that they could afford to live there.

Over the ensuing months Dominic's business expanded to such a size he soon employed some fifty artisans. They included experts in masonry, carpentry and now glazing, as more people put glass into their new sash windows. More recently he'd taken on several furniture makers to keep up with the fashion for upholstered chairs, chests of drawers and bookcases, plus an expert in the costly process called veneering. Such expensive tastes were all the rage with the wealthy homeowners of Bury.

By the summer of 1667, business was so profitable that Dominic put a man called James Hardingly in charge of the workers and their ever-increasing number of building projects. He needed a rest, a break from the day to day stress of running the business. This finally allowed him some free time, and without telling Diane he bought coach tickets for their long-planned trip to London. They were expensive, at £2 per person, plus the cost of overnight stays in the coaching inns along the way. But no matter, thought Dominic, *this is a once in a lifetime trip.* The children were old enough to be left with their reliable housekeeper, Jane, who ran the household with an unyielding strictness. They would be gone for a fortnight.

Neither Dominic nor Diane had travelled further than her sister's house in Lawshall. London was truly another world, one they couldn't wait to explore. They were beside themselves with excitement as they handed their small trunks to the coach driver. Before they boarded, Dominic pulled out a small box from his pocket and gave it to Diane. 'A small thank you for being such a wonderful wife and mother,' he said, smiling. Diane carefully unwrapped it to reveal a beautiful gold bracelet with a heart carved with the words: *'A present to remind you of this special day, July 5th 1667. All my love Dominic.'*

'Oh, Dominic, it is so beautiful, thank you, I will treasure it for all time,' said Diane as she put it around her slim wrist. She reached up and kissed him full on the lips, causing him to blush with embarrassment. They boarded the coach, squeezing in next to the three other travellers, waved goodbye to the children and were soon bumping along the road to Newmarket. Their route would take them onwards to Baldock and then south on the old Roman road to London. A trip of three days if the weather was good. For the rest of the day Diane continually looked at her bracelet in disbelief; it must have been so expensive, she thought, and it was a wonderful start to their trip. Entranced, she gently polished it with her glove as if to make it shine even brighter.

Dominic and Diane were sitting next to a dandily dressed man in his twenties, who seemed to take a fancy to the young girl sitting opposite them, accompanied by an older woman. The early part of the journey was conducted in silence as everyone seemed happy to just watch the Suffolk countryside go sliding by. Fields were one minute swathes of dense golden yellow as the wheat, barley and oats stood waiting to be harvested. They were interspersed by lush green pastures where sheep and cattle peacefully grazed, some raising their heads as the noise of the rattling coach and the snorting horses caught their attention. Dominic felt at ease with the world. Despite the recent terrible events of the Civil War, the never-ending cycle of farming life continued, undisturbed, uninterrupted by the squabbling of their political masters. It was a relaxing, reassuring sight. He started to doze off.

The silence was eventually broken when Diane asked the older woman where she and her daughter were heading.

'She's my granddaughter,' the woman corrected Diane. 'We are attending a wedding at Hatfield House; the Earl of Salisbury's daughter is getting married there. We are his cousins, and feel so honoured to have been invited,' she explained. 'You never know, we might find some eligible bachelors for Genevieve!'

The young girl blushed. 'Grandmother! Please, I am only sixteen, I do not want to be married off quite yet.'

Diane smiled, 'Maybe that is a little too young to be thinking of marriage, though we wed when I was only eighteen. Now, ten years later, we are off on our first trip to London. Indeed, our first trip anywhere!'

The ice broken, conversation flowed freely as they rumbled their way slowly towards Newmarket. The young man, who introduced himself as Sir Ian Hardcastle, quickly attempted to impress everyone with his aristocratic airs and graces, though Dominic doubted he owned any title worth having, except pretender. Nevertheless, the amiable banter made the journey pass quickly.

It was hot and uncomfortable for the first two days of the journey. The road was no more than a dirt track. The coach bumped and jarred the passengers, so by the end of each day they were bruised and exhausted. Either side of Newmarket, they were stopped to pay a toll for permission to use what the man called a turnpike.

The coach driver explained this was a new way of raising money to pay for the upkeep of the roads. 'Though they show little improvement,' he grumbled, as they continued on their uncomfortable way.

Towards the end of the second day as they approached Baldock, the heavens opened, turning the road into an impassable quagmire. The four horses, despite every encouragement from the coachmen, were unable to move the bogged-down carriage from the bottom of a hill, just a frustrating mile from the town. Desperate to extricate the carriage he ordered the passengers out to lighten the load – and then to push as best they could. It was getting darker, and the rain was slicing through their clothing. Everyone was miserable, cold and getting dispirited as they made little progress in pushing the carriage out of the mud.

'Tis a hopeless cause,' moaned Sir Ian. 'Just look at my clothes...they are—'

Suddenly, out from the forest burst three men on horseback. They galloped out of the gloom like avenging angels, the horses spraying mud and water in their wake. Slithering to a stop just feet from the travellers, without saying a word they pulled out their muskets and brandished them at the passengers. Petrified, as one they all fell back against the carriage. Dominic clutched Diane tightly to his side, shielding her from the attackers.

'Stuck in the mud are we? Such a shame. Well, your misfortune is good news for us. Let us lighten your load a little!' sneered the one who appeared to be the leader of the gang. He signalled the other men to dismount. They approached the huddled group waving their muskets inches from their faces.

'Let's not be stupid here, ladies and gentlemen, just hand over your valuables and money and we'll be on our way.' The leader had a kerchief around the lower half of his face and the words came out muffled, but the message was clear.

'You'll hang for this you...you filthy brigands!' blustered Sir Ian, the fear in his eyes betraying his blowhard words. 'My father is—'

'...Your father is a dolthead for producing such a pompous ass of a son. I care not who he is, only about the valuables you have on your person. Bert, shut him up.'

Before the young man could protest further, one of the highwaymen smashed the handle of his musket into his face, and he crumpled into the mud. Blood poured from his nose.

Bravely, one of the coachmen, thinking this distraction was to his favour, reached for a pistol hidden under his seat. Before he could lay a hand on it, the highwayman on the horse levelled his musket and fired. The shot blew open the back of his head.

Diane and the two other women all screamed, as the dead man slid face first into the mud. His blood oozed from his wound mixing with the rain-soaked earth.

The leader showed no reaction to killing the coachman, instead he calmly repeated his demand. 'Now, there's a lesson for you. Do something stupid and you will die. Now hand over your valuables. Quickly, my patience is being tried.'

The robbers dragged the trunks off the coach and forced them open, to discover very little of value. They left the contents strewn across the road, ruined in the mud. Their attention now turned to the petrified travellers. They demanded everyone hand over their money and jewellery. One quickly spotted Diane's precious gold bracelet and tried to wrench it off her wrist. She pulled back and instinctively slapped him in the face. Enraged he drew his dagger and plunged it into her chest. She slumped down, grabbing Dominic for support. Her eyes looked up into his before she closed them and her life ebbed away.

'No! No! It cannot be. Diane. Diane!' Dominic clutched his wife's dying body to his as the rain lashed down on them, a look of utter despair on his face.

He gently laid her onto the sodden ground, then uncontrollable anger welled up inside him. He screamed, 'You bastard, you killed my wife, you will pay for this!' Dominic lunged towards his wife's killer as he did so, desperately trying to reach for his own dagger. But his wet clothing hampered his movements, and before Dominic could pull the knife from its sheath and strike a blow, the thief fired his pistol at point-blank range into Dominic's chest, the force throwing him backwards, his mortally wounded body smashing into the wheel of the coach. Blood began gurgling up through his mouth caused by a massive wound to his heart. He slumped into the mud, his breathing weakened, and moments later he died, though not before reaching for his beloved wife's hand. Together in death as they had been in life.

With no alternative, the rest of the travellers were scared into submission, accepting these men had no qualms about murdering people to get what they wanted. The old woman and her granddaughter quickly acquiesced and handed over what valuables and money they had. Sir Ian, blubbering through his bloodied nose, for once lost for words, emptied his pockets and gave them his coins and gold watch. As a final insult one of the thieves ripped the bracelet off Diane's lifeless body, and stuffed it into his pocket. Within minutes the robbers fled, disappearing into the woods, leaving the survivors shivering with fear and cold. For several moments no one moved, then, speechless, they surveyed the scene of death, blood and mayhem surrounding them. Once the shock subsided, the coachman, in a whisper barely heard above the pouring rain, suggested they should immediately walk to Baldock. An hour later, still numb with trauma, they alerted the authorities of their deadly encounter, and the grim sight that would await them back at the coach.

Dominic and Diane's bodies were brought back to Bury St Edmunds, where they were buried in the graveyard next to St Mary's Church and the houses Dominic had helped build in the walls of the abbey. He would forever be close to a legacy of his work and inspiration.

Back at the house, Joan decided she and the four children could no longer stay in a home that was so much a part of Dominic and Diane's life. The memories were too painful. They should move back to Lawshall. Joan bought a house close to West Farm owned by her other daughter Jane. She lived for another two years, leaving enough money to ensure that the four children could stay with their mother's sister and not be a financial burden upon them. With Joan's inheritance, Jane and her husband, Tom, built an extension to the farmhouse and constructed a second floor, creating enough space for a family of eight to live in reasonable comfort.

Margaret and Danielle grew up and stayed living on the farm until they married two local boys. Both bore healthy and happy children. The boys, Matthew and Oliver, went back to work in their grandfather's business as soon as they left school at fourteen. After Dominic's death, Joan had sold the business at a discounted price, to the foreman James Harding, with the strict promise he would offer the boys a job, and a share in the business should they wish. Both did, and with the older man's experience and their father's innate ability buried somewhere in their genes, they grew the building company to become one of the largest in Suffolk.

When the opportunity arose, Oliver bought one of the houses his father had built into the old abbey walls, enabling him to look out over his parents' graves, while, he hoped, his father was looking down on him, happy that the business he started was still thriving.

* * * *

Still 'in residence' a century after their deaths, Maud and Grace watched events in the house from the spirit world:

'Oh, no! That cannot be possible!' Maud cried out in distress. 'My relatives murdered, their children now orphans. It is so tragic. They were a beautiful family, now torn apart by such a barbaric act. I cannot bear it, Grace. Where is our God if he allows such terrible things to happen?'

Grace held her lover's hand. They looked down on the upsetting scene as Joan explained to the children that their parents would not be coming back. 'They have gone to heaven,' she said, as if it would somehow soften the harrowing news of their parents' death.

Observing, unseen, as the family mourned the loss of Dominic and Diane, it was without doubt the most awful scene they had witnessed in their old house over the last half century.

It would not be the last.

Chapter 2
(1670)

'Yes, yes, indeed, this will do very nicely,' said Constable Francis De Vere to himself, a satisfied smile on his large ruddy-cheeked face, as he sat in front of the blazing inglenook fireplace, a tankard of wine in his massive hand. The fire was slowly thawing out his frozen feet; the cold November evening had made it an uncomfortable walk from the workhouse and House of Corrections in Moyses Hall. Though the trip had been worthwhile. He discovered two young girls that needed 'rescuing and finding of a good home' as the warden explained.

Constable De Vere was happy to be their saviour, at least that's how he saw it. Initially most girls did too, though in quick order they regretted being chosen by him to be rescued, life in the poorhouse was terrible, but a preferable alternative to his depraved ministrations.

He, of course, did not see it that way. In his new grand house it was only proper that aside from a few elderly servants he should have some young female companionship. Ones to keep him warm and amused at night. Surely the comfort of this imposing house, and his large bed, was more desirable than the cold stone floors of the poorhouse?

The two latest waifs to benefit from his dubious largesse, Mary and Janet, were orphans. That was convenient for the constable – no pesky parents to come to their aid should they complain once they were back in the poorhouse, pregnant, abused or otherwise in a state they were no longer enjoyable to him. He was assured by the warden they were both 'of marriageable age', therefore ready and capable of ministering to his needs. A small sum of money maintained the corrupt man's silence, along with the threat of gaol if he uttered a word to anyone.

The Constable ordered the elderly servants to bathe and perfume the frightened girls and give them clean clothes, but no undergarments. He was a man of simple pleasures, and this evening he would satisfy them. To his annoyance, the constable's pleasant musings and anticipation on what the night ahead would bring were interrupted by a loud banging on the front door. Grunting with annoyance, he heaved his huge, cumbersome frame up from the chair and stood to meet his unexpected visitor. One of the servants brought in a man he did not recognise. 'Master, this man says he is from the house of Sir William Crofts at Little Saxham Hall.'

With a slight bow, the man introduced himself as Edward Gardener, one of Sir William's guards.

'Sire, I apologise for the lateness of my visit. As you may know, the King is due to visit Sir William in a few days, however we have received disturbing news that there may be a plot to kill him while he stays there – or as he moves onto Euston Hall thereafter. The papists are of a dangerous disposition at this time, we fear they may be behind this plan. Sir William asks that you come to the Hall to discuss ways to protect the King during his visit. And with all speed find the plotters.'

As Constable, Francis De Vere was in charge of all law and order in the area. Though an unpaid position, it carried great influence and prestige – but with it a large responsibility to protect the citizens of the town and its visitors – none more important than the safety of the King.

The constable was well aware of the King's longstanding friendship with Sir William. His past visits to Little Saxham Hall were infamous for their debauchery, drinking and outrageous behaviour, often lasting several days. The King was so trusting of Sir William he even made him guardian of his illegitimate son, James.

Though sceptical of the claims made by Sir William's servant, with such royal connections close by, he could not ignore them. Papist plots were frequently reported to him, and so far all he achieved was arresting some low lifes for speaking ill of the King, normally after a night of drinking.

However, it could cost him more than his job, if he ignored this warning and some tragedy befell his beloved King. Trying to conceal his annoyance at being summoned so late at night, he asked in a surly voice, 'From whence did you receive news of this intended plot, may I ask, Mr Gardener?'

Still flustered from his rushed journey and the somewhat inhospitable welcome, Edward shook his head, 'I know not precisely, Constable, I am merely passing on the message from my master. He asks that you visit him immediately to discuss the matter. He wants the traitors found and arrested before the King arrives.'

Begrudgingly accepting his planned night of enjoyment with two young girls was now thwarted, he asked his servant to bring him a warm coat and send someone to get his horse. He turned to his visitor.

'Very well, Mr Gardener, you may ride ahead and tell Sir William I will be there shortly.'

Constable De Vere was a man used to getting his own way. His was neither pleasant to look at, nor to deal with. A huge man, well over six feet tall and with a waist the circumference of a coach wheel, his pock-ridden face was partially covered by an ill-kept long and straggling beard. His fearsome temper wrought terror among his other part-time constables. Criminals who crossed his path were liable to find themselves dragged off to gaol and at the end of a severe beating. Most confessed to whatever crime he claimed they committed. He ruled the town with a mixture of bribery, threats and violence. The Corporation of Bury and the other authorities turned a blind eye to his excesses, as his brutally effective methods kept the town a safe place in which to live.

He owed his elevated and influential position thanks to his sister, Denise Skinner, who managed to marry way above her station, ensnaring no other than the son of Maurice Barrow of Barningham, one of the richest men in Suffolk. A parliamentarian, he was keen to ingratiate himself into the good favour of the King and with a little chicanery had his daughter-in-law's thuggish brother made Constable, offering to pay his wages as a further act of charity to the town.

He bought the house in Whiting St, sight unseen, installing his brutish relative rent free. The only stipulation: keep the peace and protect all people and property, especially those connected to the King and any well-known Protestants. The last thing Maurice Barrow needed was the King giving his lands away to some other Royalist sympathiser.

Constable De Vere left his house as his clock struck midnight and mounted his enormous shire horse – needed to carry his bulk swiftly and in some comfort. The streets were dark and deserted. Little Saxham was only a few miles to the west of Bury, and within the hour he was being shown into the impressive great hall, where he was presented to Sir William and a cluster of other advisors: the castle chaplain, the steward and the marshall, the man personally responsible for His Lordship's safety. A gracious-looking lady seated by the fire he assumed was Sir William's wife, Elizabeth.

He accepted the offer of wine, then, standing at one end of a huge oak dining table, asked for all the information they knew about this alleged papist plot. A tall, grey-haired man, probably in his forties, guessed Francis, introduced himself as Martin, the marshall of the establishment.

'Thank you for coming here at such an inhospitable hour, Constable. To answer your question: We have heard from several sources that a dissenter by the name of John Salkeld might be their ringleader. He has been in and out of prison for his seditious words many times. He is the former rector of Worlington, though now has fallen on hard times because of his poor choices. We believe he has a group of ten or more anti-Royalists and papists following him.'

'And how do you come by such information?' asked the constable.

Martin hesitated before replying, 'We...we have a spy in their midst, constable. I would rather not reveal his name at this time.

But I can vouch for his integrity and truthfulness.'

'Do you know where they congregate to plan such treasonous activities?'

'Wisely, they meet at different places, sometimes the former reverend's home, other times in local inns. My agent informs me a final meeting will be taking place tomorrow night at the Queens Arms in Risbygate St.'

The constable was beginning to feel nervous. If what he was hearing was true, then a huge responsibility had been dropped on his shoulders. Now he knew of such a plan, if it came to fruition, and the King was injured, let alone killed, he would be joining an unwelcoming party in the Bury gaol. He shivered at the thought of what the prisoners might do to him.

'Thank you, sir, that is most useful information. Do we know whether the attack is to take place here, or before the King's visit while he is travelling? Or even when he travels on after his stay here?'

Sir William finally decided to join the conversation. 'Therein lies the problem, Constable. The King travels with many soldiers, so we believe it is unlikely he will be attacked while travelling. Which leads us to assume they will try something by stealth while he is here. The matter is made complicated as we take on many extra staff to cope with our visitor's entourage and their needs. Some of which we know, others not. We must find these usurpers with all possible haste. I can send a message to the King at his home in Newmarket, asking him to delay his arrival by a day to accommodate this.'

Constable De Vere didn't doubt his ability – if he could find them – to arrest these men and persuade them to reveal their plans. His methods were abominable, but effective. He felt no qualms about torturing prisoners, guilty or innocent, to wrench the truth from them. And if it helped curry favour with the King, then so much the better.

'My lord, your plan makes excellent sense. I will take prisoner all those at the meeting and within twelve hours provide you with details on their evil intentions against our King. You shall be hearing from me shortly.'

He finished off his wine, wiped his beard with a dirty sleeve, gave a modest bow and left the house.

Sir William turned to Martin, a look of distaste on his face. 'What a most unpleasant-looking man. I don't fully trust him.'

Elizabeth walked over to her husband. 'William, do you really believe someone will try and murder the King? In our household? It would be a bold scheme, with a high chance of the culprit being caught, surely? Why would they risk it?'

'Elizabeth, the King has done his best to treat the Catholics and other religious groups fairly, but many still feel aggrieved, and still support Cromwell. These poor misguided people are ripe for revolution when exhorted to by the likes of this silver-tongued priest. To many, losing their life while taking the King's would make them a martyr. They may number only a few souls, but they are dangerous. We must be on our guard. I hope that ruffian constable will do his job and we all will sleep soundly while the King is our guest.'

'I hope so too, William. But I don't like or have confidence in that man to do his job properly.'

"Neither do I, Elizabeth, neither do I, but we must put our faith in him, however much we dislike him. Though I will make sure we are vigilant whilst the King stays here. It would be a travesty beyond repair if anything happened to him while staying here.'

Within a day, their hopes were dashed and the King was in mortal danger.

Chapter 3

The constable and his three deputies weren't happy. They'd been waiting in the freezing night air for three hours across the street from the Queens Arms. Every few minutes the constable would send in one of his men to see if the papist group were inside. He could not go in personally; well recognised as he was in the town, his appearance would unsettle the group and probably lead to them abandoning their meeting. However, after most of the evening had passed with no sign of anything suspicious occurring, Constable De Vere, miserable, cold and angry at yet another evening away from more pleasant pastimes, decided it was all a waste of time.

From the second storey of the inn, the former reverend, John Salkeld, looked across the street and saw the constable and his men lying in wait and smiled to himself. They had done a poor job at concealing themselves. They would have to do better if they wished to capture him. John, after numerous arrests and time in gaol, was a very cautious man. He trusted no one, including those in the group planning to kill the King. Forever suspicious, continually looking over his shoulder, he was taking extra precautions for this final meeting. He now knew they had a traitor in their midst. One new member, a man with a lot of questions, indeed too many questions, aroused his distrust. He set a trap, telling him the meeting would be at the Masons Arms. The rest of his group was sent to another inn close to Saxham Hall. That traitor now sat downstairs wondering at the strange turn of events that saw him alone, when there should be six other conspirators there to finalise plans to kill the King.

In the meantime the sight of the hated constable freezing outside to no good purpose was one Reverend Salkeld enjoyed, it gave him great pleasure to see the man suffer. He was an insufferable bully and sadist, and tonight he was getting some just desserts. With midnight approaching, he saw them leave, then he too, left the Queens Arms riding to the inn near Little Saxham Hall for a final briefing with his men. Leaving a perplexed, and by now quite drunk, spy wondering how to explain his failed mission to His Lordship.

The constable, his hands and feet now frozen, told his men to go home, and he would ride out to Little Saxham Hall explaining to Sir William no such papist meeting took place at the local inn When he arrived at the Hall, even at this late hour, there was still a bustle of activity as people unloaded food, drink and supplies for the King and his retinue, now due to arrive at noon the following day. A large, bossy lady was ordering the delivery men and servants around, shouting at them where to take the boxes and to 'handle them gently; if you damage anything, I'll cut your balls off.' He guessed she must be the steward, the person who ran the household behind the scenes. The constable rode up and waited for her to pause her never-ending stream of instructions so he could gain her attention. Finally, taking a breath, she looked up, irritated at the interruption.

'Yes, sir, how can I help? Make it brief, I am busy here, as you can see.'

Not used to being spoken to with such disrespect, he thought for a moment to try and assert his authority, then decided against it. He was in no doubt she was a force to be reckoned with at the Hall, so he ignored her fearsome look and rude tone of voice. Doffing his hat he asked for Martin, His Lordship's marshall, 'It is a matter of the utmost urgency, ma'am. I am Constable De Vere, I was here yesterday. He will want to see me. Please act with haste.'

She looked up at this large, ill-dressed man on his enormous horse. He was an unpleasant fellow, in no way pleasing to the eye. She wasn't intimidated by his position or attitude but, nevertheless, thought him probably not one to trifle with. Saying nothing in reply, she grabbed a servant as he ran past, his arms full of dead pheasants. 'Jamie, go tell Mr Martin that he has a visitor, a constable. Be quick about it.'

The boy scurried off. She told the constable that he should wait by the moat's drawbridge, so he wouldn't be in her way. With that she dismissed him and continued shouting orders to her army of tired workers. 'It all must be ready for the King's visit. I will brook no tardiness or sloppiness; make sure everything is stored properly otherwise there will be hell to pay,' she warned them all, as if they needed reminding.

Becoming increasingly angry, the constable kicked his heels for nearly an hour before the marshall appeared. He ordered him inside, and without offering any refreshment asked for the latest news.

Embarrassed, the constable admitted he had nothing to report. The meeting at the inn never took place, and he had no knowledge of the conspirators' current whereabouts.

The marshall gave him a withering look. 'Well, why are you here? Get out and start a search for these killers. That's your job, isn't it? Keeping law and order? My master is well acquainted with your mentor, Mr Barrow. A word in his ear of your failure to protect the King and this household will find you dismissed from your position, and without a way to earn a living. I will make sure of it. Now go, and don't come back until you have news of their capture.'

The constable stood up, enraged that anyone should talk to him like this. But he bit his tongue, aware the influence Sir William had was far greater than his. He stood up to leave. 'I understand, sir, I will gather my forces and start a search for these men. I will do my best to find them.'

As he reached the door, the marshall shouted after him: 'Your best better be good enough, sir. Need I remind you, failure to protect the King is a hanging offence.'

'Fuck you, son of a whore,' muttered the constable as he strode out of the room, resisting the temptation to slam the door. Furious, he kicked his horse into a canter and headed back into Bury. The dawn light was creeping over the rooftops from the east, casting an eerie red glow, and a hundred chimneys coughed smoke into the still morning air as the town shook off the night and started another day. For the unsuspecting people of the town it was just another one of work and drudgery. For him it was a day when he would either end up a hero, or fearing for his life.

Within the hour he was back at home, having roused and collected six men on the way. Still seething from his treatment by the marshall he barked orders at them to find more help and then as the town woke up go to every inn and tavern asking the whereabouts of John Salkeld. He decided to offer a reward of £5 for information leading to his capture – a sum he couldn't afford but was sure the King or Sir William would offer for a successful outcome. It was equivalent to six months' wages for a working man. He felt sure it would loosen some tongues.

But it was too late. The wily John Salkeld was one step ahead of the arrogant and dull-witted constable. His men were already in place at Little Saxham Hall, disguised among the army of hastily hired helpers to cope with the King's visit. Wisely, he departed to Newmarket, well away from any repercussions. He told his followers at their final meeting that 'God and the Pope are on our side: that of righteousness and justice. The Royalists, this King, have abused their powers in God's eyes, and those of the poor people of this country. Now all of you, take and prepare your supplies of hemlock and deadly nightshade, it is a potion easy to mix in drinks or food. Let us put an end to this tyranny and reunite this country with the Church of Rome!'

With John Salkeld's exhortation ringing in their ears the men, fired up, ready for revenge, left for Little Saxham Hall. Poor, easily led, each in the past had been persecuted for their Catholic faith. They fervently believed themselves on a religious crusade. Few had much to lose if caught, and none was under any illusion of their fate if they fell into the hands of the barbaric constable. Their belief overcame fear, and their faith spurred them forward on an uncertain and dangerous mission.

The King arrived the following day in the early afternoon, with a retinue of over forty knights and servants. The monarch was in a celebratory mood, looking forward to a few (more) days of entertainment at someone else's expense. King Charles was not handsome by any means; a long face, large nose and a complexion already showing signs of his dissolute life, he'd made it his ambition to enjoy himself to the fullest, and it was at times all too obvious. He was still relieved and confident from signing the <u>Treaty of Dover</u> in May of that year, making England and

32

France join as allies in an offensive alliance against the Dutch. It was a masterstroke of diplomacy that secured his borders and his position as monarch. What he kept secret from even his closest allies and everyone at Court was a promise made to King Louis XIV that he would convert to <u>Roman Catholicism</u>. Something he would wait until his deathbed to fulfil.

As he dismounted, Charles embraced his long time friend.

'You are looking well, my friend. It is good to be back to a place I regard as my second home. Your hospitality is always abundant and of the highest quality. I am sure our stay here will live up to our expectations.' Sir William bowed, accepting the compliment. Happy to bask in His Majesty's praise.

Turning to his bastard son, James, the King exclaimed, 'My boy, you are turning into a handsome, strong man. We must find you a worthy wife! Let's see who we can find fit for the son of a King. But before we do that – I am parched from the journey, let us go inside and sample some of Sir William's excellent wine.'

Among the King's retinue were two lowly servants whose job as food tasters and cupbearers was to sample anything the king would eat or drink. Indeed, they frequently helped prepare food to prevent anyone poisoning the monarch, though in Sir William's house his own cooks would do that job. This worked well at formal dinners, but as the evening progressed and became a bawdy, drunken orgy, with drink being consumed in copious quantities, it was difficult to monitor everything the King imbibed. And that was what the anti-Royalist assassins were hoping to take advantage of. As the evening descended into chaos, the assassins saw their chances of success improve.

They planned two ways to poison the King. One man would use berries of deadly nightshade to secrete among the fruits laid out for the King and his guests to snack upon prior to the main dinner. Another made a potion from hemlock root, keeping it in a small vial hidden in his pocket, ready for a few drops to be mixed into the wine. They cared not who else might be poisoned as long as the King was amongst them.

The great room at Little Saxham Hall was one of the largest in Suffolk – as befitted a man of Sir William's wealth. The magnificent arched ceiling soared thirty feet above the large tables at which sat some 100 guests. The huge oak beams held twenty enormous round chandeliers, each sprouting fifty candles, providing a warm glow across the whole room. On each wall fireplaces that a horse and cart could fit in blazed, constantly fed with wood by the servants. As a result, the atmosphere was hot and smoky; even with the windows open the room was sweltering with a haze of smoke hovering across the room.

The noise level was already at such a pitch that people had to shout to hear each other across the table. Musicians played at one end of the hall, though those at the other would fail to hear their efforts. Jugglers and magicians wandered between the tables entertaining the increasingly inebriated diners. The poor serving girls ran a gauntlet of wandering hands and obscene propositions as the men's libido rose with the amount of alcohol they drank. Some would accept the offers, in return for a few shillings to top up their paltry earnings for the evening.

Sir William spared no money to ensure the merrymaking reached excess for all his guests. He wanted the King to have a day to remember (If he remembered anything after the amount he normally drank). However, he remained vigilant, aware that if anything was to happen to the king, he would be held responsible.

As his guest descended into an evening of dissipation, he remained sober and wary.

In the kitchens the preparations had been in full swing since sunrise. Betsy, the steward, was still barking orders to ensure everything ran smoothly. Catering for this number of people was a mammoth operation. The main meal would be served in mid-afternoon. The feast was of the highest quality with a large choice of dishes across three courses. The first consisted of meat dishes, including locally reared beef, plus chicken, swan and venison all caught on Sir William's estate. The second course of fish included eel and trout. If that wasn't enough the third was made up of sweets, cakes, comfits, cheeses and fruits, the latter where some of the lethal deadly nightshade berries would be hidden.

The drink flowed freely; homemade beer, cider, and wine were all on offer in copious quantities. Wine, especially sack white wine, was imported by Sir William in large vats, and stored in his vast underground cellars. By mid-evening many revellers were either sleeping off the effects of the strong alcohol, or cavorting in private rooms with the servant girls, or any other female company that was willing to participate. In the King's case, despite consuming a large amount of drink, he remained sober enough to expound on the merits of the new treaty with France.

One of the poisoners noticed the King had eaten a few of the deadly nightshade berries, but so far showed no ill effects. The other had put drops of hemlock in the flagons of beer, however to his horror the King seemed to be drinking only wine. His vial of poison was almost empty, and he was confused as to how to get the remaining drops into the King's goblet without being seen. Suddenly two of the guests started to vomit and then collapse to the floor, holding their stomachs, crying out in pain. Sir William immediately ordered one of the servants to find the doctor he always kept on hand during Royal visits.

Minutes later the doctor arrived, a harried elderly gentleman, dressed in black and carrying a case of medicines, herbs and potions. Deadly nightshade poisoning was not unusual; many people were still unaware of its appearance and the berries could look very inviting to eat. He quickly diagnosed it as a possible cause of the illness. The only cure was to ingest charcoal, of which he had a small jar in his case. By now several more guests were showing similar signs of illness. He quickly dispensed it to everyone, telling them to try and keep it down for it to be effective. Suspicion immediately fell upon the bowls of fruit on the dining table. A quick investigation revealed some still uneaten deadly berries.

Sir William was furious; where were the King's tasters? He demanded they be found and brought before him. The King, suddenly very sober, admitted he had taken a few of the deadly berries himself.

The doctor asked, 'Did you, your majesty, chew them or just swallow them, can you remember?"

The King looked a little nonplussed at the question. He thought for a moment, his eyes still a little glazed from too much drink, "Now you ask, Doctor, I may have chewed on one, found it somewhat bitter and just swallowed the rest with some wine? Why?'

The doctor hesitated; a wrong diagnosis could be lethal – for both of them. 'I have heard it said by other doctors that the berries can pass without harm, through your, er, system and, er...emerge...' he stuttered in embarrassment.

The King laughed, "You mean, Doctor, they will come out whole when I have a shit!?'

"Precisely, Your Majesty, precisely. However I would still ask you to take some charcoal to ensure your good health.'

Everyone breathed a temporary sigh of relief. Sir William ordered all food and drink be thrown out and disposed of in such a way that no human or animal could eat it. He ordered the drawbridge raised so no one could leave. A few minutes earlier the atmosphere was one of ribaldry and bawdy behaviour. Now, it was quiet except for the poor souls still retching in the corner of the hall. An assassin was in their midst and he must be found.

Sir William dispatched the doctor with some servants to find the rest of the party, check on their wellbeing and report back. In particular they must find the King's son to ascertain he was in good health. The group scurried off. The remaining revellers, shocked at events, started sobering up as the shock hit them – they, too, could have been poisoned. They wandered off to the corners of the great hall, or by the large fire and made themselves comfortable, hoping none would succumb to the wretched effects of tarnished food or drink. Sleep did not come easily for most.

With the King seemingly unaffected by the poison and, indeed, unfazed by the assassination attempt, then came the question, who was responsible? The two terrified tasters were hustled into the room.

They claimed to have tasted all the food being cooked in the kitchen, and the wine, cider and beer, too. And were obviously suffering no ill effects. One tried to defend himself by saying there were so many cooks and servants carrying food and drink up to the great hall that it was difficult to taste everything that was served. Indeed, they claimed, some guests arrived with their own drink. Which may have been left on the tables. These were reasonable arguments, but in the heated atmosphere where recriminations were already flying, it was to no avail.

Martin, the marshall, suggested he take them down to the cellars to have a 'private word with them.' The King shook his head; surprisingly he was in an expansive state of mind. 'I believe these men are guilty of failing to do their duty. No more. If they had wished to poison me they could have done it at any time. But they must be punished.' He paused while he considered the appropriate course of action. 'Twenty lashes each and then dismiss them from my court. Take them away. I no longer wish to have them in my sight.'

He turned to Sir William, summary justice having been dispensed. 'Now, Sir William, I believe the culprits are probably within your staff, and my guess would be those who you hired for the purpose of our visit.'

He reluctantly nodded his agreement. Thank the Lord the King did not believe him capable of such an act, it would be a terrible end to such a longstanding friendship. He would make amends by finding the men quickly and meting out his own brand of justice. He ordered the marshal to summon the guards and have them round up every worker and servant not in the regular employ of the Hall so they could be questioned. He was embarrassed that this incident occurred while the King was in his home and furious that assassins had been allowed to get so close to murdering the King, and harming his guests. He vowed to wreak a painful revenge on John Salkeld and any of his followers.

Before he could do so, worse news arrived. The doctor sent a servant back with the news that two guests were dead, and several more were in poor health. Thankfully James Scott, the King's son, was fine, though not happy at being interrupted enjoying himself with two of the maidservants.

The next few hours were a frenzy of activity as Martin arranged for all the recently hired servants to be taken down into the cellars and secured there to await his plans for them. In the meantime one more guest died and another ten became ill, though, with the doctor's help, seemed unlikely to die. The elderly physician was initially confused why some patients responded to the charcoal cure, and others had not. He then surmised another poison was being used, one which he was unable to stop causing death. The only one he knew of that was widely available was hemlock, for which there was no cure. But hemlock could only be dispensed as a poisonous liquid, which the perpetrator would surely have thrown away by now. Then the doctor remembered one way to establish if someone had been in contact with the deadly substance. He ran up to the great hall, and whispered his advice into Sir William's ear.

By early morning the interrogation of the people in the cellar started. There were fifteen of them, six women and nine men. Armed with the doctor's advice, Sir William marched into the cellars to find Martin already there with the hall's rat catcher, called Will, a small, stooped man of uncertain age, in filthy clothes, still a little confused when told of his role in these proceedings.

Sir William stood before the group, taut with anger. 'A terrible tragedy has befallen this house today. Many have been poisoned, some have died. Thankfully His Majesty is well and unaffected by the efforts of people who came here to harm him. I believe one or more of you in this room are responsible for these foul deeds. If you know who they are, it will bode you well to come forward and tell me. I offer a reward of two gold sovereigns to the person revealing the traitors within our midst. Anyone caught lying will be severely punished.'

Most of the women were crying, the men were scared and nervous that someone would name them in order to save themselves. Sir William let his threat hang in the air for a few moments. No one came forward, all kept their eyes to the ground, not wanting to attract attention.

Sir William nodded at Martin to proceed.

He ordered each one to step forward. Then like a hunting dog he asked Will the rat catcher to walk around them, closely smelling their bodies and clothing. Now he understood what was expected of him. To his surprise he had been told the smell of hemlock was the same as that of mice piss, one he was all too familiar with. Sniffing like a bloodhound he circled the bemused men and women one by one. As soon as he came across that odour on someone he was to point the person out.

After a few minutes a young man, wild-eyed with fear, and trembling, stood before Sir William as Will finished performing his weird ritual. 'It's him, you can smell it, the stink of mice piss and shit, the smell I live with every day.' Immediately the man fell to his knees, clinging onto His Lordship's leg, sobbing, grovelling, wailing in fear, 'I was made to do it, my lord. The reverend said I would rot in hell if I didn't perform his orders to kill the King. Please, I beg of you, show me mercy. I didn't mean to kill anyone.' For a few seconds the marshall and Sir

William gazed down almost in pity at the pathetic soul now squirming, prostrate on the ground.

'I will show you more mercy than you showed your victims, by ensuring you hang quickly, without pain. You are a traitor and a murderer for which hanging is too good a punishment. You should be hung, drawn and quartered.' On hearing this the young man's body went into paroxysms of terror, his hollering and screaming for mercy filling the cellar. Everyone else looked both relieved and horrified at what they were witnessing. Martin came over to Sir William, 'Can I suggest, my lord, we question him further to see if he names any accomplices? Then shall I send for Constable DeVere to take him back to Bury gaol for trial at the next assizes...or...?'

"Yes, do that. I doubt he acted alone, he doesn't look capable of planning this himself. I will ask the King but I suspect he will want to see justice passed quickly. That constable has failed in his duties. I cannot trust him to do this job properly. I will deal with him later. Summon him to take these two to gaol where they can await their fate.'

The condemned boy, with the help of some expertly applied thumbscrews, soon revealed his accomplice's name. He had managed to escape before the drawbridge was lowered, but was soon captured by Sir William's men and brought back to the Hall's dungeons. However, despite losing three fingers the boy could not provide any information on John Salkeld's whereabouts. Three days later, more dead than alive, the two men were hanged at the Bury gallows. Watching nervously by the side of the scaffold was Constable De Vere, painfully aware that he failed in his duty to find John Salkeld and his fellow traitors, and that retribution was surely coming his way.

He went home and, as he entered the house, he wistfully looked around the imposing great hall and its splendid interior, his home for just a few days-and maybe not much longer. He called for wine, and drank several goblets. Then in a semi-drunken stupor he remembered his two recent acquisitions. He asked one of the servants to send them up to his chambers. Minutes later the two girls appeared hesitantly at his bedroom door. Neither had been with a man before, so had only the vaguest notion of what was expected of them. They knew they were there to pleasure him, but how? He ordered them to disrobe and come to his bed. The two girls lay naked on his bed. He roughly fondled their thin young bodies. Probing, squeezing, indifferent to their cries of pain. Soon his huge bulk was on top of one, then the other. His sexual appetite was voracious, his predilections perverted and painful. His drink-fuelled lust soon turned to anger, then violence. For the rest of the day the other servants could hear the begging, then screaming of the young girls as he took out his frustrations, venting his lust on their once unblemished bodies. Eventually silence, as he fell into an inebriated sleep.

Very early the following morning there was an insistent banging on the door. A sleepy servant opened it to see three constables and Sir William's marshall, Martin. They barged into the house, demanding to be shown where the constable slept. The servant pointed upstairs, then ran back to his quarters to inform the other servants something very interesting was about to take place.

The constables and Martin ran up the stairs and burst into the bedroom. Initially they were unsure if the two cowering, terror-stricken young girls curled up on the bed had killed the constable – who was unmoving, splayed out, next to them. Blood was everywhere, on the bedclothes and the rugs, and on the girl's naked bodies. It took only a minute for them to realise what terrible things had taken place here to these bewildered and frightened children. Cuts and blood covered their bodies, the bruises and bite marks on their tiny breasts, and inside their legs bore witness to an onslaught of unbelievable ferocity. They were beyond crying, just hugging each other, shivering and whimpering in shock.

All four men stood still, disbelief and disgust across their faces as they took in the scene of violent debauchery in front of them. Martin quickly ordered the men, 'Cover up those girls, and take them downstairs for the other servants to look after. Come back here when you have done so – but wait ten minutes.'

Constable De Vere never saw the swing of Martin's boot between his legs. Only the roaring pain in his groin as he woke up gasping in agony. What followed, Martin hoped, was just a taste of what Constable De Vere had inflicted upon those two innocent girls. By the time the other constables appeared his face was a bloody pulp, his body a mass of cuts, with countless unseen bones fractured or broken. It was, mused the marshall, no less than he deserved.

'Take this odious piece of perverted shit to the gaol, then forget about him,' ordered an exhausted, but gratified, marshall. 'He'll not be coming back here.'

Chapter 4
(1672)

It is nearly 200 years since the old witch's spell of incomprehensible strength was cast, affecting everyone who lived in the house in Whiting Street. She had been quite specific; it should last for ten generations, or approximately 250 years. She did not know how and when the spell would finally be broken, just that its power would gradually fade.

Some of the beams within the house taken from Spinster Wordsworth's old home that once stood on the site were reused in the existing house to save money. Little did the builders know by doing this they were merely reinforcing and prolonging the evil spell's cast. However, even these mighty oak beams have a limited life. Now with some closer to six hundred years of age they were beginning to show the stresses and strains that would eventually cause them to weaken or break. Especially if exposed to damp or the elements.

Deep under the parlour was an old well, filled in by the builders in 1485. It was there the Spinster hid, in a casket, her ancient grimoire of spells and artefacts.

The inhabitants of the house for nearly two centuries were unaware of this malevolence that seeped into its every corner. They watched in horror as their new borns faced a life without the ability to see, hear or speak. Spinster Wordsworth had taken her revenge tenfold. But her spell's time was nearly over. It would soon be time for someone to finally break its evil grip upon the house.

* * * *

Standing unseen at the top of the stairs were once again two ladies, one tall and thin, with flowing blonde hair, a ready smile on her face, and the other a petite dark-haired woman, with a more serious countenance. They held hands.

'Grace, now you know the reason for your condition, and those of your children,' said Maud. 'The house was cursed, for decades poor women had babies that could not see, or hear, or have the ability to talk, like you.'

Grace said nothing; her whole life had been one without uttering a single word. Now, in the afterlife, she could speak, her earthbound affliction sloughed off in her passing.

She nodded her head and shrugged her shoulders, 'It didn't matter, it didn't stop me enjoying every moment of my life with you.' Maud, her lover, friend and partner instinctively understood Grace's reply. They didn't need to be able to talk to each other the way normal couples did. Their friendship was so deep, so intuitive, words were often impediments to their impossibly strong consociation.

'Is there anything we can do to warn other couples of this danger, this dreadful curse, I wonder?' asked Maud. She knew the answer before Grace sorrowfully shook her head and raised her hands in an act of prayer. 'Yes, yes, you are right,' said Maud, 'it is an act of the Devil that only God can reverse. All we can do is pray for those afflicted. We have watched over six decades this curse cause such misery. Let us pray it ends soon.'

They held hands, kissed and walked back into the bedroom, their images ebbing away until they were no more.

Chapter 5
(1673)

She was the gossip of the street, indeed the whole town. Lady Bellingham, as she told everyone who enquired (and a lot did), had retired from running a successful business in Manchester, then London, and now was thrilled to take up residence in Bury St Edmunds. Arriving in a magnificent carriage pulled by four white horses she swept through the town and breezed haughtily into the house, barely pausing for a glass of wine, before issuing instructions to her manservant, Arthur, to take detailed notes of the improvements needed to bring the house up to her standards. According to Her Ladyship, a lot needed doing – and quickly. She moved from room to room tut-tutting at the shabby decor, the damp spots on the ceiling and the general disrepair of the house.

'This really is a lot worse than I was led to believe by the owner,' she complained to Arthur, who nodded in agreement. Experience told him at such times silence was the best way to avoid an ear lashing. It took nearly an hour for Her Ladyship to inspect the whole house. 'Have you made a list of all that needs to be done? Please make a copy. I shall send it to the landlord and expect to be fully compensated.'

Arthur bowed extravagantly and left Lady Bellingham in the great hall bemoaning her fate, though already in her mind envisaging how the house could be transformed into a money-making enterprise.

The owner, Maurice Barrow, never visited the house. He was happy to rent it to this mysterious but apparently well connected, wealthy lady. Her credentials, as best his staff could discover, were impeccable. To further enhance her credibility, she paid a year's rent in advance, promising to be a discreet and quiet tenant. Who could want for more?

Within days of her arrival, the workmen arrived. For several weeks workmen were bustling around inside and outside of the house, repainting walls, repairing damaged windows and roofs, and making as yet unseen improvements to the interior, repairing and decorating every room to her demanding standards. Then the deliveries began: expensive furniture, particularly bedding, luxurious rugs, wall hangings and comfortable chairs, (rather a lot, one inquisitive neighbour noted to a friend, for a woman living by herself). Soon other staff arrived, all of whom were attractive young ladies, plus a young handsome man. When asked, they explained they too, had arrived from Manchester. But offered no further information.

Neighbours were abuzz with gossip and speculation, trying to find out Lady Bellingham's plans for the big house. No matter how they tried to wheedle their way inside for a closer look, they were rebuffed. The lady's intentions for the house remained secret.

Her Ladyship had all the airs and graces the people of Bury expected of someone from a big city. Graceful and statuesque, an elegant middle-aged woman, she commanded attention with her tall, regal bearing. Her impeccably styled grey hair framed a face that was always stern, some said fearsome. To see her smile was a rarity indeed. Her sophisticated air convinced everyone of her aristocratic lineage. Men were entranced by her, women jealous and wary. Though, despite all of this carefully calculated appearance and behaviour, she seemed to care little what people thought of her, seldom entering into conversation with neighbours.

Arthur was constantly at her beck and call at all times of the day and night, running errands to different parts of the town. He was the soul of discretion, never revealing what all the supplies were for, or what the workmen were doing inside the house. Nor why he was rushing around the town delivering messages and letters to the wealthy and well-connected.

After a few weeks the neighbours began to lose interest in the house and her activities. The bevy of young ladies was often seen parading around the town in their finest outfits, beguiling the men with their flirtatious looks and suggestive comments. They disingenuously told anyone when asked what they did all day at the house 'was private and educational.'

However, despite the unseemly tittle-tattle spread by people who claimed to know what was happening, nothing untoward took place. Lady Bellingham to all intents and purposes had truly come to quietly settle down in the prosperous town of Bury St Edmunds.

Three months after her arrival she secretly rented the house in Guildhall St that backed directly onto the small rear garden of her Whiting St house. A small gate was installed in the shared back wall, making passageway from one house to the other easy and discreet.

At last, the lady from Manchester was open for business. And so were her girls – and the handsome young man.

\

Lady Bellingham, real name Annette Holland, came from a long line of successful brothel owners, her mother being the famous Elizabeth Holland who ran one of London's most successful bordellos just off the infamous Drury Lane. A district well known for its high class theatres and equally exotic houses of pleasure, all conveniently placed to entertain the patrons during and after the plays finished.

When the authorities finally closed her mother's highly lucrative business, she took the money and left for Manchester. Barely had she established herself there than a severe case of the pox killed her, leaving Annette, her eldest daughter, in charge.

She inherited her mother's flair and business acumen, and continued catering to the wealthy landowners and aristocrats in the northwest of England. Ultimately, she was too successful, and despite bribes and blackmail, a new Justice of the Peace closed her down when the brothel's bawdiness and disreputable behaviour could no longer be ignored.

Promptly she and her four prettiest girls, Arthur and the young man Anteros (real name David) hastily took the coach to Cambridge then across to Bury St Edmunds. Luck was on her side when she discovered the large house in Whiting St was available for rent. The god of pleasure *Hedone* (after whom she'd named her pet dog) smiled upon her she believed when, with additional good fortune, the house in Guildhall St became available too. She couldn't believe her luck. This would allow secret access to her club catering to Bury's rich and aristocratic men at the Whiting St house.

She converted the Guildhall House into a simple tavern, where clients could have a drink then, at the appropriate time, find the hidden pathway to the luxuriously and erotically appointed rooms in the Whiting St house. And the exotic girls that awaited them.

With this final piece in the creation of her clandestine and opulent 'Men's Club' in place, she sent word she was open for business. As always, Lady Bellingham's planning was faultless and meticulous.

Her four girls, named exotically by her: Aphrodite, Eos, Syrinx and Echo (her mother insisted on Annette having a proper education, resulting in her becoming a fan of the classics) were equally well read and able to entertain with their brains as well as their bodies.

Downstairs the great hall which connected the two wings, or gables, of the house, was still dominated by the enormous stone fireplace. The furnishings were sumptuous, displaying the latest fashion in expensive chairs and chaises longues. The walls were adorned with explicit art, some painted by the girls themselves. Rare erotic books from the continent lay around for the men to read. Titles such as *The Kama Sutra, The School of Venus, The Perfumed Garden of Sensual Delight and poetry such as Venus and Adonis*, The Rape of Lucrece and A Ramble in St. James's Park among them. Frequently the girls would read from these books. On special occasions, and for a considerable amount of extra money, they might even act out, with the help of Anteros, some of the descriptions of strange and bizarre sexual acts.

Such entertainment, and what followed in the beautifully appointed bedrooms, came at a heavy price for the men who wanted to participate. A point Lady Bellingham reminded her girls each evening: "We have to act like ladies downstairs and harlots upstairs. The men must leave here having experienced nothing their wives or mistresses can ever provide them."

Eos, the youngest of the girls, a petite blonde with a perfect complexion, and mesmerising blue eyes was experienced beyond her years. 'You are right, Lady Bellingham, but from what my clients are telling me, we don't have to try too hard to pleasure them more than their wives! Most seem to be without interest in such matters after the first few months of marriage.'

'To be fair, Eos, most of these wives seem to be pregnant or suffering from the maudlins after giving birth,' said Syrinx, a vivacious redhead, always with a dazzling smile. It was she who painted some of the most outrageous murals, which never failed to excite the men as they sat waiting for their chosen girl to appear.

'Thank the good Lord for that,' chipped in Echo, a stunning girl of oriental origin who always proved popular with men, her exotic looks, sallow complexion and demure manner promising something different, new and exciting.

Saying little, the fourth girl, Aphrodite, was a beauty of African descent whose parents were once slaves. Her impossibly smooth ebony skin, dark brown eyes and slim, tall figure mesmerised the men. She had a waiting list wanting to spend time with her. This eclectic mix of beautiful girls, and the live sex shows, produced an atmosphere of unbridled hedonism, a place men could enjoy themselves without inhibitions, safely and discreetly. It soon became the most exclusive club in Bury for those that could afford its outrageous fees.

Lady Bellingham interrupted the girls' banter to offer her normal warnings, 'My little *flower sellers*, remember to clean yourself each time with the special vinegar douche, it will prevent the pox and pregnancy. We also have some lilyroot and rue now, so use that if you prefer. A pregnant whore earns a lot less, so take care!'

She turned to Anteros, smiling. 'Of course you, my sumptuous little fairy, you need not worry about such matters. It seems this quiet town has quite the yearning for the pleasures of a young man; you are making me jealous! Though the money you earn me is enough to quell such concerns,' she conceded with a smile.

Gradually, inconspicuously, the clientele from the upper echelons of Suffolk society came to know of Lady Bellingham's house of pleasure. She was careful to keep a list of the names of all those who frequented her house and when. And of their particular peccadilloes or sexual proclivities. It made for impressive (indeed eye-opening) reading and was also a solid insurance policy. Sir Edward Gage, Earl of Arlington, Lord Hervey and Sir William Gravesend to name but a few were regulars. She was careful to limit the number who could visit the house to just a handful each evening. And only those recommended by a regular member would be invited into the house.

She closed during the day (though the tavern did stay open, with the rear door remaining closed). To reinforce the image of the house being lived in by well-heeled young ladies, they all went to church on Sundays (occasionally to the embarrassment of the parishioners who were also clients) and gave generously to local charities. This outwardly impeccable, prim and proper lifestyle enabled Lady Bellingham to thrive and generate a considerable income for more than a year.

But it could not last.

The resident of the house adjacent to Lady Bellingham's was a retired Justice of the Peace, one Sir Mark Rede. His suspicions were raised that all was not what it seemed with his neighbours, when coming home late one night he passed their house, slightly the worse for wear after several tankards at the tavern, coincidentally run by Lady Bellingham. He rarely frequented the establishment, however that evening his suspicions were piqued when he noticed a small number of patrons leaving by the back door, and not returning for an hour or two. Far too long to be in the privy, he surmised. He casually asked where these guests had gone and was brushed off by the tavern owner as 'attending a private meeting upstairs.'

He thought nothing more of it until he weaved his way down Whiting St. For a second he lost his balance and grabbed onto the windowsill of Lady Bellingham's house. There was the tiniest crack between the shutters and the curtains inside, he pressed his eye to the window and jumped back in horror.

'Oh, my good heavens! Can that really be?' he muttered to himself, shaking his head to try and clear the image that had just assailed his eyes. However, curiosity made him look again. No. His eyes had not deceived him. A young man was mounting a young girl, both were naked and performing an ambitious sext act in front of several men who were cheering and clapping at their erotic theatrics.

For a moment the old man stood in the darkness, too shocked to move. Gathering his wits he stumbled the few yards to his house, up the steps and into his front room. A servant appeared waiting for instructions, only to see her master sink into the chair too dumbfounded to utter a word.

'Would the master like some wine?' asked the young girl nervously. For a few moments Sir Mark said nothing then, without looking, just waved her away. 'No. I need to be left in peace for a moment, thank you, Susan.'

For the rest of the evening, the old man wrestled with the correct course of action he should take. Do nothing, and allow a house of debauchery to exist right next door to his home? If they were discovered, who would believe him if he claimed never to have known what was going on just a few yards up the street? People might accuse him of, at best, failing to notify the authorities, at worst collusion with Lady Bellingham.

The alternative was to inform his successor, Justice of the Peace Gerald Landsworth. Not, he'd heard, the most upstanding member of the town's judiciary. However he had little choice if he wanted to alert the authorities. The days of a JP being beyond reproach and a beacon of probity, Sir Mark knew, were long gone.

It was entirely possible, he thought, Her Ladyship's extensive connections and the greasing of a few palms probably allowed such a house to operate without interference from the law. Indeed, he could not be sure, but in the brief time he looked into the front room, was it his old friend Sir William Davey of Barton, he saw enjoying the carnal spectacle? By exposing Lady Bellingham's brothel might he end up besmirching the reputation of her aristocratic clientele – and, by association, make a lot of enemies among people who were best kept as friends?

It was a conundrum that kept him awake most of the night. By the time he fell asleep a plan had formed in his befuddled mind.

Chapter 6
(1673)

Sir Mark Rede looked around his old office in the Guildhall. Nothing had changed since his departure two years earlier. The same dreary-coloured brown walls, dirty windows and threadbare rugs hardly created an aura of power. So be it, he wasn't here to comment on the decor. His wait of two days to see the new incumbent Justice of the Peace, one Gerald Landsworth, caused him to doubt again the wisdom of what he was about to do. The delay, explained the JP when he finally arrived, was due to 'those damn Quakers, who insist on not attending church. They are the bane of my life. The King in all his graciousness allows them free worship simply in return for getting a licence, yet they still fail to obey the law. Why can't everyone be Protestant and be done with it?'

'Indeed, indeed, I couldn't agree more, Gerald, they were a thorn in my side for years. I envy you not trying to control them...'

Gerald eased his expansive bulk into a large chair behind an impressive oak desk, one that had been there for over a hundred years. He poured himself some wine and offered his guest a glass. Sir Mark demurred, wanting all his faculties about him for the conversation ahead.

'So, my friend, to what do I owe the honour of your visit? How is retirement treating you?'

'In the main, most agreeably thank you, Gerald, except a rather delicate matter has arisen I would appreciate your counsel upon...I am sure I can count on your discretion.'

'Of course, of course. Your words will not go beyond these walls. Now, you have intrigued me, pray carry on, how can I be of assistance?'

Clenching his fists to calm himself, Sir Mark relayed what he had seen at Lady Bellingham's house. He finished by asking: 'To be honest, Gerald, I am in a quandary as to what to do next. I am hoping you have some sagacious advice. I am still shocked such things are taking place next door to me. I would like them to stop, I'm sure we all want them to stop, I think you'll agree. How shall we go about this?' He looked up at the Justice of the Peace expecting to see a look of horror, or at least surprise. He saw neither, instead a wry smile crossed his face. He sighed as if the news was no surprise.

'Of course I am aware of the activities in the lady's house. Indeed, I know many who have partaken of the attractions to be found therein. However, she is a devious and manipulative lady that has ensnared some of the richest and most powerful men in the county to become part of what she calls her *Carnales Club*. If I were to arrest Lady Bellingham, or close her house of ill repute down, I fear my tenure here would be short-lived. She has influential friends who like the services she provides. I am not in a position to go against them, I fear.' He paused mid-explanation. Seeing the look of disappointment on Sir Mark's face at his news, he tried to make light of it.

'Oh, don't be so downcast, Mark! It could be worse. They are quiet, discreet and provoke no trouble. He leant over the desk and in a conspiratorial voice whispered, 'Indeed, my friend, I am sure I could find someone who would vouch for you to become a member. Fair compensation, say you not, for the inconvenience, if in truth, there is any?'

It took all of Sir Mark's self-control to stifle an outburst of exasperation. Keeping a calm tone to his voice he didn't feel, Sir Mark asked, 'So, to be clear, Gerald, you intend to do nothing about a house that makes Sodom and Gomorrah look like a convent? A place, it seems, of such depravity any decent man would find abhorrent? You find the arrangement acceptable?'

In a placatory tone, the Justice of the Peace, tried to calm down the vexed older man. 'Whether I find it acceptable or not, people with powers greater than mine do not object. Come now, Sir Mark, no one is being harmed. They provide, it would seem, a service that is much in demand. In truth, compared to all the other problems I have to address, they are a low priority for me. Can I suggest you go home and let sleeping dogs, or should I say whores, lie?' He laughed at his own joke.

'I fear there is little to be done, Mark. Now, if you'll excuse me, I must see the judge about these damned Quakers.' He stood up, signalling the meeting was at an end.

Slightly puzzled and extremely irritated that the Justice of the Peace, of all people, should find an illegal brothel not worthy of their attention, disillusioned he walked home, making sure he was on the other side of the street when he passed Lady Bellingham's establishment. By the time he was home an angry Sir Mark made a decision that would have fatal consequences; if the law would do nothing, then he would take it upon himself to close down this whorehouse. Inside the Devil was at work!

Like all zealous Christians, Sir Mark knew it must be stopped. His strict puritanical upbringing made it his duty.

For two weeks his soul was tortured; how best could he accomplish God's will? His desire to see the evil-doers vanquished was matched only by the temptation to stop at the house and see what was happening inside (something to his horror he found himself drawn to on several occasions). His heart and soul were telling him one thing, his body the opposite. Seeing those beautiful young girls had awoken cravings unknown to him before. He knew these feelings were contrary to all the teachings of the Church. But, but, the women were so beautiful, so full of life. The oriental girl in particular caught his attention, raised his ardour, causing his body to react in strange and embarrassing ways.

To his consternation even in sleep he could not escape these carnal thoughts, his dreams were overrun by visions of her naked, lithe body lying next to him, stirring sensations that were disturbingly pleasurable; only to find when he awoke he was racked with guilt.

Were they souls he could save? Indeed, could his be saved? He questioned himself in thought and prayer as he spiralled into a pit of confused depression. Was he succumbing to the sins of the flesh, like those he was hoping to lead to salvation? The words of Thomas Aquinas kept coming to him:

'In the realms of evil thoughts none induces us to sin as much as do the thoughts that concern the pleasures of the flesh'

Torn as he was between these conflicting emotions, he knew deep in his soul the whores and Lady Bellingham were destined to be consumed by the fires of hell – and he was the man to send them there. He finally knew, after weeks of prayer, what he had to do. Their souls, he decided, were beyond redemption. And the sooner they, along with the house itself, were cleansed by fire, the better. God was on his side, such depravity could not be tolerated. He searched his Bible and came upon a verse in *Matthew 18*, which inspired him to act:

'What sorrow awaits the world because it tempts people to sin. Temptations are inevitable but when sorrow awaits the person who does the tempting. So if your hand or foot causes you to sin, cut it off and throw it away. It is better to enter eternal life with only one foot or one hand and to be thrown into Eternal fire with both of your hands and feet. And if your eye causes you to sin, gouge it out and throw it away. It is better than to enter eternal life with only one eye and have two eyes to be thrown into the fire of hell.'

He would burn this house of evil to the ground and all who lived in it would be consumed in the flames. It was their only chance of absolution. He would be their saviour.

The Bible may be full of advice, but it was lacking when it came to the best way to set a house ablaze. An increasingly agitated and deranged Sir Mark, in moments of lucidity, realised such an act of arson was not easily accomplished. He wasn't concerned for his own safety, or even that of his house, should it catch alight too. But what of the rest of the street? His conscience would not allow innocent souls to die if the flames took hold beyond the house of evil. He wrestled for days with this conundrum, without success.

Praying for divine guidance became a daily ritual, as did his covert trips past the house next door to surreptitiously see if the source of his pain and pleasure, the beautiful Oriental girl, was acting out his sexual fantasies for others to enjoy. He was racked with guilt each time he walked the few yards to the window and peeked in, hoping to view his tormentor, who unbeknownst to her was fast becoming his nemesis. As his life unravelled, he dismissed his servants and lived the life of a crazed hermit.

It was a hot, humid day in September 1673. Sir Mark was kneeling by his bed, praying again for a sign showing him the path he should take. He barely noticed as the rain began pummelling down on the roof. Soon the rumbles of thunder approached from the north, the rain intensified, and the room became dark even though it was early afternoon. The cracks of thunder rolled in, shaking the very foundations of his house. Every few seconds lightning lit up the leaden sky. Within minutes the storm was directly overhead, the ear-splitting thunder arriving simultaneously with the lightning. In his debilitated, confused mind Sir Mark believed God was sending him a sign. It was now, or never.

He ran downstairs to where a fire was always alight in the parlour and grabbed a large burning log from the grate. Now he would send those depraved souls to a burning hell! Their house would be burned to the ground and all those within it consumed and cleansed! As he ran towards the front door the storm delivered a cataclysmic detonation above his house. Lightning not only struck the roof, but a huge oak tree next to the house, felling it as if a giant had swung a mighty axe at its trunk. It scythed through the roof, crushing through the house. Sir Mark dropped the flaming log as he tried to flee from the tree's spear-like branches. He took only a few steps before a huge ceiling beam crashed down, pinning him to the floor in a cloud of dust and burning shingles.

Unable to move, he cowered with horror as red-hot roof tiles rained down upon him, and the discarded burning log set fire to the rugs, then curtains. The flames, fanned by the gusts of wind from the large hole in the roof, moved inexorably towards him. He was trapped. Try as he could to wriggle free, the beam was immovable. The flames like a burning snake, slithering across the floor, hungrily stalking its prey. It took just a few seconds to reach him, his coat to catch fire and the flames scorch his skin. As they consumed him, slowly, agonisingly, his last visions were not of the Lord welcoming him with benevolent, open arms, but a writhing, naked Chinese girl. He knew then his soul was destined for an eternity in hell.

* * * *

What prayer and the law failed to stop, the pox did.

In early 1674, Bury again experienced a smallpox plague. Familiar with such epidemics, the town instigated quarantine measures: burying their dead outside of the walls, and ordering the townsfolk to stay at home. Most did, but the lure of Lady Bellingham's girls and their sordid entertainment proved too much for some patrons of the Carnales Club. Smallpox cares not if you are pauper or aristocrat, and in the confines of the whorehouse and the commingling of human flesh that occurs within it, the pox ran amok. Three of the girls contracted the disease, Aphrodite, Eos and Syrinx. Only Eos survived, but her face would be forever ravaged by pock-marked skin. Echo and Anteros emerged unscathed, as did Lady Bellingham.

As before in Manchester, the lady knew when to quit. No one would visit a house where so many had contracted the deadly disease. In truth she knew her luck had finally run out in Bury St Edmunds. It had been a profitable stay, but now was the time to move on, find some more girls, and start again. She heard Bristol was an expanding city – and a long way from Bury.

Once quarantine was lifted, she, Anteros, Echo, Eos and the ever-faithful Eduard left the house complete with its luxurious furnishings, erotic paintings, and its reputation as a house of ill repute and death by smallpox.

Maurice Barrow of Barningham ordered the house stripped of all its remaining contents, fumigated and left empty for a year. Once its infamous reputation had faded from the townspeople's memory, he sold it at a handsome profit to a local solicitor.

* * * *

'Well, I thought we saw some unsavoury sights when we ran this house as a tavern all those decades ago. But this, this was...extraordinary!' said Grace.

'Yes, The Gentlemen's Rest had its fair share of such exploits but nothing compared to what we have just seen,' agreed Maud.

'And that black man...did you see the size?

'Enough, Grace!' Maud smiled. 'I thought you preferred women, in particular me, to men,' she teased.

'Of course. You were, and always will be, the object of my desires. Nevertheless, he was...impressive.'

Chapter 7
(1677)

January 1st 1677

Diary of Jane Potter.

A new year and I am so happy to be in my new home! I am staying here for a few months. I do not own this huge house; my uncle Christopher Austin, a successful lawyer and judge in the town bought it. To recoup the purchase cost (the enormous amount of £105, so I heard him tell a friend), he has rented other rooms to three law students, two young men and a charming girl, and his brother, William.

I am lucky to have my own bedroom in the north gable and use of the downstairs room, which has plenty of light for my painting. Because that is what I do. I'm a painter; to be more precise, a portrait painter. My uncle Christopher is a lover of the arts and has promised to introduce me to people who might want to commission me! I am so excited!

My cousin, Mary Beale, a local lady from Barrow and now living in London, has become famous for her portraiture. She recently painted Robert Hooke of the Royal Society and now has a commission from Lord Derby at His Majesty's Court. I cannot hope to emulate her success, but I will endeavour to make her and my uncle proud.

I have decided to keep a record of the people I am painting. Uncle Christopher, a fine man, and skilled with the written word, has suggested I do this, and send regular letters to my cousin in London to compare our painting experiences.

He paid for my education after my parents died many years ago, and now wishes me to make use of my writing and painting abilities. I am excited to oblige, I owe him so much.

In my first letter to cousin Mary, I described the house I am living in. I copy some of it here:

Dear Mary,

…Whiting St is in a very desirable part of the town, with large houses and wealthy owners. My uncle's house is one of the largest. It has two wings, or gables. Each has two large ground floor rooms; in the south gable this is where the parlour and kitchen are to be found. The other guests sleep in the rooms above, and the two servants and two cooks, in the attic rooms. Joining the two gables is the great hall where there is always a huge fire burning and we all meet for meals. The north wing, in which I am living, I share with my uncle William.

I have heard tales that the house is cursed! I don't believe it for one moment, though one of the elderly cooks tells of children being born here suffering from afflictions affecting their hearing, talking or sight. I find such tittle-tattle in bad taste, and I shall choose to ignore it.

Exciting news! Uncle Christopher tells me I may have my first commission! The son of Earl Hervey of Ickworth. Once my painting supplies have arrived from London I shall send word and start the portrait. He is said to be very handsome! I hope I can portray him to everyone's satisfaction...

Yours affectionately
Jane

January 15th 1677

I have just returned from my first visit to the famous Bury market. I was escorted by one of the (handsome!) young students, Phillip, who rents a room in the house. Uncle Christopher ordered me to take an escort as cutpurses and pickpockets are always at work in the crowded market. There was so much to see! Everything for a household was for sale – implements, pots, pans, glassware, even simple furniture. Then the food! Oh, heavens, what a sight and smell for hungry eyes and empty stomachs. Some of it I had never seen before; a large round fruit called an orange, and another named a pineapple, which is so rare only the rich can afford one. The stallholder had one on display, but not for sale.

Another was selling tea and coffee, which are now much cheaper than they used to be. I tried a small cup of tea but found the taste very bitter. They say sugar makes it more pleasing to the palate. But sugar is expensive, so I declined another cup. I have my doubts these drinks will become popular.

The market has hundreds of stalls, their owners coming from miles around every Wednesday and Saturday to sell their wares. In the middle of the market are the pillories where poor wretches who have committed some petty crime are left there all day for people to ridicule. Anyone can throw stones, rotten food or manure at them, anything to cause them the most suffering. One had received a beating, his bare buttocks still showing the marks *left by the constable's whip. And his manhood on view for all to see! Poor man, how embarrassing for him, though I suspect that is the least of his concerns.*

Philip quickly steered me away from this sordid sight and we treated ourselves to a delicious venison pie and some ale, eating them as we walked back down Abbeygate St to see the remains of the once magnificent abbey. It is so sad it has been destroyed and reduced to rubble ever since Henry VIII threw out the monks over a hundred years ago.

The day was cool and sunny so we walked across Angel Hill, and passed the beautiful St Mary's church. The Norman Tower was next on our little tour (built, would you believe in, 1148?), then we saw the peculiar houses built into the old abbey walls, some of them reaching to three storeys tall, their windows hewn out of the old flint walls that according to Philip were over 300 years old. Imagine that.

On our way back we walked across Chequer Square and up Churchgate St to Whiting St and home. It was a pleasing day in fine company. I do believe I am rather taken with Philip!

* * * *

'Looks like the lady has herself a man friend,' muttered the man to his son, as they peered across the street, watching the young couple enter the house.

The teenage son glanced at his father, Saul. He was worried. 'Won't that make it more difficult? We can't snatch two of them, can we?' The father, a tall, thin man, his pale, waxy complexion the result of years in gaol, shook his head, a slight smile cracking his dirty, bearded face. 'Na, Thomas, reckon it might prove useful. If we handle it right. Now we know for sure she's the judge's relative, we'll come back for her later. If the boy's there I've a plan for him too.'

It was three days later, a Sunday evening when they judged the opportunity was ripe. The weather was overcast, dulling the streets earlier than usual as dusk approached. The two lay in wait inside an empty stable across the road. They'd seen a succession of young people, some looking like servants, some young people and another man, leave the house walking up the street to go, they guessed, to evening Mass at St Mary's Church. It meant the house should be empty except for the girl and her male friend.

Saul turned to his son, a look of determination on his face. "OK, son, let's do this and make ourselves rich and get my revenge on that bastard judge – do as I've told you and we'll be fine.'

They opened the stable door and cajoled a complaining donkey to pull a small cart out onto the darkening street. There was just enough light to see a few feet in front of them as they stopped outside the house. The father had a large knife tucked into his trousers which he unsheathed and handed to Thomas. From the back of the cart he retrieved a hefty hammer, swinging it by his side feeling the weight, imagining the damage it could do if struck against someone's head. It gave him confidence, a sense of power.

'Ready?' he asked, in a whisper. 'Remember we don't want to harm her. Not yet, anyways. If her man friend appears, we knock him out. I'll clobber him really hard with the hammer. Then get them both in the cart. Gottit?' Thomas nodded obediently, trying not to show his fear. If this all went wrong they would be hung. Kidnapping anyone was a death sentence, the relative of a judge and he might impose the barbaric hung, drawn and quartered punishment as well.

He'd never been enthusiastic about this plan, but his father was hell-bent on revenge, and would brook no argument from his son that there might be a less dangerous, less risky way to get his own back on the judge. 'The beauty about this plan,' he explained to his son, talking to him like he was a five-year-old, 'Is we get the judge scared out of his miserable wits – and make some money too. Just beating him up would yield us nothing'.

So Thomas agreed to play his part. His fear of being involved in the kidnapping was only exceeded by his fear of what his father would do to him if he failed to help.

Before he could say anything, the old man was banging on the front door. There was, for a few moments, no movement inside the house, then a faint glow from a lantern could be seen through the windows making its way towards the front door. It opened and Phillip's half-lit face appeared, and behind him stood the young girl, the reason for this whole criminal exercise.

The young man immediately looked concerned. 'What do you want?'

Before he could finish his question the two men rushed into the hallway, slamming the door shut behind them. Saul knocked the young man to the ground with a hefty blow to his head. As Phillip collapsed, the lantern fell to the floor, smashing into pieces, its light promptly extinguished. In the dark, Jane screamed. Before she could escape further into the house or utter another sound, Saul pushed her to the floor and quickly covered her head with a stinking old sack and secured it with a length of rope which he tied tightly across her mouth to form a gag.

Jane found herself being manhandled outside and thrown into the back of a cart. Her hands were roughly tied behind her back once she was lying down. She felt Philp's limp body being dumped alongside her and some kind of cloth then thrown over them. Seconds later the cart moved off down Whiting St. The whole attack had taken just a few minutes, and she was still too stunned to comprehend what was happening – or why. Any thought of escaping was dashed as someone sat on her, making it impossible to move. Then a hand clamped over her face, forcing the revolting old sackcloth further into her mouth, stifling any chance to cry for help.

She heard a man's voice chuckling with pride. 'Well, boy, that all went to plan. See, just trust your old man, he's never let you down yet.'

Thomas listened to his father's gloating, deciding there was no point in arguing that the main reason they had both ended up in Ipswich gaol in the first place was because of a previous ill-conceived caper involving stealing cattle. Trusting his crooked father that time cost him three years in gaol and 25 lashes, courtesy of Judge Austin. His father's company for all that time sharing a cell made a terrible ordeal even worse.

When they were finally released, neither could find work; no one wanted to employ people who stole from farmers. They'd scratched an existence cleaning chimneys, rat catching and taking on jobs no one else wanted to do. When they had been sent to clean and sweep the chimney at a house in Whiting St, Saul's resentment erupted when he discovered it was owned by his nemesis, Judge Austin. From that day forward Saul was consumed by the desire for retribution. The girl staying at the house led him to the plan to kidnap her and demand a ransom.

Initially Thomas wanted nothing to do with Saul's hare-brained scheme. But arguing only got him a cuff round the ear. Even though he was now big and strong enough to fight back, Saul was still his father, and in truth, cleaning chimneys was a loathsome way to earn a living.

As they trundled out of Bury, Thomas realised there was no turning back now. If it worked they would be rich; if not, they'd be dead. He felt the girl beneath him squirming in discomfort, muffling something through her gag he couldn't understand. He bent down, putting his face close to her head under the cloth. 'Just lay still and shut up if you know what's good for you. It'll be a while until we get where we are going. I'm not going to hurt you.' Jane grunted something and stopped squirming, though he could hear her muffled sobbing.

For, it seemed, hours the cart bounced its way along the rutted tracks. Jane tried not to panic, but her stomach was in knots of fear. She struggled to breathe at times, and passed out on a couple of occasions. When she was conscious the only sounds she heard were the grunts of one of the men as he urged the donkey to speed up. Petrified that at any moment she might be murdered, Jane prayed like she had never done before. The weight of the man sitting on her was suffocating and uncomfortable. She was consumed with worry for her and Phillip's life, but was helpless to do anything to help either of them. Frustratingly, she had not heard him utter a sound, or even move. Please God that blow to the head had not killed him.

Eventually they stopped. The person sitting on her jumped off the cart. The cover was pulled back and Phillip's still semi-conscious body dragged from her side. She heard a thump as he hit the ground and grimaced at the further injuries being inflicted upon him as he was dragged away. Next, hands grabbed her, pulling her roughly off the cart and pushing her into a building that smelled of hay and manure.

She heard a man's voice, harsh, and sinister, spoken in a broad Suffolk dialect. 'Alright, you rich man's trollop, here's what's happenin'. You'll stay here until we get ten gold sovereigns from your rich uncle. Fair payment, and reward for his so-called justice in sending me and my son to rot in the bowels of Ipswich gaol for three years. He's a cumberworld and he's goin' to pay us back for our piss-poor treatment. I'm going to make him suffer the way we did. I've waited a long time for my revenge, now you're my way to get it. Understand?'

Jane was shocked. So this was what this was all about? She shook her head in despair, still unable to ask any questions, or plead for her life. A feeling of hopelessness descended upon her.

The man's menacing voice continued. 'So your dolthead of a friend, once he's woken up, will be dumped back near the town with the message to your rich uncle. Ten sovereigns for your safe return or he will never see you again. I call that a fair exchange.' He grunted a short laugh, then she heard him walk away, telling his son to tie 'the bitch' up tightly to a stall. As an afterthought, he ordered him to take out her gag, warning her, 'You can scream all you like, no one lives close by, so don't waste your breath. You may not have many left.' He chuckled at his sick joke. The barn door slammed and another person moved behind her, untying the rope around her head that was forcing the hood into her mouth.

With the gag taken out, and breathing more easily, Jane asked her unseen captor for a drink. She heard a younger voice mutter something about 'shutting up and don't move', before returning a few minutes later with a flagon of cider.

'You can lift up the hood to drink but don't turn around. If you see me, then my father will probably kill you,' Thomas instructed Jane. She lifted up the front of the hood and put the flagon to her parched lips, gulping down the rough, sour drink. 'Now put the hood back down, lady, for both our sakes. Don't try to escape. We'll find you and make your life even more miserable. Just sit still and say nothing. I'm going to leave you here while I take your friend back to town. I'll have to tie you up again; I'm sorry.' With her back against the post he expertly bound her hands leaving her no room to move. She was uncomfortable, but for the moment unharmed.

A few minutes later she heard Phillip, obviously still groggy and in pain, complaining loudly as he was forced back into the cart and the reluctant donkey pulled the creaking contraption off into the distance. The silence that followed allowed Jane to regain her composure and plan a possible escape. Tugging on the rope around her wrists brought home the reality that it would not be easy. They were tied tightly and strongly. Slumping back in pain and despondency, she sat in the gloomy barn and worried about how she would be treated while their prisoner. These men were clearly desperate and dangerous; having a young girl at their mercy might lead to other indescribable acts being forced upon her. She shuddered at the thought. Then, God forbid, what if for some reason her uncle could not find the money for her ransom? He was rich, but ten gold sovereigns was a fortune, which even he might find troublesome to raise at such short notice.

What had she done to deserve this terrible ordeal? Jane started to cry, heaving sobs that shook her body, praying, pleading to God to be rescued, her life saved. The question that kept repeating itself, spearing her mind with dread: Would they really kill her if her uncle failed to pay the ransom?

Chapter 8

It was early morning when Phillip stumbled into the house to find a distraught Judge Austin and two other men, sitting around the dining room table, clearly in a state of great agitation. They had been struggling to devise a plan of action. But with so little information to hand Christopher and the two constables failed to come up with any viable suggestions as to where Jane might be and the reason for her disappearance.

Seeing Phillip immediately raised their hopes – only to have them dashed when they saw his plight. All three ran to support him as he staggered into the great hall, blood congealed across his face and neck. His clothes were ripped and filthy. He was a sorry sight to behold, but they all prayed he would have news of Jane's plight.

'Please God, Phillip! It is good to see you at last! Tell us, what happened? We have all been worried as to your whereabouts.' Christopher half hoped to see Jane follow him into the room. He tried to hide his disappointment when she didn't. He ushered Phillip to a chair by the fire.

'Come here and sit down, boy, tell me what on earth is going on; where is Jane? We have been worried out of our wits.'

He ordered one of the servants to fetch water and some cloth to cleanse Phillip's bloodied face. He poured a large measure of brandy into a glass and handed it to the young man, who, with shaking hands, downed it in one swallow. Impatient for answers he sat next to him, took his hands, trying to get Philip to concentrate on providing some coherent answers. He asked again:

'I am sorry to press you, my boy, but can you tell us what occurred and where Jane is now?' He tried not to sound fearful, however he assumed time was of the essence and he needed answers now.

As the servant wiped the cold water across his face and cleaned the wound at the back of his head it helped clear Phillip's mind. In a weak voice he tried to explain the terrible events that had befallen them the previous evening.

"Tis still a blur, sir, so forgive me if I ramble a little in the retelling of this incident.'

'It matters not, Phillip, do your best to recall every detail,' urged the judge.

For the next ten minutes he recounted the attack, the journey in the back of a cart, for how long he could not tell as he was unconscious for most of it. Being woken by two men, both with kerchiefs covering their faces. Then given the important instructions that Jane would only be returned unharmed on payment of ten gold sovereigns. After which he was bundled back into the cart with a hood over his head and dumped in Southgate St.

No sooner had he finished his inarticulate description of events than Christopher and the two other men, both constables, bombarded him with more questions, trying to extract any further snippets of useful information.

'How long was the journey? In which direction did you travel? How old were the men? What was the farm you were taken to like? Did the men say anything that might identify them, names, places? Did they harm Jane? Did you see her or talk to her?'

He apologetically shook his head, 'I am so sorry, gentlemen, I was dealt a heavy blow to my head and I am still feeling a little befuddled. All I know is you have two days to pay the ransom or they say Jane will be killed. These men are ruffians, I have no reason to doubt they will do so without any qualms.'

Judge Austin slumped back into his chair, his mind already calculating how best to find the money – and Jane. He looked at the two constables. They were amiable men, probably facing their first case of kidnapping. He doubted they would have anything helpful to suggest, but he asked anyway.

'How do you propose we proceed, gentleman? These men clearly are dangerous. Even if I can find the money they ask for, how do we pay it? Where, when? More importantly, how do we rescue Jane?'

The constables looked at each other, their faces devoid of any bright ideas. The elder one made the obvious suggestion: 'Perhaps, sir, we should wait and see what the kidnappers do next. They might be bluffing. It takes a lot to kill a girl in cold blood. Maybe wait another day to see if you receive a message from them with further instructions?' Much as he hated to agree, the judge concurred for the moment; that was all they could do.

Jane was hungry, uncomfortable and, to her embarrassment, in need of the privy. Still with her face covered by a sack she called out for help. No one took heed of her cries. By the time Saul came into the barn many hours later, she'd had no choice but to relieve herself where she lay. He was quick to mock her humiliating condition.

'Oh, my word! Little stuck-up miss trollop has wet herself like a baby. My, my, what a sight. Well, now you know how we felt in gaol when they kept us in chains for days at a time. Sitting in our shit like pigs. The guards always found it amusing to mock us so, missie, you can suffer like we did; see how you like it.'

Her anger flared up and, despite her shameful plight, she cursed her unseen captor. Spitting her defiance through the hood, she said, 'Sir, you have no cause to treat me like this. I have done nothing to harm you. Do you have no conscience? No sense of decency? You should be ashamed of yourself for treating a woman in this way!'

'Save me your lectures, I could accuse your uncle of many of the same things. He treated us like animals. Showed no mercy, dispensed justice with no concern for what tortures we faced. I only wish he was here instead of you. That would be revenge enough to satisfy my anger. Say no more, wench, I may decide to put you to other uses while I wait out these two days.'

'You wouldn't dare! Attack a defenceless woman!' Jane shouted her defiance, knowing she could do little to stop him.

'I would, and I will if you keep annoying me. You have been warned. Shut your mouth for your own good. Otherwise things will just get worse for you.'

Jane heard the man move closer and then felt him beside her. Suddenly his hand was inside her bodice, the other roughly pushed between her legs. He massaged her breast, his calloused hand groping for her nipple. Between her legs he prodded his fingers into her most intimate parts. She tried to squirm away from his attack but her ties were so firm she could not escape his probing and painful molesting.

'Please stop, you are hurting me.' She cried out in terror, but he was not to be dissuaded from his enjoyment. Sensing her fear, her expectation that worse was to follow, he found exhilarating. He leant close to her inhaling her perfume. He breathed into her ear, 'I will have you all to myself before the day is out...'

'Father! For God's sake, what are you doing?' demanded Thomas, who unexpectedly appeared at the door of the barn. 'Stop it! At once! Do not harm that girl. Do you have no honour? What would my mother say if she saw you behaving in such a way?'

Hearing his son's accusation, Saul stopped pawing Jane's body, and stood up to face him, eyes seething with annoyance at the interruption. 'Your mother was a whore, just like she is,' he kicked Jane to emphasise his point, 'She spent her life allowing men to do as they pleased with her, stupidly for no reward. I'll do what I like with this young strumpet, and you'll not be telling me otherwise.'

He strode over to his son and backhanded him across the face, then walked out the barn door, still muttering threats and insults. Wiping the blood from his cut lip, Thomas ran over to Jane kneeling down beside her, he asked, 'Are you hurt, ma'am? My father is a dangerous animal; neither of us must do anything to raise his ire. It will bring us only harm. He will have no conscience hurting you for his pleasure. I have seen him do it before. I will try and protect you from the worst of his behaviour. Best not to say anything, that is what I have learned.'

Still mortified from the man's disgusting attack, Jane stammered a thank you to Thomas for his concern. She asked if she could be untied and clean herself. 'Also, some food and drink I would be most grateful for, if you have any.'

'We have no food, ma'am. I can bring you a bucket of water to clean yourself. Though I will have to keep watch over you. If you escape, my father will kill me. Do you promise you will not put me in such danger?' Jane nodded her agreement. She might detest his father but this young man was showing her a modicum of care, and she could not risk being the cause of him coming to any harm. His gesture of kindness sparked an idea in her mind: if she could befriend him, appeal to his sympathies, maybe, just maybe he might help her escape. The thought, however remote, gave her hope. The boy was obviously terrified of his father, and probably, she reasoned, doing this criminal deed under pressure, unwillingly ,and in fear of the consequences if he disobeyed him. Her spirits rose as she saw a possible way out of her predicament.

Before she could attempt to put her plan into action, the father returned, ordering his son outside.

'Now listen to me, son, this is important. In the morning you're to go back into town, find some street urchin, give him a penny and tell him to deliver this message to that high and mighty judge: *Put ten gold sovereigns in a bag and leave it beneath the Plague Fountain before dawn on Saturday morning. Once we have it, he will be told where to find his niece.* Make sure they get it right. Now get some sleep and be up early, get into Bury and find someone poor but clever enough to deliver that message. Follow them from a distance to make sure they do it. You understand me?'

'Yes, Father. Once we have the money, who will let them know where to find the girl? She has not been fed and will become ill if she is not cared for.' Thomas waited for a tongue lashing for showing he cared about the girl's wellbeing.

Instead his father gave a malevolent grin and grabbed his son by the shoulders, explaining, 'With ten gold sovereigns in my pocket, I care nothing for the girl's future. If you want to come back here and release her, that's up to you. Just like your mother – you're a soft-hearted piece of shit. Boy, I intend to be out of Suffolk and on a ship to the Americas within two days of getting that money.'

His father's callous attitude shocked Thomas. He knew this was a risky venture, but if successful could mean a huge amount of money and no harm done to their victim. Now he recognized the scheme concocted by his father all along meant the girl was dispensable. He cared not if she lived or died.

Disgusted at the turn of events, Thomas was determined to make the young girl's safety his responsibility. He made his way into their tumbledown shack to get a few hours sleep. At dawn the following morning he got on his complaining donkey and plodded back into town. The weather had turned cold, and wind whistled across the open fields, slicing through his thin clothes. By the time he reached Bury he was frozen, miserable and disillusioned about this whole escapade.

He toyed with the idea of going directly to the house and telling the judge where his father and the girl could be found. However, much as he loathed the way his father was behaving, he couldn't bring himself to betray him, at least not yet.

Making his way to the poorhouse, he found two children crouched in the doorway out of the biting wind begging for money. Thomas looked at the two young boys, dirty and emaciated, probably thrown out of the poorhouse for bad behaviour, or because the warden had taken a dislike to them. Bury had a well organised system for helping the impoverished off the streets. The workhouse, or poorhouse, was the final ignominious step as a person slipped from a life of near-starvation to one of confinement, drudgery and misery.

Thomas whistled from across the street: 'Hey, you two, come here.' The two urchins ran over, the prospect of money, food or shelter making their coldness disappear. 'See this penny, it's yours if you deliver a message to a large house down the street. All you have to do is just knock on the door and repeat exactly what I'm about to tell you.'

He led the children to the corner of Churchgate St and Whiting St, then pointed out the house where the message was to be delivered. He made them repeat it several times and gave them a halfpenny, with the promise of the same again once they returned with confirmation the demand had been repeated to someone in the household.

He shooed the children away and watched as they hesitantly walked up to the house and knocked on the huge oak door. It was opened by a female servant. Even from a distance he could see the kids laboriously repeating the message he drilled into them. The astonished woman looked up and down the street, though Thomas had taken cover behind a water trough so as not to be seen. She left the children standing there and ran back inside. Thomas whistled at them to scarper before they were taken into the house. They came running back, panting with exertion and holding out their hands for the rest of their money.

'Did you do exactly as I said?' asked Thomas, 'Repeat precisely what I told you?'

'Yes, mister, we did what you told us to say. She was real surprised, wanted to know who sent us. We said we didn't know. That's the truth, innit? Then told us to wait. Didn't fancy that, so we're back here for our other halfpenny.'

Thomas couldn't help but smile at their innocence. They had no idea what they had inadvertently become involved with. Nor did they care, he guessed. They'd just made enough money to buy food for a few days. However, the sooner they were on their way, the better. He handed over a halfpenny coin to each of them and told them to disappear. They did, scampering off down Churchgate St, already planning on what food to buy with their ill-gotten gains.

Inside the house Judge Austin listened as the woman repeated the message. The strain of the last 24 hours showed on his face. A sleepless night and worry over his niece's whereabouts had turned his face to an unhealthy pallor, and lines of worry creased from his eyes.

'Is that all he said? Are you sure?'

The nervous servant confirmed it was: 'Yes, sir. The boy said ten gold sovereigns to be left under the Plague Fountain by tomorrow dawn. That's what the young lads said before they ran off, I saw not in which direction.'

Phillip, who had kept the judge company since early that morning, didn't help matters by saying, 'Tomorrow is Saturday, and there will be hordes of people around the stone washing their money. It will be difficult to keep an eye out for the one who grabs the purse with the ransom in it.'

'Well, thank you for that helpful comment, Phillip.' The judge gave him the kind of withering look he saved for prisoners pleading their innocence on hearing the imposition of a heavy gaol sentence. He needed constructive suggestions, not negative ones.

'At least we have to assume she is still alive. Which is good news,' suggested Phillip, trying to be positive. 'Sir, do we have to plan how to catch the kidnappers as they take the money? Shall we follow them? Or do we just wait for another messenger telling us where she is held?'

The judge thought for a moment, 'I think we need to talk to the constables; we cannot take the law into our own hands. These are violent men.'

An hour later the two constables were back to hear the latest news and devise a plan to arrest the kidnappers as they collected the ransom.

'Constable, how many men can we assemble in the vicinity of the Plague Stone? I am willing to pay whatever is necessary. I fear if we allow these men to escape, we will never see my money, or Jane, again.'

The constable, trying to conceal his surprise, asked, 'You are actually going to leave twelve gold sovereigns under the Plague

Stone? There is always a danger that someone else may discover them and steal the coins.'

The judge allowed himself a strained smile, 'That is a risk we have to take. No, I will place some counterfeit coinage there. I have plenty confiscated in the court house. I doubt these thieves have ever handled a coin of such little value, so will not know it is worth nothing. Until they try and spend it.'

The constable nodded, appreciating the deception involved. 'That's an excellent plan, Judge Austin. I will recruit as many men as possible to be on duty from dawn tomorrow morning. I have every confidence we will catch these scoundrels and bring them before your court. I do not envy their fate when we do so! Do you wish me to return and collect the coins, sir?'

'No, I will take care of them and place the bag under the Plague Stone myself. Thank you, Constable. I trust you will find enough men to cover all possible escape routes? I shall see you again before dawn on Saturday. Let us meet, say, at the Norman Tower.'

Thomas arrived back at the farm at noon. Cold, tired and hungry, all he wanted was some food and sleep. He let the donkey into the pasture and made his way to their tiny cottage. The peace was fractured by sounds of a girl's voice screaming and pleading for help. Rushing into the barn he faced the repugnant sight of his father, naked from the waist down, lying on top of the young girl, trying to force her clothes up around her waist. Despite being restricted by her hands tied to the stable post Jane's struggling and kicking was making it difficult for him to easily complete his loathsome task.

'Just keep still, you whore. This is all your type are good for...'
he grunted in frustration as he tried to force her legs apart.

'Father! What in God's name are you doing? Get off her. Now!'
Thomas ran over and grasped Saul's coat, pulling him off the
petrified girl. Caught in his frenzy of lust his father stood up and
lashed out at his son, catching him on the side of the head. Stunned
at the force of the blow, Thomas fell back heavily, cracking his
head on the floor. Dazed, for a few seconds he lay there; his father
meanwhile was back on top of Jane still attempting to force himself
upon her.

Jane kept struggling, shouting and kicking, hoping in vain to
dissuade this disgusting man from raping her. Her increasingly
desperate cries brought Thomas back to his senses. He pulled
himself up and looked around the old barn for something to use
against his father, anything that would stop him from this animal
behaviour, this insatiable desire to have this girl at any cost. He
ran over to the woodpile and grabbed a large log. Running back,
he stood over his father and brought it down with a sickening
thud onto his head. Instantly he collapsed, motionless, on top
of Jane. For a second no one moved.

Thomas, seeing Jane trying to roll his father's unconscious body
away from her, bent down and dragged him to the other side of
the barn. He returned and without a second thought untied her
hands. Jane sat up, quickly tore off the hood and for the first time
saw both her kidnapper-and rescuer.

Holding her hands to her face, she sat on the ground crying
uncontrollably, huge sobs shaking her body. Thomas stood there,
wondering what he should do next, about his father, and Jane.

'Thank you...thank you,' Jane stuttered after a few moments, still heaving between her tears of relief and now shivering with shock. The young man was at a loss as to how he could help, or what he could say. Jane, the words tumbling out as her panic started to subside, asked, 'Who...who are you? What are you going to do to me now? Please...please, I just want to go home.' Fearing her ordeal might still not be over, Jane, trembling, wrapped her arms around her body, hugging herself as she looked up pleadingly at Thomas.

He realised he was now in an impossible position. The kidnapped girl had seen his face, so if he set her free, she could describe him to the authorities. To make matters worse he had attacked his father, who the girl could also describe if asked. He did not have the stomach to harm, let alone kill the girl, unlike his father who surely, once he came to and saw the scene in front of him, would have no hesitation in disposing of her – and possibly him.

He knelt down beside Jane, who shied away, keeping her distance fearing he may tie her up, or do worse. 'Don't you come near me. Just let me go and I'll say I never saw you. I promise on my mother's grave.'

Thomas, with a disconsolate shrug, said, 'I believe you, lady. But my father won't. He will probably kill both of us given the chance. He will awake long before you can safely get to Bury and sure as day follows night he will find you. He knows where you live! You are worth a fortune to him, and I would not be surprised if he tried again to somehow get his revenge on the judge. I fear we must come up with a plan that will save us both – you from my father and me from the hangman's noose.'

Chapter 9

Diary of Jane Potter.

February 21st 1677

*I*t has been nearly three weeks since the most awful experience of my life, and only now do I feel able to write down what transpired. I will try to be as honest as possible, though I know it will be difficult to stop my emotions taking over as I put pen to paper.

My abduction and treatment by the boy and his father is not something I wish to yet recount in this diary. To write about it, and then read at a later time would bring back too many painful memories. Indeed, I do believe there are parts of it that have already been erased from my memory. I have no desire to relive them.

Let me start by recounting my escape and how my two abductors' fate was sealed, in two very different ways.

The boy, Thomas, who I fervently believe was forced into this inopportune scheme by his horrible father, found himself in an unenviable position. He knew that, once his father discovered I escaped with his son's help and he would not collect any ransom, both our lives would be in danger. I persuaded the poor boy that he should accompany me back to my uncle's house. At first the young man, knowing he committed a crime, did not wish to go to my house for fear (quite rightly, I presumed) of him being arrested. To flee was the alternative, though with no money and *the prospect of the constables and his father pursuing him, it was an unattractive choice.*

With great reluctance he returned with me. I pledged to Thomas that I would take it upon myself to plead his case with my uncle, and ask for his mercy. And so it was that we made our way with haste back to my uncle's house, where a warm welcome greeted me, but not so for Thomas. I explained to Uncle Austin that he was forced into this ill-thought-out crime, then, realising the error of his ways, helped me escape and, perhaps of greatest import, he knew where his father was hiding.

Initially, Uncle Austin was unsympathetic to my entreaties and requests for leniency. However, I eventually won him round (it seems even my crusty old uncle is not immune to my feminine wiles!).

After much consideration, when Thomas finally appeared before him at the Assizes Court he sentenced him to just three years' transportation to the Americas. Preferable to the fate that befell his father, who was captured still unconscious at their barn in Alpheton. The miserable, evil man received his just rewards and was sentenced to hang. As I write this, his execution will take place in four days. I have yet to decide if I shall attend.

Thomas was taken to Ipswich Docks and is now somewhere on the seas heading for his new home. I don't doubt it will be uncomfortable and at times harsh, but it is better than hanging.

Saul Davies was found still unconscious at the farm. His trial lasted but a few hours and he was found guilty of kidnapping. He was hanged on February 25th 1677.

Two months later Thomas departed for Virginia in the Americas with 200 other criminals. For the first time in his life he was lucky. His new master worked him hard in the tobacco fields, but the young man soon showed an aptitude for all things mechanical. He became an expert blacksmith, repairing the ploughs and making gates and horses' harnesses. At the end of his three-year sentence, he stayed on the plantation as a paid worker, so valuable were his skills. While there he married an Irish girl in March of 1680 and produced a family of six children. They moved to Charleston, North Carolina in 1681 where he started a successful business as a ship's chandler. Thomas never returned to England.

Chapter 10
(1680)

'God, I just love this city,' exclaimed Davy as he stood by the window of his office overlooking the docks of New York. 'There's a hundred ships out there that must have come from every continent. Truly, brother, we are at the centre of the world! I'll take these sights and smells with me wherever I go.'

'I wish you would take them, there's nothing romantic about the smell of horse shit, rotting fish and stewing rubbish,' replied Dan with a smile. 'But why should you worry, you're off to England. Leaving me with this unforgettable stink. Never mind, I'll manage.'

'I have every confidence you will, brother, I shall be gone only a few weeks at the most. I shall miss you, and of course New York. But I am looking forward to being back in England, though 'tis unfortunate that the circumstances are unhappy ones.'

'I sincerely hope the news when you arrive will be of a pleasant nature. Maybe next trip I shall join you.' Dan stood up from his desk, and put his arm around his brother's shoulders. 'Now you take care of yourself on your adventure, no womanising or gambling!' laughed Dan, adding on a more serious note, 'Please pass on my best wishes to Henry and Louise, I do hope our venerable stepfather recovers from his illness, though I fear, reading the letter from Mother, his time may have come. I wish I could join you but there is much to do here, and I cannot trust my managers to run the business properly in our absence. Please return with all due haste. If your stay proves to be a long one, promise me you will write?'

Knowing full well it was unlikely, Davy still threw out the promise to keep his brother happy. 'Yes, of course I will keep you informed of what is happening. And indeed what's changed in our old home town. Twenty years is a long time to be away. Maybe I shall find a fine English wife while I am there!'

Dan replied, grinning, 'Well, no American woman wants you, so maybe you'll find a gullible English girl to fall for your...your raffish charms! At least you are wealthy now, that must count for something. Makes up for your many other faults!'

'Thanks for the vote of confidence, brother. We shall see, we shall see. First I must attend to Henry's affairs, it seems his mind is failing him, and he has no other person to help. 'Tis such a shame both his children died early, so it is now down to me to sort matters out. Who knows what I am walking into?'

'Who knows, brother? Whatever it is I am sure you will sort it out in quick order. Now go or you will miss your boat.' They exchanged heartfelt farewells, then Davy gathered up his luggage and left.

As his coach carried him to the docks and his ship bound for England, Davy marvelled at how much New York had grown in the twenty years since the British had taken it over. With a population of over 5,000 it was one of the largest cities in America, expanding quickly as it became the hub for the country's imports and exports. Dan and Davy became rich handling Henry's business after he sold the plantations in Virginia and moved into exporting pelts, wood, tobacco, indeed anything that would satiate the demands of England's burgeoning wealthy classes. Three years ago they bought the business from their stepfather. Since then it continued to grow, making the brothers one of the largest exporters to Great Britain from New York.

Davy was unsure exactly what business interests Henry still ran in England. As a successful lawyer Henry loved to invest in all manner of enterprises, so Davy expected some surprises, not all good, he suspected. Henry and his wife, Louise, lived a modest lifestyle with a house in Guildhall St and a farm somewhere near Sudbury. Whatever the state of his business interests Davy was confident he could sort them out. Twenty years helping Dan build up the enterprise in New York made him street-smart, quick-witted, and careful with every penny.

As his ship, *The Atlantic Rose*, left the harbour for the four or five-week journey, it gave Davy time to reflect on how his life had changed since meeting Henry back in 1650, when he was but a lad of ten.

He and Dan were languishing in Bury gaol having stolen some candlesticks from a house in Whiting St that Henry owned, but at the time was renting to a wealthy moneylender and his wife. If found guilty they would've been hanged. Fortune had favoured them when Dan remembered Henry was a distant uncle, and a lawyer, who they'd met only once. He sent a message from gaol begging him for help. Henry initially refused but, at his wife's insistence, reluctantly came to their aid, persuading the judge to sentence them only to a day in the pillories, under the proviso he took Dan and Davy under his wing. He did so, providing them with an education and a decent home. Subsequently Henry adopted the boys as his own sons. They proved quick learners and in their stable environment excelled at their studies in the local grammar school. So much so that when Dan was old enough Henry sent him to run his plantations in America. A few years later Davy followed. Neither had returned to England since.

On board Davy began to see why so few people made the trip across the Atlantic unless it was imperative. The cramped quarters, called the aftercastle, where the few passengers and crew all slept in hammocks or bunks, had such a low ceiling Davy continually banged his head. The food was monotonous, chosen for its ability to not go bad rather than for its taste, with offerings such as hard bread, ship's biscuit, meat and cheese always on the menu.

His fellow passengers grumbled about their seasickness, from which Davy was grateful not to suffer, the food, the smells and the discomfort. They made for poor companions, too concerned about their own wellbeing to strike up a conversation.

The Atlantic Rose was of modest size. Davy paced the deck one day out of boredom and managed to count just 25 long steps from aft to stern. Packed to the gunnels with 300 hogshead of tobacco, the ship was fully loaded and wallowed precariously in heavy seas. In the main the wind was favourable and on some days he heard the captain say they had covered over 100 miles. Halfway through the voyage on a bitter March morning a seaman shouted the warning, 'Iceberg to the northwest, five leagues away.' Everyone rushed to the port side to see this floating white mountain. Close enough to admire, far away enough to be safe. They sailed lazily past it, clawing their way eastward towards England. It was one of the few moments of excitement on the voyage.

On some days the temperature dropped below freezing and the passengers huddled below deck around a brazier to keep warm. On others a thick, dense fog brought the ship to a becalmed, frustrating halt which tested everyone's patience as they waited for a breath of wind to fill the sails, push away the fog and allow the journey homewards to continue.

After four weeks *The Atlantic Rose* sailed past the Scilly Isles, docked in Portsmouth and then continued as part of a convoy of sixty ships headed up the English Channel to London. Two weeks later Davy wearily trudged down Guildhall St to Henry and Louise Jermyn's home. The street had changed little in over twenty years. The magnificent Guildhall was yet again being renovated; parts of it dated back to 1220, and it was in need of a new roof and windows. Davy nodded to the workman who was meticulously replacing the panes of glass, a highly skilled job. One breakage was a month's wages to these artisans.

He knocked on the door of the house and waited; even though it was his home of old, he felt uncomfortable walking in unannounced. He knocked again, finally the door opened, and an old lady, with grey hair falling around her shoulders and sallow complexion, looked up at Davy. He was just about to ask for Henry or Louise, when the woman's face lit up with a welcoming smile, 'Please God if it isn't my boy, Davy!' She flung her arms around his neck and hugged him with a ferocity that belied her slight build. Too shocked to say anything he realised it was Louise, his mother, looking so different from when he'd last seen her waving him off at Ipswich docks some two decades ago. Once tall and strong, her eyes always so bright and alive, she was now a shadow of her former self. Her face a picture of loss and grief. Her slim frame stooped with the weight of her unhappiness.

Trying to conceal his surprise at the dramatic change in her appearance, he waited for the fierce embrace to end, then kissed her on both cheeks. 'Mother, my dear mother, it has been too long to finally see you again. You look...wonderful. I am so happy to be home.'

Even though he knew the answer, he held back from asking about his stepfather's health. They walked into the main room of the house where a fire lit up an otherwise gloomy room. Louise, too, seemed unwilling to broach the subject. For a few minutes Davy answered Louise's questions about his trip from New York. Both not wanting to dispel the happiness of the moment. Finally he asked:

'It has been a long, tiresome trip, Mother, I am in need of a decent meal and some good English food!'

Louise smiled, 'Davy, Davy that's a refrain I haven't heard in a long time – you asking for something to eat. I never was able to keep up with your appetite. Of course, come into the hall, I will get one of the servants to bring sustenance and ale. Sit down, we have a lot to talk about.'

Davy stood in front of the huge inglenook fireplace holding his hands out to the flames, bringing the circulation back into his cold fingers. He looked around the large room; it had been redecorated, with curtains and wall hangings, all of excellent quality from what he could tell. Plus new furniture. It was the dwelling of a comfortably well-off man. Anxiously he waited for Louise's return – he could no longer delay wanting news of Henry's wellbeing. The fact he had not come to welcome Davy created a sinking feeling in his stomach, and he felt bad news was about to be delivered. Louise came back into the room and sat down, beckoning him to sit next to her. She took hold of his hands, delicately rubbing his fingers as if it would somehow help her control his reactions when she told him about Henry.

'I know you are waiting to hear about Henry. For too long it has been a weight around my neck, knowing you would be arriving too late to see him. Davy...your wonderful father is no longer with us. He passed away over a month ago after a long and painful illness. He wished and tried so bravely to live long enough to see you, but the malady from which he suffered for many months was relentless and he succumbed at the end of January. He fought well, stubborn as ever until the end, but God finally extinguished his pain, for which I am grateful. He was a great man, a caring husband and I miss him dreadfully.' Louise let go of Davy's hands and pulled a kerchief from her pocket, stopping the tears falling from her eyes. Davy knelt down before his distraught mother and hugged her, trying to absorb, somehow take away, the pain she still felt deep inside. He whispered in her ear. 'My brother and I owe everything to him, he rescued us from the worst possible existence, and we are grateful beyond words to him – and you – for the lives you gave us. We are all honoured to have known such a man.'

Louise gently pushed him away, the wisp of a smile now on her tear-stained face. 'Davy, you and Dan have made us both so proud. Your achievements in America delighted us beyond measure. He never stopped talking about how successful you were and how fortunate we were to have you as our sons.' Standing up, she shrugged off her melancholy and poured some ale from a pitcher, filling two tankards. She held hers aloft, 'May God bless his soul, and we thank the Lord that we knew and loved such a marvellous man. Cheers!'

Davy joined in a toast to his departed father, then descended like a vulture on the platter of meat, cheese and bread.

The sad news now out in the open, the atmosphere lightened and they reminisced, laughed, and tried to catch up on twenty years of separation. The food, drink and a comfortable chair in front of the fire, took its toll on Davy, making him drowsy. He asked Louise if he could take her leave and sleep for a few hours. He barely noticed that she showed him to his old bedroom up in the eaves of the house. Though redecorated since he last slept there as a boy, much of the furniture was the same. As he fell asleep fond memories of the time he spent in the room came filtering back prompting a deep, dreamless rest.

The following day, after a welcome night's sleep and a breakfast fit for a king, Davy asked where he should start to try and gather an understanding of Henry's affairs. Louise showed him into the study. Both were determined to put on a brave face, the room and its contents a poignant reminder of Henry. Davy sat at the bureau looking at the piles of papers, agreements and ledgers encompassing Henry's numerous business interests. It was a daunting sight.

Looking a little deflated, Louise explained, 'I have done my best to keep up with it all while he was ill and unable to attend to them, but in all honesty I am sure I missed a lot. And now he has passed, it really has become overwhelming. His old friend Judge Austin, who lives up the road, has been of great assistance. Oh! He now owns the house in Whiting St, which you....know, of course. How could you forget the scene of your crime, that led you here?' She laughed, though Davy did not find it so amusing.

'Well, that is a long-past incident in my life I would rather forget, Mother! Let me spend some time looking through all these papers, then I may go and see Judge Austin for further advice or information.' He flipped through one of the mountains of paperwork and sighed. 'This is going to take some time, Mother, to get organised. But fear not I will prepare a full list of all his business interests as quickly as I can. Then we can decide on the best course of action to ensure you have a comfortable future. That is my priority.'

For a full week Davy worked night and day. Twice he paid a visit to Judge Austin, who proved not just knowledgeable about any legal problems associated with agreements Henry signed, but a vital source of information on who some of the people were that his father had done business with: who were honest and who weren't, which businesses were doing well, which were struggling. During the course of these meetings, the judge was interested to know more of Davy's life in New York, his and his brother's businesses, and America in general.

'Is it really the land of opportunity everyone says it is?' he asked one day.

'It can be, no doubt about it, sir. But it requires a lot of hard work. The rules and regulations are not so onerous as here, however the law is worryingly slack at times, with little legal recourse if arguments arise or dishonesty takes place. It can get, shall we say, a little brutal at times? Outside of the cities, life can be dangerous, the Indians are beginning to realise that us Europeans are going to take their land without or without payment, and in the western areas they are protecting it violently at times. I have heard many a story of murder, kidnapping and rape of pioneers. It is not for the faint of heart.'

The judge was fascinated by Davy's stories; so much so, one day he suggested, 'We are holding a double celebration for my niece Jane, it is her birthday, and the completion of her most important painting commission so far. I would be honoured if you could attend on Saturday and maybe entertain our guests with anecdotes of your life in America?'

Davy happily accepted the invitation and went home to tell Louise about it. She was thrilled. 'Jane is a lovely girl, who went through a terrible ordeal a few months ago, being kidnapped and I gather almost raped. She seems to have recovered and has become quite the local celebrity with her portrait painting. I am sure you will have a wonderful time and the guests will be enthralled with your stories from America.' Adding with a mischievous grin, 'She has become quite the eligible young lady, so I understand.'

That Saturday, intrigued and a little nervous, Davy presented himself at the judge's house. A servant led him to the great hall where some twenty people were chatting and laughing. In the centre of the room a large picture hidden by a velvet cloth resting on an easel in the middle of the room. The judge saw Davy and signalled he should join his group of guests. Collecting a glass of wine along the way he walked over and shook hands, 'Judge Austin, thank you again for the invitation, it is a pleasure to be here. A break from poring over my father's books is most welcome.'

'Please call me Christopher, and let me introduce you to the person we are all here to celebrate. Jane!' He called to attract her attention. 'Please join us. This is the young man I was telling you about who lives in New York. He is the son of Henry Jermyn, who actually used to own this house, many years ago.'

Davy barely heard Christopher's words of introduction, his attention diverted to what he thought was the most attractive woman he had ever set eyes upon. As she shook his hand and bowed slightly he was at a loss for words. Holding onto her hand for probably longer than was appropriate, he finally found his voice and managed to utter a few words of congratulations on finishing her painting. Taking a sip of his wine allowed him to collect his thoughts, as Jane asked him questions about his stay in England. Had it changed much since he was last here? How long would he be staying? How was his mother? Embarrassed at his social inadequacy he gamely tried to answer her, but feared he just babbled nonsense. Eventually gaining control of his nervousness and his tongue, the conversation flowed smoothly.

Jane smiled inwardly. There before her stood a strapping, handsome man who had forgotten, if he ever knew, the niceties of informal conversation with a woman. Feeling a little sorry for him, she continued talking and made sure he was included in the chatter with the other guests to help him relax. She noticed his eyes were roaming all around the room as if he was trying to find or remember something, so eventually she asked, 'Sir, you seem to be anxious to find something in the room, have you been here before-with your father when he owned it?'

Davy felt himself blush. 'Er, no, ma'am, I was just admiring the beautiful wall hangings.' Jane didn't accept the explanation; however, deciding it was a topic for some reason her guest did not wish to pursue she enquired no further. She felt her uncle's hand gently touch her arm. 'Shall we do the unveiling now?' Jane nodded and went to stand beside her covered picture. Her uncle then proceeded to embarrass her with a lengthy eulogy as to her talents as a portraitist, before with a theatrical flourish she pulled the cloth away to reveal a portrait of the young Lord Hervey of Ickworth. There was a generous round of applause and numerous favourable comments from the guests as they looked with admiration at her work. The young man himself went over to Jane and gave her a kiss on each cheek. 'Ma'am, you have done me more than justice with this painting. I fear anyone meeting me after seeing this will be mightily disappointed,' he said

'Not at all, my lord, I believe I have captured your true looks and your inner self. At least I tried to. I am glad you are pleased with the result.'

'Perhaps you and Judge Austin could come out to Ickworth sometime, and see the picture in its...proper place?'

'I would like that very much, my lord. I thank you for the invitation.'

Hearing this exchange, Davy felt a slight tinge of jealousy. 'You are indeed most talented, Jane,' said Davy, a few minutes later, when she had extracted herself from the conversation with Lord Hervey.

'Aside from being an accomplished artist you have reached the grand age of 21. If you were in America you would be married with a brood of children by now! Are the English less inclined to wed at an early age, I wonder? Are you not at least courting?' Davy suddenly realised his rambling, pointed questions might be seen as improper. Before he could apologise, Jane answered coyly.

'I'm not sure a lady discusses such things with a man she has just met, sir. But since you ask in such a polite way, no, I'm neither betrothed, nor attached to any young man, If truth be told the pickings in Bury are lacking in choice. It seems self-important young aristocrats are the only ones my uncle thinks I should meet.' Before she could stop herself she added, 'I think I need a little more adventure in my life to balance the serious and painstaking work involved in painting portraits.' *Oh, Jane, she chastised herself, what are you saying to a man you barely know?*

What will he think of me being so honest and outspoken? She cast her eyes downward to hide her embarrassment.

"I'm sure some rich, worthy young man will soon beat a path to your door,' said Davy, grinning.

Regaining her composure, Jane led Davy over to the centre of the room and announced to everyone that their guest from America was going to entertain them with stories about life in the colonies.

Overcoming his awkwardness at being the centre of attention after a few stuttered sentences, he found the words flowed easily as he described life on a tobacco plantation, slavery, and the painful and dangerous progress westward. He added a few interesting anecdotes about New York and how it compared to London.

Asked about how they were governed, he explained, 'There are difficulties in creating any form of local government; people are too busy scraping a living to worry about such things, and the Indians and their attacks on the pioneers are a constant and dangerous reminder there is no real order, no one there to ask for help – except your neighbours.'

The questions came in a rush from the other guests: How easy was it to travel there? What was the voyage like? How big were the cities? (When he pointed out that New York was one of the largest but no bigger than Bury, people were astonished.) What were the main occupations? Were all religions really allowed to conduct their affairs in the open? Had he actually met an Indian? After half an hour Judge Austin decided that Davy needed rescuing from the friendly inquisition and announced dinner was to be served.

Delighted, he found himself seated next to Jane, who continued to pepper him with questions. Exhausted at her endless interrogation he interrupted her and facetiously suggested the best thing she could do 'is go out there to find out for yourself.'

Deploying her best pout, she answered. 'Well, who knows, I might just do that one day. In the meantime, my birthday wish is that you come here again for supper and allow me to ask as many questions as I like. You cannot say no to such a request.'

'Is it a request, or an order, or maybe even a threat?' asked Davy jokingly.

'Turn me down and you shall find out, sir. I am available next Wednesday, at five o'clock. Can I count on you honouring my birthday wish?'

Try keeping me away, thought Davy, before replying with mock seriousness, 'I am a man of honour and would not dare to upset a lady's birthday request. I look forward to seeing you then. I will be recollecting more anecdotes for your pleasure.'

'I expect nothing less! I might even sketch you while you talk. Yes! I shall practise my charcoal drawing while you entertain me. Perfect!' she trilled, trying to contain her excitement. With difficulty she tore herself away from Davy when a guest annoyingly tapped her on the shoulder to ask a question about the painting.

By the middle of the evening the dinner ended and people began to depart. He thanked his host, and Jane demurely reminded him of his visit to see her on Wednesday. Davy, his mind racing, walked back to Louise's house. While only five minutes away, by the time he opened the front door he knew something had happened to him that was giving his stomach butterflies, and putting a stupid grin on his face.

Louise looked up from her book as he entered the room, and asked, 'So what are you looking so happy about? Too much to drink at the party?' He avoided answering her question, for fear of embarrassing himself, and went upstairs to continue ploughing through his father's business correspondence. It proved a hopeless task. His mind was on one track only, the thought of spending time alone with Jane in just a few days.

Next day Davy knuckled down again and, after nearly two weeks, a clearer picture of his father's at times Byzantine business interests emerged. He wrote copious notes to make sure he had all the facts to present to Louise. One evening after supper he felt confident enough to put his mother in the picture regarding Henry's legacy.

'I think I can finally explain to you in general terms the size, scope and possible value of Henry's businesses. There is some good news, actually a lot of good news, but some also difficult decisions will have to be made over the next few months. Let me explain.'

For the next hour Davy went through his notes. There were a dozen properties in Bury that she now owned and were rented out and two farms near Whepstead producing a regular, if unspectacular, income. Plus, a flour mill, two shops in the Buttermarket, an apothecary, a bakery and one ale house. More problematic, in many other cases Henry lent money to people to start, or rescue their businesses, but appeared to have done little to get the debt repaid.

'So, by my estimates and having talked to some moneylenders and people who know the value of properties in Bury, I think if the houses, businesses and farms were sold at their full value, you would receive over £5,000. On top of that if you pursued all the money owed, it would amount to another £2000. In short, Mother, if Father's estate is handled properly you are a wealthy woman!' He glanced up, a triumphant look on his face. Instead of seeing his mother smiling, she looked worried. 'Of course that is wonderful news Davy, and it is a relief that the poorhouse does not await me. But in truth, I have no knowledge or experience in running businesses, selling property, let alone collecting debts. It all sounds overwhelming if I am to be honest.'

She left an unasked question hovering in the air. It took Davy a few seconds to read the silence, to understand what was being wordlessly suggested. He decided to give himself time to think over the answer.

'I understand, Mother, it must be daunting to be faced with such tasks. Allow me time to look at the options concerning disposing of Henry's estate and let us talk again tomorrow.'

Louise nodded her head, grateful Davy had not dismissed out of hand her implied proposal he should stay in England to manage her former husband's businesses, and do whatever was necessary to realise their full value. She knew it was selfish of her to expect him to stay for a much longer time than he originally planned, but at the moment no acceptable alternatives came to mind. She hoped he would agree to stay; unbeknownst to her, an ally was coming to her aid.

Jane was apprehensive, yes, jittery even, at the prospect of meeting Davy again. Had she been too forward in asking him to come and visit her so quickly, and on the flimsiest of pretexts?

Was a sense of decorum pushed aside in her enthusiasm to spend more time with this handsome, eligible young man? Too late now, she thought, he was due to arrive in a few minutes. She spent most of the day doing her hair and trying on different dresses she felt appropriate for such *a tête à tête.*

She'd finally chosen a pale blue dress sporting a white brocade with the new fashion of a *mantua bodice,* though she eschewed the large ruffles on her sleeves as these could interfere with her drawing or painting. In a moment of daring she let her long fair hair loose, leaving her *fontange* thrown carelessly on her bed. Her maid was aghast at Jane's impetuousness; if Judge Austin saw such an outfit he would surely castigate her, claiming it was unbecoming a young lady. Jane didn't care – she knew that in America things were less formal and she was anxious to show Davy she was a woman happy to cast aside old, stuffy customs.

Chapter 11
(1680)

Diary of Jane Potter.

March 31st 1680

*H*ow quickly does time fly when you're in the company of a young man who is attractive, fascinating and enjoyable company!

This afternoon passed in a whirl of laughter and delectation. Drawing Davy gave me the opportunity to scrutinise his every feature, and ask him endless questions about his life in America and his plans for the future. Poor man; it must have been like an inquisition at times, but he seemed willing to satisfy my quizzing, except for his life in Bury before he went to America. Then he was evasive, but no matter; 'tis of little importance, it was such a long time ago.

From an artist's perspective he is an interesting study. As befits a man who has spent a lot of his time outdoors his skin is weathered and rugged. His chiselled jaw is framed by a neatly trimmed beard, with just some flecks of grey appearing! Even at such a young age his eyes are etched with lines, telltales of resilience, or a tough life, I wonder. Whenever he looked at me, his thoughtful gaze made it feel like for every question I asked him, I was also giving away a little bit about myself.

We interrupted the sitting for some refreshments. It was a wonderfully relaxed afternoon and I do believe at times he was actually flirting with me, or was that just wishful thinking?

To be honest my sketch of him was by no means my best work! He was a distraction of the most pleasant kind, so the result was one I hesitated to even show him. However, polite man that he is, he showed delight and appreciation at my efforts, asking if he could take the drawing home to show his mother.

Not once did he make any forward or importune comments; he was a perfect gentleman, and to my pleasure seemed genuinely reluctant to leave when the time came. He asked if we could meet again, and with a shameful lack of discretion I immediately agreed.

April 6th

It was a beautiful warm spring day, so when Davy arrived he suggested we go for a walk around the town. As it wasn't a market day, the streets were uncrowded and, after a stroll across Angel Hill, down Eastgate St and along the banks of the River Lark, we walked back to the Traverse and found the new coffee shop at the recently renovated Cupola House. One part of the ground floor being an apothecary, the other providing refreshment in the form of tea or coffee. It has become quite the meeting place for local writers, artists and others of a creative persuasion. As an unaccompanied woman I would not normally have been welcomed in such an establishment, but on the arm of a dashing young man, no one seemed to mind. While sipping a cup of strong coffee (from the distant lands of North Africa, so the owner proudly explained), Davy revealed his dilemma concerning Louise's veiled suggestion that he should stay and run his father's businesses. He understood her desire, but he felt a duty to go back and help his brother in New York. It took all my self-restraint not to persuade him to stay in Bury – for purely selfish reasons, of course! We discussed the matter at some length, he reached no conclusion and I remain hopeful he will decide to remain here.

And then it happened! As he bade me goodbye at the front door of the house, he kissed me! It took me completely by surprise and all my strength to stop my knees from giving way! It was only the briefest of intimacies, our lips just touching for a second, but as I write this an hour later I do believe my hand is still shaking. Is this what love feels like?

April 30th

Davy has made an appointment to see my uncle, Judge Austin; he is going to ask permission for my hand in marriage!!! I am giddy with excitement, and only hope he finds no reason to deny Davy's request. I know we have been acquainted for barely two months, but I believe deep in my heart this man will fulfil everything I want and need in a husband. I have been praying like a nun all day for a favourable outcome from this meeting.

May 1st

He said yes! Davy and I are to be married this summer, I am hoping in early August. I met with Louise, who was delighted at the news. I am sure her joy is doubled at the prospect her son will remain in England and continue to run his father's affairs. I am so happy for her, and beyond jubilant at my own good fortune.

* * * *

The wedding took place on August 3rd at St Mary's Church. The weather was sunny, a perfect reflection of the day's lighthearted and celebratory atmosphere. Even the curmudgeonly Judge Austin, who gave Jane away, made an amusing speech at the festivities afterwards, claiming his niece was so pretty 'men came from far-off continents to seek her hand in marriage.' The bride and groom made a striking couple, Jane's radiant and smiling face beguiling all who saw her. Davy, a little overwhelmed at all the attention, stood tall, an imposing figure happy to let his new wife soak up the admiration of the guests. He was exhilarated and enthralled with his beautiful new wife.

Louise, too, was delighted. Knowing Davy would be here for the foreseeable future to run her late husband's estate took a huge weight off her mind. He was not the only one at the wedding who remarked she looked brighter and happier than she had for many months. And she had gained a talented daughter-in-law whose portraiture skills were becoming recognised beyond the town of Bury – her commissions now coming from Ipswich and even Norwich. She was on a path where her abilities would make her famous. Unfortunately his brother, Dan, could not attend the wedding, but sent congratulations and the present of two large silver candlesticks (only Davy and Louise understood the joke – these were similar to the items many years before which, as young boys, they had stolen from the house – leading to their arrest and subsequent extrication from the hangman's noose by their soon-to-become stepfather).

The couple moved into the house in Whiting St. A few days later Judge Austin came to see them.

'I have a present for you both.' Another rare smile creased his face as he handed over a parchment roll. Davy opened it. 'My lord, are my eyes deceiving me, or are these the deeds to this house?'

'They are, Davy. It is only befitting that a couple of your stature should live in and own a house of this grandeur. As I get older I have no need for the responsibilities involved with its upkeep; you are young and now have the means to make this house a magnificent home for you and your future family. I hope you all will be happy here.'

Jane embraced her uncle, spluttering copious thanks amongst her tears of joy. As soon as the judge left they rushed round to see Louise, whose face on hearing their news showed no joy, only despair.

"Mother, you seem upset. I thought you would be happy that we own such a wonderful house! Why are you not so? Is there something wrong?" asked Davy.

Louise sat down, asking the couple to do likewise. She took their hands, while she explained in a quiet voice, the curse she believed lurked in the house which led to her first child being born with no hearing. They had lived there for only a short time, before moving out for fear their next child might be so afflicted. She wasn't, though tragically died a few years later, soon after their deaf son had succumbed to a mysterious pox, leaving them childless. The young couple listened disbelievingly until Louise added she also knew of previous owners whose children had suffered similar fates.

Davy was not convinced. 'Curses? Spells? I believe it to be hogwash, Mother, just a terrible coincidence that children are born in that house with such conditions. I am so sorry it happened to you, Mother, but I have no fear it will happen to any of our children. We are both healthy, and I promise you a grandson before the year is out!'

Jane was not reassured by her husband's aplomb; Louise had seen it happen firsthand within her family – and others. They left the house, Jane despondent, Davy angry. Later that evening she broached the subject, suggesting maybe they should move.

'What, sell this magnificent house? What would your uncle say if we told him the reason why? He would, I am sure, laugh at us for subscribing to such strange beliefs. No, my dear, we are staying here, and will bring up a brood of healthy children, just you wait and see.'

As if to prove the point, he grabbed Jane's hand and led her to the bedroom, where he made love to her twice within the hour, as if eager to impregnate her as soon as possible. Jane, still discovering the unknown delights of her body, and his, fell back exhausted after Davy spent himself inside her for a second time, shuddering and groaning as he did so. She was anxious as he to start a family, however Louise's warning lodged in her mind, like a splinter in her finger, worrying, painful, and difficult to ignore. Never mind, she reasoned, that was all in the past; there must be a sound reason why it happened to her mother-in-law. The days of witches and curses were for the superstitious. Jane decided to carry on trying for a family as soon as possible.

It was May 16th 1681 when she went into labour and produced a healthy-looking boy, they named Henry. Davy was ecstatic – a son! He fussed endlessly over the baby whenever he came home from work. All seemed well to start with. However, it was in July when they first noticed the baby seemed to hear no sound they made, their voices failing to generate any reaction from him. He smiled, gurgled happily, his eyes were bright and alert, but something was amiss. A doctor came from the local hospital to test the boy's hearing. Once completed he gave them the terrible news; Henry was profoundly deaf.

Jane was distraught, then angry for not heeding Louise's advice. If the house was to blame, then Jane knew she no longer wanted to live there. She wanted more children and would never forgive herself if they too suffered such illnesses. Reluctantly she decided they must leave the house as soon as possible. It was such a lovely house in all other respects, but, despite her unwillingness to believe in witchcraft and spells, she convinced her Uncle Christopher, and then Davy, that they should leave. They moved in August into Louise's home in Guildhall St, never to return to the Whiting St house, leaving all the furniture, expensive hangings and rugs behind, fearing whatever may have caused the baby's hearing defect was somehow lurking within them.

Yet despite the move, despair fell over Jane like a weighted blanket. Her interest in the baby waned. She worried endlessly about his and their future. Her depression seemed to worsen every day. The new home, with Louise looking after her and the baby, could not shift the desolation and melancholy that meant for days at a time she uttered not a word. Davy was worried about her and the baby's health, but the doctor and his mother advised him to give Jane time to recover from the trauma and despondency that often follows a difficult birth.

Diary of Jane Potter.

September 3rd 1681

My poor darling baby boy, I still feel so guilty that you will never be able to hear my voice, or the deep American twang your father speaks with. Music, the sound of birds, rushing water, the laughter of your gruff uncle, all will be unheard by you.

How will your life be fulfilled missing such beauty? Yet your eyes sparkle with happiness and you are already, I believe, trying to form words of some kind. You seem unconcerned that you have no hearing, content with your lot. But I am not. I fear for your future when we are not here to take care of you. Protecting you from ridicule, harmful and insensitive people who will make your life a misery.

I cannot bear to think of you suffering without Davy and me there to offer succour and love.

It is all my fault, no matter what my beloved husband says, or the priests (though behind my back I am sure they somehow blame past sins of mine for your affliction). It is best for both of us that we end our lives while I am capable of administering this poison. You will feel little pain. I shall follow you soon, my beloved son. I shall be with you in death as I was for both of us in life, but in a safer and happier place.

Davy, when you read this I shall be with Henry and our Lord Jesus. Forgive me, my love, but I have prayed and prayed for guidance from God and forgiveness from you for what I have done. Please be happy for me and your son. Once your grief has waned you will know I did the right thing. I will love you always. Jane

* * * *

Distressed and tormented, her mind unhinged after months of guilt, believing she alone was responsible for Henry's deafness, Jane lay back on her bed. She undid her bodice and freed her milk-swollen breasts. The baby squirmed in her arms, sensing it was time to feed. She uncorked a small vial of hemlock, an irreversible poison, and rubbed it onto her swollen nipples. She slowly brought the baby to her breast. He quickly began suckling, hungry for her goodness. Every time he stopped, she rubbed a little more of the deadly potion onto her nipple. It took several minutes before his small body spasmed and then lay motionless, still latched to her breast. Then Jane drank the rest of the vial. She lay quietly with her dead child until the hemlock took her life.

Davy sank into a pit of depression. He blamed himself for his beautiful wife's death, since it was he who disregarded the advice given by Louise concerning the danger of having children in the house. As a result the two most important people in his life were no more. To compound his desolation, two months later Louise passed away. A sense of disconsolation consumed him. He drank himself senseless every day. Although now a wealthy man after inheriting his father's extensive business empire, he let matters slide, and his creditors and tenants took advantage of his indifference. Eventually Judge Austin convinced Davy he should either sell up and go back to America, or stay and manage his business properly.

Davy took the former course. Just eight months after the death of his wife and child, he was on his journey back to his brother and America, a land that was full of happy recollections and a bright future far, far away from England, a place of melancholy and memory.

The spinster's curse had not fully run its course, but its end was drawing near.

Chapter 12
(1688)

*I*n the last decades of the seventeenth century, the country was still riven with strife as the different religions and their adherents fought for recognition. Catholics, Protestants, Jesuits and non-conformists fell in and out of favour with the King and Parliament. Various bills and laws were passed, then rescinded to try and maintain the peace. Increased freedom to practise their beliefs only seemed to inflame one group or another. With the birth of a son by James II's second wife, Mary of Modena, many feared the likelihood of a new Catholic dynasty arising again. Concern among non-Catholics was now at its highest, and then the unthinkable happened: Several prominent politicians and aristocrats invited the Protestant king of what is now the Netherlands, William of Orange, to invade England to protect Protestantism. William obliged and, along with his fleet, landed in Brixham, Devon, on November 5, 1688. The event is often referred to as the 'Glorious Revolution' because the transition of power was relatively smooth and bloodless. James II fled the country on 23rd December, 1688.

* * * *

Monsignor Patrick de Voight was worried. A month ago he was able to practise Mass in the great hall of the house, regularly squeezing in over forty worshippers. Some Sundays he held the service twice as the number of Catholic adherents increased and his services grew in popularity. Now with the Glorious Revolution sweeping the country, Catholics were again under attack and being driven underground, imperilling his weekly meetings and those that attended.

Pondering over the wording of his next sermon, divine inspiration was failing to work his quill pen across the paper. All he could see was the progress made over recent years slowly evaporating and his flock being forced to worship in secret and fear for their lives. He put his pen down in frustration. 'Please, Lord, send me guidance, send me words of comfort and reassurance to my supplicants,' he prayed quietly to himself.

Sitting across the room, her back to his desk, was his companion, Mary. She looked over her shoulder and offered her own advice. 'Patrick, my dear, much as it pains me to say it, I think you and your worshippers need a miracle and a place to hide, not kind or inspiring words. I hear there are riots in Cambridge, that they attacked a Catholic chapel in Cheveley, razing it to the ground. Someone has now accused the mayor of trying to blow up the Guildhall, a fabrication no doubt, but one that I am sure will result in his removal from office, as he is a Catholic. We have to face the ugly truth, Patrick; with King James gone, the demon Protestants are taking control again.'

Patrick walked over and sat next to her. His face was drawn and grey, a picture of despair. His normally alert eyes were now dull and rheumy. He shook his head, still unable to grasp the turn of events that within weeks had reversed years of progress.

'After all our hard work, our prayers finally being answered, now in order to continue our mission we will be in hiding like hunted rabbits, running from the bloodthirsty Protestants again. It does, Mary, test my belief in God's purpose at times. But I will not run from these heathens. We will continue to open our Mass here to anyone wanting to pray with us for salvation in these heretical times. This house will be our, and their, sanctuary. We must be discreet and constantly on our guard, but we shall continue the Lord's work.'

It was a vow that would prove difficult and dangerous to keep over the coming months and years. The riots that tore apart Cambridge, London and other cities swept into Bury St Edmunds in the middle of June. As Mary predicted, Mayor John Stafford was stripped of his office and his home in St Andrew's St burnt to the ground. The rioters swarmed through Bury seeking any homes or businesses run by Catholics. A mob of nearly 100 invaded the abbey grounds where the Jesuits had built their college, known as Mass House. The terrified inhabitants were dragged out, beaten and threatened with hanging if they didn't leave the town immediately. Many did; however not all were so easily cowed. One tall, strongly built young Jesuit priest stormed out of the building, wielding a large heavy cudgel as if it were a wooden spoon, his brown cassock an incongruous sight as he launched into the mob screaming verses from the Jerusalem Bible.

'Ye shall all burn in hell!' he bellowed, his rage giving him strength and dissolving his fear. The other Jesuits stood back cowering by the door as they watched him wade into the mob, his vows of peace and non-violence lost in the heat of the moment.

He felled three men with mighty blows to their heads, two never to get up; the sheer ferocity of his attack momentarily halted the crowd's efforts to enter the college. It was a valiant attempt, though doomed to failure as the baying attackers, outraged at his unexpected bravery, soon surrounded him shouting insults and threats. For a few minutes he defended himself against them, but many had pikes, much longer than the reach of his wild swinging club. Slowly the slashing and stabbing of their weapons began to take its toll. As blood stained his cassock from a large wound in his neck, the brave Jesuit fell to his knees. The crowd surged forward raining blows with their weapons on his fallen body. Still weakly cursing them the huge man finally succumbed to their remorseless onslaught when a sword was plunged deep into his neck. The horrified Jesuits watching the murder of their Brother fled inside the college, frantically barricading the door. The senior Father screamed at his students to escape by the rear entrance into the old abbey grounds and head for the River Lark.

"Head towards Thomas Burton's house at Beyton with all haste, don't stop for anything or anyone, these barbarians will be upon us within minutes!' The ten petrified students stumbled over one another in their haste to escape; barely had Father Michael followed them, than he heard the old oak door crack and splinter into pieces, allowing the horde to surge into the college. Their looting and ransacking of the house allowed the Jesuits time to flee along the river bank and to safety.

When Father Michael caught up with the frightened students he led them to the safety of a Catholic sympathiser, Thomas Burton. They would never worship again at the Mass House.

Mary walked into the house carrying fresh produce from the Bury market to find Patrick pacing the great hall. His agitation was clear.

'Praise be! You are safe, Mary; whatever tempted you to go to the market when the rioters are still rampaging around the town? I heard they attacked the Jesuit college, and killed one of their students. They are assailing and murdering anyone with

Catholic connections, it seems. You cannot be seen outside, it is too dangerous.'

'Calm down, calm down, Patrick, they are more interested in stealing and damaging property than in killing women. Though I was told of their murderous behaviour towards the Jesuits, I understand most escaped. However, little is left of the building; it has been torn apart, everything of value now gone.'

The monsignor looked more despondent than ever on hearing this news. 'Our position here is becoming more dangerous by the day, but I cannot desert my flock at a time like this, when they need us most. It is my duty, to them and to God.'

Mary walked over and put her arms around his neck, drawing his face towards hers. 'And it is my duty to aid you in whatever way I can, and that includes helping you relax for a short time and forget about these troubles.'

'Mary, oh Mary...' Patrick moaned quietly. He knew what she was doing, and his resolve quickly melted.

She kissed him gently, but with a passion that together with her hand slipping under his cassock and gently massaging him, brought a groan of expectation and pleasure. Wordlessly she led him upstairs to their chamber, and playfully pushed him onto the bed and said, 'You may start your prayers now, Patrick.'

As she loosened his clothing and slid her hands between his legs, Mary heard his familiar, whispered, refrain, '*Lord please forgive me for my sins, I am weak and unworthy of your love...Lord, please forgive me....*'

She stroked him until he was ready for her, his prayers becoming more urgent as his excitement increased. She pulled up her dress to reveal no undergarments. Patrick looked at her, lust in his eyes, saying, 'You are displaying the root of all evil to me! You are a wanton harlot, sent to tempt me! I am but a weak man of mind and flesh, and you take advantage of me!'

'Indeed I do, Monsignor, but I have needs to satisfy, and your body serves me well. You shall pray for my and your salvation while I assuage my desires on you. You must feel no guilt.'

Mary lowered herself slowly, agonisingly onto him. Patrick closed his eyes, finally tearing them away from what he called her passage of pleasure. Mary's words were well chosen, the perfect mix of contempt and the carnal. His passion was now so inflamed that, barely had Mary straddled him and begun moving her hips in a circular motion than he felt his release becoming unstoppable. He babbled, the heat of passion making his words indecipherable, *Lord please forgive me for...sins, I am weak...unworthy of your love...*Mary increased her concupiscent movements, thrusting against him as his hips rose and fell with increasing urgency.

Mary lent forward whispering in his ear, 'Now! Now! Empty your sacred seed into this whore's passage of pleasure. I command you...the Lord will forgive you.'

Later, as they lay entwined in a post-coital stupor, Patrick turned on his side and looked at Mary, smiling, for a brief moment his problems forgotten, 'Your words were well chosen today, my love. You are getting more imaginative each time. Thank you, it was a most enjoyable release and one I needed. But now I must go and recant for the pleasures you have given me, and suffer my penance. I feel three days in a sackcloth and twenty lashes would suffice; do you think that will allow the Lord back into my prayers?'

Not waiting for her answer he quickly dressed and walked across the chamber. Suddenly his voice took on a serious tone. Turning to her, he pointed at her unclothed body. 'Please cover yourself, Mary, your nakedness is unseemly; this is, after all, a house of God. Please act with a sense of decorum.'

Mary, used to Patrick's instant mood switches, did not reply. She knew well, hypocrisy was all part of his warped disposition: a zealous priest but one with insatiable sexual demands. For how much longer she could maintain this charade – in public a housekeeper, in private a mistress – she didn't know. Not for long if this house became a focal point for Protestant vengeance. She'd stay until it became too dangerous, then move onto the next holy man with not-so-holy proclivities. There was something about them that she found so appealing, almost addictive. But then she'd been introduced to their unquestioned defilements, their persistent carnal demands fifteen years ago when she first entered the convent as a virginal novice, a postulant ripe for the taking. By the time she took her vows she had lost count of the number of monks and priests who visited her chamber. Some didn't rape her; with a warped logic they asked to be pleasured by her hands or mouth, believing this allowed them to maintain their vow of celibacy.

She left when she became pregnant, refusing to abort the baby despite the insistence of the abbot. In the end it was a pointless gesture, because the baby died at birth. She might no longer be a nun, but years in a convent had perversely taught her how to keep men of the cloth satisfied in and out of bed. Those skills ensured a comfortable living and a roof over her head. A nun turned whore, she laughed to herself: *Well, I wasn't the first and I won't be the last.*

She continued to lie on the bed, slowly covering herself up, not because of his request, but now it was time to cater to her own pleasure. Patrick was a good man, she mused, but a selfish lover. He rarely considered her needs, too busy grappling with his mental gymnastics, simultaneously trying to appease his good Lord and his libidinous urges, to worry about her. It did not matter, her pleasures were to be found with her own hand, or occasionally when a nun or another woman stayed at the house. She found their ministrations gentle and selfless. Plus from time to time Patrick seemed happy to watch her cavorting with another woman before he took his own gratification. Jealousy was not one of his vices, though he made it clear none of these women could remain in the house for any length of time, anxious to avoid any unseemly rumours. That, Mary pondered, could be the least of his worries.

As the rioting continued, the town was awash with rumours about how the new Bury Corporation would be run, and whether the Catholics, long in a position of power, would remain so. It would be many months before this was decided. In the meantime the anti-Catholic mobs were silenced by the magistrate and some heavy-handed constables. By the time they were quelled, ten people died, but the seeds of distrust were now sown. It would be decades before all the religions would accept the others' beliefs.

For the next few months the house became a secret venue for Catholics to practise their faith. Monsignor de Voight risked his, and Mary's, life every Sunday to deliver Mass to a small but devoted congregation. Just when the atmosphere seemed to be calming down, to everyone's shock Alderman Ambrose

Rookwood, one of Patrick's congregants, was found guilty of a plot, along with others from Suffolk, to assassinate King William. Anger in the town flared up during his trial, at which he was inevitably found guilty. His hanging was the talking point of Bury. Fearful that if they didn't attend the execution Patrick and Mary would become suspects among the Protestant militia, they decided to discreetly watch from a distance.

The day of the execution was overcast, cold and miserable. The execution site was packed with people restless to watch the spectacle of a man lose his life. One which never seemed to tire. The food and drink sellers were doing a brisk trade, many selling warm mulled wine to ward off the chilly day. The atmosphere was one of gaiety at the prospect of a traitor being hanged. King William was a popular monarch; anyone who dared to threaten his life deserved to die.

Patrick whispered to Mary, 'These Rookwoods seem to court traitorous enterprises. Another Ambrose Rookwood was hanged for his part in the Gunpowder Plot, some time at the start of this century. They are not the most successful conspirators, it seems!' Patrick allowed himself a quiet chuckle, despite the sombre circumstances.

From Abbeygate St, a rumble of jeers and catcalls could be heard as the cart carrying the victim trundled down the hill and turned onto Angel Hill making its way slowly across to the scaffold. In chains, Ambrose looked bewildered and seemingly unaware of his surroundings. The crowd grew more vociferous in their insults. Some threw stones, rotting vegetables, anything they could find to make his final journey as uncomfortable as possible. Many in the crowd booed when the judge on the scaffold announced he was not to be hung, drawn and quartered – the normal manner of death for traitors. His family connections, and money, had influenced the judge towards the swift and less painful death of hanging only.

A worried look crossed Mary's face. 'He looks as though he has been tortured. See his hands...they are bloodied, it looks like the thumbscrews have been at work on him. And his face is brutally injured, I pray he did not reveal anything about where he takes Mass. We could be in serious jeopardy if he has.'

Patrick agreed. 'You are right, Mary, though I think if he'd betrayed us we would already have been arrested. They call themselves Christians, yet here they are hanging a man for daring to have his own path to following the Lord. They are all hypocritical heathens; may God send his retribution down on them...'

Mary roughly elbowed him in the ribs, 'Shush, Patrick, there are many people here who agree with what is happening today – you must learn to silence your opinions; save them for your sermons.' As she finished her warning the crowd erupted into a huge roar, almost animal in nature, as Ambrose made his way up the scaffold steps, stumbling as he did so. When asked by the judge if he had any final words, he held himself erect and looked directly into the crowd. Through one eye, the other closed by a huge swelling, he surveyed the howling crowd with a look of disdain. Shouting to make himself heard, he spat his final words out, 'I stand before you as I stand before my own God and Lord Saviour. Steadfast in my belief that the Catholic Church is the only true and righteous one...' He paused, gathering his thoughts, the crowd had gone quiet. He spoke again, his words echoed eerily around Angel Hill. 'I go to my death knowing that one day this country will be rid of the Protestant scourge and Rome will become our true masters again. King William is an imposter, whose soul along with all his believers will burn in the flames of hell! Long live King James!'

Before he could say anything more inflammatory, his hands were tied behind his back and the noose roughly pulled over his head and tightened around his neck. Seconds later he was pushed off the scaffold, plunging several feet before being caught with a sickening jerk. His fall was halted with such force that, to everyone's horror, his head was ripped from his body. His torso fell to the ground and, for a few seconds, those close by saw his legs twitching, his death throes mercifully short. His head rolled several feet away from the scaffold before stopping at the feet of one of the crowd. Delighted at this macabre gift, the man picked it up and tossed it to the executioner, who held it aloft for the roaring crowd to see. He shouted as he waved Ambrose's head by its hair, 'A deserved end to a traitor! May he rot in hell! May all Catholics rot in hell!' The baying crowd cheered at his words – they had seen justice successfully dispensed. Ambrose's decapitated head was thrown into a sack to be taken to the west gate and mounted onto a pike. The day's macabre entertainment over, the crowd quickly lost interest and started to leave.

Mary and Patrick hurried back home. Suddenly he stopped and, holding Mary's arm, he pulled her in the direction of Hatter Street.

'Where are we going, Patrick?' asked Mary.

'I want to talk with Nicholas Stafford, to see what has happened to his brother John, the former mayor. I am trying to discover how much danger we are in or whether the worst is now past us. I believe he can help us decide whether we should stay in Bury, or leave.'

'Leave Bury? And where would we go that's safe? I have heard of no place that offers sanctuary to Catholics. The country is a cesspit of Protestantism. The only place to go would be France or America; at least we would be welcome there. Otherwise we may as well stay here and keep quiet until this tyranny ceases.'

'I know, I know, Mary. But I fear for our safety and that of our worshippers by asking them to come to the house for Mass. Heaven knows what our neighbours are thinking; it only needs one to tell the judge and we could all end up in gaol. I am torn between preaching the word of God despite the danger, or accepting we must lay low until, as you say, this persecution stops. I have prayed for guidance without receiving a clear sign. Maybe this visit will point us in the right direction.'

They arrived at a modest house, in need of some repair. The roof was sagging under decades-old rotting shingles, and the window and door frames were rotten too. Most of the glass panes were broken, the holes patched with cloth. Patrick knocked and waited for a response. Then knocked more loudly again. No one came to the door, and he heard no movement from within. Hesitantly Patrick pushed on the door. It opened with some effort and they walked inside, calling out their presence. Barely had they gone a few feet down the hallway before the smell hit them.

'Oh, good Lord, what is that foul odour?' asked Mary, holding her sleeve up to her nose in an effort to smother its unwholesome effect.

Patrick recoiled as the stench reached him too. 'My Lord Jesus, that is vile. I wonder what could be its cause. I am fearful of what I might find, but I best investigate. Though my senses are telling me we should leave immediately!' He started to move down the hallway. 'I believe it is coming from the scullery. You stay here, Mary, let me discover its source.'

Mary pleaded, pulling at Patrick's arm. 'No, please let us depart immediately. I have a bad feeling about this house. It has an evil miasma; let us go now before we discover something we shouldn't.'

He shook off her grasp and disappeared into the gloomy interior of the house, and was soon lost from Mary's sight. She moved back to the front door to breathe less foetid air. It took only a minute before Mary heard a muffled cry and the sound of Patrick clumsily rushing back towards her. Out of the lightless hallway he barrelled past her into the fresh air of the street, his face pale, a picture of revulsion. Tears streaming down his face, he said nothing, words failing to form, his mind unable to describe what he had seen.

'What? What did you find, Patrick? You look like you have seen the Devil, you are as white as snow! Tell me, please.'

Patrick bent over, hands on his knees, trying to control the urge to retch up his lunch. He finally controlled his breathing and stood up, his face still ashen. He took hold of Mary's arm and silently led her away from the house towards home. She said nothing, accepting it served no purpose forcing him to recount what he'd witnessed. Once home, he sat down by the fire and collected his thoughts. Mary sat patiently by his side, holding his hand. Speaking slowly, he recounted the awful sight that met his eyes in Nicholas Stafford's house.

'I found Nicholas's body, so badly beaten I barely recognised him. His murderers had also slain his wife. I believe from the way her body was left she may have been...violated as well, she was barely clothed. Blood was everywhere. It was a scene of such horror I shall never be able to wash it from my mind. She suffered an appalling indignity, Mary...' He paused for a moment, gathering his thoughts, trying to erase the memory of what he had just seen.

'But maybe...maybe this is the sign I was seeking. For there was a note affixed to Nicholas's chest with a knife saying "*Let this be a warning to all Catholic heretics*". Mary, these people have no soul, no decency, they are not Christians, they are murderers; they will not stop until they have killed us all. I believe this is God's way of telling us to leave Bury for safer pastures.'

He cupped his face in his hands and sobbed, rocking backwards and forwards in his grief. Mary comforted him, saying nothing. She stared into the fire imagining them as the flames of hell. There was so much evil in the world at the moment it was a place so many souls were destined to endure for eternity. She did not intend to be one of them.

Mary gently lifted up and held Patrick's face in her hands, and kissed him on the lips. 'You are right, my love, this house, this town, even this country is not for us. Let us pack up and leave immediately after next Sunday's Mass.'

Three days later in front of a packed congregation, Monsignor Patrick de Voight announced his intention to leave Bury. His fellow Catholics, already cowed and in fear of their lives, now had no place to meet and conduct Mass; they were disappointed at the news, but sympathetic to his decision. For many it would be the last time they attended a Catholic service, and others would take the vows laid down by the law of the land and become Protestants, the only way to ensure they lived safely, free from persecution.

* * * *

In 1689 King William's Act of Toleration was created to thank the Protestant groups for helping overthrow James II. It gave freedom of worship to non-conformists, or any Christian group that didn't conform to the Anglican Church, except Catholics. These groups were allowed to have churches and worship in public. In the Bill of Rights, Parliament declared that no future monarch could be a Catholic or be married to a Catholic, and that law remains in force to this day. It wasn't until around 1760 and afterwards that various Acts of Parliament allowed full emancipation of Catholics to worship in public.

Chapter 13
(1700)

Sir Dudley, the new owner, was not impressed at the ever-increasing expenditure needed to repair the house, and made his feelings clear to the builder tasked with the work, when he visited one day to inspect progress. He surveyed the scene before him; the piles of rotting beams smouldering as a fire slowly consumed them, discarded wattle and daub lay in huge piles to be disposed of (conveniently, to the bottom of Angel Hill, which was being raised to prevent flooding). As for the actual rebuilding, little seemed to have been accomplished since his last visit a month earlier.

He beckoned for the foreman to approach, and wasted no time lambasting the poor man: 'Mr Foreman, work here is intolerably slow, it seems to me. What is the cause of the delay? I am employing you to complete this work with all due haste. Since I was last here little seems to have happened.'

The foreman, called Isaac, bowed and doffed his cap, ''Tis a fact, my lord, work here is slow, but the sill plates are in poor condition, and under the floors is damp where the rain settles, causing the floor joists to rot as well. It is a lot more work than we expected, my lord; we still have more floor to remove so we can dig out underneath to drain the water away from the foundations. We haven't found why the water is resting under the house as it does.' The foreman shrugged an apologetic shoulder.

Ancient Hallways

His Lordship was not appeased. 'Well, get more men to work on this. I need it finished by Christmas at the very latest. I have promised my daughter she will move in after her wedding in November. I shall return in two weeks and I expect to see rebuilding work started. Do I make myself understood, sir?'

'Yes, my lord, crystal clear. I shall employ more men and make every effort to meet your deadline...this will mean, of course, an increase in the wages each week.'

Sir Dudley gave the man a withering look. 'I am well aware of the costs involved; leave that to me, you just get the work done, otherwise I promise you there will be consequences, none of them palatable, for your reputation.'

He climbed back into his carriage and disappeared down Whiting St in a cloud of dust, leaving the foreman pondering if it was all worthwhile. Working for the aristocracy paid well, but the aggravation and intimidation meant he earned every penny. He turned back to the house and the workmen who'd stood watching the altercation. He snapped at them, 'If you want to keep your job, stop gawking and get working. His Lordship is on the rampage; if I lose my job, so will you...get to it now!'

It was a week later when one of the workmen, digging out earth from under the scullery floor, shouted to the foreman. 'Isaac, come 'ere, I think I know the cause of the flooding, there seems to be an old well here. 'Tis covered with some rotten wood – shall I remove it?'

Isaac walked over. This was news he didn't want to hear; more problems, more expense, more abuse from His Lordship. Arms akimbo, he sighed, looking down at the splintered wood, beneath which was some murky, black water. 'Rip the wood away and see how deep it is; use some rope.' One of the workers did as he was ordered and plopped a weighted rope into the water, and announced a few minutes later it was over twenty feet deep. It was an old well, covered up years ago. But how long ago, wondered Isaac. Why hadn't the original builders filled it in? No wonder the floors rotted away.

'Sweet Jesus,' cursed Isaac, 'Alright, get some buckets and empty it out, then fill it with the old wattle and daub, and be quick about it.' He strode away, annoyed at yet another delay, another problem, hopefully one that would be short and easily fixed.

It wasn't to be.

An hour later Isaac heard the men chattering excitedly as they peered down the hole. He walked over demanding to know what was causing them to stop work this time. One pointed down the well. 'There's summ't down there, shall we see what it is – or fill the 'ole in?' asked one of the workers.

The foreman peered into the black depths and caught sight of something solid, a box or trunk of some description. Exasperated, he ordered, 'Just stop chattering like a bunch of housewives, one of you get down there and bring whatever it is up for me to see. And be careful – who knows, it might contain something valuable.'

Using the longest ladder they could find, they dropped it into the well and, clutching a candle, one of the men hesitantly descended to the bottom. His voice echoed up to the men watching his rescue efforts.

'Isaac, 'tis too heavy for me to lift and carry up the ladder, best get a rope.'

One was found and minutes later the man reappeared clutching one end of the rope. He handed it to Isaac. 'I have loosened it from the mud, and I think if you pull hard it should come out.' In fact it took two men's strength to drag the box up from its watery resting place to the surface.

The box was not large, though it seemed disproportionately heavy for its size. Isaac estimated it was about two feet square. He wiped off the mud and slime to reveal that, surprisingly, the wood was in excellent condition considering where it had been resting. He found himself in a dilemma, should he just dispose of the box and pretend it was never found? Or dutifully inform Sir Dudley, as he should legally do? He decided on the latter course of action, knowing how the men might gossip about it, and word get back to His Lordship. He despatched one of his men to run to Sir Dudley's home, about two miles away. Within the hour His Lordship appeared, a little frustrated at being torn away from his favourite pastime: gardening in his huge orangery.

'Good Lord, my man, what is it now? Some buried treasure, I am led to believe by your messenger.'

'Of that I am uncertain, my lord, but I thought it best for you to be here when we open it. I wanted no one accusing us of theft.'

Sir Dudley walked to where the box lay on the ground. 'Quite, quite, well let us get on with it. Open it now, I am intrigued as to what might be inside. Be quick about it. The box looks of good quality and well made. I reckon it must be oak...most interesting.'

Isaac replied, 'Indeed, my lord, considering it has been buried in water. I am surprised it hasn't rotted to pieces.' Not wanting to delay matters any further, he picked up a hammer and iron bar, and with some effort pried open the top of the box, finally revealing its contents. Immediately he removed the lid and a waft of warm, foul-smelling air arose from the box, strong enough that even the men standing some distance away felt it brush their faces. Sir Dudley screwed up his face from the offensive smell. The other men feeling the warm, malodorous draft emanating from the box moved further back to avoid its nauseous effect. Suddenly everyone became wary of the box and its contents. Something wasn't...right. The lighthearted atmosphere changed to one of caution, and for some, fear.

The obnoxious odour soon dissipated and within seconds everyone regained their composure, creeping forward as Isaac leant over to look more closely at the box's content. It consisted of a large book covered in vellum, dyed dark red. He looked at Sir Dudley for instruction, 'Stop hesitating, man, lift it out – I want to see inside. Be careful; it could be fragile.' Issac obliged and gingerly put his hands underneath the book. Immediately he emitted a squeal of surprise, let it go and fell backwards.

'What on earth is the matter with you, man? Stop dallying, pick it up and let me look inside,' demanded Sir Dudley, oblivious to the shocked look on Isaac's face, who rubbed his hands together as if freezing cold.

Isaac explained, 'Your Lordship, that book, it, it has a cold slimy feel, and something jolted through me when I touched it. I am not a superstitious man, but it has some kind of power that renders it painful to the touch. I will not try again.'

Sir Dudley, sceptical of the foreman's complaints, pushed him aside and reached down into the box, only to call out in surprise, as he too, felt something painful coursing through his body. 'Good God, you are right man, this is most strange. What can be causing it? Perhaps if we use some gloves it will mask its effect. Fetch me some at once.' Moments later one of the workmen handed Sir Dudley a pair of old leather gloves and he gingerly reached in, pulling out the book and gently putting it down on the floor.

'Ah, the gloves helped keep that strange feeling at bay. Let us look inside. Everything appears to be in remarkable condition, and my hope is that somewhere we will find a date and name of who made this strange object. It looks like a book, but is far too heavy to be just paper.'

Sir Dudley was correct. The 'book' was in fact a smaller box made to look like one, complete with a heavy leather cover on metal hinges. Warily he opened it and peered inside to find sheets of old vellum bound to one edge. They were covered with strange symbols, and words in what looked like old English. Gently he peeled them back. He looked in horror at what lay underneath: the most bizarre collection of artefacts he had ever seen.

Collectively, the men also gasped, then were struck silent by the macabre sight that met their eyes. Carefully laid out, with intricate precision, were a collection of five crystal stones, set in a pattern on top of a pentagram made of bones, each stone resting on one of the five points. Around the edge of the box were scattered the leaves of herbs and plants. And in the centre, the gruesome sight of a cat's head. As if this wasn't hideous enough none of them showed any sign of decay or age. It was as if they had been placed there yesterday.

'My Lord Jesus,' exclaimed Sir Dudley, hastily making the sign of the cross. 'What can this possibly mean? It is an abomination! What is the intent of this vile collection of objects?'

The foreman cautiously looked into the box, then shook his head, 'I do not know much about witchcraft, my lord, but this bears all the signs of it. Someone wanted to cast a spell of some kind on this house. Only a priest will be able to fully comprehend what it means.'

Gently Sir Dudley covered up the remains and shut the lid. As he did so Isaac saw something odd. 'My lord, look, the box is much deeper than the book. It appears to have room for some other objects underneath it, maybe. A kind of false bottom, I think.'

Sir Dudley leant over and looked closely, running his fingers around the edges of the box. His foreman was right. Warily he opened the box again and ran his finger around the inside. In one corner a tiny piece had broken off, enough to allow him to put his finger in and pull. Isaac was right, there was a false bottom which, though tightly fitted, could be removed. Hesitantly, he pried open the hidden compartment, and the hideous smell that assailed them earlier discharged itself with even greater force. Sir Dudley turned away, putting his arm across his face to block out the disgusting smell. He then looked back into the box, and met a sight that would remain with him to his dying day – a human embryo with an inverted cross skewering its tiny heart surrounded by animal bones, a glass jar and other strange objects.

Chapter 14

After the gruesome discoveries in the exhumed box, Sir Dudley instructed it to be lowered back into the well and a new, secure cover placed over it. He threatened that any workman who spoke of these findings would be punished and jobless. He knew he must discover what the contents of this box meant - and what he should do with them. Over the next few days work ground to a halt on the house while Sir Dudley, using his influence and wealth, sought out those most knowledgeable about all things witchcraft. For that is what he believed the box contained - something beyond his experience or comprehension - but he was aware that, unless it was handled correctly, his reputation and that of the house might in some way suffer.

His investigations and search for help led him, inevitably, to the Church and less...conventional experts.

The bishop of Suffolk himself replied to His Lordship's request and agreed to conduct an exorcism at the house. Further enquiries located an elderly woman, called Luna, living in the town whose lifelong vocation was the study of witchcraft. Sir Dudley invited them both to the house.

Luna arrived at the appointed time, riding up the street on a mule that looked as old as she did. Wizened and of tiny frame, with thin grey hair, Luna looked - and smelled - unkempt and impoverished. Her sallow, lined face offered a startling contrast to her piercing blue eyes, which seemed to have defied her ageing. Rumour had it that in her youth she belonged to a coven of witches in Stowmarket, but nothing was ever proven. She survived the hysteria and witch phobia that surrounded the last trials in Bury in 1662, despite the fact that one of the women found guilty and hanged was her cousin, Amy Duny.

The bishop arrived, with his retinue, a few minutes later-and could barely conceal his contempt at finding the unprepossessing Luna also there to offer advice.

Sir Dudley was no fan of the bishop, who he regarded as a pompous little man. He waddled arrogantly around in expensive robes that could not conceal his enormous girth: so much for a life of abstinence and temperance, he thought to himself.

He wanted this whole process over quickly. Though the images of what he saw in the bottom of the box were still vivid in his mind, he did not relish seeing them again. Isaac already had the box pulled up from the well, and a pair of thick gloves ready to be used by whoever handled its contents. Sir Dudley was not keen to repeat that experience either.

He started the proceedings formally: 'Bishop, men of the cloth and er, Luna, thank you for coming to offer your advice on how we should conduct the investigation of the contents of this box found buried beneath my house. I have viewed them already, and they are...how can I put this...distasteful, repugnant to look at and exude an odour of the most unpleasant kind. I find the whole thing inexplicable but believe it to be some form of witchcraft – hence the purpose of your presence here today. I wish to know how best to dispose of its artefacts, and dispel any lasting effects it may have on this house.'

Sir Dudley scanned everyone's faces. The bishop still had a look of disdain on his face, whilst Luna remained impassive. 'Isaac, would you remove the top, please?'

Wearing the gloves, Isaac removed the book from the wooden box, placed it on a table, and slowly turned back the cover. The smell was immediately evident to everyone, and in unison the clergymen made signs of the cross. For a few moments nothing was said as everyone examined, from afar, the bizarre collection of artefacts.

The bishop harrumphed. 'Please, Sir Dudley, this is undoubtedly some kind of pagan ritual, hardly worth my time being here to investigate it, if truth be told. Any priest could have dealt with this.'

Sir Dudley ignored the bishop's dismissal and ordered Issac to remove the lid and reveal the hidden chamber beneath the book to reveal the rest of the contents: the cat's head and the embryo. No sooner had he done so than even the bishop looked shocked. 'Oh, my Lord Jesus, this is too abhorrent for words...is it what I think it is?'

Luna quietly made her way forward so she was now standing beside the box. In a calm voice she explained the disgusting sight in front of them: 'Yes, gentlemen, it is what you think – the embryo of a baby, a human baby, and the other bones around it are also those of young children, I would guess no more than a few months old when they died. The small wooden carvings are figurines of children as well. Ah! Look, each of them have been altered, one has no eyes, one has no mouth and the other no ears. I wonder what this all means?' She continued to investigate and muse out loud her findings. 'Yes! This small glass container is called a Sour Jar. Its contents represent the person or people you wish to harm with the spell. These look like babies' teeth. And the herbs are, I believe, acacia, fleabane and tannis root all have the power to kill or injure babies in the womb.'

Luna stopped her examination, stood back from the box and looked at the men. 'I can assure you this is no prank, Bishop, this is the work of a witch of considerable prowess and skill.' She paused and gently ran her hand over the cover of the book – whatever force had affected the men when they first touched it did not seem to concern her. She asked, 'Has anyone read the pages in the book yet? It may offer evidence to help identify what the meaning was for all of this. Though I am beginning to see the purpose of this elaborate bewitchment. Whoever did this spent many months creating it.'

No one moved, let alone offered to open the book but, unfazed, Luna took it upon herself to do so. On the first page, she saw a riddle and read it out loud:

In this house where a child is born,
A curse lingers, a witch's sworn.
Beware, young souls, its cruel root,
Their journey, a soundless one, a bitter mute.
Never to utter a spoken word,
Their voices will be forever unheard.
Others never to see or hear,
Living their lives in pain and fear.
For ten generations, this curse will last,
A payment for all the evil children past.

On the next pages were further symbols, hexes and written incantations, which Luna read carefully. The rest of the group stood in silence, allowing this peculiar old lady to do her work.

On the very last page were the words:

On this day of Hallowtide MCDLXXXV, I, Jane Wordsworth, High Priestess, do command this spell last for ten generations. May this house, and those who suffer from its curse, be released after this time, my retribution having run its course.

As Luna finished reading, for a moment there was silence, then Sir Dudley asked the question on everyone's mind: 'Fascinating indeed, but what exactly does it all mean?'

Luna sat down and said nothing, mulling over the contents of the box and the riddle in the book. At last she spoke, her voice wavering a little, realising the importance, the ramifications, that the spell Witch Wordsworth had created all those years ago would have had on the people living in the house.

'I cannot be sure, gentlemen, without conferring with my Grand Grimoire and an old copy of Forbidden Rites, or even *The Grimoire of Solomon*, but it seems to me that this spell, created by High Priestess Wordsworth, was made to cruelly affect any baby born in this house, by afflicting them with no hearing, sight or ability to speak. Why she did this, we will never know, but that is my belief. As to how effective it has been...well, does anyone know of a child being born here with such a condition?'

Behind the bishop an elderly priest held his hand up to his mouth in horror. 'Oh, my Lord Jesus, yes, yes, I do remember such an occurrence. It was, let me think, over twenty years ago; I baptised a poor child who could not hear, and his parents I believe lived in this very house. I can check the parish records to be sure. They were distraught, as they had been warned by a relative that such things happened in this house in the past, but chose to ignore the warning. Oh! Please God, does it mean this evil magic really works?'

Sir Dudley was about to reply when Issac, still staring down at the book, blurted out, 'My Lord, some of those symbols in the book…there are similar ones on beams in a room upstairs; I saw them and wondered what they meant. Could they be part of this…this spell?'

'Take me to them,' said Luna curtly. Despite her apparent old age and infirmity, her voice carried an authority no one ignored under these strange circumstances. Several minutes later she returned, out of breath from climbing the stairs, clutching Isaac's arm for support.

'Indeed, I believe those symbols and runes may well be connected to this book and the spell. Isaac tells me he thinks they are beams older than this house, likely from a previous home on this site which we have to assume is the one Witch Wordsworth lived in, though we shall never know for sure.'

Sir Dudley, now fully accepting that Luna had the most knowledge about this whole strange episode, asked her, 'So, how do we stop the curse, or whatever it is, and its evil effect on this house? And, it seems, the people that live here? I cannot have my young daughter in residence and the risk that her children might be born with such terrible conditions.'

Luna walked over to Sir Dudley and gently moved him away from the men still standing transfixed around the box. When they were out of earshot, with a smile she said, 'Such advice does not come without some recompense, my lord. This is a spell, a curse of such strength and longevity I will need to return in a few days with a plan that will nullify its effects.'

'How much?' asked Sir Dudley, bluntly.

'I am thinking two gold sovereigns would be sufficient.'

'So be it; when shall you return? I wish this whole terrible ordeal to be over quickly.'

'It will take time to discover what is required; you cannot hurry such matters. Let us say three days from now...'

'Shall I ask the bishop to return at the same time?'

The old lady waved a dismissive hand, 'By all means, my lord, let them pray and practise their exorcisms on your house. It can do no harm, but it likely will do no good either. And I will wager he will charge you a lot more than I for his services.'

'Luna, I thank you for your advice and guidance. I shall see you in three days. Is there anything we should do with the box and book in the meantime?'

She paused for a moment, deep in thought. 'Yes, there is, my lord. This is what you must do: You should burn it, but not where it now lies. Take it far away, close to no habitation, and a place no one is likely to visit, build a house, or grow any crops. Not a lake, as it will infect any living thing it touches. Bury it in a deep hole and, before filling it, set the book and box alight; burn every fragment. Let the ashes not touch anyone or anything. When nothing remains, sprinkle a layer of lavender on the ashes and fill the hole. Leave no markings. It is important you follow these instructions – the strength of this curse is beyond any I have ever seen. This is the only way to forever stop its evil effects on anyone else.'

Nodding his head, Sir Dudley said, 'I understand, it shall be done immediately.'

At that the old lady walked back to her mule, with difficulty mounted the complaining animal and left. Sir Dudley went to the bishop and asked if he could come back in three days to conduct an exorcism. He saw no reason not to use both homespun magic and the power of the Church in this spiritual battlefield to fight the evil that infected the house.

The bishop said he would gladly do so, but could he discuss the delicate subject of a donation to the Church to cover such a procedure? Sir Dudley smiled to himself as a figure of four gold sovereigns was suggested as an appropriate amount for the bishop's time and trouble.

I wonder if they are twice as effective as an old lady and her strange concoctions will be, he thought to himself as he walked back to talk to Issac. He explained in detail to him Luna's advice on how to dispose of the offending box and its contents, promising a gold sovereign for his efforts once the risky job was satisfactorily completed. Issac's initial reaction was he wanted nothing to do with this grotesque box of curses, but a sovereign was a month's wages, it was worth the risk, he decided. He set to work immediately – using the gloves he carefully picked up the box and put it in an old sack, then in the back of his cart. All the time whispering a prayer under his breath.

He threw in a spade next to it and trundled off towards the forest near Rougham, stopping on the way to gather some wild lavender growing by the road: He knew of a boggy, marshy area that was good for neither living nor hunting near the small village. He hoped a sovereign would be the only reward for distasteful endeavour, and not some lifelong curse. Within the hour he completed his task and on the way back stopped in his local church to light a candle and pray for protection from whatever evil magic may have infected him.

True to her word, three days later, Luna returned, carrying a small sack slung over her shoulder.

Sir Dudley was present with his son-in-law, Robert, soon to be the new resident of the house, at least once he was assured this unbelievable spell, or whatever it was, had been eradicated like a plague of rats.

'Good day, Your Lordship.' Luna walked over to the two men. She looked tired and even more careworn than when they last met. 'I have consulted many books on how to rid a house of such a curse. Normally it is a person who suffers from such black magic, not a building. To prepare the potions to dispel such a spell for a whole house is a lengthy process. But I have consulted the best advisements going back to the days of King Arthur and believe this will rid the house of its terrible disposition.'

Sir Dudley nodded his understanding; after the last few days nothing about this problem surprised him. He took her words on trust – there was no reason not to.

'Now please leave me to get on with my work.' With that she went into the house.

Robert gave his father-in-law a quizzical look. 'Heavens, she's a weird one; are you sure she isn't a little mad?'

'Maybe she is, Robert, but I have to believe the ritual she is about to perform is the only way to solve this peculiar mystery.

We have little to lose; it is a subject of which I am woefully ignorant. Strangely, I have faith in what she says and what she intends to do. However, as a backup I do have the bishop conducting an exorcism tomorrow!'

Luna, by now inside the house, extracted some ground sage, mugwort, basil and bay leaves – all well-known herbs designed to reverse a witch's spell. These she mixed with the urine of a cat, creating a pungent eye-watering smell. Luna took a small brass spoon and poured tiny amounts around every room in the house. Then out of the sack came a small glass container filled with rosemary, pine needles and red wine, called a Witch Bottle. She mixed enough to deposit a drop in every room in the house.

As she moved from room to room she ululated words in old English that attacked the old witch's spell.

'In the name of Jesu Crist, I now rebuke, breke, and lossen this house and any kin therein from any and all y cursyes, fetiches, charmes, vexaciouns, hexes, spelles, eche jynx, alle psychic powers, sorcerye, bewitchments, enchantments, wicche craft, love potions, and psychic prayers that has been set upon me, even unto ten generaciouns. I breke and lossen this house from any and all connected or related spirits from any person or persons or from any occult or psychic sources. I praye Thee, Hevenly King, to send them back unto þe senders now. Let him þat loveth cursyng receyven it unto himself.'

The bottle itself and the remains of the concoction would be buried beneath the house, along with the final element of her anti-diabolism ritual: a small wooden container within which was the heart of a bird with pins stuck in it to be placed on a pattern of overlapping circles of fresh nightshade, to further rebuke and extinguish the old witch's grimoire. She would instruct Sir Dudley where to place this. For three hours she moved from room to room, muttering incantations and conjurations, stopping from time to time for no obvious reason, seemingly concentrating on certain parts of the house more than others, bending over them and whispering words in strange languages. At times Luna was in some kind of trance, the two men believed.

Sir Dudley and Robert could not understand what she was saying or doing. But without doubt something was happening. Occasionally the men felt great waves of pungent-smelling air wafting past them out of the door. It wasn't cold, but still sent shivers down their spine.

They both decided to wait outside. 'Sir, this is most uncomfortable, can she really be removing some kind of deadly miasma from this house? It feels too incredible to be true, but something strange is definitely happening; do you feel it?' Robert asked, worried he was making a fool of himself in front of his future father-in-law.

'Loath as I am to admit it, Robert, yes, something incomprehensible to me is taking place in there. As a man of science I have never believed in witchcraft and devilry, but my mind is changing by what is happening here today.'

When Luna finally rejoined the two men she looked exhausted, her face more drawn and grey than before. Her hands shook as she took Sir Dudley's hand in hers. 'My work is done, my lord. Ensure this bag is buried in the hole where Witch Wordsworth's box was found. It is the last part of the expelling process. I believe her spell was coming to its end in a few years, so all that I have done has merely foreshortened its demise. One final thing; make sure any beams in the house with strange symbols or signs carved in them are removed and burnt.'

She wearily turned to Robert. 'I believe your new home will now be a happy one with no danger that children will be born with the terrible afflictions that ones in the past suffered from. Witch Wordsworth has caused enough melancholy over the last 200 years, but her spell is now, I pray, over, her evil power removed. I wish you all well.'

'How sure of this are you?' asked Robert.

'Young man, nothing is certain in the spiritual world. Evil and good are constantly at war with each other, but I have done what I can. Witch Wordsworth created a spell of power and longevity the likes of which I have never seen before. But for every harmful one there is an antidote, something that will destroy its power. I believe I have done that, but only time will tell.'

With that, the old lady pocketed the two gold sovereigns proffered by Sir Dudley, collected her old mule and walked slowly down Whiting St. She was tired; this sordid business was too much for her ageing mind and body. Purging an evil of such power had depleted her inner strength, and her discarnate gifts were used up. Never had she felt such a lethal and long-lasting spell – its wickedness pervaded everything that she touched in the house. Luna had no doubt some part of it had affected her too, in some sublime, unseen way. Shivering and exhausted, she made her way home to her small cottage in Northgate St, a fever already brewing up inside her.

Delirious, she slumped in front of her small fire, visions of dead children and deformed babies flashed before her eyes. Despite drinking a herbal mixture known as *Queimada* and reciting

Conxuro, a spell to ward off evil, she felt herself succumbing to a malevolent force she could not fight. She knew expelling the house in Whiting St of its deadly bewitchment had taken a fatal toll on her health, mentally and physically. A weakness descended upon her; she felt her sight waning, she heard no birds at dawn, nor could speak properly her incantations.

By morning she was dead, the two gold sovereigns still clutched in her gnarled, lifeless hands.

* * * *

'Thank the Lord for that old lady and her white magic; what a horrifying curse was upon our old home!' Now I know my daughters were born without speech and hearing, and me without the ability to talk, because of a witch's curse. I am not sure if I am relieved or filled with anger.' Grace was walking amongst the unfinished renovations, gliding through the new walls, unfamiliar with the house's new layout.

Maud followed her, then stopped in what was once a study, but now a bedroom, and looked up at the marks and carvings in the oak beams in the ceiling.

'I often saw these and wondered what they meant', she said, gently moving her hands across the strange symbols and figures etched deep into the five-hundred-year-old wood. 'Now I know. I wonder what other secrets this old house holds about which we know nothing.'

They were about to be surprised again.

Chapter 15

Early the following morning the bishop and his entourage arrived with much pomp and ceremony, in sharp contrast, thought Sir Dudley, to the old lady's modest, unassuming behaviour.

Sir Dudley met him as he alighted from his luxurious carriage. 'Good morning, Bishop, thank you for coming to perform the exorcism. I have every faith the Lord's power will break whatever curse is afflicting the house.' It had better, he thought, for what it is costing me. The price for God's help was not cheap nowadays.

He didn't mention Luna's visit the day before, her peculiar emanations while she conducted her own exorcism, or the strange potions she left around the house. He certainly kept to himself his feelings that somehow he felt more confidence in her efforts than that of the Holy Church.

As a man of science he preferred to work with objects he could prove, or see, existed. Not figments of imagination, flights of fantasy, talk of spirits and grimoires, whatever they were. Nevertheless, whatever secrets this house held, whatever malevolent forces were at work within it – he wanted rid of them, by any means necessary. He was prepared to put his scepticism aside and let both the unconventional and conventional ideas of how to deal with such unworldly matters be put to use.

He spoke to the bishop, concealing his dislike of the officious little man. 'I will leave you to your...modus operandi, and pray God will resolve this problem quickly and satisfactorily.'

Pompously, the bishop agreed: 'I believe it will be so, Sir Dudley, His potency over the powers of evil has stood the test of time. I shall commence now. Can I ask you to stay outside of the house while we conduct the exorcism?' He hesitated, and gently took Sir Dudley's arm, whispering 'Ahem, could we dispense beforehand with the matter of the donation?'

Sir Dudley's four gold sovereigns disappeared inside the bishop's robe with a deft sleight of hand, unseen by the rest of the clergymen. He doubted a farthing of the donation would ever make its way into the church coffers. It seems the closer to God people perceived they were, the greater their corruption. So be it, the exorcism was more for public consumption, reassuring neighbours, and his son-in-law, that all had been done to rid the house of its spiritual stigma. The money was not important.

The bishop signalled the four priests to follow him inside the house; each was carrying, the bishop told him, a bottle of 'genuine Lourdes holy water, blessed by the Virgin Mary herself,' I bet it is, thought Sir Dudley sceptically, more likely scooped up from the River Lark this morning.

The holy men disappeared into the house. Through the open window he heard them chanting:

Crux sancta sit mihi lux
Non draco sit mihi dux
Vade retro satana
Numquam suade mihi vana
Sunt mala quae libas

Ipse venena bibas.
(May the Holy Cross be my light
May the dragon never be my guide
Begone Satan
Never tempt me with your vanities
What you offer me is evil
drink the poison yourself.)

They moved from room to room and, after a short time, left the house looking suitably solemn, but satisfied. The bishop came over to Sir Dudley, smug as ever. 'I am confident whatever evil lurks in the house has now gone. We have left holy water in each room. We have prayed at length that any demons should leave never to return; your house is now cleansed and exorcised, Your Lordship. We shall now depart...'

'Bishop! Bishop! Pray look at this!' One of the elderly priests was looking down at a piece of wood lying among the old and rotted beams, about to be burnt. 'I have seen these letters before...I am trying to remember where. I know they were amongst some old parchment scrolls describing the history of the great St Edmund's Abbey...'

The bishop walked over and looked at the scrap of wood, trying to read the letters scratched haphazardly across it.

Reliquiae sancti h...
Ab...
Tutus ab...
Requi...

'What of it, Father Cassipierre? It looks like an inscription, or part of one.' He turned the crumbling piece of wood over to see carved, *'Found by Harold in 1550, tunnel under Angel Hill.'*

'Translated it means: *Reliquiae sancti*, 'the relics of...and Tutus ab, means "safe from",' said the priest helpfully.

'I am well aware of what it says, I understand Latin,' snapped the bishop, 'but what does it pertain to? Is it of any import? Who was this Harold person? It looks like some prank to me. Father, what do *you* think it means?'

The elderly priest hesitated; he knew in the back of his mind this inscription was somewhere to be found in the abbey archives. He just couldn't remember where or when he'd seen it many years ago.

'I am not sure, Your Worship. Not all the old abbey records were destroyed by Henry VIII's men after the Dissolution. I believe it references a tunnel under Angel Hill. There were persistent rumours that the old abbey had escape tunnels to a dozen places in the town. 1550 was just after the abbey's destruction; maybe this man found something in one of the tunnels.'

The bishop was dismissive. 'I too have heard such rumours, but I have never seen any proof the tunnels existed. In any event that was over 150 years ago. I doubt, even if they did exist, there is now a way to enter them. By all means keep this memento, but I doubt it means anything of import.'

He turned to the rest of the men and ordered them into the carriage. With a casual wave he bid Sir Dudley farewell, ordering the driver to take them back to the church. Father Cassipierre sat quietly clutching the old piece of wood, gently stroking the carved letters as if hoping some divine intervention would explain what they were describing.

In an unexpected turn of events, no sooner had work finished on the house than Sir Dudley decided to sell it. Matters had changed and his daughter would no longer be moving in as originally planned. For her engagement to Robert was over. The boy disgraced himself by getting another girl pregnant, and Sir Dudley would have no more to do with him as a result. Heartbroken, his daughter announced she would travel to London to stay with her uncle, wanting nothing more to do with Bury St Edmunds, or the house.

Back in the church archives Father Cassipierre continued to look for clues that would explain the mysterious scrap of wood's enigmatic inscription.

Chapter 16

His prayer for an act of God, a revelation, was realised a few weeks later when one of the worst storms to hit East Anglia bore down from the north, depositing a biblical amount of rain across the whole county. In past days, the River Lark that ran through the old abbey grounds was navigable all the way to Ely, and thence to The Wash and the North Sea. It was kept clear and well dredged and would have normally coped with such a torrential downpour, one that continued for three days and nights. But alterations to its path, and the draining of wetlands to the north slowed its flow to such a level it silted up, thereby not only becoming unnavigable, but unable to drain the unprecedented volume of water the storm created.

It was by the end of the second day of the storm that residents on Eastgate St saw the bridge over the river was now clogged with debris brought down by the roiling current from miles upstream. It became a makeshift dam causing the water to swiftly rise up along the banks of the river all the way back to the River Linnet and Southgate St.

With frightening rapidity the water soon covered the whole of the abbey grounds, flooding the old ruins in places to a depth of ten feet. Relentlessly it surged until the bottom of Angel Hill was awash in filthy, muddy water. The earthworks built to prevent such a catastrophe were swept away by the swollen waters like children's sandcastles on the beach.

And still the river kept rising, until it forced a breach in the bridge across Eastgate St, reducing the centuries-old crossing to rubble and flint in a matter of a few hours. Like a plug pulled from a sink, the water cascaded with unstoppable force through the meadows and on towards Fornham All Saints leaving a trail of debris and destruction in its wake.

Back in the abbey grounds, as the water subsided, it left a thick layer of silt and jetsam, with wreckage from downed trees and buildings caught in the floodwater now beached in a sea of mud. In many places it damaged the ruins of the old abbey, wearing down the old walls and toppling over some of the remaining roof pillars. As the town's residents began to clear the debris they discovered next to what was a wall of the cloisters, a large hole leading down to a tunnel. They surmised the force of the water had swept away its ancient cover. They informed the town corporation of their find, and a few days later an officer arrived to investigate.

He was accompanied by a priest from St Mary's Church, the mayor of the Bury Corporation presuming this might be a matter requiring their attention as well as his. Father Browning, the archivist at St Mary's Church, was assigned the task. Already soaked and covered in slimy mud, the two men peered down into the hole. It stank of rotting vegetation and human waste.

Jonathan from the town corporation was a small, thin man, with a busybody attitude, full of his own self-importance. He stood back from the stinking dark hole and said, surprise in his voice, 'I heard rumours about these tunnels for years. I never thought they existed, but it seems they do after all. I think we'll just have to fill it in before people get the idea they can go exploring. It is too dangerous to leave like this...'

'Not so fast, sir,' interrupted the priest, holding up his hand. 'These tunnels lead in many directions under the town. Initially they were built as a means for the abbey monks to hide, or escape when they were attacked. But from what I have read, they were also used for storing or archiving the abbey's records and artefacts. I will check with the bishop, but I think he would like the tunnel examined before it is sealed up again.'

'Really?' I am not sure the corporation will want to delay dealing with this matter,' huffed the little man impatiently. 'I can't see the point of waiting – whatever was in there will have been ruined by the water. And we don't want any children wandering in there, it's too dangerous. I am sure the mayor will want it closed up very quickly.' His tone implied that the mayor trumped the bishop's authority when it came to matters such as this.

In his most solicitous tone, the priest countered, 'I think it best if the bishop and mayor meet to discuss this. If there are historical items or relics relating to the church down there, it is important they are found and saved. I shall report back to His Excellency the bishop at once. Please do nothing hasty in the meantime.'

Reluctantly, Jonathan agreed, saying he would put a temporary cover over the hole, adding 'he couldn't assure it would not be removed by the local children, and any injuries suffered by them if they entered the tunnel would be the fault of the church.'

Ignoring Jonathan's idle threat, the priest trudged back through the thick, cloying mud to the church, and wrote a message to the bishop in Ipswich, requesting his involvement in persuading the town corporation to allow the tunnel to be searched. Having sent the messenger on his way, he went into the church's private quarters to clean up. There he bumped into Father Cassipierre, to whom he relayed news about the tunnel.

'You say there is a tunnel exposed, Father Browning? One that may go under Angel Hill? Praise the Lord, I believe my prayers have been answered.'

'And what were you praying for, aside from our normal requests, Father Cassipierre?'

'Guidance as to what an inscription on a piece of wood we found when we exorcised that house in Whiting St might mean. It is unfinished, but according to whoever wrote it way back in 1550 the full inscription is to be found in one of these tunnels. It alludes to something being safely stored there, but I know no more. But as the Lord is my witness I believe the opening up of this tunnel is an act of God encouraging us to discover its meaning.'

Father Browning was sceptical. 'Well, you better keep on praying, Father; I have just written to the bishop asking he stops the corporation from filling it in until we have looked in the tunnel ourselves. It is uncertain if he will agree to my request. I too, have read in the archives that these tunnels were used for safekeeping the abbey's records. Maybe there are other things to be found down there – including a solution to your puzzle.'

'I believe so, Father, I believe the answer to my search will be found down there. I have been unable to find any reference that might complete the inscription, and it has been occupying my thoughts daily. I shall pray the bishop grants us the opportunity to search that tunnel.'

It was a frustrating two weeks before Fathers Cassipierre and Browning could access the tunnel. The bishop and mayor finally agreed they could have just two days to search the tunnel, once it had drained of water and dried out sufficiently for them to enter safely.

Chapter 17

The workmen struggled to clear the sticky, malodorous mud left by the flood. Progress was slow as they removed it bucket by bucket to the surface. Mercifully, as they worked away from the river and up the tunnel's incline under Angel Hill, the depth of the debris decreased. Finally, the two priests could descend into the murky tunnel to begin their exploration.

They asked that some of the workers remain at the base of the steps down into the tunnel in case they needed further help – or rescuing.

The going was slow as they struggled through the ankle-deep mud and detritus left by the flood. After some 200 paces it began to dry out, then, unexpectedly, the tunnel divided. They decided to take the right-hand route. Despite burning brightly, their flambeau only lit the tunnel a short way in front of them. They were in a cocoon of silence, within an orb of light extending just a few feet around them. It was painful progress, and the air was becoming stale and foetid. They continued on for several minutes. Both noticed the floor of the tunnel was increasingly covered in rocks and earth that seemed to have fallen from the roof. But at least it was becoming drier; they were now beyond the extent of the floodwaters, it was possible anything they might find would not be ruined.

Several minutes later, Father Browning, now out of breath, couldn't hide his disappointment. He said, 'There seems to be nothing here, not even the remains of any parchments or books; I am beginning to become discouraged. I was hoping to find something of interest. Shall we continue? Do you think it is worth all this discomfort, Father? The tunnel looks increasingly unsafe and in poor condition – perhaps this is a dangerous fool's errand after all. Also, this foul air is making me feel unwell. What do you think, Father?'

Father Cassipierre wasn't prepared to give up so soon. Clutching the inscribed piece of wood in his hand like some talisman, he still believed it was his guiding spirit that would lead him to finding the full inscription, and whatever it might reveal.

He pleaded, 'Let us continue for a few minutes, please. We have come this far; what is a few more paces? I just have a feeling we are close to finding what this person found all those years ago. If you prefer, I will go on alone.'

'No, I cannot leave you in this godforsaken hole by yourself, it is too dangerous. We will continue a little further until it becomes too unbearable. I do not share your optimism, but let us keep searching.'

The tunnel became more difficult to traverse – at times it was almost blocked by rocks and earth dislodged from the roof. Suddenly, Father Cassipierre, who was now leading the way, stopped and peered closely at a large flat stone fixed into the wall. 'Oh, my sweet Lord Jesus, here it is; a stone with the rest of the inscription. We have found it, Father, we have found it!!'

Out of breath, Father Browning leant wearily against the wall, held his flambeau close to the inscribed stone and read out loud in full the words carved upon it:

'Reliquiae sancti hic iacent.
Ab angelis custoditur.
Tutus ab infidelium direptione.
Requiescat in pace aeterna'.

Both were familiar with Latin and quickly translated it.

The relics of the saint lie here.
He is guarded by angels.
Safe from the plundering of the unbelievers.
May he rest in eternal peace.

An almost speechless Father Cassipierre looked, mouth agape, at his companion.' Does...does this say what I think it means? Because if it does we may have found...'

'Yes, it could be, my dear Father. But let us not jump to conclusions, and think for a moment of the repercussions; if it is indeed the remains of St Edmund, such a find could be of incalculable damage to the Protestant Church and a blessing to the Catholics. It could cause untold trouble, stir up resentment. Let us consider its ramifications before we do anything hasty.'

Father Cassipierre was quivering with excitement, deaf to any reasoning. 'Yes, I am well aware of the consequences but, Father, if we have found the remains of St Edmund himself it is a momentous discovery. People have been looking for these since the Dissolution. No matter what religion you follow, these are of immense historical value – as an archivist surely you cannot ignore this.' He paused to control his excitement and catch his breath. He looked imploringly at Father Browning, incredulous that he should be questioning this historic moment.

He continued, trying to convince his friend, 'This could contain the relics of one of the most venerated saints in Christendom; its value, its importance goes beyond our church, can't you see that?'

For a moment Father Cassipierre stopped talking, realising the incongruity of their situation. Here the two of them were having a theological argument in a cramped, filthy tunnel, likely to collapse at any time. Discussing a find of such ecumenical importance, its discovery could rock the foundations of the Protestant Church.

'Maybe we are getting ahead of ourselves; should we not try opening this vault and see what is inside?' suggested Father Browning. 'It may be empty, in which case we are arguing over nothing.'

It was a reasonable argument, one Father Cassipierre reluctantly agreed with.

Both then realised they carried nothing with which to lever open the heavy flat stone fixed securely into the tunnel wall.

'I shall return to fetch the workmen,' said Father Browning, turning back down the tunnel.

'Wait! No! No one must know of this until we are sure of what it contains. If it is the relics of St Edmund we have to decide what to do. Just ask to borrow a spade and metal bar of some description. We shall open it ourselves. This must be our secret, Father. Hurry back, I am desperate to discover what is in here. I fear this tunnel is likely to collapse at any time. Pray, make haste!' he urged.

Father Browning walked away, and the glow of his flambeau was soon swallowed by the darkness.

As Father Cassipierre stood in the tunnel, alone, his mind began to play tricks on him. Would Father Browning come back? Would he die here, so close to finding the holiest of relics, and never live to tell the world about them?

As his thoughts became more whimsical, he lost track of time. Then there came an ominous rumble from far up the tunnel, and seconds later a wave of dust came roiling down, choking him and stinging his eyes. What little air there was seemed to be sucked away, making breathing more difficult. He realised part of the tunnel had collapsed. It was clearly unstable after all the rain. Fear grabbed him and for a second he thought of running back towards the entrance. Was all this worth his life?

However, clutching the inscribed piece of wood, looking at the stone with its prophetic inscription, hiding what could be a relic of incalculable value, he knew what he had to do: stay and confirm what every bone in his body was telling him, that he stood inches from the remains of one of the most famous saints ever to have lived. No, he wasn't moving until he knew for certain what was in there, no matter the consequences.

The elderly priest sat down on the cold, damp floor, exhausted, the physical exertion and the lack of breathable air combining to drain his strength. Minutes passed with no sign of his fellow priest returning. He felt drowsy despite his discomfort. Just as he closed his eyes a louder, closer rumble shook the ground he sat upon and seconds later another gust of debris filled air blasted past him, almost bowling him over. He scrabbled to his feet, dizzy and disorientated. He felt a large rock fall against his feet. Somehow his trusty torch remained alight and, lowering it, he saw the vault stone was now lying on the ground, shaken from the wall by the tremors running through the tunnel.

The old priest's befuddled mind had a moment of clarity – the Lord had opened the vault for him! Now he must look inside the small vault and see if his prayers had been answered. His unwavering belief was that the relics of St Edmund were now within reach. He knelt down and with the aid of his flickering torch looked inside to find a beautifully carved and ornately decorated box the size of a small trunk. He pulled it gently onto the rubble-strewn floor, his heart racing with excitement. On top of the box were the words EADMUND REX ANGLORUM (EADMUND, KING OF ENGLAND).

Father Cassipierre clasped his hands together in a prayer of thanks, crying with emotion, overwhelmed by the magnitude of his discovery. Words from the Bible came to his mind:

Rejoice always, pray without ceasing, in everything give thanks; for this is the will of God in Christ Jesus for you.

Meanwhile, Father Browning was wrestling with a different set of emotions as he struggled slowly back towards the tunnel entrance. He heard the distant rumblings and guessed the tunnel was collapsing, which further fuelled his dilemma. Had Father Cassipierre been killed? Was it too dangerous to return to find him? Was it also dangerous to encourage his obsession with opening the vault in the search for what may or may not be St Edmund's remains? He knew the consequences for the Protestant Church would be shocking, unpredictable, causing much upset, even revolution. Did he want to be the one to have caused these terrible acts by finding the relics? They could defrock, even excommunicate him as a punishment.

He slowly ascended the steps into welcoming daylight and fresh air. The workmen looked at him, covered in mud and dust from head to toe. 'Are you well, Father? Did you find anything?' asked one of them. 'Where is the other priest, is he in need of help?'

Struggling to regain his breath, the priest finally answered, 'No thank you, everything is satisfactory, but I need to borrow some tools to open a vault we have found. I shall go back and help Father Cassipierre; you must remain here.'

The men needed no encouragement to remain above ground. They certainly didn't want anything to do with vaults and human remains, and they, too, heard the unsettling noises coming from the tunnel - they had no wish to be buried alive.

The workman took hold of the priest's arm, 'Father, I think it best if you stay here, or quickly return for the other priest. The tunnel sounds in a dangerous condition. We can come back another day when it is safer.'

'I appreciate your concern, sir, but this is something that has to be done now. I fear we will not get another chance. We shall return shortly, I promise. Do not endanger yourself by following me.'

With that he descended back into the treacherous passageway, clutching a fresh flambeau to light his way. It took a frustrating amount of time to reach Father Cassipierre, the pitch dark now mixed with choking powder and grit, reducing the effectiveness of the light from his torch to such an extent he could barely see a few inches in front of him. Along the way more rumblings shook the tunnel and filled it with yet more unbreathable air. Finally he found the elderly priest staring, awestruck, into a wooden box. Prayers were babbling incoherently from his mouth.

'Father, Father, what is it? What have you discovered? Are you in distress?'

The old priest looked almost paralysed with emotion. He failed to acknowledge the question, so Father Browning moved closer to the box, shining his torch so he could ascertain its contents. Instinctively on seeing them he stood back, made the sign of the cross and fell to his knees.

'Oh, my sweet Lord,' he whispered, awestruck. 'Are those truly the relics of St Edmund?

Father Cassipierre replied, 'I believe they are, Father, we have found them after nearly 200 years! Just look at all the artefacts buried with his bones – they are all the proof we need.'

Whatever concerns Father Browning may have harboured now vanished when he realised the truth of what they had discovered. The Church, no matter what denomination, he now believed, needed to see St Edmund's relics and restore them to a place of honour, for everyone to see, pray to, and revere his memory.

Another closer, more intense shaking in the tunnel brought him back to reality: unless they moved quickly, they and St Edmund's relics would be buried again. The tunnel was unstable and collapsing around them.

'Father, we must leave now, or we will never escape.' The young priest grabbed his elderly companion's sleeve trying to make him stand up. He refused to move, pleading, 'Unless we can take these relics with us, I am not leaving. You must help me carry them.'

With a desperation in his voice Father Browning said, 'Father, we cannot – the box is too heavy, and liable to fall apart. Let us put it back in the vault for protection. We will return when it is safer.'

'NO! I will not leave!' Father Cassipierre was adamant – there was no fear in his eyes, only determination. Or was it madness, wondered Father Browning.

He was scared and worried. How could he persuade this old man he would die unless he left immediately? He tried again to pull him away, but the priest held doggedly onto the box, protecting it with his body. Suddenly, just a few feet up the tunnel from where they stood, the roof collapsed, sending an avalanche of rocks and earth crashing to the floor. The force extinguished both their flambeaux, leaving them in total darkness and smothered by a fog of dust and debris.

Father Browning heard the old priest cry out in pain, then in a weak voice tell him, 'Go, Father, go! I am trapped here, my legs are stuck under the rocks...you must leave now. Please worry not, I am at peace, leave me to die next to St Edmund! My path to heaven is assured.'

As he uttered his dying words, the young priest saw a gentle blue light shimmering from the box, illuminating Father Cassipierre's dust-covered face which, far from revealing the pain he must be suffering, showed him with a beatific smile, a look of calm and peace radiating from him.

One last indecisive thought crossed his mind: should he take some of the relics with him, proof of their discovery? Then he quickly realised that without the box and other artefacts, a few relics were meaningless.

He tried one last plea: 'Father, this is no place to die, I must try and free you...'

In a quiet, steady voice, he replied, 'My son, this is the perfect place to die, besides the remains of our greatest saint. No, please go...I command you to save yourself. His light will show you the way.' With these last words Father Cassipierre's head dropped slowly onto the floor, the mysterious blue light dimming; as it did so, by some miracle one of the torches burst into life, illuminating the tunnel. Father Browning picked it up, made the sign of the cross over the prostrate figure of the dead priest and ran towards the entrance. The rumble and crash of the collapsing tunnel followed his stumbling, petrified race to the surface.

As he clambered up the steps into the sunshine and fresh air the entire tunnel seemed to disintegrate behind him and a fresh fall of stone and earth sealed the entrance. The workmen helped Father Browning to his feet, and one asked after the other priest. Shaking his head disconsolately, Father Browning explained in between gasping for breath, 'He was trapped...I could not save him...God rest his soul, and please God, save my soul, for I shall live with the memory all my life that I was unable to help him.'

Later in church, he prayed for forgiveness, and for guidance: should he tell the bishop of their discovery, or bury the memory deep in his soul, never to be revealed to anyone except his God?

No answer came. Deep down he knew no good would come to the Church of England if the whereabouts of St Edmund's relics were exposed. The Catholics would attempt to find them and use them as a rallying point for yet more religious strife. So he kept the secret, telling the bishop that nothing was found, but the life of one honourable holy man was tragically lost, along with the inscribed piece of wood found by Harold 150 years earlier.

History would barely register the incident. A footnote in Bury's long and fractious progress towards religious toleration. One not to be achieved for another 150 years.

Chapter 18
(1716)

There, 'tis done! A true labour of blood, sweat and tears! Look, my first issue of *The Suffolk Mercury!*'

Thomas Bailey held up a single sheet of paper covered on both sides by news and gossip from around the town, county, and from London too.

His wife, Sherry, looked on admiringly. 'Well done, husband, that is a noble and worthwhile achievement, this town's first newspaper. I am so proud of you! It has been a long time in the making. I am so pleased after all your efforts. Now you have produced the first issue, how often will you be publishing it?'

A look of concern crossed his face, 'I need to get more people to advertise in the Mercury to publish it regularly. Paper is so expensive, at twenty shillings a ream, I can only afford to print about 250 copies. Then we have to pay back the moneylenders for the printing press, that costs fifteen guineas, and we are taxed a halfpenny on each copy we sell. Damn that stamp tax! At the moment I will only charge a penny for a copy; it is not enough, but people will not pay more until they see stories of interest to them. At the moment, I do not envisage we will become wealthy doing this.'

'It will take time. Well, we are lucky my father has been generous in paying the rent for a year on our house, as his contribution to your business. That is one less thing to worry about. I am sure people will begin to support your endeavour; they are desperate for news, and you are the only one that can provide it. You'll just have to be patient. I am sure it will be a tremendous success.'

His wife's encouraging words meant a great deal to him. Her support for this risky endeavour was essential to its success. Sherry had no real interest in publishing a newspaper. But she accepted it was a vision he'd harboured for many years. Today was a day to celebrate – and worry about the finances tomorrow.

Thomas looked at his wife. Although petite in stature she was strong of character and, once on a chosen path, she would rarely be dissuaded from her objective. Quietly spoken, with a beguiling smile and warm eyes, he had fallen in love with her the day he met her two years ago at a hunt ball. Wed within months of that meeting, she patiently watched – and helped – as he planned the launch of *The Suffolk Mercury*.

Since then her loyalty throughout the long and arduous process launching the newspaper had been invaluable. Her gentle persuasion convinced her father to assist financially until the newspaper produced an income that would support them.

With a resigned shrug, Thomas agreed, 'I know, I know. But being in such debt is always a concern to me. We need to find some news that will make people want to buy the newspaper...' He paused mid-sentence, exhausted after a long day printing the first issue. 'Anyway, I am too tired to worry about it now. I have to be back at the printing works early tomorrow; thankfully the walk to Long Brackland is short.'

Two weeks later news came to Thomas of a murder in Northgate St, an insalubrious area of the town renowned for its brothels, distilling of illegal alcohol, gambling and vagabonds looking for easy prey.

The victim was a young girl, apparently a prostitute, found naked with her throat cut.

Thomas was shocked; murders were rare in Bury St Edmunds, but this was the kind of news, macabre and salacious though it was, that would help sell extra copies of his newspaper.

He decided to find out more before committing the story to print. First stop would be the local constable and any watchmen that were patrolling the area at the time. It was two days after the discovery of the body when Thomas tracked down the constable who first attended the murder scene. Despite the severity of the crime he had only just recruited a search party to visit all the houses in Northgate St to gather more information. Thomas was not impressed at his tardiness. He found the man in a tavern in the Buttermarket, not far from the town gaol.

'Constable Cooper?' asked Thomas as he approached the man, clearly already the worse for drink.

'Who wants to know?' he demanded, belching, his bloodshot eyes having difficulty focusing on Thomas's outstretched hand.

'I am Thomas Bailey, publisher of *The Suffolk Mercury* newspaper. I am writing a story about the murder. I understand you are the person trying to find the culprit. I was hoping to ask you a few questions.' He sat down at the table before the constable could say no.

'Not much to tell,' he said, 'though my memory improves with a full glass of ale in my hand.'

Thomas asked the landlord to bring a drink over 'for the esteemed constable.' Then asked if he could describe the murder scene and any progress he'd made towards finding the killer.

'She was a whore, probably got into some argument with a customer, and got her throat slit to keep her quiet. They are attacked all the time, the dangers of doing such a disgusting job if you ask me. Girls like her don't last long.' He slurped a mouthful of beer, wiped his mouth with his sleeve, and slumped back into his chair. His indifference to the girl's fate – and finding her killer – annoyed Thomas.

'Yes, I can see such girls are likely to find themselves in unsafe situations. However, someone out there is a murderer; they must be caught, don't you agree? Have you made any arrests, or have any suspects?'

With a sense of finality in his voice, the constable shrugged, 'No. No one seems to know anything. That Northgate St area is a pit of vice and crime, doubt we'll get any help from the people who live there. My men only get paid a penny a day for their time, so they'll not want to waste more than a few days looking for the killer of a young strumpet.'

Sensing he was wasting his time, Thomas asked one last question, 'Could you at least give me the girl's name?'

For a moment the constable said nothing, as though he couldn't remember her name. 'Er, yes, it was...Jenny Paperlace. I was told she lived near the Kings Arms alehouse. I haven't been able to find out where yet. I wouldn't recommend going to that part of the town without some protection, they'll rob you of that nice watch before you can ask a question. Now, if you don't mind, I have more important work to do than talk about a dead whore.' He stood up, drained his tankard and unsteadily made his way out of the tavern.

Thomas was unimpressed with the constable's attitude. He couldn't accept that a young girl's murder, whore or not, would be of so little concern to him. He decided to disregard the lawman's advice and visit Northgate St to ask a few questions for himself. He found it strange that a murder, a rare occurrence in Bury, was not being investigated with more fervour. Finding and convicting a killer would be a feather in any constable's cap, so his lack of enthusiasm in attempting to solve this crime was puzzling.

The intrepid publisher waited until the evening before venturing down to Northgate St. He did take off all his rings, hid his watch and dressed in old clothes hoping the overall effect was to make him an unlikely target for any ne'er-do-well. Sherry was not impressed – she sternly rebuked him for taking on the role of an investigator.

'Thomas, this is not your job. It is dangerous, the constable warned you not to go to that part of the town. Can't you take Richard with you? He is a strapping young man, he might afford you some protection.'

He was not to be dissuaded by his wife's concerns. 'Sherry, if I find out who committed this murder, it could help our newspaper succeed and make money. I cannot turn the opportunity down. As for taking Richard, he is our apprentice. He may be a big lad, but he would be useless if things turned ugly. He can't even kill any rats he finds in the print shop, so I doubt he will handle himself in a useful manner when confronted by some cut-throat...Not that I am expecting any such trouble,' he added hastily as Sherry's face went wide-eyed with worry.

His wife wasn't finished. 'Thomas, you must not put yourself in jeopardy. You will do no one any good if you are found robbed and beaten. And all for what? A good story? Let the constables do their job and then write about it when they have found the culprit. There are more important responsibilities than the newspaper; your wellbeing and your family are both of greater consequence.'

He had always loved her quiet determination, her persistence and optimism in the face of the trials and tribulations they had faced while starting the newspaper. Indeed, he believed they would probably never have launched it without her dogged resolve. Now, however, her arguments were making him waver, doubt his motives in going in search of Jenny's killer. But Thomas knew if he abandoned his plan then the poor girl's murderer would likely never be caught. And, of course, if he did find him, or her, then the story could be the making of *The Suffolk Mercury.*

He walked over to his wife and took both her hands in his, 'Darling wife, what you say makes eminent sense, but based on my discussion with that idiot of a constable, nothing will be done to find this girl's killer. She deserves better, no matter what miserable trade she plied, she shouldn't be forgotten, treated like a dead dog. Something tells me there's more to this than meets the eye. I promise I will take extra care, I will take my pistol too, if it makes you feel better, but please let me do this, I feel I have some kind of duty to find the truth in this matter.'

Sherry, her eyes wet with unshed tears, said nothing. Then she embraced Thomas, whispering in his ear: 'You are a stubborn and honourable man, Thomas, and I love and hate you for it! So go now before I lose my temper. I shall expect you back before midnight, otherwise I will come and find you myself. And I warn you, you'll regret it if I do!'

Northgate St was a twenty-minute walk from Whiting St, but it was a world apart from the elegance of the large houses in that area of Bury. The lanes and alleys off Northgate St were pitch dark, barely lit by the candles in the houses' windows. Thomas found the Kings Arms tavern in Pump Lane. It was a run-down, dilapidated building with boarded-up windows and a broken door. Outside three men lay sprawled unmoving on the ground, covered in their own vomit. As he entered, the noise of a room full of raucous drunks and the smell of beer and unwashed bodies almost took his breath away. He elbowed a path to the bar. Everyone was either too inebriated to notice him, busy pawing and groping the whores or had passed out on the floor. In the small bar he had to shout to make himself heard to attract the landlord.

He ordered some ale that arrived in a filthy, unwashed tankard. As the landlord served him, he introduced himself and explained what he was doing there, asking if he knew Jenny Paperlace. The answer surprised Thomas. 'Didn't know her, she wasn't from around here. Just heard the poor girl's body was found 'round the corner. Terrible thing to 'ave happened. It's not good for business, you know?'

Thomas was confused. 'So she...she wasn't a...whore? That's what the constable told me she was.'

178

'Not as far as I know. Think she worked on one of the big estates out near Great Barton. No idea how her body got here...now, if you'll excuse me, sir, I have people to serve.' Thomas didn't bother to down the murky-looking ale in the dirty tankard, but left quickly, heeding Sherry's words of warning if he was late back home.

As he walked across Angel Hill and up Churchgate St to his home, Thomas was perplexed, turning over in his mind why the constable had lied to him, and why someone would take the trouble to dump Jenny's body far away from where she lived. Clearly they wished to confuse anyone looking into her murder, that was understandable, but the constable's untruths? Now that requires further investigation, thought Thomas as he walked into the house and met a relieved Sherry who had waited up for his safe return.

'So...having risked life and limb, what did you discover, if anything?" Sherry couldn't keep the scepticism out of her voice.

'In truth, dear wife, I am more confused about this whole incident than when I left. The landlord was most helpful. But it has set me off on an altogether more interesting path, I think.' He then repeated what the tavern owner told him. Sherry finally seemed to take an interest in the story:

'So, what are your thoughts now? Do you have any ideas on how to use this information? It now seems you have half a story. Not one you can really use in the newspaper until you find out more about this girl, what she did and, of course, why she was murdered.'

'You're right, Sherry, it is indeed a conundrum, and one which is getting more complicated to unravel. I assume my next move will be to visit the Earl of Northumberland at Barton Hall to see if Jenny worked there. Maybe that will shed some light on this mystery.'

The next day, Thomas rode out to Great Barton, a distance of some five miles, to the huge estate owned by the Earl of Northumberland. He did not expect to meet the earl himself. A conversation with the head housekeeper would tell him if the murdered girl had been in service there. He found his way to the servants' entrance and announced himself to a cook who was skinning some rabbits on a table near the kitchen door. Soon a stern-looking, rotund, middle-aged lady, hair tied in a severe bun and impatient look on her face, stood arms akimbo in front of Thomas demanding to know what he wanted.

Thomas explained the reason for his visit and, as he did so, her expression softened, 'Yes, we have just heard the terrible news about Jenny; she was such a sweet, hard-working girl. To come to such an untimely and violent end is so, so sad. Do you know if they have caught her murderer?'

'It appears not, ma'am, which is why I am here to see if I can help the authorities catch him. Though at the moment they seem reluctant to pursue the matter for some reason. Can you think of any reason why someone would want to kill her? Had she upset someone here or in the town that you know of?'

The housekeeper suddenly became evasive. 'I wouldn't know about that, sir, all I know she was a lovely girl, but who she knew, or if she had any male friends, I cannot say. Now, if you please, I have a lot to do, we have a houseful turning up this weekend. I wish you well.' She turned and strode back into the kitchen.

Thomas watched her go with the feeling she knew more than she told him. He never said anything about 'men friends', so why mention it? Why did this murder have so many lies buzzing around it like flies round a honeypot?

As he turned to leave, a young butler approached him. In a quiet, hesitant voice he said, 'Sir, I just heard your conversation about Jenny. She was my friend and I am heartbroken at her death. She was a good girl, not the whore people are saying she was.' He looked over his shoulder, as if to make sure no one was watching him from the house. 'I have an idea what may have led to her murder. But I cannot be seen to be talking to you here, I may lose my job.'

Intrigued, Thomas suggested they could meet that evening. The butler gave his name as Matthew, agreeing to meet again at the local tavern, the Rising Sun, at nine o'clock.

By ten o'clock Matthew had not arrived. Thomas was loath to venture back to Barton Hall to find out the cause of his delay, so he returned home to find Sherry furious with worry. She lambasted him for disappearing all day without any message explaining what was happening, or where he was. He tried to calm her down, by revealing the latest twists and turns in his search for Jenny's killer, but she was beyond reasoning with.

Her eyes glared with fury as her worry turned to anger. 'You've been gone twelve hours, Thomas! I was fearing the worst. The more you involve yourself with this matter the more I worry for your safety. I believe you when you say there are now more questions than answers, but it's not your job to seek an explanation for all of this. That is why we have judges and constables. You are a newspaper publisher, stick to what you know – it is safer for both of us. I beg you stop this folly before ill befalls you. You are meddling in affairs that are not your business. No good will come of it, husband.'

'I understand your worries,' Thomas said, 'But I cannot sit by and watch this girl's murder go unsolved. I will return tomorrow to speak to this boy Matthew at Barton Hall, then I promise I will inform the constables of my findings, and leave them to do their job. I beg you to let me do this. My conscience will then be clear.'

Sherry sighed, 'As you wish; I know I am not going to persuade you otherwise, but I will keep you to your promise: talk to that boy, then leave it to the authorities – remember you have a newspaper to publish at the end of this week, the staff need you there to help them.'

'I know, I know, you are right,' agreed Thomas. 'I shall do as we have agreed, no more.'

Next day, his best-laid plans came to nought when, on returning to find Matthew, he was told by a nervous servant the boy was no longer in the employ of the earl, and no one knew of his whereabouts.

Chapter 19

N ow, watch me carefully,' said Thomas to his assistant, Edward, as they crouched over the printing machine setting the type for the next issue of *The Suffolk Mercury*. They were putting the individual letters of each word inside a wooden frame, laid out in a mirror image of how it would appear on the sheet of paper when printed. Patiently Thomas explained the process again to his young apprentice:

'Take each letter and put it face up and create the words of the story in a line inside this wooden frame; it's called a galley. Then between each line of words put these little spacing bars of lead, called leading. Follow the layout I have sketched on this piece of paper and exactly the words I have written. The main story at the top. Take the big letters for the headline from this tray, and then for the smaller letters in the story take them from the other tray underneath it. That way we don't mix up the big and small letters.' The young man stared intently as Thomas laid out the first few rows of type.

Thomas employed Edward as he was well educated, good with words and a keen learner. Indeed, at times his spelling was sometimes better than his own. But setting out a page of lettering in the right order with no spelling mistakes, based on what Thomas had written, was a day-long process. Eventually the whole page of letters and words was laid out and put inside a wooden frame called a *forme.*

When that was done he continued his explanation of the printing process to Edward. 'We now have to put ink over the type using these two balls. They are expensive because they are made of dog skin leather, which has no sweat pores, and stuffed with sheep's wool. We soak them in ink and run them over the lettering inside the galley, see?'

Edward nodded his understanding of the delicate process. 'And now we start printing?' he asked.

'Not quite yet, we will run just one copy and read it from top to bottom to find any mistakes. Then, if it is satisfactory, we start to print.' Thomas laid a slightly damp sheet of paper over the forme which was now secured onto the printing press's bed. He rolled under the <u>platen</u> and screwed it down onto the paper and ink covered type, pressing hard to produce a printed copy.

He unscrewed the platen, carefully lifted up the paper and turned it round to read the page:

The headline shouted in the largest typeface he had – 48pt – '*Murdered girl was servant at Barton House*'

Underneath in 24pt it read: '*Killer still at large – constables have made little progress in his capture.*'

The main story went on to reveal what had been discovered so far in Thomas's brief investigation (not much, he had to admit) and ask his readers why so little was being done to find the culprit. Why was her body left near Pump Lane? And why had her close friend at Barton Hall gone missing?

'Well, that should stir things up a little, don't you think, Edward?' said Thomas, rather pleased with his little exposé.

The rest of the page consisted of smaller news stories about two robberies, some buying and selling of land, a forthcoming auction and the deaths of three prominent local citizens (and to compensate, four births to members of the local aristocracy). The other big news story: the River Lark was again navigable after a long fight by Henry Ashley. People were now able to transport goods from Eastgate St to Mildenhall by river.

The other side of the sheet had several small advertisements placed by local traders offering everything from fresh meat to grain, horses and animals for sale to a new contraption called the seed drill to help farmers, it said, sow seed more quickly and with less waste. Mentally Thomas added up the money such adverts generated; around fifteen shillings, he estimated. Just enough to cover the paper costs, ink and stamp tax, and pay his group of young boys and girls a ha'penny for every ten copies they sold.

It took all day to print 250 copies, allowing for the ink to dry on one side of the paper before printing on the reverse. The following morning he gave each of his group of newspaper sellers fifteen copies each, kept fifty for himself to sell from his printing works, and the rest in case one of his team needed extra copies. *I should be so lucky, Thomas thought, normally I end up burning the unsold ones because I printed too many, a terrible waste of money I cannot afford to keep losing.* Quietly he prayed that this issue, with its provocative headline and story, would be the turning point for his fledgling newspaper.

Within hours it would bring him both good and bad news.

* * * *

By lunchtime, all the young newspaper sellers were back at his printing works, their coin bags full of pennies, asking if Thomas could provide more copies to sell. The word was spreading about the murder story and people wanted to read it for themselves. Delighted, Thomas gave them each some of his spare copies and worked through the night printing another 200, then another 250. By the end of the week he'd sold over 900 copies.

He arrived back home, exhausted after working non-stop for two days, smelling of ink and sweat. He told Sherry how many extra copies he'd printed due to the popularity of his main story.

'Thomas, congratulations!' said Sherry, beaming with pride. 'That is the most you have sold of any issue. I take back everything I said about that murder story, it has piqued the town's interests – and boosted our coffers. I'll get the cook to bring some food and ale. You look as tired as a wilted flower; come sit by the fire.'

'Tired, but happy,' said Thomas, a wan smile on his face as he slumped into the chair, the heat of the fire quickly making him feel drowsy. 'That issue has certainly made us a name in the town. I hope it not just helps find the girl's murderer, but puts our business on a sounder footing. Heaven knows we need the money my dear. If this continues, maybe at last we will no longer be so dependent on the kindness of your father.'

Sherry's father, Sir William Elkins was a wealthy landowner, farmer and moneylender, living in Lavenham. Sherry was his only daughter, on whom he doted, lavishing gifts and patronage of her artistic efforts with embarrassing generosity. When approached with the idea of supporting Thomas's new publishing enterprise he agreed to buy the house in Whiting St and let them live there rent-free for a year as his way of helping. He was not optimistic about its prospects. But property, he reasoned, unlike his son-in-law, was a solid investment.

'I know the King hates these publications,' he expounded to the couple over lunch one day, 'He thinks they incite sedition, allowing people to write the most outrageous lies about him and his government. I have it on good authority that the stamp duty will go up again soon to try and quash this rash of so-called newspapers.'

'But, Father, they are common now in London, and some publishers are becoming wealthy and influential as their popularity increases. I think it is too late to stop their spread now across the country.' Sherry knew it was pointless arguing, though the mention of their influence on matters of business and local politics went some way to dispelling her father's objections – anything that might benefit his interests was worthy of consideration. Buying the house for them was a risk-free way of helping, she knew.

'It will be a good investment, even if your newspaper fails. Though I wish you the best of luck, of course,' he added with lacklustre encouragement.

In the meantime, at his manor house, he pointedly displayed his daughters' paintings, frequently encouraging guests and visitors to buy them at (Sherry considered) inflated prices. The cost, Sir William suggested, of doing business with him. As a result there was a steady demand for her landscapes of the countryside around Bury, and flattering renditions of the streets and people in the town. It produced a steady, modest income which kept food on the table and servants paid, but that was about all.

Now, they were both hopeful The Suffolk Mercury might become financially viable. The latest issue proved popular with the townspeople. The challenge now, as Thomas pointed out, 'was to keep people reading and buying the newspaper – we won't always have exciting stories like this murder to report on.'

That would be the least of their troubles. Unbeknownst to the couple, this story was not welcome with one very powerful person; the Earl of Northumberland.

* * * *

'Hell's bells, boy! What stupidity have you done now?' roared the earl at his cowering son. 'Was this murdered girl another one of your dalliances? I know she worked here. Don't lie to me, Louis, I shall beat the truth out of you.'

Louis, next in line to inherit the vast wealth of the earl of Northumberland's empire – and the power and prestige that came with it – was looking far from a worthy candidate to take on such responsibilities. He stood before his father, blubbering with fear, his thin, reedy body shaking in the face of the earl's threats. At 21 years old, he'd been given the finest education, showered with his father's largesse, mixed with the great and the good of the realm, but shown no willingness to accept any responsibility, or act in a manner befitting the station his father held – and which he would take over in due course. He was a grave, irredeemable disappointment the earl frequently told his mother, the countess, who doted on her son despite his all too obvious failings.

'F...F...Father, I can explain...' the boy stuttered in panic, trying to find some words that might prevent his father inflicting any more pain upon him. His ear was already bleeding from a hefty swipe and he knew that would just be the start unless he could calm down his irate father.

'Yes, yes, the girl stayed in my bed on occasion, but I was always careful to avoid...you know...making her with child. Then when she came to me saying she was expecting a baby and I was the father, I panicked. I didn't know what to do. She wouldn't get rid of it and wanted money, otherwise she would tell everyone downstairs. So...I...'

'Quiet, boy! You continue to be a disappointment to myself and your mother, and now further embarrassment is to befall us because of your habit of sticking your spindle in every willing honeypot you find. And now...now.' He waved a copy of The Suffolk Mercury in front of his son's face, 'this, whatever it's called, newspaper, has the finger of suspicion pointing at us...' He threw the paper to the floor and pulled Louis to him, their faces inches apart, the earl asking in a menacing whisper, 'Look at me, boy, were you involved in this girl's death? Lie to me and I will disinherit you faster than you can wipe the snot off your miserable face.'

'Not...not directly, Father,' he stammered, avoiding his father's eyes. 'I asked the head butler to dismiss her...'

'And then what else? Tell me everything, boy.'

'Then, I...I asked one of the gardeners if they knew someone who might be able to keep her quiet...you know, scare her into silence, persuade her to leave Bury. I gave him money for the girl, so she could move away...I am unsure what happened thereafter.'

'At a guess, you foolish boy, the thug kept the money and killed the girl,' said the earl sarcastically.

Louis nodded his head, misery written all over his face, 'I suppose that might be the case, Father. I am so sorry.'

Ignoring his son's apology, the earl said, 'My Lord Jesus, what have I done to deserve such stupidity from one of my offspring?' He paused for a moment, then said, 'Well, here's what's happening to you, my boy. Tomorrow you will leave for our estate in Scotland and stay there until I order you to come back. Furthermore you will work as a farmhand while you are there. It is time you had some discipline and order in your life. Do I make myself clear?'

'Father, you can't do this to me,' wailed Louis, 'that is worse than transportation to the Americas! I will be treated like a slave! Please father, I beg of you...please reconsider...'

'Actually, that is not a bad idea now you mention the Americas. My friend the Earl of Cornwallis has a plantation in Virginia; I am sure he would welcome some extra help out there...Would that be a preferable alternative, I wonder...' The earl could barely stop a smile coming to his face, enjoying seeing his son squirming with fear.

Louis was immediately contrite. 'Father, of course, Scotland is a wonderful idea. I shall start packing forthwith...I am so sorry for the problems I have caused...I promise I will make amends...make you proud of me.'

'That would be a first. Now get out of my sight,' said the earl brusquely, 'I will see you next year for the hunting season, and if you get another girl pregnant again I will cut off your balls.'

Louis bolted out of the room, leaving the earl pondering how to stop publication of any more damaging stories in that pesky Suffolk Mercury. Unlike his son, he was loath to try threats, coercion or violence. Gentle persuasion was more his style, and if that failed, then the offer of a delicate bribe normally did the trick. However, a lot was at stake. If the gentle approach didn't work, more drastic action to halt further damage to his reputation would be required.

He called for his valet. After a brief discussion, he sent him to Bury with instructions to find out more about the publisher, his business, and any relatives that might be 'persuaded' to help stop his ill-conceived pursuit of justice.

Chapter 20
(1717)

West Farm in Lawshall, still owned by one of Grace and Maud's descendants in the early eighteenth century, was now a substantial enterprise growing produce for sale in Bury market, as well as rearing cattle, sheep and horses. Several fields were also let to neighbouring farmers.

Grace's great-great-great grandson Humphrey Debenham, the current owner, a young man in his thirties, was reading a copy of *The Suffolk Mercury* his brother brought back from Bury.

Humphrey scanned the story about the murdered girl. He noticed with interest the owner listed the house in Whiting St as the address of the newspaper business. He mused out loud to himself, 'I see Grace and Maud's old house in Bury is in the news again – that place seems to attract attention. Thomas Bailey, who lives there now, is the owner of this *Suffolk Mercury*, and he's writing quite scandalous news about the Earl of Northumberland. That man could find himself being sued for libel if he isn't careful. He could lose his house if he lost.'

Mary walked into the parlour and gave a mug of ale to Humphrey, 'Were you talking about that house in Whiting St? I walked past the house a few weeks ago; it is still an imposing place. I have often wanted to go inside and see what it's like. Grace's letters tell such fascinating stories of their time there, running the tavern, the people they met. It has truly seen some interesting times.'

'Not that I wish him ill, but if his fortunes wane, maybe we should look at buying it sometime, open up a shop for all our produce and meat. It might be an opportunity for us if this reckless publisher continues to upset the local aristocracy; they'll show no mercy if they think their reputation is being besmirched. Mind you, I'd be delighted if someone took that arrogant earl down a peg or two. Those arse-licking Royalists think they can do whatever they like. I will wager this poor girl was being bedded by one of his sons, and then caused trouble.'

'Husband! Keep your old-fashioned Cavalier sentiments to yourself,' warned Mary, 'Talk like that, even now, could get you in trouble. Just accept aristocrats like the earl are above the law. You cannot fight them, so just ignore their arrogant ways, it will only upset you.'

'You may be right, Mary, I cannot do much about those pieces of horseshit, but it seems this Thomas Bailey has no fear of them. He deserves our help if he ever needs it. Anyone who can make life uncomfortable for those, those, lobcocks has my support.'

'You be careful what you say and do, husband,' said Mary, suddenly sounding serious, 'We have toiled long and hard to be where we are; a reckless word or deed could see us in the poorhouse if we upset these people. I dislike them too, Humphrey, but let us vent our ire in private, not in public.'

Humphrey didn't answer, realising he'd probably spoken out of turn. Though even six decades after his grandfather had been hanged by the Royalists in 1656 at the height of the English Civil

War for daring to speak out against the King's excesses, he still felt aggrieved and bitter at his death.

However, he didn't need his wife to castigate him any further, so he changed the subject. He'd spotted an advertisement for a seed drill which he was now reading and, as far as Mary was concerned, the previous conversation was seemingly forgotten, 'Now this looks interesting, this new machinery reckons it can save time and money on seed planting. We've over twenty acres of barley to sow next season, this could be a godsend. We could rent it out to other farmers when we've finished with it...I'll get one of the boys to see the man in Bury selling them.'

Mary, relieved that Humphrey had moved on from his political rant, said, 'You and your fascination with all this new machinery never ends; a new Dutch plough was the last one, wasn't it? They all cost money, do they not? Are they worth it? I often wonder, isn't it less money just to hire more men?'

'Men are unreliable, and their wages just keep rising,' explained Humphrey. 'What with a new plough and this seeding machine, I believe this is the future of farming. One day they'll probably find a replacement for horses and oxen to pull the equipment! I look forward to that.'

'You are such a dreamer, Humphrey; nothing will replace horses.'

'Maybe not in our lifetime, Mary. But the farm our Benjamin and Richard will run will be a lot different to the way we do it now....anyhow, enough of guessing the future. The present demands I go and check on the cows' feed and water. I shall return for supper.' Humphrey eased himself slowly from the chair. Rubbing his aching back, he walked outside, his mind wandering back to the newspaper and the article about the Earl of Northumberland – his ancestors had been rabid Royalists – but now maybe he could make the aristocrats' life a little uncomfortable by offering some help to this Thomas Bailey fellow, who surely was going to need it if he continued to incur the wrath of the earl.

He mulled over the best way to do this, deciding to send the publisher an anonymous letter of support and a donation of £5; that would be a start. Humphrey smiled to himself: he hoped this new publication would cause that arsehole earl maximum embarrassment. Any way he could make that happen would be some small revenge for his grandfather's death.

The family would indeed end up owning the house in Bury again, and would face a challenge that would test their friendships to the limit.

Chapter 21

Thomas was perturbed at the disappearance of the young servant Matthew from Barton Hall. He recognised the boy was nervous at the prospect of talking to him about the murder of Jenny Paperlace. Clearly he knew something that would cause trouble in the earl's household, but what? Nevertheless, having seen the way sales of his newspaper rocketed when he published his story about her death – and the unanswered questions it raised – he believed morally he must continue his investigations, which in turn created a financial benefit for the newspaper.

He'd returned home from the printing works to find his wife sitting in front of the fire. She said nothing as he entered, no welcome, barely a recognition he was in the room. Instead she stood up and handed him a letter that arrived earlier in the afternoon.

'We had a visitor who delivered this, he said he was from Barton Hall,' said Sherry, a slight tremble of fear in her voice. 'I didn't want to open it before you came home.'

Thomas looked at the back of the letter and saw the Earl of Northumberland's initials embedded in the wax seal. Saying nothing he ripped it open and unfolded the paper. The letter was short and to the point:

Sir,

I read with dismay and outrage, the spurious accusations in your publication, The Suffolk Mercury, insinuating that this household, or someone connected to it, was involved in the death of Jenny Paperlace. I can categorically deny any knowledge of how, or why, she was murdered.

If you continue to repeat unfounded allegations of this nature I shall have no alternative but to ask my legal counsel to sue you for libel, with the purpose of permanently closing your newspaper to stop the spread of such malicious gossip about myself and my household.

Furthermore I will seek financial damages from yourself for the maximum allowed by law.

Please cease and desist publishing any further stories implicating or impugning Barton Hall and its occupants with this crime.

George FitzRoy, 1st Earl of Northumberland,
Barton Hall.

Sherry was furious, 'I told you to stop this stupid business, Thomas, trying to find the murderer of that girl – now look at the trouble you have caused. Unless you take heed of his threats we will be ruined. Tell me this matter will cease now, Thomas, promise me this is the end of it?'

But where his wife saw a threat, Thomas saw an opportunity. A chance to put his newspaper on a pedestal, fighting the wrongs perpetrated by the rich and entitled. He came from a poor, underprivileged family, practically indentured servants on a vast estate near Cambridge. He'd seen his parents' helplessness when evicted for not paying the rent, the suffering and ignomy they endured as they tried to raise him and his brothers on next to nothing. Now this was finally his chance at retribution for the wrongs the earl's ilk inflicted on his family all those years ago.

He knew his wife feared for their safety, their livelihood, but somehow he needed to convince her that she should not let these threats dissuade him from finding the truth.

'Sherry, please, understand what is going on here,' he said, trying to be cool-headed as the temperature of the argument rose. 'The earl is a bully, using his power and money to smother the facts I am trying to uncover. This letter, this threat, makes it clear to me that the earl is hiding something. I owe it to the murdered girl and her family to expose his lies. My credibility – and the newspaper's – is at stake here. I cannot back down. I have spent my life watching these people ride roughshod over ordinary folk. Now, with The Suffolk Mercury, we have a way to draw attention to their callous indifference to others' suffering. Indeed, talking of letters I have received several of support, including some donations, so it would appear others feel the way I do.'

Sherry walked over to him, enraged at his stubbornness. Her eyes were alight, flaming with anger. His unwillingness to see reason as she saw it could cost them everything. She rarely lost her temper with him, but the prospect of financial ruin was more than she could bear.

'Please God, Thomas, are you out of your mind?' exclaimed Sherry. Her body was practically vibrating with rage. 'We have toiled so long and hard to make this venture a success, to have a good life, now you want to risk it all for nothing...a...a...'

'...A worthless servant girl? Is that what you mean, Sherry? Is she worth 'nothing' to you?' Thomas was shouting, horrified his wife could be so dismissive of a young girl's murder.

'No, that isn't what I mean, Thomas, I mean this is not our fight. That's why we have the law, to deal with such matters. I am begging you to concentrate on writing stories that don't offend people, especially people like the earl.'

Thomas wasn't backing down. 'But isn't this what a newspaper is supposed to do? Highlight injustice, give a voice to those that have none? Report the truth? Or would you rather I just write about births, deaths and marriages?'

He slumped down the chair, resting his elbows on his knees, staring at the floor. 'Sherry, I cannot in all conscience let this matter rest. You know from whence I came, the injustice people like the earl inflict so casually on lesser mortals like my family, like this unfortunate girl. I cannot, will not, walk away from bullying threats like these. If the earl is hiding something about this murder then the people of Bury should know about it.'

He paused and then, looking up at Sherry, he whispered, 'I beg of you, my love, let us be strong together and pursue this awful matter to discover what really happened. If Jenny was our daughter would you not wish us to do so?'

'But she wasn't. And this is not our battle, Thomas,' replied Sherry. 'Remember the earl probably knows my father; if he feels threatened then he may start making life difficult for him too. If he does I am sure the monetary help he is giving us will be withdrawn unless we accede to the earl's demands – and then where shall we be?'

Thomas was taken aback at Sherry's stubbornness. Normally she acquiesced when it came to matters of the business, but not so this time. He was waiting for her beguiling smile to lighten up her face, the captivating flash of her eyes that finally intimated the argument was over. But not so this time. Her defiance was unnerving, unexpected. Thomas finally realised that whilst he had met his match in this argument, he would continue his quest without Sherry's knowledge. And ultimately ask for forgiveness – as her permission was in no way forthcoming.

Trying to bring the matter to a close he suggested, 'Enough of this bickering, my dear. I am weary, let us retire and discuss this again in the 'morrow.' He turned towards the stairs, climbing them slowly, his body and mind numb with tiredness. Sherry waited a few minutes then joined him, her unhappy feelings torn between protecting Thomas, herself and their home, and his determination to take the honourable course of action.

Scullery maid Agnes Featherstone peered around the door from the kitchen watching her master and mistress go upstairs. She'd listened with interest to their lengthy altercation. She wondered if such information could be worth money. Her uncle was head butler at Barton Hall – surely the earl would pay handsomely to know what his foe was thinking and planning, ahead of time. Tomorrow was Sunday, her day off – she would take a trip to the earl's mansion, see her uncle and reveal what she knew – and discover if it had any value.

The following day Thomas rose early to visit the printing works, deciding further discussion with Sherry would only inflame matters and achieve nothing. He disliked the idea of going behind his wife's back to pursue the truth about Jenny's murder, but his conscience pushed him forward, ignoring the damage it might create in his marriage. Optimistically he hoped the whole story might blow over soon, the girl's murderer be found and amicable relations restored with his wife.

As he left, he bumped into Agnes as she hurriedly left the house, barely able to meet his eyes as he wished her a pleasant day off from work.

Agnes walked across the town. Few people were around early on a Sunday. It took her an hour to reach Barton Hall. Nervously she approached one of the servants carrying leftovers from the previous night's dinner, on their way to feed the pigs. She was directed into the kitchen which was a flurry of activity as breakfast was being served. Agnes stood in the corner out of the way as platters of cakes, rolls, bread, toast, boiled eggs with coffee, tea, and hot chocolate, were rushed upstairs. It was a far more lavish menu of dishes noticed Agnes than at her master's house. Her mouth watered at the smell of the freshly baked bread and pastries.

She waited silently for over an hour until her Uncle Theobald came downstairs from serving breakfast to see her. Despite the frenetic, harassed atmosphere he smiled and gave her a warm embrace.

'Agnes, this is a pleasant surprise,' he said with genuine delight. 'What brings you to Barton Hall?'

She suddenly realised that her visit might not be such a good idea. If she was discovered spying on Thomas and Sherry she would lose her job – all for the sake of a few shillings. As she stood there slack-mouthed with indecision, her uncle took both her hands in his and gently enquired, 'Are you unwell, child? Is something wrong? You have gone very pale.'

'No...no...I am in good health thank you, Uncle,' said Agnes, 'Can we talk where there are not so many people?'

Minutes later they were sitting on a wooden bench by the stables; the only sound was the shuffling of horses in their stalls and the crunch as they ate their fresh hay.

Still concerned that her visit was a dull-witted venture, Agnes struggled to explain her plan to her uncle. 'Er...I am unsure where to start, or if I should say anything at all.'

'Child, whatever you say I will not repeat it - unless you want me to. What is it that concerns you?" asked her uncle.

'Well...you...you have heard of that girl being murdered in Bury?'

'Yes...of course. Who hasn't? I have read about it in that newspaper. Do go on.'

'And I believe my master, who owns The Suffolk Mercury, has accused the earl of some involvement, in some way?'

The old man's interest was suddenly piqued... 'I have heard him comment on this,' he replied noncommittally. 'What are you trying to say, Agnes? These are matters that are way beyond your station.'

'I know, Uncle, I know...I just thought, that well, I could listen to my master's conversations about this matter and report them to the earl. He might find them helpful...maybe worth a shilling or two?' Agnes asked, now more in hope than expectation.

The head butler hid his surprise on hearing the young girl's suggestions. He said nothing, mulling on the implications and how useful it might be to him – and the earl – to have inside information about the troublesome publisher's determination to sully the House of Northumberland.

He looked at Agnes. The girl was an innocent waif, wading into waters that would drown her if the tide turned to her disadvantage. However, it would enhance his position in Barton Hall if he became a source of information the earl found useful. In truth he guessed the wayward son was somehow involved – his exile to the Scottish estate at short notice implied some guilt in some way. And while the earl had the money and power to survive even the most egregious attacks on his family, knowing in advance what the newspaper might publish would allow him to take the necessary action to thwart its effect.

'You did the right thing by coming to see me, Agnes,' he said, in a calming, avuncular tone. 'Let me talk to the earl and see what he says. If you wish to wait here I will see if he can spare a few minutes to talk to me. I shall be back shortly. Would you like some breakfast while you wait?'

'Please, Uncle, I would be most grateful for something to eat.' He left her in the kitchen where, minutes later, a platter of meat, cheese and biscuits was brought out by one of the servants. For the first time that morning Agnes felt more confident she had done the right thing.

Half an hour later, her uncle returned. He sat beside her and quietly whispered to her, 'The earl has agreed to your idea.' He promised to pay her a shilling for every piece of information she brought to him from the household of Thomas and Sherry.

Agnes left, her mood buoyed by the expectation of making some extra money, but deep down inside, her stomach churned at the idea she was betraying her master and mistress, who had always been so kind to her. She put her doubts aside and decided the money was of more value than loyalty.

Chapter 22

After a few days of talking to his contacts around the town, the earl's valet hadn't much to reveal about Thomas and Sherry, or their business, that could be used against them. His most useful discovery revealed they were running the The Suffolk Mercury on a shoestring, surviving only with financial help from Sherry's father, Sir William Elkins.

'Now that is interesting,' said the earl. 'I know Sir William. Maybe I should invite him to dinner here on Friday. See if some pressure can be brought to bear that way.' He instructed the valet to personally deliver the invitation today and impress upon Sir William that he wished to discuss a matter of 'some importance'. In other words it was an invitation not to be refused. The valet bowed and scurried away. A slight smile crossed the earl's face as a plan formed in his mind. 'There's more than one way to skin a libellous rabbit!' he said to himself. 'And this rabbit is about to be caught in my very own snare.'

Back at the house, Agnes tried to remain as inconspicuous as most servants should, but at the same time get close to her master and mistress to overhear their conversations. She offered to take on extra duties, such as cleaning their bedroom, lighting the fires and candles in all the rooms, anything that would keep her in close proximity to them.

She noticed the following day the angry atmosphere between them had subsided a little. At least they were conversing, albeit tersely, over breakfast. Thomas left the table without discussing any further the contentious topic with Sherry, thus providing Agnes with no useful information. Suddenly she felt a heave in her stomach and rushed outside to the privy and vomited. Oh, please, Jesus. No! No! Ever since she had missed her monthlies after a night of drunken sex with her now long-gone boyfriend, she was petrified this might happen. This retching confirmed her worst fears.

Agnes knew she was suffering from morning sickness. Soon it would be difficult to conceal her pregnancy from the other servants, and her mistress. The young servant knew that unless she found some valuable information to pass to her uncle and the earl, her prospects for earning extra money were looking very dim. Under normal circumstances a pregnant servant was dismissed as soon as they couldn't perform all their chores. She needed to find out something – and quickly.

Later that morning she heard Sherry announcing she would be going out to the market. Soon after she left, Agnes ran upstairs to Thomas's study. Surely there must be something here of use.

Hastily rummaging around the piles of paper strewn across his desk she saw little but bills (many long overdue), ledgers and some issues of *The Suffolk Mercury*. Frustrated at finding nothing of interest she ran back downstairs, across the great hall and into the scullery, only to feel the urge to be sick again.

And so it continued for the next few days. The atmosphere between her master and mistress remained frosty, and to her chagrin the topic of the girl's murder and Thomas's investigations was never discussed. To make Agnes's mood even more despondent her morning sickness became worse, so much so, the housekeeper noticed and felt the need to pull her aside.

'Is everything alright, girl?' said Violet, a middle-aged, comely woman with a warm smile and caring manner. 'Come sit at the table, let me get you a cup of tea, you look real washed out.' As Violet bustled about the kitchen making a pot of tea, Agnes could no longer hold back her tears.

'Mistress Violet, I am with child! I don't know what to do, all I see now is my future in the poorhouse! I have been so stupid. What shall become of me?'

Violet came over and put her arms around the trembling girl's shoulders. 'Oh, you poor child! Who is the father? Is he willing to marry you?'

Agnes, head in her hands, mumbled. 'No...no, he has gone to London. I am alone...'

Violet sat beside the distraught girl, put the cup of tea on the table and hugged her until she calmed down. 'You are not alone, you are in service with a good family who I am sure will help in any way they can. They are fine people; you need to tell them of your plight at once, and see what can be arranged. All is not lost, child.'

Agnes nodded. 'Thank you, Mistress Violet, you are most kind.' Her sniffling subsided as she sipped her warm, sweet tea. Now, however, Agnes slowly grasped the awkward position she found herself in: Betraying her employers' confidences to the earl for money, or throwing herself at their mercy and begging them for help with the baby? She knew her uncle would be furious if she failed to provide the information she promised – it would reflect badly. An embarrassment for him in front of the earl – for failing to produce something of use in his battle with the newspaper. Yet, she reasoned, she never promised the conversations she overheard would be of any use. Or perhaps she could make something up? Would they ever catch her lie if she did?

Torn between her divided loyalties, miserable and sick, she left the kitchen and went upstairs to bed. Her once safe and secure future now looked increasingly uncertain.

* * * *

The dinner was a splendid affair. The earl and his wife Margaret and Sir William Elkins and his wife, Daniella, were joined by the earl's eldest daughter, Victoria, and her dreary husband, Phillip.

Even if the company wasn't, the meal was outstanding. Sir William was a man of some wealth, but the lavishness of the food, priceless table ornaments, silver cutlery and plates impressed even him. There were three courses, the first being soup and fish, followed by fricassees and ragouts and finally a course of meats and roasts. The huge table was completely covered as all the dishes were served at once. Then the beautifully embroidered tablecloth was removed and replaced (as it had become stained by the guests who used it to wipe their mouths). The dessert was served: a mouth-watering selection of fruits, nuts and sweetmeats displayed in beautiful china baskets as well as jellies, ices and syllabubs.

All accompanied by the finest wines from the earl's vast cellar, reputedly one of the most extensive in the country.

After three hours of tortuously polite conversation, the earl suggested he and Sir William retire to his study to discuss some 'business matters'. *Finally*, thought Sir William, *we are getting down to the real purpose of our visit.* He wasn't stupid, he guessed it was something to do with his son-in-law's stories about the earl's household. And while he was several ranks lower in the aristocratic peerage, he was not awed by the Earl's position.

Glass of excellent vintage port in hand he waited for the earl to start the conversation. He looked around the sumptuous study; huge pictures of the earl's ancestors stared lifelessly down into the gloomy room, lit only by the huge log fire and a sparse number of candles.

'Thank you for joining us tonight, Sir William', said his host solemnly, 'However, there is a matter which I wish to discuss with you'. Sir William said nothing to help the conversation along. Let the upper class twerp suffer a little, he decided. Clearly feeling uncomfortable, the earl continued, 'Er...as you may have read in that newspaper, *The Suffolk Mercury*, my name, and this household has become embroiled in the search for the murder of a servant girl from the Hall.'

Feeling no need to help his host struggle with this delicate matter, Sir William merely nodded non-committally. In fact he quite enjoyed seeing the pompous man fighting to retain his reputation, when everyone knew his son was a dissolute wastrel – and more than likely had something to do with the servant girl's death.

'It seems the owner of the newspaper, your son-in-law, appears hell-bent on finding the murderer, and in the process besmirching my reputation to boot.'

'Is that so?' Sir William asked, injecting a note of surprise into his voice.

'Yes, I'm afraid to say it is. You can rest assured if I had any knowledge of the culprit I would, of course, inform the authorities.'

'Of course, I would expect nothing less of you, my lord.' The earl was oblivious to Sir William's sarcasm.

'However, your son-in-law's persistence in investigating this sorry affair is proving an embarrassment, and an unnecessary one, which I would ask you to intervene and stop.'
'How so? Why should he take any notice of me...my lord?' Sir William replied unhelpfully.

'As I understand it you are the money behind this venture with this newspaper. Surely you must carry some influence with him – and your daughter?'

Sir William was expecting some such request, but saw no reason to acquiesce. He'd discussed the invitation with Thomas and Sherry earlier in the day. They provided him with all the information they had garnered so far (which wasn't a lot – but the earl didn't know that).

He wanted to be prepared. He was quite enjoying the earl's discomfort and was not in the mood to be dictated to by this upper-class bully.

'So would I be correct in saying, my lord, that while you object to being the subject of an investigation yourself, you have been prying into my affairs at the same time?'

'If you have nothing to hide, Sir William, why should you be concerned?'

"The same could be said of you, my lord.' He couldn't help taunting the earl.

'Be careful who you criticise, sir, I need not remind you of the influence I have in this county.'

'Are you now threatening me? Clearly if you have nothing to hide you should welcome the newspaper's investigations that would clear your name, or that of your son's, once and for all.'

'What has my son got to do with this; what gossip have you heard? I demand to know, sir!' The earl stopped pacing around the room and confronted Sir William, menace in his beady, rheumy eyes.

'I don't know, my lord. Why don't you clear up the rumours once and for all and explain why your son left so quickly after the servant girl's body was found?'

'That is a slanderous accusation, sir. If I were a younger man I would call you out for such an insult.'

'I am accusing no one. Merely asking the question that many people want answered,' replied Sir William calmly.

The earl, exasperated that the conversation was not going the way he intended, started pacing back and forth again in front of the fire, his portly figure casting outsized shadows moving across the room. Sir William continued to nurse his port, now at room temperature and smooth as silk to the tongue. While he waited for the earl's response he took a sip, savouring the sweet, delicate taste. He didn't envisage he would be offered a refill.

The earl sat down, leaning towards Sir William, collecting his thoughts. Then said abruptly: 'How much?'

'How much?' asked Sir William.

'Please do not play dumb with me, how much will it cost to make this all go away?'

Sir William hadn't become a successful businessman by revealing his thoughts when an unexpected offer was made. Keeping his face devoid of emotion, he paused, weighing up his response. He had the earl on the ropes; however, now was not the time for a knockout blow and to make him an enemy. No, just a bloody nose, to make him think he had got off easily, would be the best approach.

'I believe, my lord, you have three people to satisfy and keep quiet. The law, the newspaper owner and the servant girl's family. I cannot speak for how you handle the constable's interests, nor that of the family. Those I am sure you can deal with yourself and provide a satisfactory outcome. I shall consult with my son-in-law and reply with a figure that he finds acceptable – if he is prepared in the first place to let the matter drop in exchange for a financial incentive. I can offer no guarantees his silence can be bought, but I will ask him.'

'I am grateful for your understanding, Sir William – and your advice – I shall contact the constable and the girl's family forthwith,' said a relieved earl, finally hoping this awkward matter was reaching a satisfactory conclusion.

Thomas was, predictably, incensed on hearing about the after-dinner negotiations and the blatant act of bribery being offered by the earl for his, and *The Suffolk Mercury's*, silence.

'This is completely unacceptable; it's an affront to me, and the integrity of the newspaper. I cannot, and will not, take his money stained with the blood of that young girl. He is tantamount to admitting his son was involved in her murder - he must face justice!'

'Thomas, you can be as indignant as you like, the truth is, even if you did prove his son was involved in that girl's death, loath as I am to admit it, the earl has such power and influence he will make sure it never goes to trial. The boy will never see a day in gaol, let alone the hangman's noose. Unpalatable it maybe, but that is the world in which we live. Now I suggest you take his money; shall we say enough to buy this house from me? That will allow you to keep the newspaper running without getting into debt. Pick your fights, Thomas, this is one you cannot win.'

Sherry weighed in, 'My father is right, Thomas, you know it. Why ruin ourselves, even put our lives in danger, when you will in the end achieve nothing but a self-righteous glow of vindication? What use is of that if we are penniless? Please, I beg of you, Thomas, call a halt to this madcap investigation.'

In his heart Thomas knew he should continue to unearth the facts about the murder and hold, by all accounts, the earl's son, responsible for the servant girl's death. Then publish his findings and...and what? Make an enemy of the most powerful man in the county? Who would make sure his son was never brought to justice and at the same time do his utmost, probably, to sue his newspaper into bankruptcy.

All so he'd feel exonerated, a successful example to all of taking the moral high ground, while fighting off his creditors. Not for the first time he had to accept that wealthy men like the earl would always come out on top. 'Pick your battles, Thomas'; he had to agree with his father-in-law. It pained him, but he saw little alternative but to accept the outcome negotiated by Sir William.

And so the matter of the murder of Jenny Paperlace, with the transfer of large sums of money, quietly faded from everyone's memory – and the newspaper headlines. The constable and the girl's family were handsomely rewarded for their silence, and the Whiting St house became the property of Thomas and Sherry Bailey. The earl's son remained in Scottish exile until the old aristocrat's death, following which Barton Hall was sold.

Agnes finally revealed to Sherry and Thomas she was with child, mentioning nothing, of course about her ill-conceived plans to betray them to the earl.

Thomas and Sherry said she could stay at the house. Closer to the birth the three decided it would be for the best if they adopted the newborn, providing it a safe and well cared-for upbringing. She remained in their employ for several years, watching over her child as it was brought up in the house of a now successful newspaper publisher.

The Suffolk Mercury continued for many years with Thomas at the helm. It became known as the St Edmund's Bury Post and was published until around 1740.

* * * *

'Will this child be afflicted like my daughters, do you think, Maud? I pray it is not the case. I would not want them to suffer like my children did,' said Grace.

'We can do no more than observe and pray,' said Maud.

'This will be the first birth in this house since the exorcism, what, seventeen years ago? I hope that the evil spell has finally been broken. I wish we had known about it when we lived here; could we have somehow warned the house's later occupants? Helped them and their children avoid the pain and suffering?' wondered Grace.

'We can only observe and pray, we cannot interfere with fate's often upsetting choices. I wish we could,' Maud answered.

'Come, my love, let us leave this happy family to its celebrations, hopefully to be repeated when the baby is born.'

As they silently receded into their spectral world, Maud and Grace felt an unease about the future of the house and its occupants. Turbulent times lay ahead.

Chapter 23
(1742)

Colonel John Masterson-Phillips gave his two sons admiring looks, puffing out his chest; he could not conceal his pride. Standing to attention before him, they were in full military dress, their red coats lined with contrasting colours, the distinctive white bands in an X across their chests. It was enough to make any father, especially a former colonel of the Suffolk Regiment, proud and just a little nervous.

'You both look splendid, boys, ready to take on those Prussian upstarts. I'm sure you will repay my investment in your commissions with blood on your sword and the death of our enemy. You're captains in the best-trained army in the world; I expect you to return with tales of victory and derring-do. Your dear departed mother would have felt the same, I'm sure. God rest her soul.'

Frederick, the elder son, smiled inwardly at his father's bombastic little speech. It wasn't the first time he had delivered some flowery speech congratulating them on their achievements – albeit they had been helped amply by his money. Truth be told, he couldn't wait to get away from home and into battle, prove his mettle and achieve the higher ranks with as much speed as possible. All he knew is they were off to some part of the Continent he'd never heard of until a week ago. Now he was itching to see some action.

He stole a quick glance at his younger brother, Leo, who he knew was inwardly cringing at his father's urging to commit murder and mayhem. A bookish boy of slight build, he was reluctant to join the army in the first place, let alone the Suffolk Regiment where his father excelled himself in the War of the Spanish Succession. It was an impossible act to follow, they both knew, but they had little choice in the matter. Comparisons were already being drawn between his father's brave exploits and leadership qualities and those of his sons who, as brand new officers, had yet to prove their worth.

Poor Leo, thought Frederick, *this whole process must be torture for him.*

At that moment Leo caught his brother's look and rolled his eyes in mock horror as his father's speech droned on. He knew his elder brother was likely to return home a hero from whatever war they were pushed into. Eager to see action, it was almost a foregone conclusion Frederick would excel in the battles ahead. He was born to lead and to fight. His father's blood ran thick through his veins.

By contrast, all Leo wanted to do was keep out of harm's way and come back with all his limbs intact, to pursue his dream of teaching, writing and publishing fine historical books. Army life so far had been a painful experience at which he barely passed his training to become a captain alongside his gung-ho brother.

'Boys! Let us drink to your success!' The colonel gave his sons each a large glass of brandy, and, taking one for himself, raised it in the air, 'For King and country and to vanquish the enemy wherever they may be!' The three raised their glasses and threw back the stinging spirit in one gulp.

'Thank you, Father, that was most...inspiring,' said Frederick. 'I am confident we will both do our duty. I for one am looking forward to seeing some action. I am tired of the months of training, and I am sure my men are too. They are a formidable fighting force, all now keen to get the enemy in their sights.'

Leo said nothing, and quickly left the room to finish packing. They departed tomorrow for Harwich, then across the North Sea for Holland. Neither knew their final destination.

Angel Hill was packed with over 600 soldiers and officers making final preparations to depart at noon. Double that number of civilians were there saying their farewells to the soldiers. The officers' horses snorted and whinnied at the noise and the crush of people, anxious for the quiet of the open road.

The square was festooned with flags, and a band played patriotic, stirring music. The mood among the soldiers was optimistic, promising friends and relatives they would be back before Christmas. As the time came for departure, and the realisation that they would not see these young men for months, indeed some never again, the women began to cry, while the soldiers did their best to show no emotion and hold back their tears.

Eventually they formed into battalions and marched off in precise formation down Southgate St. Their numbers would be swelled to over 800 as they were joined by other battalions along the way to the port of embarkation.

By June of 1743, the Suffolk Regiment became part of what was known as the Pragmatic Army totalling over 17,000 troops, fighting in what became known as the Austrian War of Succession. It was a war of confusing and changing alliances that saw Britain fighting alongside, at times, the Dutch and Hanoverians, against a chaotic, back-stabbing alliance of France, Prussia, Spain and Sweden. It was into this melee of conflicting allegiances that the Suffolk Regiment fought in the Battle of Dettingen. It became famous for being the last time a reigning monarch, in this case George II, led an army into battle. However, it was an inconclusive victory, but enough to stall the French advance. The Suffolk Regiment suffered light casualties, and both Leo and Frederick were unscathed.

For the next two years the war continued, with battles being fought across a wide swathe of central Europe. It was in May 1745 the Suffolk Regiment saw action again at the Battle of Fontenoy against a numerically superior French army. It was a short, bloody and ultimately unsuccessful one for the Pragmatic Army, and the Suffolk Regiment in particular. The regiment sustained its highest number of casualties in any battle, some 322 dead and wounded – almost a third of their number.

On their return to Bury the regiment was met with none of the pomp and celebrations seen at their departure two years earlier. The crowd on Angel Hill was sparse, not just because it was pouring with rain – but there was little cause for jubilation. Most of the townsfolk knew someone who had been killed or wounded, the latter returning earlier that year. The remaining officers and soldiers as they entered Bury that miserable day in November tried to keep their chins held high, hiding their disappointment from the few people welcoming them home.

It was a desultory occasion, the soldiers wanting nothing more than to return to their homes, the comfort of their loved ones and to recover from the trauma of battle.

'Frederick, as you would expect, was leading from the front as he always did,' explained Leo, his voice a whisper, as if merely speaking the words caused him physical pain. 'In every action we saw, he was always fearless, and determined to show everyone his courage by example. He was an inspiration to his men. A true officer who set himself the highest standards.' It was a speech Leo had rehearsed for his father, knowing he would want a glowing report of his dead son's exploits. It wasn't a difficult task; Frederick was an inspiration to his men, the consummate British officer. Although now a dead one. Try as he might, he could bring no enthusiasm to his words.

Colonel Masterson-Phillip's normally stiff upper lip was quivering with grief. His elder son blasted beyond recognition leading a charge against the French artillery. It was an officer's death in the finest tradition of the British army, but his pride could not conceal the depth of his grief. Tears rolled down his cheeks into his grey whiskers. He hastily wiped them away with a kerchief. Despite his best efforts to control his emotions, he couldn't hide his feelings of loss and pain.

After a few awkward minutes, and a hefty tipple of brandy, he composed himself and walked over to Leo, who was sitting staring vacantly into the fire. His mind still seeing the carnage on the battlefield, his body feeling the unbearable pain of his injuries.

'And how are your wounds healing, my son?' He looked at the stump of Leo's right leg. The rest of it lay somewhere on the battlefield, sliced off by French grapeshot. His right hand, now with only two fingers, courtesy of a tiny piece of shrapnel almost surgically removing them, compounded his sense of failure.

'I am recovering, Father, though it will take time to adjust to eating with a fork strapped to my hand. I am hoping to get some kind of wooden attachment to strap to the remains of my leg. I am going to the hospital in a few weeks when it has healed.' Leo described his wounds as though he was reading from a book. His voice was flat, emotionless, his eyes blank and expressionless. Still shocked by his brother's death and his life-changing wounds, he drifted from day to day in a laudanum-induced haze, aided by large amounts of brandy and gin. At times, in the pits of depression and self-pity, he envied his brother; at least he didn't face a life of pain, of people staring at his disfigurements, relying on help from friends and relatives to do the simplest tasks. What did the future hold for him? Certainly not writing or teaching. Only the drinks and drugs kept him from focusing on the pitiful life ahead of him.

Trying to be optimistic, his father, in a rare display of affection, gently patted Leo on the shoulder. 'Cheer up, my boy, many have come back from battle with worse wounds than you and have lived a long and productive life. You can stay here as long as you like until you recover, then we can look to the future and see what a war veteran like you can do to make a living. Maybe find yourself a nice young lady to marry?'

Leo looked up at his father, with bitterness slicing through his voice said, 'Father, we have to accept the fact I have no prospects to speak of in terms of a career or marriage and a family. If you can't face the facts, I have to. I am, and will continue to be, a burden on you – and of no use to society. All I wanted to do was teach and write books. You insisted on paying for my commission into the army, you gave me no choice in the matter. As always, being the dutiful son, I went along with your demands, for the sake of the family name and honour – whatever that it is. Well, that didn't turn out as planned, did it, Father? One dead son, and another crippled. A legacy to be proud of, Father.'

The colonel stood speechless in front of his son. No one had ever spoken to him in such a manner. His son may be horribly wounded, but his comments were disrespectful no matter the circumstances.

'I should mind you to watch your tongue, young man. I will put your ill-advised comments down to your condition. However, I expect you to buck your ideas up, accept the position you now find yourself in and make the most of it. You have a lot more to live for than you realise at the moment. Be grateful and thank the good Lord you did not suffer the fate of your brother...'

'...Go on, Father, say it. Frederick would have suffered in silence with such wounds and gone on to great things no matter his disabilities...he was always your favourite son, the one you had such high expectations for in the army. Well, he's dead, Father, blown to pieces by some Frenchie gun, so you're left with me now...sorry if I'm such a disappointment. If I could change places with him, I would; maybe that would make you happy.'

Without waiting for a response, Leo struggled to his feet, and hobbled slowly up the stairs to his room, leaving the colonel stunned at his son's outburst. He shakily refilled his brandy glass, sat down and wondered just what he should do to deal with his disturbed son, knowing deep down inside what Leo said was uncomfortably close to the truth. He needed to reconcile his own tortured emotions on this matter, and recognise that Leo would need help for many months, if not years, to come. He brought up his sons to be independent, self-sufficient, reliant only on their own abilities, perfect officer material. Now he had one son drowning in self-pity and the other just a memory.

In the army backsliders, shirkers and weaklings were soon knocked into shape, given some backbone, a sense of purpose and camaraderie. However in civilian life such tactics didn't work. Floundering to find a solution for his son's melancholy, the colonel visited the local apothecary in the hope some medications might help.

Bury's biggest apothecary was in Cupola House in the Traverse, a short walk from his house. It was owned by Thomas Macro, whose father started the business many years earlier. If anyone could offer a cure, the colonel believed, this experienced apothecary would be the person to talk to.

As he entered the shop his senses were bombarded by the smell of dozens of herbs, flowers and fruits, stored in hundreds of jars neatly lined up on shelves running from the floor to ceiling. A small, bald man with glasses and a kindly expression smiled and asked how he could help.

The colonel was grateful he was the only customer; it wouldn't do for everyone to know his son was suffering some kind of sickness of the mind. He explained his son had come back from the war and was 'not himself'. 'Despite my best efforts I cannot shake him out of his lethargy and despondent frame of mind. I was hoping you could recommend something that might help.'

Thomas nodded his head sympathetically, 'Your son is not the only one suffering such after-effects of being in battle. Many young men are in a similar position in the town, sad to say. I have heard that a combination of regular cold baths and a diet of lean meat, fresh eggs, freshwater fish and particularly grapes are recommended by many. Though I do not know how efficacious such foods are. I would avoid giving opium as it can become addictive, but as a last resort it can dull the senses sufficiently that the upsetting memories fade away.'

He turned to look at the array of herbs behind him, 'However, let us try to start with some ginseng, lavender, St John's wort and chamomile to calm his disposition. Would you like to try these?'

Happy that someone seemed to have some answers, the colonel quickly agreed to buy some of each herb – and return later in the day once the apothecary had prepared them for use. In the meantime he would ask one of the servants to visit the butcher and fishmonger to buy some of the healthy foods that might also help. Anything was worth trying.

He arrived home to find his son still in bed, even though it was past lunchtime. He was about to call him downstairs when there was a knock on the door, and moments later the butler appeared with a letter, presented formally on a small silver plate.

The colonel didn't recognise the writing, so opened it with some curiosity. It was from his sister, Isabel, in Cambridge, from whom he had heard little in over two years. The message was short and to the point:

'Dear brother John,

I hope this letter finds you well, and I apologise after all this time in asking for a favour at such short notice. It concerns my daughter, Marie Anne. She is, in truth, proving to be a difficult child to bring up as she reaches the age of seventeen. Without a father, she is becoming rebellious and argumentative. Even with her disfigurement, she seems to attract the attention of the college boys far too easily. Which is a cause of some concern, as she seems only too willing to entertain their advances.

I am at my wits' end in trying to control her behaviour, and begin to fear the worst may happen...need I go into detail? I was hoping a few weeks at your house, under your...guidance and discipline, might rein in her wilder antics.

If you cannot help, I may well have to seek her admittance to the local asylum, a move that would cast shame on all our family. One which would be a last resort, but serves to illustrate to you how desperate my situation is with my daughter.

If you are acceptable to this proposal I will arrange for her to arrive in the next week or two.

I do hope you can assist me with this extremely troublesome matter. I await your reply containing, I hope, a willingness to help myself and your niece.

Kindest regards, your loving sister.

Isabel

Chapter 24

Two weeks later, the colonel stood on Angel Hill waiting for the Cambridge coach to arrive. He felt he had little choice but to answer his sister's plea for help. Plus, he hoped the distraction of a young lady in the house might shake his son out of his torpidity.

As the coach stopped, and the passengers climbed down, he quickly recognised the challenge ahead of him. Before he could offer a word of introduction Marie Anne shouted tartly up to the driver, 'That was the most uncomfortable journey I have ever experienced. Did you purposely drive through every pothole on the road? And why should I pay the tolls as well - that is what the fare is for, is it not? I believe you are just pocketing that money - you should be ashamed of yourself!'

The driver mumbled an apology, and quickly handed Marie Anne's bags to the colonel, who promptly steered his irate niece away from the coach to prevent any further argument. He then saw, all too clearly, what her mother meant by 'disfigurement'. Her otherwise flawless skin - and extremely pretty face - was sporting, from her cheek bone down to her jaw, a scar that still looked as though it was healing. The colonel couldn't help but stare, and in doing so was caught in his niece's fierce glare. 'Not pretty, is it, Uncle? Did my mama tell you how I acquired it? Quite the story if you're interested.'

'No...no, she didn't say anything,' the colonel stuttered. 'Let us get back to the house and if you wish to tell the story, I am happy to hear it, but please don't feel obliged if it pains you in any way.'

Calming down, she took her uncle by the arm and walked along beside him as if nothing had been said. She was equally forthright with her next comment. 'So, Uncle, it is you who my mother has turned to, in a last attempt to make a lady out of me? Let me start by saying I am not as bad as she would have you believe. As long as I get my own way you'll find me easygoing and accommodating!' She flashed a disarming smile, though the Colonel was unsure if she was teasing, or threatening him.

'Ah! Well, um, I am unsure how to answer that demand. In my household I expect you to do as I ask...'

The young girl playfully tugged his arm and laughed. 'Uncle, I jest with you, I know I have been a thorn in my mother's side. However I am here now, a fresh start – I am sure I will have a fine time sampling the delights of Bury – and meeting Leo again, who I have not seen in, what, ten years? How is he after all this time?'

'In truth, Marie Anne, he is not well. He came back from the War badly injured and having lost his brother as well. For weeks he has barely left the house. He needs to be dragged out of his malaise, and that is where, to be honest, I hope you can help me.'

Marie Anne looked surprised, 'I didn't know I was being sent here as a nurse. It's not something I have any experience in, but if I can help my cousin, it's the least I can do. In exchange, how can I put this...I am sure you will be, shall we say, less draconian in your efforts to turn me into a lady?'

She smiled coquettishly at him, and the colonel knew this girl was trouble for sure. Though if by some miracle she saved his son from his lassitude and brought him back to his former self, then he was happy to go along with her suggestion.

'Marie Anne, we have an agreement!' he said, grinning at the girl's demand.

Over the first evening meal, having persuaded Leo he should at least welcome his long-lost cousin over dinner, the conversation was stilted. Leo was morose and monosyllabic. Even the light-hearted chatter that Marie Anne poured forth like a babbling brook, in an effort to fill in the painful silences, did little to lighten his mood. In fact Leo barely acknowledged her presence except for a few perfunctory words of welcome. As soon as the meal finished he excused himself and went back to his room.

Little changed for a few days, then like a ray of sunshine after a cloudy day, Leo bluntly asked Marie Anne how she had acquired her scar. 'Ah! He speaks!' she said jokingly. 'I have seen you staring at my face and there I thought it was my blue eyes or blonde hair that attracted your attention. So is it time to compare war wounds?' The colonel inwardly winced at her directness, fully expecting his son to retreat back to his room upset at her directness. But no, with a ghost of a smile crossing his face, Leo said, 'Ladies first...'

'Well I am sure my story does not contain the derring-do and bravery that surrounds your war wounds. Mine are a result, I'm afraid, of my own stupidity, though I would call it misguided bravado.' She settled back in her chair to tell her story.

'I was with a group of students on the Backs at Cambridge, when they dared me to jump off one of the bridges into the Cam. I said I would if they all did, first. They called my bluff, all jumped off without incident. Never one to back down from a challenge, I proceeded to follow in their stupid footsteps. Little did I know, or see, a small boat going under the bridge behind me. As I jumped off the bridge the boat appeared beneath me and I caught my head on the rudder. I was knocked senseless, rescued by my friends and taken to hospital where a surgeon sutured my wound, and mercifully kept all infection out. So...My moment of madness will be remembered every time I look in the mirror.'

Marie Anne took a sip of wine, looking at Leo expectantly for him to start his story.

For a moment he seemed unable to form any words; then, his voice cracking with emotion, he recounted the horrors he suffered during the battle. 'The French had practically surrounded us, their artillery was blasting from every direction. Bodies were thrown around like ragged dolls as the shot ripped through our ranks. I didn't even feel the shrapnel take off my fingers, until I tried to lift up my musket and it just fell from my hand. Like a fool I remember standing there with the noise of the guns, the screams of my men thinking...how am I going to do up my bootlaces? Truly, that was my first thought!'

Leo paused and took a sip of brandy. Without thinking, Marie Anne reached over and took his hand in hers, ignoring the wound she now covered with her delicate fingers. 'Go on, Leo, please don't stop halfway through your story...' She smiled encouragingly. After a moment's hesitation, he drew breath and continued.

'It soon became clear our regiment was decimated and the colonel gave orders for us to retreat to higher ground and regroup. Reinforcements were due to arrive at any time and we still believed we could rout the French before the end of the day. Then...then from the north another battery of cannons opened up, cutting through us like a scythe through hay. I felt an explosion beneath me. I remember flying through the air...then nothing. Until I awoke in the field hospital to see a surgeon wielding a saw above my leg. As he pressed down on my knee, I am ashamed to say I passed out, only to awaken with half a leg.'

The colonel was speechless; not only had his niece managed to get Leo to talk of his injuries, but also he'd even made a joke about them. Marie Anne continued to hold Leo's hand for a few moments then got up and pecked him on the cheek. 'There, Leo, we both bared our souls a little this evening, I feel better, how about you?'

Leo stood up, bowed slightly to Marie Anne and said simply. 'Thank you for listening, now please excuse me. It has been a most...enjoyable evening and I am feeling tired.' He clumped up the stairs using his home-made crutches to take each step in a painful hop. By the time he reached the top he was, as usual, exhausted.

The colonel watched his son finally hobble up to his room. A few moments later he broke the silence: 'Marie Anne, that was incredible, you made Leo converse more in the last few minutes than I have in three months. I hope and pray this may be the start of his recovery. Though I shall not raise my hopes too quickly, but please keep talking to him, he responds to you more than he has ever done to me.'

'I will do my best, Uncle. He has suffered greatly. It will take a long time until he regains his confidence. However, as I said before, I love a challenge, and Leo is my next one.'

As the days turned to weeks and spring arrived, Leo was gaining a little more confidence every day. His conversations, particularly with Marie Anne, moved beyond his war experiences into their shared love of books and writing. The house contained hundreds of books, which the young couple devoured, reading quietly to themselves by the fire, or to each other when they found chapters they felt the other would enjoy. They obtained back issues of The Rambler by Samuel Johnson. It covered topics such as morality, literature, society, politics and religion, aimed very much at the middle class. Both laughed at his caricatures and advice on entering the upper classes of English society. But it was a copy of *Fanny Hill* that set them giggling with embarrassment at its explicit content.

'No wonder this has been banned and the author arrested; it is quite shocking, indeed obscene, in places, don't you think?' asked Leo.

'Why do you think sex is something abhorrent? Do I detect some prudishness here? Come, Leo, you were in the army. Did you not have camp followers and harlots following you everywhere you went? Men need the release women can offer, even in war. Are you saying you never partook in such pleasures?'

'Yes, of course such women were everywhere, but knowing it's happening is a lot different to someone writing about it in detail, for everyone to read.' Leo was squirming with embarrassment at the way the conversation was unfolding. He desperately tried to change the subject. 'Maybe we should put this book to one side, and read some parts from Shakespeare's latest play, Richard II? What say you?'

'I say you're acting like an old maid, Leo.' Her voice dropped to a whisper: 'Don't you find reading such books stirs the loins a little?' She had a suggestiveness in her tone that Leo found both alarming and worryingly attractive.

Leo tried again, 'Maybe that is a topic for another day, Marie Anne? I do believe it is time for bed. Tomorrow I thought we could take a walk around the Bury market, if the weather is favourable.'

Marie Anne decided to stop teasing him. His offer to take her into the town was becoming more frequent as he adapted to walking with his wooden leg. It had taken him painful hour after hour to harden his stump, but he walked a little further every day. Now the excursion up to and around the Buttermarket was within his capabilities.

'Today I will try and use just walking sticks,' announced Leo as they prepared to leave the house the following day. 'I believe I can manage without my crutches–with your help maybe?'

Marie Anne was impressed at his new-found confidence. 'Bravo, cousin, let us go and show the townsfolk how much progress you have made!'

The day was warm and sunny, in synchrony with their happy disposition. It was Saturday, when the market was always busier than the one on Wednesday. The fine weather was encouraging more people to spend time browsing the stalls, buying fresh produce and household goods of every type. The noise of so many shoppers crowded together added to the cacophony of all the animals in cages awaiting their fate; some quietly, others not so much.

'Oh, look, Leo, someone has puppies for sale; we should get one. We could take it on long walks, or with us when we go riding. Wouldn't that be so much fun?' Leo wasn't sure if Marie Anne was serious until she picked up a mewling little brown and white pup and held it to her chest. The dog immediately stopped crying and nuzzled into her coat.

'He's taken a fancy to you, miss; you have a way with dogs, I can tell. Why not take him home? That breed is kind and easy to raise. Yours for only a shilling,' said the stallholder. 'Take two and I can do both for one and sixpence. They'll keep each other company.'

Leo was shaking his head, 'We cannot do this, Marie Anne, without asking my father first...'

'Nonsense. Who doesn't love dogs? Everyone does! And these are just so adorable. I am sure I can persuade your father to welcome them into his home. Do you have some money on you?'

Leo knew at the moment as far as his father was concerned Marie Anne could do no wrong, and he did not doubt her powers of persuasion would allow the two puppies to be welcomed into the house. He tried to think of an argument to dissuade her from the purchase, but he knew he was wasting his time. Leo handed the money to the beaming stallholder, who gave them each a squirming bundle of furry friendship.

'Father will not be pleased, I can assure you; he is no lover of dogs. However, the die is cast. You better be prepared to deploy all your charms, young lady...'

'Oh, they are just adorable!' cooed the colonel. 'What a wonderful idea to have some pets in the house. Liven things up a little. We must get the cook to find them some food, they are probably hungry. Have you named them yet?'

Leo stood mouth agape as his crusty old father fawned over and petted the puppies, letting them clamber all over him and the furniture. *That girl could charm the leaves off the trees, even get away with murder, he thought. I should not be so ungrateful, not only is she making me happy, but my father too.*

He looked at her, realising she was a true ray of light driving out the darkness he and his father had wallowed in for too many months. His heart ached with pleasure, a feeling unknown to him in years. Marie Anne came to this house so they could restrain her headstrong foolhardiness, but instead she rescued him from the pits of despair, and his father too.

Now, to complicate matters, could it be that he was falling for this wayward young lady?

As Leo's health improved, both mentally and physically, his feelings for Marie Anne deepened too. In just two months she became the sole focus of his life. Gone were the days of misery and self-pity. While his physical problems would never go away, they were no longer the focus of his daily life. They took to riding out into the Suffolk countryside often, as far as Lavenham, Stowmarket, even Newmarket to watch the horse racing. Their two energetic puppies, now named Romeo and Juliet, followed them everywhere. But as the summer weather started to turn to the cooler days of autumn, their carefree existence was threatened by some harsh realities.

Leo, courtesy of his father's connections, was offered an administrative post back in the army, based near Norwich. Meanwhile, Marie Anne's mother, having been informed by the colonel that she was 'the perfect guest, a transformed young lady' decided the reformed young girl should return to Cambridge and set about the serious task of finding a husband.

Marie Anne and Leo sat underneath a huge oak tree discussing a future apart from one another. A question hung in the air, unspoken; what did they see as their future? Suddenly Marie Anne leant over and kissed Leo full on the lips. Leo kept his eyes closed long after she had pulled away from him. 'I was hoping that would happen, now I'm not so sure.'

'Why, was it that horrible?' she asked, perplexed.

'No, on the contrary, it was wonderful. But I knew if you did that, I may find it difficult to control myself. I have longed for that to happen, but our circumstances make it impossible for us to become more than friends.' Though they had flirted often and on occasion behaved in a manner more akin to young lovebirds than distant relations, both resisted the urge to take their feelings any further. Until now.

'Are you saying you don't want me to kiss you again?' Before he could answer she pushed him gently to the ground and lowered her face close to his. 'Tell me when to stop...'

He didn't. He couldn't. So absorbed in the moment he barely noticed as her hand slid down into his trousers and started to gently stroke him. He tried to say something but the force of her kiss on his mouth smothered any half-hearted words of resistance. She seemed to know precisely what to do. The strength and tempo of her hand all too quickly brought him to a peak of pleasure and continued until he had released himself with a final thrust of his hips and a groan of contentment.

'My God, I cannot believe that just happened,' said Leo once he caught his breath. 'I know not whether to feel guilt or delight that you have just given me such pleasure.'

'Oh, Leo, to be sure the pleasure was all mine; to see you lost in the throes of ecstasy, to feel you lose control because of me, is a satisfaction in itself. I shall give you a few minutes to rest and then try something I read in *Fanny Hill*. It will be a new experience for both of us...'

Minutes later she moved her head down to his waist and where her hand had been earlier, replaced it with her mouth. Leo was shocked at her carnal knowledge – had she gained it all from that book? He knew the camp followers performed such acts, often in preference to sex itself, as it avoided the danger of unwanted pregnancies. The men in his regiment retold of these in graphic detail around the campfires, but never, never could they possibly describe to him the intense gratification he was now experiencing.

Just as he felt he could hold back no longer, Marie Anne stopped her ministrations and in one quick motion mounted him, hastily pulling aside her dress and undergarments and slowly, oh so slowly, lowered herself onto him. In unison they moved, lost in each other's pleasure. No thoughts as to whether it was right or wrong, no thoughts at all except an uninhibited desire to enjoy the moment. It was over too quickly for both of them. The weeks, months of pent-up desire lost in a few minutes of uninhibited lust.

They both cried out in unison, as they finished their lovemaking, satiated and exhausted.

They lay together unmoving, struck silent by the magic of the moment. Neither wanting to break the spell that lovers feel after such passion. Soon the air cooled as the sun went down, and self-consciously they dressed and made ready to leave.

'Say something; anything,' said Leo, 'I need to know what you are thinking. I believe we have crossed some kind of line. Are you not concerned?'

'Only annoyed that we should have done this weeks ago. Just think of the fun we could have had doing that each day?' She grinned mischievously, unworried at his moral dilemma.

'Can you please be serious, my dear, just for once? How does this change things between us, our future – whatever that may or may not be? Or was this just a taste of something that cannot be repeated?'

'Actually you tasted very nice, you'll be pleased to know,' replied Anne Marie, suggestively putting a finger in her mouth.

'Dear God, you drive me insane! I am falling in love with you and all you can do is jest and tease me! I have told you my feelings – I will not let up until I know what you are thinking.'

'I'm thinking we should go back home and ask your father if you can marry me.'

The following day, Leo asked his father for permission to marry Marie Anne. It was rare for the colonel to be speechless, but words failed him on hearing his son's unexpected request. Well aware they'd become close friends, he didn't realise they'd fallen in love. He promised to give them a decision once he visited Marie Anne's mother to seek her opinion.

His sister was surprised but delighted: 'If you have tamed my daughter's excesses and Leo thinks he can make a decent wife of her, I say let them be wed!' Isabel could barely contain her glee at the thought of someone else taking on responsibility for Marie Anne's welfare. So, with her blessing, the colonel saw no reason to deny Leo's request.

Preparations for the wedding ceremony, to be held a week before Christmas, included a fresh coat of paint inside and out for the house - and new furniture in the rooms the married couple would live in until they found their own home.

The colonel, now in his sixties and increasingly housebound, hoped they would stay in the Whiting St home indefinitely. Selfishly, lacking a wife to look after him in his dotage, he hoped they would be prepared to accept this responsibility, in return for living in a large, comfortable house, which would become their own on his death.

The wedding was a modest ceremony, attended by a few relatives and some soldiers who served with Leo during the war. The celebrations at the house afterwards were full of laughter and the drinking of copious amounts of wine and beer. Soldiers the world over knew how to take advantage of free alcohol.

If anyone noticed, nothing was said about the tiny bump in Marie Anne's stomach pushing against the tight bindings of her wedding dress.

On June 16th 1743, to everyone's surprise, she gave birth to twins, a boy and a girl. They named the boy Frederick and the girl Mary, after Leo's mother, who had passed ten years earlier. The colonel, now riddled with arthritis, beamed with joy from his chair by the fire. In October 1744 another child was born, a boy named Isaac. All were born fit, healthy and with none of the afflictions previous newborns in the house suffered from.

Spinster Wordsworth's curse was finally broken.

Colonel John Masterson-Phillips died on July 8th 1745, leaving behind a family that still cherished every minute they spent together in the large comfortable house in Whiting St. Leo never returned to army life. He studied to be a teacher, learnt how to write with his good hand, and taught History and English at the King Edward's Grammar School.

They lived in the house for several more years before buying a small estate near Barrow. The new owner's connection with the house went back over 200 years.

Chapter 25
(1752)

So let me try and understand this change,' said a bemused Humphrey, 'Following the second day of September, we lose eleven days of the year and the next day becomes September the 14th? Explain to me again why we are doing this.'

'That I don't know, Father,' said his frustrated son, Benjamin. 'All I know is we have to make this change, and that the year now begins on January the first, not March the 26th. It's all been decided by the Church and Parliament. Something to do with how long the year is based on the sun's cycle rather than how something called the Gregorian calendar works. I am no astronomer, Father, just a humble farmer, but it seems this year will be shorter than before.'

It was the third time he'd tried to describe this change to his aged father. In truth he didn't really understand it himself; as a farmer he was ruled by the weather and the seasons, so reducing the year's length or changing when it started, would make little difference to him. But for those paid a daily wage, some were already noisily airing their anger at the prospect of losing twelve days' pay. He'd seen one riot by workers in the Market Square last week, and he heard others were planned. Even their MP, Admiral Augustus John Hervey raised the issue in Parliament, but neither the government nor the Bury Corporation wanted to be involved.

'Father, I have to be getting back to the farm in Lawshall,' said Benjamin. 'Richard will be here later in the week, and the servants will take care of you in the meantime.' He looked at his father, then realised the old man was already dozing by the fireside, his interest in why, inexplicably, September the 14th followed September the 2nd quickly forgotten.

For the third time in the space of two centuries the families in West Farm, Lawshall and the Whiting St house were intertwined. The house was bought by Humphrey two years earlier after its previous owner, a solicitor, moved to the country. The fact a distant relative in 1578 owned and ran a successful tavern in the house, and much later in the 1660s another far flung relative lived there was of little consequence to him. Despite being nearly 300 years old it was still a handsome townhouse, one of the biggest in Whiting St and a sound investment, though it was never turned into a shop as Humphrey had wanted many years earlier.

Since buying the house, it was now a home for his ailing father to live nearer the hospital, and a temporary storage for the produce from the farm, en route to the Bury market. The house had been extensively renovated and urgent repairs to the roof completed. It wasn't lavishly furnished, but comfortable for an old man and the three servants who looked after him. Benjamin hated leaving his father, but their farming business now spread across 200 acres in and around Lawshall, and even with his brother as a partner, it still demanded a lot of his time.

A servant, Charles, came into the great hall to inquire if everything was satisfactory, and whether he or his father needed anything. Benjamin disliked the man, though why he couldn't quite explain. Charles shuffled quietly and obsequiously around the house, appearing to do a lot of work, though in practice the house always looked untidy. He wanted to dismiss him on more than one occasion for his failure to properly look after his father. Several times he arrived to find his father distressed, dirty, and uncared for. But in his moments of lucidity Humphrey insisted Charles should be given a second chance.

Charles was employed just a year ago and soon insisted two friends should be taken into service; the woman as a housekeeper and a teenage boy. Both being of 'better character' than the existing staff. At first, they all seemed to genuinely care for Humphrey. However, in recent months Benjamin noticed standards slipping.

Neither he, Richard, nor indeed the rest of the family could pinpoint their concerns about the house's upkeep and their father's welfare. Aside from the poor condition they occasionally found him in, they began to notice items such as silverware, paintings and ornaments missing. When they asked their father what was happening, the bemused old man brushed aside their worries, explaining he had sold them as he no longer wanted them in the house. When they questioned the staff, all of them professed ignorance, just agreeing Humphrey had wanted them gone. As for where the money went, no one knew.

'I require nothing, thank you, Charles. I am leaving now. Can I trust you to take fastidious care of all my father's needs until my next visit?' Benjamin said pointedly.

'Of course, of course, sir, he will be looked after to the highest standards, you can be assured of it.' The servant grovelled as the glib promises slipped from his lips.

'That had better be the case, Charles, otherwise there will be consequences, unpleasant ones. Do I make myself clear?'

'Yes sir, clear as the water in a mill pond.'

Very lyrical, thought Benjamin, *this man is an insufferable creep.*

'Either I or Richard will be in town again in a few days. Make sure my father is given every aid for his comfort in the meantime.'

Benjamin leant down to kiss his father's head, but the old man, now fast asleep, showed no reaction. He whispered a brief term of endearment, stood up, nodded a curt goodbye to the hovering Charles and left the house. It was an over an hour's ride to the farm in Lawshall, and he wished to be there before dusk.

All the family worried about his father being alone with just the servants, but it was an arrangement that suited all of them and worked well for a couple of years. Though as Humphrey's health deteriorated in the last few months, Benjamin wondered what was the best course of action. He decided to discuss it with the rest of the family: maybe now was time to bring him back to the farm in Lawshall for his final days?

Four days later Richard, Benjamin's younger brother, galloped into the farmyard, leapt down from his horse before it skidded to a breathless halt and ran into the farmhouse. It was lunchtime and his brother and wife, Eloise were eating at the kitchen table. Both were startled as Richard flew into the room, tears streaming down his face.

'Benjamin, Benjamin! Quick! Father is seriously ill, I have just come from the house. He is all alone! It seems the servants have left; the place is empty except for Father lying in his bed. We must go now. I have a neighbour waiting with him until a doctor arrives. Please hurry! I fear the worst.'

Under an hour later the two men rushed into the house, strangely empty not just of people, but of most of its decorations and household pieces. The great hall's furniture was strewn around the room with overturned chairs and broken glass everywhere. Ignoring the mess they ran up to the first floor into their father's room to find a doctor and priest in attendance, the latter kneeling beside the bed holding the frail man's hand, quietly praying.

'How is he, Doctor?' asked Benjamin.

'I'm afraid he's very ill, sir. I believe he has only hours to live at best. I took the liberty of summoning a priest to comfort him. He is close to starvation and has been neglected, as you can tell by the malodorous condition he is in. Where are the servants and housekeepers who are supposed to look after him, do you know?'

'That I do not, Doctor, but I intend to find out. Is there anything you can do for him? Anything to ease his pain?' asked Richard.

'I fear it is too late to reverse his decline. I have given him some laudanum that will help alleviate his suffering. Of course, if someone could clean him and make him comfortable that would help too.' Without offering to help, and with a slight shrug of his shoulders he turned to leave. 'I shall return later today to administer some more pain relief. Now if you'll excuse me, gentlemen, I must be going to my next patient. I have done all I can here.'

After the doctor left, with help from the priest, the sons bathed and cleaned their unconscious father, moving him to the adjacent bedroom, away from the disgusting mess he had been lying in for several days. Humphrey groaned quietly as they lay him down on the clean bed. He gave no indication he recognised his sons, or could retell what had happened to him.

As they sat by the bed, watching their father's life force quietly fading away, both sons could barely control the fury inside them, witnessing what the servants had done to their dear father. Not only did they take advantage of his illness and frailty, they stole from him, then neglected him to the point of death.

'I shall see those thieves and murderers hang,' whispered Benjamin to his brother. 'I knew something was amiss here in recent months, I was just too busy to stop and look further. I am ashamed of my poor judgement, my lack of action, brother.'

'Don't shoulder all the blame, Ben, we are all guilty to a degree. We trusted the servants here to look after our father, paid them well, and they thanked us by doing this. We shall have our revenge, whether father lives or not.'

'Indeed we shall, Richard. No matter where they are, we shall find them. Justice will be served, by the courts, or maybe us. We shall see.'

Humphrey died before the day was out, his last breath coming as dusk descended. Richard went back to the farm to tell the rest of the family of his passing. Two days later the funeral took place at the local church in Lawshall, his body laid to rest in the graveyard alongside family ancestors going back three centuries.

Richard's daughter wandered through the gravestones reading the inscriptions. 'Father, there is one here, I can barely read it...I think it says something about a lady called Grace; she has the same last name as us, and died in 1611! Who was she?'

'From what I have heard, Grace was a very special lady, she bought the farm we now live in, and also the house in Whiting St. By all accounts she was a beautiful, talented woman. She left us letters she wrote to her friend Maud. We have them somewhere; you can read them when you are a little older. She wrote them because she was born unable to talk, but despite that she started several businesses and was very successful. Reading those letters you'll get to know her and how they lived in those days...it was a lot different from today.'

'But I can read, Father, and I'm nearly eleven! Why can't I see them now? Please, I would love to know more about her! She sounds so interesting.'

'Soon, Jane, soon. Now we must get back to the farm, I have work to do.' Richard now regretted bringing up the subject of Grace's letters. He knew from reading them, all still carefully bundled and handed carefully down the family generations, that Grace and Maud were more than just friends. Some of the correspondence between them described in explicit detail their deep love and physical intimacy, topics he did not feel the need to discuss with an eleven-year-old. It had been embarrassing enough with his wife.

Days after the funeral the family sat round the large oak table in the great hall, trying to understand how they had been deceived and allowed their father to be so mistreated – and how the servants fooled him into selling off so many valuable items.

'Do we know what is missing?' asked Richard. 'Are we to presume whatever was stolen and sold, the proceeds went to the servants? Might Father have kept the money?'

'I think that the servants stole most of the valuable items is a fair assumption, Richard,' replied Benjamin. 'The problem is he filled the house with so many things it's difficult to know what has gone. However, surely our first plan must be to find these thieves and bring them to justice. I have asked the constable to come by so we can tell him what's happened – let's leave him to go after those criminals. He is due here this afternoon; in the meantime we should tidy it up and try and fathom what was stolen.'

The family was disappointed at the constable's reaction to their claims. As he wearily pointed out, 'Even if you can provide us with a list of at least some of the items that are missing, who is to say they were stolen, or not sold willingly by your father? That is what the servants will claim should we ever catch them.'

'What about leaving him to die, unfed and ill-treated?' demanded Richard, annoyed at the unhelpful attitude of the constable. 'Is that worth your time?'

'I agree, sir, it was a terrible thing to leave your father in such a condition, but he was old and infirm. They are not doctors, and maybe they were not able to minister to his needs, through ignorance or even fear. I believe it would be a difficult case to prove, though of course we will do our best to find them and discover what happened. Unfortunately there are only three constables for the whole of Bury at the moment, and it will not be a priority, I am sorry to say.'

The constable stayed a few more minutes and noted the names of the three servants and some of the more valuable items the family believed stolen. His lack of enthusiasm made it clear little more would be done by him or his fellow law enforcement officers. He bade them good day, offering words of condolences as he left the house and vague promises they would be hearing from him.

'God's strewth, that man is as useful as a candle in a snowstorm. He will do nothing, of that I am sure. Are we just to let him walk away from this atrocity? Someone murdered our father, and he says it's not a priority!' Benjamin was seething at the constable's indifference. He banged the table with his fist and jumped up. 'Well, I am not going to rest until I have found those servants and meted out some of my own justice; what do you say, Richard – are you with me?' His brother agreed: they should both seek out the culprits themselves.

It was easier said than done.

On checking the references for the old servant, Charles, they discovered that the household he claimed to have worked in for many years had no recollection of his service there. The other servants they knew even less about, so were unable to make any headway about them. They started to feel foolish and irresponsible, letting three, it turned out, strangers into their father's house and leaving him alone with them for days at a time.

Staring into a tankard of ale in the Masons Arms Inn close by the house, Richard was angry and frustrated, 'We let him down, Benjamin, left our father in the hands of thieving rogues. I feel disgusted with myself, guilty of such selfishness. And to make it worse, we are no closer to catching those ne'er-do-wells. Where do we look next?'

'We could try the local churches. If I remember, the old man always took Sunday morning off to go to church, something tells me he was a Methodist...doesn't say much for them if they harbour thieves and murderers! Maybe we should seek out where these people meet. I know it is a long shot, but it has to be worth trying. If they are not there, maybe the priest might know something,' suggested Benjamin.

Unenthusiastically Richard agreed; there were few other alternatives to pursue.

Luck was with them. The famous evangelical and Methodist preacher, John Wesley, was returning to the Assembly Rooms on Angel Hill as he had on many previous occasions. Any Methodist, or indeed Anglican, would be there to hear his thoughts and advice on how to live a pious and healthy life. Richard and Benjamin hoped that if Charles was indeed a devout Methodist he would almost be obliged to attend the meeting.

They arrived an hour before the start of the proceedings and already people were queuing along Angel Lane all the way to Churchgate St.

'Heavens, I heard he was popular...it seems half the town is wanting to hear this Wesley man preach,' said Richard, awestruck at the size of the waiting crowd. They eventually squeezed into the large meeting room, which was packed, with standing room only. They stood near the front so they could turn back and see the congregants' faces. Benjamin, being a head taller than Richard, could surreptitiously survey the room for Charles or his two companions.

'Maybe we should try praying they are here,' said Benjamin sarcastically. 'Not sure how a man who steals and murders can also be one who prays. Mind you, these types have a strange way of asking forgiveness, maybe his conscience is bothering him...though somehow I doubt it...'

'Benjamin, just hush with the complaining, people can hear you. I know it's a long shot any of those three will be here, but it's worth trying. Anyway, a little praying won't do your soul any harm!'

'Very funny, Richard...'

Before he could finish his reply, a hush descended on the crowd as a tall, thin man clutching the Bible, mounted the stage. His long auburn hair was uncombed and fell untidily, partially obscuring his face. He had a long aquiline nose and a small, tight mouth. However, when he raised his hands in welcome a broad smile broke across his face, which transformed his looks to one of genuine pleasure at seeing such a large audience.

Wesley was joined on the small stage by his wife, who he introduced as Mary Vazeille. She sat down and participated little in the proceedings.

He held his hands up in supplication, and asked that everyone bow their heads in prayer. For the next hour he kept the audience spellbound with his rhetoric, expounding as much about ways to keep the body healthy as he did about the audience's spiritual well being. They were hushed and attentive, hanging on his every word, hoping he would somehow throw them a lifeline to a better existence, physical and spiritual. Frequent cries of 'Amen!' and 'Praise the Lord!' rose from the crowd in response to Wesley's entreaties.

But Richard and Benjamin were only half listening, too busy scrutinising the faces in the room.

Benjamin was becoming frustrated. 'There are just too many people here, brother, I cannot see anyone who looks like Charles. Maybe we can try and get out early and then watch everyone as they leave?'

'Good idea, brother. It won't be easy, people are packed in here. Let us try, though.'

It took the brothers several minutes to force their way to the exit, generating a good many very unchristian-like comments from those they pushed their way past. Offering copious apologies, the brothers finally fell out onto Angel Hill. They waited by a table selling copies of John Wesley's book, The Primitive Psychic outside the main entrance to the Assembly Rooms. It was nearly an hour later, after a rousing finale of 'Author of Love Divine' that the crowd began to leave.

'Eyes peeled, Richard,' instructed Benjamin, 'I still think we'll need a miracle to find that crook here, but we have waited so long, what's another few minutes?'

The crowd swarmed out of the Assembly Rooms, chattering excitedly, in high spirits after hearing John Wesley's uplifting words. Richard and Benjamin had difficulty scanning the sea of faces as they rushed past onto Angel Hill. Within minutes the surge of people had dwindled to a trickle and then to nothing as the last few stragglers wandered out into the bright sunlight.

'God be damned, not a sign of any of them! What a waste of time that was!' muttered Richard to himself.

'What now, brother?'

With a resigned shrug, Benjamin answered, 'I have no idea where we should look next, Richard. Let us go back to the house and plan our next move. Though truth be told, I am beginning to lose hope we shall be successful in this endeavour. It pains me to think we have spent so much time to no avail – and those scoundrels will get away with their crimes.'

Richard said nothing, walking alongside his brother, past the Norman Tower and cutting up Churchgate St towards Whiting St, passing the new, huge poorhouse built on College St to house over 200 impoverished souls. Those who had fallen to the very bottom of society. It was a harsh refuge from an even harsher life of begging on the streets. Ironically, the adjacent streets were still an affluent area with many double-fronted houses proudly displaying the wealth of their owners. As the brothers approached their house they saw a young man peering through the front windows.

'Hey you, young man, can we help?' asked Benjamin. When they saw who it was, Richard rushed forward and grabbed him by the arm. 'Come back to steal some more?' he asked, his fist raised to hit the young man.

'No, no, sir, I have come back to explain what happened to your father. I saw you at the Methodist meeting earlier, and guessed you might be looking for one of us. I decided that I must come and see you, to beg for your mercy and understanding. I know you owe me no favours or kindness, I just need you to know that I am truly sorry for what happened to your father.'

The boy was clearly frightened; both Richard and Benjamin stood menacingly close to him, barely restraining themselves from giving the former servant a good beating. However his pitiful look, and obvious fear of their retaliation, weakened their desire for revenge sufficiently to drag him inside the house.

'You are Stephen, if I remember correctly. How old are you?' asked Richard.

'I'm seventeen, sir.'

'Old enough to hang for your crimes,' said Benjamin pointedly. 'So before we take you to the gaol, explain yourself, and what happened to our father. And don't lie. If necessary we will beat the truth out of you.'

His voice trembling with fear, he offered a rambling explanation of his time as a servant at the house with the woman his mother, called Judy, under the controlling influence of Charles, his stepfather.

'My stepfather has made a living out of fleecing elderly people he supposedly cared for. When he married my mother, it made his life easier. People trusted an old man with a woman and a young boy in tow. He chose his victims wisely, making sure they were too old or sick of mind to notice what was happening to them. He made extra money by selling my mother's services as a whore. A big house like this made it easy to accommodate the men who came here, charging them extra for staying the night if needs be. It was these men we sold some of the valuable stuff to, and others went to the pawnbroker.'

The boy dropped his voice to an embarrassed whisper. 'Sorry to say, sirs, my mother even serviced your father if he showed an interest in her. It all helped to keep him quiet and persuade you all was well.'

Richard and Benjamin looked at each other aghast at the boy's story. This happened right under their noses, and they suspected nothing? How gullible had they been!

'So why did you all decide to leave in such a hurry?'

'You have to understand, sir, I was just doin' as I was told. If I argued, Charles beat me, and my mother too. He is an evil man. We had no choice.' Stephen paused as he then revealed the full, dreadful story.

''Bout a month or two ago we could see your father was getting worse. Out of his mind at times. Charles was scared he might say something to you, not realising it. We could see his body was failing too. Charles knew it was time to leave before he died and our game would be up for all to see. He was clever, you know, always knew when to quit before he got caught. Unfortunately your father took a sudden turn for the worse, so we upped and left, taking what we could carry. Both my mother and I said we shouldn't leave your father alone in such a state, but he threatened us again, so we left...I am so, so sorry, it was a terrible thing to have done.'

The boy was now sobbing, catching his breath as he tried to control his emotions. He felt a sense of relief at his confession but was also now fearful of his fate at the hands of the two heartbroken sons, who he still feared might take out painful retribution upon him.

'Stay here, don't move,' ordered Richard. He took hold of his brother's arm and steered him towards the parlour. 'Benjamin, let us talk in private.'

Still shocked at Stephen's revelations, they sat down at the large kitchen table. Neither said a word for a few minutes as each considered what to do next.

Richard spoke first: 'It is tempting to take our revenge out on this young boy, but I do believe he was too young to refuse his stepfather's orders. And to see his mother sold to men for sex right before his eyes, I almost feel sorry for him. Maybe he can...'

'...Maybe he can lead us to the old man?' Benjamin interrupted, guessing his brother's next words.

'Exactly what I was about to say. If we can bring him to justice, I am happy to let the boy and his mother go...are you?'

His brother nodded in agreement, 'Now we have to persuade him to tell us where Charles is hiding. I shall not hold back, I warn you, brother. I will be as persuasive as necessary! Play along with me...don't interfere no matter what I may say, or threaten.'

The two men strode back into the house, Benjamin shoved him onto a chair, roughly grabbed hold of the boy's hair and pulled his head back. He brought a large kitchen knife down onto the boy's throat. 'Now listen, boy, we need you to tell us where that devious little shit is hiding. If we catch him, we will take him to the courts for justice to be done. Then, we may consider letting you and your mother go. If you have lied to us, or cannot help us find this man, you will spend the rest of your life in gaol, or worse, hanged. Do I make myself clear, boy?'

Though almost choking, the boy agreed. 'Yes, yessir. I am willing to help, I trust you as gentlemen to keep your word too.'

'We will. Now tell us, where is this evil bastard to be found?' demanded Richard.

'He is staying at the Swan Inn in Hawstead. I heard him say that we would be moving on to Cambridge tomorrow. He sent me into Bury today to sell some of your father's possessions to help pay for the journey. If you hurry he should still be there.' Stephen looked expectantly at the two men, hoping this information would keep his throat from being slit.

'For your sake, he better be,' replied Richard.

'Let us put this snivelling wretch in the cellar until we return; a little hunger and thirst is small penance for him to pay. What say you, Benjamin?'

'It sounds like a fine plan, brother. Let us depart at once. Time is of the essence; it sounds as though he is about to run away.'

They unceremoniously bundled the hapless boy down the rough-hewn stairs into the cellar and slammed the trapdoor shut, dragging the heavy table over it to ensure he could not escape.

Hawstead was only an hour away, and it was mid-afternoon when they arrived at the Swan Inn, a small, thatched roof building, with some broken-down tables and chairs outside. Two horses harnessed to a small carriage were tethered to a nearby tree. The rear of the carriage had several crates and boxes strapped to it. Sounds of merriment came from within the tavern; several people were obviously well the worse for drink already.

The brothers stopped, suddenly unsure of the soundness of their plan.

'What is our course of action, Richard?' We cannot just march in and drag this man out, he may have friends in there for all we know. I only have my knife with me, not my pistol – I am not well armed for a fight.'

'Me neither,' admitted Richard. 'Unfortunately he knows both of us by sight, so we cannot surprise him.'

'Maybe we wait until he leaves. That could well be his carriage.'

'Yes, we could, but that might be hours from now. I would prefer to act sooner rather than later.'

As they sat on their horses pondering their next move, a young boy rode up to the inn, dismounted and walked towards the door.

Suddenly an idea came to Richard's mind. He called across the yard, 'Young man! Come here. There's sixpence for you to earn by doing me a small favour. Are you interested?'

With a little hesitation the boy walked over, a look of suspicion on his face, 'Depends what you want me to do, mister.'

'I want you to go inside and ask for a man named Charles, an elderly gentleman. Can you tell him Stephen is waiting for him by the carriage, and he has some money for him? Be discreet, whisper it in his ear so others do not hear what you say.'

'Is that all?' The boy looked relieved.

'Yes, that's all. Will you do that for me?'

'Where's my money?'

Richard smiled at the boy's nerve, reached into his pocket and counted out three pence.

'There is half; when we have finished talking to the man, then you'll get the other three pence.'

The boy snatched the coins, and ran into the inn. The brothers rode over to the carriage, keeping their backs to the inn entrance so Charles would not realise who they were until, they hoped, it was too late.

A few minutes later they heard the inn door slam and a voice slurred by drink call out, 'Stephen? Stephen, where are you? You snivelling little bastard, have you got my money?'

Charles staggered towards the carriage still calling out Stephen's name. His brain, addled by beer, took a few moments to register who the two brothers were when they turned to face him. Once he did, the blood drained from his face. He made a half-hearted attempt to run back to the inn, but his movements were slowed by his drunkenness, and the brothers quickly manhandled him to the ground. Suddenly in his fear he found the strength to struggle and start shouting for help.

Nothing happened for a few seconds, then the inn door crashed open and three men stumbled out, one bellowing in a voice that brooked no argument, 'What are you doing with my brother? Leave him alone or I'll beat you to a mash!' The large cudgel in his hand gave weight to his threat. The two other men, though unarmed, were well built, and ready for a drink-fuelled fight.

'Wait, wait, all of you. This man killed our father and we are here to take him to face justice. We mean no harm to any of you.' Richard's voice of reason momentarily stopped them. But only for a few moments.

'Don't care! Go get the constable! You're not the law,' said cudgel man. 'My brother wouldn't do something like that. He's a good man.'

'And he'll be dead before you reach us,' said Richard as he pulled out his knife and held it tightly to Charles's neck. 'Move a step closer and I'll slit his murderous throat. Now you all just go back to your drink, and we'll be on our way.' One of the men moved a step towards Richard who, with a flash of the knife promptly cut off Charles's ear, throwing it at the cudgel man's feet.

Charles howled in pain, clutching the bleeding stub of his ear, blood pouring between his fingers. All three men looked in horror at the piece of bloody flesh lying before them in the dirt. None moved.

'Now do as I say, or I'll take his eye out...' threatened Richard.

Benjamin had never seen his brother so violent, or so fearless. He was awestruck. 'Good going, brother, now let's get this pile of shit on the carriage and out of here before they try something stupid or brave. You drive, I'll get your horse.'

The fear of God spurring their actions, within seconds Charles was dumped in the carriage, Richard sat on him so he couldn't move, and in a flash they were bouncing down the track towards Bury. The drunken trio's threats and insults followed them, but that was all.

In the confusion they had forgotten one thing. Where was the woman, Judy?

'Dammit, Benjamin, we forget this turd's wife. Now what? We cannot go back, they will murder us!'

'Shit and damnation!' In frustration, Richard kicked the old man beneath him. 'Was your wife at the inn? Or had you pimped her out like some street harlot?'

Charles replied angrily, 'She isn't my wife, she's Stephen's wife. She's no harlot, just a scheming bitch who has set me and you up. I heard her cooking up something last night with him. Seems you've fallen into whatever trap she set you! Think she reckons if you have me, you won't bother looking for her and the boy.'

Furious at falling for such a deception, the brothers rode back to the house. They knew as soon as they entered, the old man was right. The table covering the trapdoor was pushed to one side and the cellar was empty.

'Well, we have been duped good and proper, brother. That boy was a good actor,' said a rueful Benjamin. 'But at least we have this one to hand over to the constables, so all is not a complete waste of time. And we have some of their booty in the carriage! A small reward for our efforts?'

'I hope it's more than a small reward, we nearly got ourselves murdered because of that woman.'

But the mysterious mother fooled them again. They went outside to the carriage to examine the luggage. It was a huge disappointment. The cases and trunks contained nothing but cheap clothing and personal effects, nothing of any value.

'I was hoping some of Father's possessions might be here. Guess it is not our lucky day!' said Richard, disappointed after all their efforts. 'This quest for justice is becoming frustrating and more dangerous every day.'

'Well, all is not lost, we do have the old man to take to the courts. Let justice serve its due desserts on him at least,' said Benjamin, in a resigned voice. 'We could go after that couple, but I am losing the taste for this fight, to be honest. We have a farm to run, a family to take care of; I think spending more time chasing them would be a fool's errand.'

'I agree, brother, let us take this little shit to the courts and go home to Lawshall.' The justice system did not fail them. Within the month Charles was tried and found guilty of thievery and manslaughter, and sentenced to fifteen years transportation to the Americas. For a man of his age, it was as good as a death sentence.

As for Judy and her young husband, or son, no one really knew what their relationship was, nothing was heard from them again. Richard and Benjamin informed the local newspaper of the tragic story surrounding their father's death, naming the couple, in the hope that it would serve as a warning to others not to fall for their scheming, dishonest ways.

Two weeks later, Richard, Benjamin and their families sat at the large table in the great room, discussing what to do with the house. Everyone agreed it was a beautiful home, though its upkeep was becoming more expensive by the day: something always needed replacing or repairing. The expense they could afford, the farm in Lawshall was producing a healthy income. There was also the emotional attachment; their predecessors lived here, and they all felt an unspoken connection to its past. However, the most important question was whether they wanted to let it and become landlords.

They debated the pros and cons, each member of the family having their say. Richard's teenage daughter suggested optimistically, 'it would be a wonderful place for me to live, when I get married, which may not be too long into the future!' They all laughed; she was only twelve. 'That, I hope, is a few years away, young lady,' replied her father.

In the middle of their discussions, Benjamin received a letter from his brother-in-law, Jameson, who was now living in London. He had just moved there from the West Indies after marrying a 'local girl' as he described her. He wrote that he was keen to leave the 'squalor and danger' of the capital and did he know of any houses in Suffolk to rent?

Benjamin wrote back offering the house in Bury. It seemed like the perfect solution.

It would, however, bring a divisive force not just into their home, but the whole town.

Chapter 26

I am excited to finally meet Jameson and his new wife,' said Eloise, as she climbed into the carriage taking the family into Bury. She was dressed in her Sunday best for the occasion and looked very much a country lady, thought Benjamin. Her straw-blonde hair was tied tightly back into a bun, accentuating her high cheekbones and clear blue eyes. *I am one lucky man*, he reflected as he sat down beside her and took the reins. His two daughters, Jane, twelve, and Henrietta, nine, also looked clean and smart for their first meeting with Uncle Jameson.

It was a warm, sunny late autumn morning. As they left Lawshall and took the track via Stanningfield to Sicklesmere, Benjamin looked across the recently harvested fields. Thankfully, the barley and wheat produced good yields this year, making up for the decline in wool prices as the once-thriving cloth-making industry declined across East Anglia.

All in all it had been a good year, he decided, and now an unexpected visit from a long lost relative was a pleasant diversion from running the farm.

No one had seen Jameson for nearly ten years. When his father-in-law asked him to help run his plantations in the West Indies Jameson went, never to return, until now. By all accounts he'd made a success of it, and since the death of his father-in-law the lands had passed to him. Some one thousand acres producing mainly sugar and some cotton, making Jameson a wealthy man.

His return to England was to take an extended holiday, a break from the crushing heat and humidity of the Caribbean and let his family visit England for the first time.

However, a brief stay in noisy, polluted and crime-ridden London convinced him it was not safe there for his wife and young daughters. Speculatively he wrote to Benjamin to find out what properties might be available to rent, only to discover to his delight they owned one in Bury! Unsure of his long-term plans he agreed to rent it for six months. He and his family arrived a week ago and promptly sent an invitation for everyone to join them for a family get-together.

Benjamin hitched the horses outside the house and, as they approached the front door, Jameson was there to greet them. A tall man in his late thirties, he looked in robust health, ruddy cheeks and bushy grey sideburns that sprouted copiously down to his chin. He was all smiles as he embraced Eloise and the two young girls, then warmly shook Benjamin's hand.

'It has been too long since we last met, and now we convene in your beautiful townhouse! A perfect place for our families to celebrate this auspicious occasion,' gushed Jameson. 'Come in and meet my family!'

They all bustled excitedly into the great hall, and stopped dumbfounded at the sight that met their eyes. Standing before them were Jameson's wife and two young daughters, with beaming, welcoming smiles...and skins the colour of mahogany. For a few seconds no one said a word; clearly the three women were expecting some kind of reaction – it was an all-too-familiar reaction since their arrival in England – and waited to see what it would be. Eloise looked at Benjamin, not sure what to say, and he was equally dumbfounded.

Jane broke the silence with a childishly simple question: 'Mother, why are their skins so...so black?'

Eloise, recovering from her own shock at the unexpected turn of events said, 'Jane, that is a very rude thing to say. I apologise to the ladies for my daughter's ill manners.'

So there it was: Jameson had married a black woman and produced two children, though with a much lighter skin colour than their mother. Eloise didn't know what to say, so said nothing for fear of embarrassing herself.

A few more awkward moments followed as the question, for the moment, was ignored, and Jameson carried on making the introductions. 'This is my wife, Violet, and my children, Desdemona and Juliet.' The atmosphere still remained tense; no one was sure what to say or do in case they might cause offence.

Jameson, sensing the need for an explanation, said:

'I know you find this all a little surprising and unconventional. Believe me, I understand the sight of a white man married to a black woman is a strange one in this country, but 'tis not the case so much where we have been living.' He paused, aware that what he was about to say might shock his family even more. 'Violet was actually my father-in-law's...er...companion...and lived in the main house for many years. And it was where she gave birth to Desdemona and Juliet; they are his children. Sadly, he died some six years ago, and suffice to say Violet and I subsequently fell in love. We married four years ago and I adopted these two lovely girls as my daughters. I know this news will come as a shock to you all, but I do hope you will accept, and welcome us as part of the family.'

The few moments of silence that followed was broken by Eloise, who walked over to Violet and hugged her, then the two girls. 'I don't care a jot what colour your skin is. What the two of you may have done might be unconventional, but it is not wrong, at least as far as I am concerned. Though I fear others may not be so accepting. I am so happy to meet you all. I believe it is now time to celebrate your love, and bravery. Welcome to our family.'

The look of relief on Jameson and Violet's faces was obvious. Too often they had been shunned, berated and ostracised, especially since their arrival in England. Finally, they felt no sense of judgement or criticism. It was a weight off their shoulders, and they finally felt at ease, at home.

'You cannot know how wonderful it is to hear those words,' said Violet in her soft, lilting voice, filled with gratitude. 'We thank you from the bottom of our hearts. Now, shall we eat and drink?'

While the four girls went off exploring the house, the adults sat and discussed events of the last decade, each keen to discover the others' family history. Benjamin was fascinated to learn more about how the exotic crops like sugar and tobacco were grown, while Violet and Eloise chatted amiably about their children and their lives in such different parts of the world. Violet avoided talking about life as a slave, and Eloise didn't press her even though she would have liked to know more.

Richard and his wife, Penny, and their two boys, Mark and Aaron, arrived later. Likewise, after the initial shock of seeing Jameson with a black woman, they, too, joined in the celebrations. All seemed well as the children played noisy games around the large house, and the adults gossiped, discussing business and politics. Jameson explained in some detail the operation of his vast plantation. Though slavery was not practised in England, the transportation of slaves was still a huge business since it started in the early 1600s.

With no shame, Jameson explained he owned some 150 slaves (Violet having been one, but who was granted manumission in his father-in-law's will). 'Without their labour, the cost of sugar, cotton and tobacco would be out of reach for most people in this country. It is an economic necessity in order for us to survive. Those clamouring for its ending will find it hits their purses all too quickly if they succeed in their objectives,' argued Jameson.

'Yes, but is it not a cruel system? Are not the slaves treated badly? Kept in chains, denied their freedom? How can that be fair?' asked Richard.

Jameson was undeterred by the implied criticism. 'It is true many slave owners do not treat them well. I like to believe I care for mine; ask Violet.' Without waiting for her to comment, he continued, 'Slaves are expensive to buy; they are an investment which only repays itself if you look after them.'

Richard persisted: 'They have little choice, though, do they? Why would they want to come to a foreign land and work for nothing, so far from their homes, wherever they may be? I am not sure how this all works. But I have to be honest and say I find the whole system less than satisfactory.'

Jameson tried to enlighten him. 'The whole process is now a huge business, Richard. Slaves are brought across from the west coast of Africa to the Americas, both North and South continents. It may be unpalatable for you English, but it is a way of life, of business, for us.'

'Sorry; it might be a normal way to do business in the colonies, but here it is frowned upon. But how do you find them all?' asked Richard, Jameson's justification of slavery failing to convince him of its merits.

'Oh, that part isn't done by us slave owners or even the transportation ships. The countries on the west coast of Africa have numerous slave trading ports. Other Africans bring people captured in war, or bought from other traders, and transport them to the coastal cities .That is where they are loaded onto the ships. The whites don't go hunting for them, we just buy them from other blacks.'

'So these African traders are selling their own people into slavery?' Richard was incredulous.

'Oh yes! Didn't you know? They were doing it long before us whites turned up, they used to sell slaves to Arabs, or just each other. It's a fact of life to them. Though it's a much bigger enterprise now. It's just money as far as they are concerned. Like selling diamonds or timber,' said Jameson matter-of-factly. 'I understand if people in England find it all rather distasteful, but if we weren't buying them, other people would. At least we look after them. You forget that thousands of criminals from this country are transported to America where they are treated like slaves, are they not? What is the difference? I see no one trying to stop that practice!'

Richard remained silent; he didn't accept the argument but did not wish to disrupt the gaiety of the afternoon by starting a quarrel. So, seemingly satisfied with Jameson's justification for being a slave owner, the conversation drifted onto other less contentious subjects.

It was only later, as they shared a carriage back to Lawshall, Richard raised the topic again with Benjamin: 'Brother, I am having difficulty accepting a white man marrying a black woman is a holy partnership. Many say they are an inferior race, that the offspring are often soft of mind. In truth, I feel uncomfortable having them as part of our family. Folk around here, I'll wager, may not be as welcoming as us. I fear it might affect our business, even lose us friends if we are associated with them. As for owning slaves, that is abhorrent to my mind, and in the eyes of the Lord too, I believe.'

Benjamin was not surprised at his brother's antagonism at the marriage, and the fact that Jameson was a slave owner. He sensed all afternoon a simmering dislike, and was grateful that he was raising it only now.

'I know you find this uncomfortable, and so do I, but I think from what Jameson said to me in confidence, he may be selling the plantation and moving back to England. I get the feeling this visit is to gain a sense of what living here with a black wife and children would be like. Indeed, for all his attempts at justifying slavery I believe he sees that its time is coming to an end, that soon it will be outlawed, rendering his plantation worthless. He wants to get out while he's ahead.'

'Well, I don't blame him for that, but that still leaves the question of his wife and children...how will they be accepted in Bury, if that's where he intends to stay? Heavens, these locals don't like people from London, and they are of the same colour!'

'You are right, Richard, but that is not our problem. We can only support him as any family would. How the people of Bury react to them is beyond our control. I don't envy them at all but they must be able to count on our support if no one else's. Do you not agree?' He knew he was pushing his brother into a corner, to persuade him that the family should project a united front.

Non-committally Richard replied, 'I see your argument – let me think on it, talk it over with my wife. I am willing to support them, but not if it puts our family or our business at risk.'

'As you wish, brother, you must follow your conscience in matters such as this. Let us talk again in a few days.' They rode the rest of the way home in uncomfortable silence, each wrestling with their thoughts about how best to handle this unexpected dilemma, one which could severely disrupt their lives if the wrong choices were made.

Three weeks later as Richard was supervising the last of the wheat stubble being burnt off in the field, his brother came riding at speed to his side. 'There is a problem with our guests. It seems Violet was attacked and Jameson was involved in some disagreement. I am unfamiliar with all the details, but I think we should make haste there to offer our help.'

'I warned you that they would attract trouble, Benjamin. Now they have and we are involved; no good can come of this, I fear.'

'You must be so pleased you're right,' spat Benjamin, unable to contain his anger. 'However, he is our relative and he needs our help. But if you're not willing to get involved, I shall go by myself.' Saying no more, he urged his horse into a canter and headed off to Bury.

'A duel? You have been challenged to a duel? God in heaven, how did that come about?' asked an incredulous Benjamin.

'I think it best I explain from the start,' said Jameson. His face bore the cuts and bruises from his earlier, violent, encounter. Though in pain, he was unruffled as he recounted the incident that took place on Angel Hill that morning.

'I was walking with Violet and the children near the abbey ruins when two men of some rank made a derogatory remark about my wife. In truth it is not the first time such comments have been made as we go about our business in the town. Mostly I decline to give them the pleasure of showing any reaction to their crass obloquy. But this man called my wife a particularly distasteful name, so I stopped and asked if he cared to repeat it, and risk regretting his rudeness. With the support of his equally boorish companion he did, then continued his insults by calling my children "monkeys".'

'Oh, Jesus,' moaned Benjamin, guessing what happened next.

'So I felt I had no alternative but to defend my family's honour. I struck him with my walking stick, and he punched me in retaliation. Before the altercation could continue, bystanders separated us, and in a moment of bravado I challenged him to a duel, so the matter could be settled like gentlemen. I was somewhat taken aback when he agreed. Unfortunately, with so many witnesses, I feel obliged to see the matter to a conclusion. To back out would leave me open to accusations of cowardice.'

Violet so far had said nothing but now asked, 'Can't someone go and talk to this man? Make him see sense? I am prepared to forget his insults if he agrees to call off this stupid duel. Someone could be killed – it is not worth it. I, and my children have been called worse. I thought England was a civilised place; this is no way to settle an argument. Benjamin, please do something!'

271

'I agree, Violet. But English custom makes it difficult to reverse a request for satisfaction. Both parties must agree to it. I can visit the man and see what he says. Do you know his name?'

'I have the name of his second, Mark Burberry – here is his card.'

'I will go there forthwith and shall return with hopefully good news,' said Benjamin.

The home of Mark Burberry was on the outskirts of Bury near Hardwick Hall. Benjamin immediately saw a potential problem. The house was large, in generous, immaculately kept grounds, its owner obviously rich, which made him wonder just who was the person that accepted the invitation to a duel? Unfortunately, the more wealthy or aristocratic, the less likely they were to change their mind. Honour and reputation ran in their blood; any sign of weakness was to be avoided.

A servant opened the heavy, ornate oak door after Benjamin had been kept waiting for several minutes; someone was making a point, he felt. He explained why he wished to see Mr Burberry, and after a further wait he was shown into a well-appointed library – and made to wait another fifteen minutes.

'Mr Benjamin Debenham? I assume you have come to sort out details of the duel,' said Mark as he strode into the room, not bothering with any introduction or welcome. 'Nasty incident, I must say, your man completely overreacted by attacking Sir David. He still is in pain after the unwarranted attack, but will be ready for the duel, say in two days' time?'

'Sir David?'

'Yes, Sir David St John Westerby, son of Lord Cornwallis; I'm sure you've heard of him. Not a man to be trifled with, or, of course, insulted.'

Benjamin's heart sank, but he persevered. 'I beg your pardon, sir, but I believe it was he that insulted my brother in law's wife and children, because of their skin colour. Is that how a man in his position behaves?'

'It was a passing comment, perhaps a little inappropriate, but nothing that warranted such a response. Clearly the man must expect such a reaction in this country when he decides to take a slave as his wife.'

The man's arrogance was beginning to rile Benjamin, who fought to control his temper.

'Sir, while I cannot agree with what you are saying I am here to see if common sense can prevail and honour be satisfied without the need for a duel. I am sure no one wishes to see any more blood spilt over such a matter.'

'Ah! So your man wishes to renege on the arrangement? It doesn't surprise me, his sort always do...'

'His sort? Now what are you implying, Mr Burberry? If I may say, it seems you delight in making unfounded accusations, throwing insults around with little regard for the truth. My brother-in-law is merely trying to avoid further bloodletting, in spite of his belief you have grossly slandered him.'

'Be careful, Mr Debenham, otherwise we may have two duels happening at the same time. However, I shall choose to ignore your disrespect this time – I appreciate you are concerned for your brother-in-law's wellbeing. But as to your request the matter be settled outside of a duel, I am afraid the answer is no. Sir David's reputation is of paramount importance to him. Therefore, I propose we conclude this matter and meet at dawn the day after tomorrow at Sexton Meadows...Now if that is all, Mr Debenham, my butler will show you out.' With that curt dismissal he left Benjamin standing there irate at the man's rudeness.

Benjamin returned, relaying the bad news to the couple. Violet was angered and worried. 'Why was he so unreasonable? Surely he must see someone could die in this duel? What else can we do to stop it?'

'I see only two alternatives,' said Jameson. 'I either face this man and hope to God I am neither injured nor killed, or we leave Bury and return to the plantation. Though indirectly, Benjamin, that could have a derogatory effect on your reputation, I would guess. No one wants to be associated with the relatives of a coward.'

Benjamin hadn't considered this, and Jameson was probably right. Richard would certainly claim it was the case. He was coming to the uncomfortable conclusion that a duel was the only way out of this mess.

And so it was, two days later, that Sir David St John Westerby, with a smug-looking Mark Burberry as his second, presented Jameson and Benjamin a beautifully engraved box containing the two pistols to be used in the duel. 'Please make your choice, gentlemen, check the gun over and load it as you wish.'

There was a cold indifference from the two men, as though this was something they had done before: a simple transaction, with no deadly consequences for either party. Merely some game to indulge in on a misty autumn morning. By the time the sun broke through there was a possibility one of the two duellists would be dead. This is not a day for dying, thought Benjamin, it's a beautiful, peaceful morning, the dawn birdsong in full chorus, oblivious to the tragedy about to be enacted on the dew drenched field beneath them. What stupidity is this? Here in the midst of Nature's dawn splendour, two men are fighting over something as pointless as their honour?

'Gentlemen!' Benjamin blurted out, feeling the need to make a desperate last attempt to stop this foolishness. 'Cannot, I beg you both, common sense prevail here, today? Is spilling blood over one's reputation a sensible way to resolve an argument? Please, reconsider your actions before it is too late!'

His words were met with scornful looks by Sir David and his companion. 'Too late sir, the die is cast,' sneered Sir Mark, 'Such distasteful actions and words that have been made by your friend require we cannot offer a compromise. The duel must commence forthwith.' Without waiting for any further comment he turned to the two men holding the pistols.

'Now let me explain the rules:

'You will stand back to back with loaded weapons, walk ten paces, and then turn to face your opponent. You may fire simultaneously or in sequence. Now I ask once again, do you believe your case is just, your testimony true, and that you carry no weapons other than these pistols?'

Both men nodded. Jameson, though nervous, seemed confident. He regularly used a pistol on the plantation for sport and protection. He knew that he should stand sideways to his opponent to present a smaller target, and take his time when aiming and shooting. He had the choice if his adversary shot first and missed, to merely fire his ball into the ground. Killing his opponent was not a necessity to finish the duel to everyone's satisfaction.

Benjamin shook Jameson's hand and wished him well, then stood several yards to one side. The two protagonists stood back-to-back. Jameson's face was white, taut with fear. His eyes were staring off somewhere into the distance. Benjamin wondered what a man thought about at a moment like this. His family? His past? Where to aim? How best to survive the next few minutes? He hoped he would never find himself in such an unenviable position.

'Gentlemen, start your ten paces now!' said Mark, quickly retiring back several feet from Sir David.

Benjamin would later swear that time seemed to stand still as the men walked slowly away from each other, that a quiet descended like a blanket over the meadow and the birds were silent, as each man walked slowly away from the other. They both turned practically at the same time and levelled their pistols at arm's length, shoulder high. For a second neither man fired. Then Sir David with a practised pose held his arm steady and pulled the trigger. A second later Jameson did likewise. But then in a tragic, fatal twist to the whole lamentable affair as Jameson fired, he was hit, his body flung sideways by the shock of the ball entering his chest. His shot flew wide of Sir David, instead hitting Sir Mark, some fifteen feet away, in the neck.

Benjamin ran to Jameson's side; blood was already oozing from a large wound below his left shoulder. Groaning in agony, blood started gurgling from his mouth, and he pleaded to be taken back to Violet as quickly as possible. 'She may be able to...save me. Don't let me die in this godforsaken field, let me feel...her embrace...one more time...I beg you.'

He hoisted Jameson onto the back of their small carriage and quickly left the Meadows. Glancing back, he saw Sir David cradling his second's head in his lap. He cared not if he was dead or alive, the man was an arrogant cad who got what he deserved.

The journey to the house took only a few minutes, though by then Jameson had lapsed into unconsciousness, his white shirt now drenched crimson, his face deathly pale, his breath ragged as it fought against the tide of blood in his throat.

Violet heard their arrival, and showing remarkable self-control helped her husband into the house and onto the table in the great hall. Quickly taking charge she ordered Benjamin to get a doctor. The two servants were dispatched to boil water and find cloth for bandages. She shouted after Benjamin as he ran out of the room, 'And stop at the apothecary to get clove, goldenseal and...yes, garlic and turmeric compounds, now quickly, time is of the essence!'

For all her outward coolness, in her heart she could see the wound was likely to kill her husband. The shot had gone through his rib cage, grazing the arteries just above his heart, and with the blood still bubbling out of his mouth, she deduced somewhere his lungs had been punctured. In her time as a slave she was familiar with the most horrendous wounds, normally inflicted by the lash, and became competent at stemming the flow of blood and preventing infections. The carnage caused by a pistol shot inside the body was beyond her knowledge, but she was determined to try and save her husband, no matter the odds stacked against him.

Within the hour Benjamin returned, a still half-asleep doctor behind him. 'I will go to the apothecary now and be back shortly, I felt it best to get the doctor here first.'

Violet ignored Benjamin's explanation and turned to the doctor, who could not hide his surprise at seeing a black woman administering to a white man. Dispensing with any introductions she briefly explained the situation:

'My husband has been shot just above the heart. I am unable to control the bleeding, despite using flour. I have asked Benjamin to get some turmeric and other potions which may help too. What do you suggest? Doctor, I know of no other remedies to stop the flow.'

The doctor rolled up his sleeves and gently prodded the wound, eliciting a groan of pain from the semi-conscious Jameson. He shook his head. 'Ma'am, I have nothing to give as a treatment that will help. The wound is deep, and by the looks of it the shot disintegrated inside his body, causing much damage. All I can offer you is some laudanum to ease his pain. I wish I could render you more assistance but, tragically, such wounds are normally fatal.' Looking genuinely distressed, he wiped his hands on one of the cloths and then took Violet's hands in his.

'I will stay a little longer to see if I can help close the wound, and stem the bleeding.'

'Thank you, Doctor,' said Violet. 'That is most kind of you. I am waiting on some herbs that could help. It might all be in vain, but I have to try.'

Shortly thereafter, Benjamin returned clutching the various vials of herbs and potions Violet requested. She busily started to grind them down in the mortar. She then added echinacea oil, garlic and turmeric to the mixture, creating a paste she spread all over the wound. 'Where I come from we used this to stop the bleeding from the slaves' wounds after they had been lashed or injured.' Her explanation was said without rancour. It was a fact of life they lived with every day on the plantations.

The doctor stood back and admired her skills as she mixed the herbs, and applied them to the wound. It was not the way he would have ministered to such an injury, but he was always willing to learn alternative treatments. He knew his training and experience would be of little help.

As Violet worked on her husband's wounds she spoke of the limited supply of medicines they had in the West Indies, how they experimented with different plant, tree and vegetable extracts to find cures to the myriad of diseases afflicting people in the brutal tropical heat. 'The slave owners didn't want to spend money on doctors, but always expected the women to cure the ill slaves to make sure they could get back to work. It is a horrible way to live, Doctor, you cannot imagine what slaves have to put up with, especially if you had a vicious or mean owner. Here in England you are so far away from seeing the horrors of slavery I am surprised to hear there is a stirring voice amongst the Quakers to ban this country's slave trade...not a moment too soon...'

Her knowledge of natural remedies for a wide range of ailments he found fascinating. As she spoke his admiration of her nursing abilities deepened. He found himself in awe of her expertise. Finally, she finished her ministrations and, wiping her hands on a bloodied cloth, she stood back, looking at the wound.

'Once that poultice has dried and hopefully stopped the bleeding I will put on this mixture of clove and goldenseal which will stop the wound becoming full of pus and infection. Is that how you would do it, Doctor?' Violet asked.

'That is not how we have been taught in this country. The normal treatment would be applying carbolic acid. But in my experience it is not always effective. I will be intrigued to see how your salve works. Maybe I can put a few drops of laudanum on his lips now to ease his pain and send him to sleep?'

'Yes, Doctor, please do. It will help my husband through this difficult time. Now, for the moment, I believe there is nothing more we can do but let Nature take its path.' She turned to him, 'I feel the need for something to eat; would you care to join me?' If he was taken aback by her direct invitation, he concealed it. To be invited to stay for lunch, albeit with Benjamin in attendance, and by a black woman at that, seemed a little forward. However, he could see no harm in accepting her offer, and in truth he found her intriguing and her dusky looks, well, attractive.

Careful, he told himself as he looked across the dining table at Violet, she is a married woman, from a different race. No good would come to him if he let his feelings progress beyond a mild fascination.

Chapter 27
(1753)

Violet managed only a few hours' sleep as she stayed by her husband's side, rebandaging his wounds, reapplying the poultices and compresses. Disappointingly they seemed to have little effect. The blood still seeped from his wound, and dribbled from his mouth. A fever developed during the night, and despite her best efforts Jameson's condition was worsening by the hour. The doctor unexpectedly returned early the next day to see if he was improving. Gloomily Violet relayed that her husband had shown little improvement. The doctor examined him and reluctantly agreed with Violet's diagnosis. He administered some more laudanum, 'I am sorry, Violet, but my feeling is your husband will not live much longer. I am bereft of ideas to help him. You have done more than I, however sometimes the task of saving someone is too much no matter how hard you try. You have my sincere condolences. Would it offer him comfort if I ask a priest to visit? It is the least I can do.'

Knowing only too well the doctor was confirming her own fears, Violet disregarded any propriety, leant into him and let the tears flow down her cheeks. He hesitated for a moment, then put his arms around her. Within seconds she was sobbing, huge gasping heaves, her body quavering, with the dreadful realisation that she would soon be a widow, in an unwelcoming and hostile country.

He felt helpless, as he always did when a patient died, and did his best to comfort her.

Jameson died within the hour. By then Violet had accepted the inevitable and started preparations for the funeral. The doctor – she finally learned his name was Timothy – stayed with her. One of the servants went to the Lawshall relatives to inform them of Jameson's passing. Violet, unsure of the procedure in England for the handling and display of deceased bodies, sought the doctor's advice.

'In the West Indies, because of the heat, bodies are often buried the same day as death occurs; how is it done here?' Violet's voice was calm, unemotional. She would mourn properly later. Timothy suggested they wash the body and wrap it in a large cotton sheet. Once done, she called the children to the bedroom and explained that their father had passed away 'to a better place' and they should all pray for his soul, remembering the happy times they had with him. Not quite old enough to fully comprehend the sombre circumstances and the fact they would never see their father again, they did as their mother requested, then left in the company of a young girl servant to look after them.

A few hours later Benjamin, Richard and their families arrived to view the body and pay their respects. They arranged for the funeral to be held two days later at the Independent Chapel just a few doors down from the house. There were few others besides the family at the funeral. Jameson's body was taken back to Lawshall and buried alongside the other members of his extended family.

Violet and the two children returned to the house, to ponder on their future. As a widowed black woman Violet knew her options were limited: Selling the plantation as Jameson intended would make her a rich woman. But would that be enough for a happy life in England? At the age of 29 she saw no likelihood of finding another husband if the attitudes she'd experienced so far were anything to go by. But at least the spectre of slavery was almost unknown here, and maybe in the near future would be banned altogether. Would this make people's attitudes less hostile towards her?

Or she could go back to the West Indies and run the plantation. As a former slave the prospect was unappealing, indeed abhorrent. The final option would be to sell the plantation and use the money to buy a house close by, and be near the few people she knew as friends in that part of the world. But still, on a day-to-day basis, she would see firsthand the degradations of slavery everywhere around her.

Thankfully Jameson brought a substantial sum of money and gold with him to England and on arrival deposited them in a London bank. At least in the short term she and her children wouldn't starve.

While she grieved for the past and planned for the future Violet wanted to ensure the Lawshall relatives were willing to accommodate her staying at the house. She decided to visit them and discuss her future. She presumed Benjamin in particular would be approachable and helpful; Richard, not so much. She hoped her changed circumstances would soften his attitude towards her.

The farm was winding down for the winter. Barns were piled high with hay stalks, sacks of wheat, barley and oats were stacked three high. Most to be sold, some to be kept back for feed and making their own food to see them through the fallow months ahead. Violet had only been to the farm once on a short visit with Jameson. Now she was happy to be taken around the farmyard and buildings, Benjamin clearly delighted to explain how it all worked.

'We have nearly 200 acres of land, mostly down to crops, but we keep enough sheep and cows for our own needs. If they produce too many calves or lambs, then we sell them at Bury market. We lease another fifty acres of woodland for hunting, not that we have much time nowadays,' explained Benjamin.

'How many people work your land?' asked Violet.

'Most of the time it's just me, Richard and maybe two or three others. Harvest time, everyone pitches in and helps each other, then there might be twenty of us. We've bought with two other farmers a winnowing machine that helps us sort the wheat from the chaff so much quicker than by hand, and now we understand more about rotating the crops each season we are getting much better yields...'

'All this land and so few people...and they are all paid for their labours?'

Benjamin laughed, following her thinking, 'Yes, Violet, no slavery here! Everyone gets paid, though I'm sure some would still say it's not enough! Might even claim they are treated like slaves. But no one forces them to do anything they don't want to. A lot different from your plantation?'

'Yes, so different, you have no idea. Slavery is just accepted as the way it should be. Some divine right the white man has over the blacks, to treat them as subhuman, just two-legged workhorses. Expendable when they can no longer do their job. These people working your land have no idea how lucky they are. However, now you have brought up this matter, it is why I have come here today, to seek your advice on what I should do next. The best way forward for me and my children.'

Paul H Rowney

'We will be happy to help you in any way we can! Let's go back for lunch and discuss your future plans,' said Benjamin.

Over a simple meal of mutton, potatoes and home-grown vegetables, Violet outlined, as she saw them, her alternative future paths. Benjamin, she noticed, was still more amenable and friendly towards her than Richard, offering sound advice about each of the options as she explained them. Richard said little, but sat across the table scowling and silent.

'May I ask how much your plantation could be worth?' enquired Richard, finally joining in the conversation.

'I do not know exactly, but I heard Jameson saying to a banker in London that it could be worth in excess of five thousand pounds. But most of the value is in the slaves we own. If I free them all, then the value falls, and I am practically penniless. I am torn between protecting my family's future and not want for money, or follow my conscience, free the slaves, then sell the plantation for a fraction of its worth.'

Richard felt compelled to ask, 'If you freed the slaves, what would become of them?'

'It doesn't happen often, but when it does they normally carry on working at the plantation, and get paid a pittance. They have their freedom, but there is not much they can do with it.'

Richard nodded, but said no more. His silence making it obvious which choice he would make.

After much discussion, all agreed Violet's final decision would not be easily made. All the options had advantages and disadvantages; trying to placate her conscience by freeing the slaves or creating a safe future for her and the two girls was a conundrum that she'd yet to find an answer for.

When she did, it came from a most unexpected quarter.

It was several weeks after Jameson's death that one of Violet's children, Desdemona, became ill. She sent for the doctor. In fact, he had been an occasional visitor, from time to time checking on her wellbeing. Each time he stayed a little longer. Their conversations, initially about medical matters, soon ranged across slavery, politics and the challenges of living in England as a black woman. The doctor found himself drawn to her astute intellect, and her dusky good looks.

One day over a cup of tea, she recounted the day she and her family were captured in Borno, far from the Atlantic coast, and made to walk for two weeks chained together until they reached the port of Ouida. There, she was made to lie next to her parents and brother in a suffocating, filthy hold for three weeks until they reached Jamaica. She was only ten years old at the time and lucky that her entire family were bought by Jameson's father. Violet became a housemaid and within a few years was bedded by the owner. He kept her as a mistress until his wife died.

'And then I was lucky for a second time when Jameson and I fell in love and married. No one was more surprised than I that he was interested in me after being with his-father-in law for so long. However, despite the nasty whispers around the island suggesting I had cast a voodoo spell to make him marry me, we did, way back in...when...1742, I think.'

Timothy sat quietly listening to her rags to riches story, one which had come to a shattering halt with her husband's death a few weeks earlier.

'And now you are here in a small market town in England, what do you plan to do next?'

Violet decided to confide in him her uncertainty over whether to sell the plantation, or not, asking his opinion. Diplomatically he did not try and steer her towards one solution as opposed to another. Ultimately he knew it was her decision alone, although he was happy to be asked, and pointed out some considerations she may have not thought of.

When he arrived to see Desdemona, he found the child with a high fever, and red blotches over her body.

'I think she has smallpox, Violet, we must quarantine her – and you – until she recovers. If you have some herbs that can ease her fever, then I would suggest you use them. I think they might be more effective than anything I can give her.'

'The only one we use in Jamaica is from the pitcher plant. The island's original inhabitants found it was quite useful. I doubt the local apothecary will have it, though. I will use ginger and chamomile and see if that helps.'

He stood up from beside the sick girl's bed, and without thinking took Violet's hands in his. 'Try not to worry. She is young and strong. The pox is not the death sentence it once was. I will leave at once to see what I can find that will help her.'

By the time Timothy returned two days later, Desdemona was sitting up in bed, her fever abated and her skin almost devoid of the ugly red pustules.

'I see the patient is making a full recovery; that is wonderful news. I must investigate further this whole business of innoculation, it seems to be offering great hope against the evils of this disease.'

'It was kind of you to go to so much trouble.' said Violet. 'By way of a thank you, would you be acceptable to have dinner with me this evening?' She added hastily, 'The servants will be here too, of course, should you be concerned about any...any lack of decorum.'

Smiling, he answered, 'You owe me nothing, but I would be delighted to join you for dinner. I shall go home and change and be back here at...?"

'Shall we say seven o'clock?' suggested Violet.

'I look forward to seeing you then.' Timothy closed the front door and walked jauntily down Whiting St. He tried his best to control the huge smile spreading across his face.

The dinner was a kaleidoscope of tastes that Timothy found intoxicating. Somehow Violet obtained herbs and spices which turned the meat and vegetable dishes into exotic delights the like of which he had not seen nor tasted before. Along with a bottle of locally made wine bought as his contribution, the evening was a delight. She continued to amaze him with stories of life on the plantation, her education under the auspices of her husband – who demanded she become as well read as any white woman, of any rank – and her less savoury experiences in London, where a black woman married to a white man was greeted with shock and disdain.

'I fear it will be a long time before such a marriage is accepted in this country,' Violet said, a note of sadness in her voice. 'Though I heard the local Quakers have invited Ignatius Sancho to talk at their church here in a few weeks. I shall certainly go and listen to him; he has become a leader in the abolitionist movement in England. Maybe he can broaden a few narrow minds in this town!'

Timothy thought it wise to offer some words of caution: 'Violet, I know you are not a woman to follow convention, but there is generally a period of mourning a widow endures before being seen in public again. Also are you sure you want to be seen in the company of Quakers and...well...revolutionaries, some might call this...Ignatius man?'

'Bah! I am a pariah anyway in this society, so why should I worry, or keep to their norms? I care not what they think, as they care not for what I feel. As for Ignatius, he is a man of the highest probity and deserves all the support he can get to end this ghastly era of slavery. I hope he stirs up the people of Bury; they are too comfortable in their ignorance of this issue. They need to know the truth. I hope he drowns them in it!'

'OK, I see I shall now have to call you Violet the Firebrand!' said Timothy, grinning. 'Jesting aside, I for one would never stop you from doing what you feel is right, and I concur with your belief that the people of Bury should be enlightened about slavery. If you'll permit me, I would love to accompany you to this meeting.'

The audience was small, but attentive, and they listened to the diminutive Ignatius Sancho thump the pulpit as he delivered his message. A former slave, who was brought to England when he was eighteen, he ran away and was lucky enough to be employed as a butler by the Duke of Montagu, who educated him, eventually allowing him to leave and start his own business in London. Now he could talk freely about the need to abolish slavery. He quickly became a spokesman for the movement and spent a lot of his time travelling the country pressing the need for slavery and the slave trade to be abolished.

His words resonated with Violet as he implored the audience:

'In Africa, the poor wretched natives blessed with the most fertile and luxuriant soil – are rendered so much the more miserable for what Providence meant as a blessing: the Christians' abominable traffic for slaves and the horrid cruelty and treachery of the petty Kings encouraged by their Christian customers who carry them strong liquors to enflame their national madness – and powder – and bad fire-arms – to furnish them with the hellish means of killing and kidnapping. This must stop!'

She had been thrilled when Ignatius at the end of his speech made his way through the crowd to meet her. As the only other black person in the room, he was anxious to hear her story. On a whim she suggested he come to the house for refreshments that evening, to which he'd readily agreed.

'Did you not find his words so inspiring?' asked Violet as they walked back from the Quaker meeting hall, 'I cannot wait to talk further this evening...you will stay I hope?'

He was finding it difficult to say no to Violet. Aware he was becoming embroiled in matters about which he knew little, but could affect his reputation with the townsfolk, and his patients, his caution weakened each time he spent time with this strong-willed woman. She seemed determined to take on the world, no matter the consequences. Even by associating with her, he knew he could find himself ostracised from the very community that was the source of his livelihood. Despite these persistent concerns, he was drawn to her like a moth to a flame; he just hoped this deepening friendship would not prove fatal to his reputation.

Ignatius kept both of them spellbound with his story of being born on a slave ship, sold into slavery in New Granada, then brought to London, escaping bondage to the house of Montagu. He was now a successful shopkeeper and landowner, allowing him the rare privilege as a black man of being able to vote – the first in England to do so.

'But that is just the start, Violet, us free black people must fight for abolition with every breath in our body. We owe it to the thousands of our kin still chained to the anvil of slavery in the Americas.'

Does this man ever stop preaching? wondered Timothy as they sipped on a glass of port in front of the warming fire in the great hall. Violet soaked up Ignatius's rhetoric like a sponge, sitting entranced, hanging on his every word, peppering him with questions about how the abolition movement could persuade more people that slavery was an abomination that must be stopped.

'We can only do so much, Violet, but whatever it is, we cannot falter in our quest. Too many lives are at stake for us to say the path to abolition is too difficult or dangerous. People like you and me – freed slaves – and the increasingly powerful voice of the Quakers, are duty bound to fight this obscenity with vigour and persistence. We will win in the end, but when that will be, I cannot say.'

His words even pricked Timothy's conscience, and he could see Violet was fired up ready to join the cause. By the end of the evening Violet knew what she should do; a plan of action for her future was forming in her mind. She was excited, yet fearful for what it might transpire.

It was late by the time Ignatius left. Both were tired yet invigorated by the energy from the evening's discourse. Before he could say his goodbyes, Violet came up to him, wrapped her arms behind his neck and pulled him into a long, delicate, probing kiss. She whispered in his ear, 'Will you stay with me tonight?'

He pulled back, looked into her large soulful eyes, an expectant smile on her face. Her skin in the shadow cast by the fire was a lustrous mahogany. She was the most alluring, sensual woman he'd ever met. Her dark colour only made her more irresistible to him. He knew he should leave; the consequences of staying were too unsettling to even consider, yet, yet he also knew the woman standing in front of him was unlike any he'd known. There were a hundred reasons to say no to her invitation, but he couldn't.

'You hesitate, Timothy, have I misjudged your feelings?

'No, no, not all, just...what will people say?'

'I wasn't intending making a public display of it!' she grinned. 'Is it because I am black? Be honest with me.'

'No, no, not at all...I find you irresistible.'

'Timothy, you are still hesitating. Can I ask...have you bedded a white woman?'

'Well, just one...'

'I can assure you we are all formed in the same way! God merely changed our skin colour, nothing else!'

It was his turn to grin. 'Yes, I guessed that much!'

'So are you staying or leaving? I am close to changing my mind.'

'Yes, of course I'll stay, I have dreamt of this moment for weeks. I was never sure how I would react if it ever came to pass, but now I know I want you more than ever. More than anyone.'

She was uninhibited, at times wild, in her lovemaking. Caring little about displaying her lithe naked body, she disrobed quickly and lay on the bed as he fumbled out of his clothes. 'Are you going to keep me waiting much longer?' she teased him as he struggled to unbuckle his shoes. 'I shall start without you...' she said, putting her slender hand between her legs, moving it in a suggestive, stroking motion.

He lay down beside her, and quickly decided he would abandon himself to her experienced, uninhibited behaviour, which promised a night of sensual delights the likes of which he'd never known. Her hands and lips roamed over his body, exploring, teasing and arousing him. Within an embarrassingly brief time his release came. But she seemed unfazed, whispering, 'Don't worry, it will be but a few minutes before you are ready for me to take my pleasure...'

Her hands resumed their stroking, probing and caressing over every inch of his body; her mouth licking, kissing him in places that made him cry out in pleasure, soon made him desperate for her. She pushed him back, and in one fluid movement straddled and consumed him, their hips quickly rising and falling in unison. She soon started moaning, panting, her breath quickening. She leant forward, hands either side of his head, her breasts swinging just inches from his face. He moved his lips to her nipples, and that was all it took for her to lose control and reach her peak, crying out in ecstasy, then collapsing exhausted onto his chest. As she did so the last movements of her hips caused him to shudder to a climax again.

'Violet...'

'My love, please, say nothing, nothing at all. Just let me float in this sublime moment of pleasure, in peace, something I have not experienced in a long time...'

After minutes of silence she spoke wistfully, not in anger, 'Why is it white men so often revile black women, insult us, yet so many want to bed us? They call us animals, yet seem willing to use our bodies for their satisfaction; doesn't that make them animals too?'

He thought for a few moments before replying, 'I cannot begin to comprehend the degradations and indignities you and your kind have suffered for so long. I only hope the time will come soon when we can start making right the wrongs you have endured. I will do all I can to make that happen for you.' He leant over and kissed her.

'Mmmm, well, before we start that crusade, I feel the need for some more...of you.'

'I am not sure I am quite yet ready for a repeat performance,' replied Timothy, glancing down.

'There are other ways to pleasure me...your mouth and tongue seem to be working well...She gently pushed his head towards her thighs.

'Oh! You want me to...to?'

'Yes, my lover, that's exactly what I wish you to do, women love it when a man uses his tongue...'

'But I must be honest and say I have never done this before.'

'In that case I will enjoy it while you learn. Remember the saying 'practice makes perfect'? I am sure you will get the idea very quickly, but not too quickly...'

The following day Violet decided what to do about the plantation, and her future. She sat down with Timothy to explain her plans.

'While I would be lying if I denied what happened last night has affected my thinking, in truth my mind was made up some days ago. I will sell the plantation, with the stipulation the new owner grants manumission to all the slaves, and offers them paid jobs. Most will stay, they have little opportunity to go elsewhere. I know it will reduce the value of the plantation by a considerable amount. But I believe slavery's hold on my people is being weakened by the day. Soon the English plantation owners will have no choice but to free their slaves. I hope a new owner will see this, and accept my terms – for all our sake.'

Yet again, he was awed by her willingness to sacrifice herself for the benefit of others. It was a huge risk which at worst could leave her destitute – black women could find little employment except as servants or maids. Though it was one she was prepared to take.

'I think what you are planning is admirable and a selfless act, my dearest. However have you considered the consequences if the sale fails to produce enough money to secure an income for you and your daughters?'

'I have, and I will worry about that at the time. I am resourceful and hardworking, I will always find a way to make ends meet.'

Timothy said nothing for some moments, then to Violet's astonishment he bent down on one knee and took her left hand in his, 'My darling, you are the most amazing woman I have ever met, indeed I am sure will ever meet. Will you do the honour of marrying me?'

The next few months were a whirl of activity. The marriage was planned for March. The Lawshall relatives, after their initial consternation at the news, were delighted for the couple, and as a wedding present suggested they stay rent-free for a year at the house.

The wedding took place in the Quaker meeting hall in St John's St. Aside from Richard and Benjamin, and their families, Timothy's cousin Elias attended with his young family, making the long trip from Ireland for the celebrations. Various Quaker friends swelled the congregation to nearly fifty people.

No mention of the wedding was reported in the The Suffolk Mercury newspaper.

Initially some of Timothy's patients moved to other doctors, but most found his advice and medical knowledge more important than his choice of wife. Indeed some found his newfound remedies (courtesy of Violet) highly effective against their illnesses and injuries.

In mid-June they received news from their solicitor in London that the sale of the plantation had been completed. All Violet's requirements would be met by the new owner. The price paid was £3000, just over half its worth than if it had been sold with all the slaves in bondage.

Financially secure, Violet threw herself into the abolitionist movement, giving lectures and talks across the country, revealing to horrified audiences the truth about life as a slave, especially a female one. On several occasions she joined Ignatius Sancho as he forced the issue of slavery into the public eye and the political arena.

She met regularly with Members of Parliament including local MP Augustus Henry, to press the case for abolition. She wrote countless articles for newspapers pressing her case for the abolition of slavery. She met Olaudah Equiano, who came to England after purchasing his freedom in America. Equiano helped organise a group of black Londoners known as the Sons of Africa to campaign for abolition. Of particular resonance to Violet was his belief in the idea of interracial marriage, which he argued 'would eliminate colour barriers and inspire racial harmony'.

Violet was indefatigable in her efforts, though she did admit to Timothy one day that, 'Winning over people on this issue is like pushing a large stone uphill, no sooner do I think I have reached the top than it slips from my hands and tumbles back to where I started.'

'Violet, you and I know that it will be many years before all aspects of slavery will be abolished in this country. It has been a profitable business for too many people, for too long, for it to change overnight. I am sure your persistence will pay off, but I believe it will be later rather than sooner.'

'I know, I know, it is just I am impatient for change; too many people are still living lives of untold misery until we abolish this terrible trade in human beings.'

Even falling pregnant and producing a son did not stop her crusade. However, after staying in Bury for five more years, she felt her work would be more effective in London, the English centre of slave trading.

They left Bury in the summer of 1758. The house was used intermittently thereafter by its owners in Lawshall, often lying empty for weeks at a time. In 1760 Richard and Benjamin decided it was best to sell the house before it needed more money spent on it.

Before they could complete the sale, unbeknownst to them an intruder on a cold November evening decided to break in and light a fire to keep warm. The chimney, unswept and blocked with leaves, caught on fire. The great hall and the rooms above it were severely damaged before neighbours extinguished the flames. Faced with a huge bill for repairs, the house was sold for a fraction of its worth to a local builder.

(In 1807, Parliament passed the Slave Trade Act, which outlawed the international slave trade, but not slavery itself. In 1823, the Anti-Slavery Society was founded in London and pushed for The Slavery Abolition Act, which became law on 22 July 1833, just a week before William Wilberforce, the man famous for his anti-slavery activities, died.

The Act provided for payments to slave owners as reparation. The amount of money was set at £20m (approximately £3.8bn at 2024 values). Under the terms of the Act, the money was to pay out for the loss of the slaves as business assets to their registered owners. Half of the money went to slave-owning families in the Caribbean and Africa, while the other half went to absentee owners living in Britain.)

Chapter 28
(1760s)

By the 1760s Bury St Edmunds, with a population of 7200, was expanding in all directions away from the original grid of streets. To make way for new buildings and to improve the flow of traffic the medieval gates on the east, west, south and north of the town were all demolished. The need to defend the town was no longer of concern.

Though it was not the largest town in East Anglia. By comparison Ipswich's population was 10,000, Norwich's 30,000 and Colchester's 10,000 (the original capital of England under the Romans). London dwarfed them all with 575,000 inhabitants.

The wool industry, and the myriad of associated activities surrounding it, was still the main employer in the county, but much reduced compared to previous decades. Bury was no longer the important commercial centre it once was, compared to 200 years earlier.

In 1766 silks and velvet imports were banned into Great Britain. This saw a revival in the town's fortunes, as the skills needed to make these cloths were already available. And with improved communications, convenient for London's markets. This was a short-lived boon as the demand for silk products would never provide the amount of employment that the declining woollen industry had in its heyday.

Increasingly, farming became a major industry and employer, as it became more intensive and productive. In an area to the north of the town called the Woodlands, or High Suffolk, dairy cattle became important for their milk production. Daniel Defoe had written that Suffolk made 'the best butter and perhaps the worst cheese in England.'

By 1765, another brewery opened in St Mary's Square, opposite Wright's Brewery. By the end of the century Greene King would be founded and Bury become a centre for a prosperous and long lasting brewing industry.

Communication to London and other major cities was improved by the introduction of turnpikes on all the major routes out of the town. These roads increased the speeds at which coaches could travel, particularly to London. Many coach services now offered a Bury to London trip completed in just one day (a distance of over 80 miles).

In the town, Whiting St and the likes of Guildhall, College, Hatter and Churchgate Streets still attracted those looking for larger houses within walking distance of the town centre and the twice-weekly market. Some houses succumbed to the fashion of putting Georgian brick or stone frontages onto the original medieval building. With their distinctive large windows uniformly spaced with the front door precisely in the centre, they attracted wealthy residents keen to follow the latest architectural fashion.

Bury was changing with the times, but at heart it was still a medieval town – the majority of the buildings in the centre survived from the mid and late 1400s. Soon the Industrial Revolution would impact the town with new industries, technologies and rapid changes in lifestyles, especially for the wealthy.

Chapter 29
(1766)

Henry Steward went to bed early; the bitter cold March evening was too much for even the roaring fire in the great hall to dispel. The bedroom was even colder, though his bed had the damp chill taken off it by the warming pan his servant Mary left between the blankets.

An auctioneer, or 'broker', Henry became wealthy by disposing of land, goods and chattels through his monthly auctions. He'd purchased the house from the builder who spent two years renovating it following the devastating fire that burnt the middle of the house down to the ground. It was a fortuitous coincidence; the builder approached him to auction the house, only for Henry to buy it for himself. Since then he'd spent lavishly on furnishings, wall hangings and rugs to reflect his newfound prosperity. The house boasted a fresh coat of white whitewash, and a Castrol oven, which allowed the fire in the oven to be completely contained and reduced smoke and heat from escaping – and lessened the likelihood of another fire.

Currently a widower after his wife died two years earlier giving birth to their first child, who sadly did not reach his fifth birthday, Henry now lived alone with just two servants, Mary and Jonathan. Mary was a comely girl, just seventeen years old, but willing to share his bed on occasions in return for an extra shilling or two in her weekly wage packet. He had met her while selling off the estate of her recently deceased father, and took her into his employ, deciding to sack the incumbent, Elizabeth Burroughs (who was, as it happened, older and not so...accommodating).

Little did he realise these actions would lead to a terrible tragedy.

This particular evening Mary was sleeping in the servants' quarters behind the huge parlour with the warmth from the oven radiating through the wall. It took the worst of the chill off the room, though she could still see her breath as she lay down on her straw bedding. Even her pet dog, Millie, snuggling up by her feet, failed to get her warm enough to fall asleep quickly.

Suddenly Millie growled; she'd heard something outside in the rear garden. Someone had knocked over a metal pail. Seconds later Mary heard the window in the buttery at the back of the house pushed open. The sash weights banged inside the window frame – someone was breaking into the house!

Millie ran into the buttery barking, and Mary followed, grabbing a large copper saucepan with which to defend herself. It was dark except for one candle, permanently left alight by the back door. In the gloom, Mary saw someone running towards her and before she could lift a hand to defend herself, let alone hit the intruder with her makeshift weapon, she felt a stab of pain as her head was hit hard by some metal instrument. Crying in pain, she fell to the ground clutching her head, feeling the blood starting to seep between her fingers.

The noise made by Millie's barking woke Henry, who ran from his bedroom at the other end of the house to see what was causing the disturbance. Where was that boy Jonathan when you needed him, thought Henry, as he raced across the great hall towards the dog's incessant barking – quickly remembering the boy had gone to see his parents for a few days.

As he entered the parlour, his candle partially illuminated a hooded woman hitting Mary with a hammer as she lay on the ground.

'Stop this! Now!' bellowed Henry. The intruder stopped and looked at him. For a moment Henry thought he recognised her, but the light was inadequate to see properly.

'You scheming bastard! You think she's better than me?' screamed the woman. 'You'll be the next to die!' She lifted the hammer above her head and rushed towards Henry. With no way of defending himself he put his arm before his face. He felt a sharp pain as the hammer smashed into his shoulder. He stumbled back towards the door, falling to his knees. His assailant, satisfied for the moment she had seen him off, turned back to Mary, who was struggling to stand up, and raised the hammer again...

Henry, who many would later accuse of cowardice, made no attempt to stop the intruder and, instead, ran out into the street to try and find help. At that hour, however, there was no one around. By the time he reached the courts, roused a sleeping constable and both returned to the house, the burglar had left and Mary lay bleeding on the floor, wounds she would not recover from. By morning she was dead.

A burglary that turned into a murder was a rare occurrence in Bury, so the full complement of constables and law officers were soon searching for the perpetrator. Henry told them what the woman shouted at him, adding while he couldn't see her face, she did sound familiar. He assured the constables he would do his damnedest to recollect where he might have heard that woman's voice before.

But not all the constables believed Henry's story. 'Women murders are as rare as hens' teeth; what could the victim have done to deserve such an attack?' said Senior Constable Whithers to Judge Heartsone as they reviewed the progress of the case a few days later. He added, 'The fact the man ran away while his servant was attacked, and we could find no evidence of damage done by someone forcing their way into the house, is, shall we say, curious?'

'Possibly, Constable, however we mustn't jump to conclusions...And the hammer was found in the parlour?' asked the judge.

'Yes, so it is possible they fought over something, about which we do not currently know, and Mr Steward killed her. It would not be the first time a master disposed of a woman in his employ, especially when, according to the other servant, she was a regular visitor to his bed?'

'Though why would he do the deed in his own house, then come to us to report it?' pondered the judge.

'True, that is a risky way to try and place the blame on someone else. Let us see if he remembers who the assailant might be, and if we find her, hopefully the truth will come out.'

'A sound course of action, Constable, keep me informed of your progress. We need to conclude this matter as soon as possible.' The judge dismissed the lawman with a wave of his hand. Despite the constable's scepticism, he couldn't accept that a successful and wealthy businessman would resort to such violence. Henry, he knew, was an honourable man, and he hoped the matter would be resolved in his favour.

Later that day, Henry finally thought he recognised the voice of the female attacker. He made haste to see the constable with his revelation. Just two days later a woman by the name of Elizabeth Burroughs was brought before the judge. The woman, he learnt, was previously employed by Henry as a servant but, so she believed, had been thrown out in favour of the younger Mary. According to the constable who questioned her, she was jealous enough to want to take Mary's life. In addition, Elizabeth knew the layout of the house and that the rear window was never locked, a perfect way to gain entry without breaking anything. Furthermore she could find no one to vouch for her whereabouts at the time of the murder.

In her defence she claimed to know nothing of Mary's death and accused Henry of the crime, saying that Mary was with child by him, something he did not wish to be made public.

The judge was unsure about the innocence, or guilt, of Elizabeth or Henry. Both had reason to wish Mary harm, especially if she was indeed pregnant. But to go as far as murdering her? Neither seemed capable of such a deed. He decided that both should be put on trial, and let another judge decide the outcome.

On March 25th the trial began. Normally it was a day-long exercise which involved a confrontation between the prosecutor and, if alive, the victim. With no victim it turned into a straightforward argument between the prosecutor and the defendants. It quickly became clear Henry was not involved in Mary's murder. There was no evidence against him.

That left Elizabeth to face the prosecutor alone. It was an uneven match, an experienced lawyer against an illiterate woman. Who, with no adequate alibi, and Henry's dubious claim he recognised her voice, stood little chance of persuading the judge she was innocent, despite repeatedly claiming that was the case.

Justice was swift, uncompromising and some would say arbitrary. Elizabeth Burroughs was found guilty and sentenced to hang. On the scaffold she maintained her innocence; her last words were, 'I know a lie will avail me nothing; I am innocent of the murder for which I suffer at the hangman.' She was executed on April 4th, 1763.

The Suffolk Mercury reporting on the case described her as 'a cold blooded murderer, driven to the edge of insanity by envy and jealousy'.

But was she innocent? Confusingly, four years later, in 1767, a wool comber in the town, called Samuel Otley, confessed to the murder of Mary Booty, but his claim was dismissed, as he was found to be insane. It transpired that Henry Steward allegedly refused to pay him for some goods sold on his behalf. Enraged at what he saw as an act of thievery he claimed he entered the house, after one too many drinks, with a view to confronting Henry and demanding his money. Mary Booty tried to stop him, and in a drunken fury he bludgeoned her to death. By the time he 'confessed' to the murder, years of drink had reduced him to an addled pauper, and no one took him seriously.

Henry's business continued to prosper. He became the leading auctioneer in the town, the commissions he charged generating a healthy income. Though he was always quick (too quick, his detractors would say) to buy a plot of land, or a valuable household item at less than market value prior to the auction, promising the seller that at least he was avoiding the risk of no one bidding on it.

He expanded to Newmarket, Ipswich and Cambridge, selling anything from furniture to cattle, horses to houses. But as his wealth grew, so did his reputation as a man who would soon as swindle you for a 'penny if he couldn't for a pound.'

Now in his forties, portly, with a ruddy complexion, and a pronounced limp due to gout, he confided to a his new business acquaintance one evening over a fine glass of Madeira, that 'I wish to be married again, and have some children to inherit my legacy. Despite my age I feel I have much to offer a young woman.' Without a tinge of modesty, he continued, 'She will want for nothing and be left very rich when I die.' His drinking companion, Kevin de Bragg, was a struggling wool trader who found Henry only too willing to sell goods on his behalf without asking too many questions as to how he'd obtained them. Auctions, Kevin soon found, were a quick and anonymous way to cash in on 'unwanted' household items. And he always seemed to have plenty of them, and Henry was happy to help dispose of them. It was a mutually satisfactory, if verging on a dishonest, arrangement.

Never one to miss an opportunity, he quickly calculated that Henry's search for a wife could be a way to procure himself a handsome sum of money. He knew a likely match. Charlotte, at age twenty, might appeal to this middle-aged widower. Keen to move up in the world and make money, she would see the potential of this plan as much as he did. Simply, with her wed to an ageing, sickly husband, upon his passing they could all share the wealth he left behind.

'Henry, if I may be so bold, I think my, er, sister, Charlotte might be worthy of your interest as a possible wife? She is comely, well read, an excellent cook, and is wonderful with children, so I am told! I would be the first to say she is no oil painting, the pox has left her face with scars. But she is excellent company and of an age to settle down and produce you some fine heirs.'

Grateful for Kevin's suggestion, and lacking the will to actively seek a potential wife himself, he agreed to meet Charlotte. After all, he thought, *I am of an age when I cannot be too fussy about the attractions a wife should have, despite my wealth.* Her ability to produce children was his main concern, the female servants were more than willing to service his other needs. But he wanted a child in wedlock to avoid any problems with his estate once he died. Henry didn't think he was being maudlin, just practical. A lifetime of hard work had left little time for pleasure. Now, he decided, his last few years should be spent in the company of a fine young woman and a brood of children, one of whom would inherit his fortune and good name.

All went to plan for both Henry and Kevin. Charlotte proved to be an attentive and considerate young lady, interested in everything Henry had to say, and remarkably well versed in the value and appeal of the myriad of items Henry stockpiled in his warehouse prior to an auction. A useful skill, Henry assumed, acquired through her association with her brother Kevin. Within weeks Henry decided Charlotte should become his wife. He was surprised, but acquiesced, when she told him a quiet wedding with just a few relatives in attendance was her preference. Henry agreed it would cost less money, a positive start to a marriage!

And so on August 14th 1770 they were married in front of just six people.

Quickly Charlotte became an indispensable part of Henry's auction house, from acquiring and listing the ever-increasing number of items to be sold at each auction to managing the finances. Henry was thrilled to have someone who wanted to learn every aspect of his business, helping it grow and prosper.

Kevin de Bragg became an almost daily visitor to their house, or to Henry's offices, paying at times, Henry thought, too close attention to Charlotte. He frequently brought along two young children that she seemed particularly fond of, introducing them as his nieces.

However, to Henry's frustration, she seemed incapable of becoming with child. Notwithstanding her willingness to suffer his frequent attempts to impregnate her, nothing happened. Henry was growing concerned at the lack of an heir.

'Charlotte, I know it is not me that is failing to make you pregnant, I had a son several years ago – do you know of any reason why you are not conceiving?'

She looked contrite, 'I do not, husband. I have been taking potions but they have not worked. I shall go to the apothecary and see if they can suggest something that would help me conceive.'

The weeks turned to months, and by 1773, no child was conceived, Henry was becoming a worried man. That September he held one of his biggest auctions of the year. Land and buildings were on the block; if they sold for good prices, Henry's commission would be substantial.

Dressed in his smartest business attire, Charlotte at his side, they departed for the first day of the auction at Great Barton. In the carriage was a trunk full of papers, deeds and legal documents. Henry was excited; he loved the thrill of the auction, watching the bids go higher, mentally calculating his earnings. The smack of the wooden gavel down on his portable desk at another successful sale was most gratifying. The fact that fourteen acres sold that day for the astronomic price of £240 meant he was in the right place at the right time. Nowadays, due to his gout, Henry sat some of the time, and occasionally, for the less important items, let Charlotte conduct the bidding, a novelty that did no harm to his reputation as an innovative and successful businessman. Indeed he became convinced some bidders overpaid just to try and impress Charlotte with their deep pockets. No matter, it was all about the money for Henry, and he was making more than he could spend.

But still no sign of an heir. His libido now declining as his age and health took its toll, he knew the chances were decreasing of him having an heir. Every month that Charlotte failed to fall pregnant was an increasing worry. Finally he decided to confront her as they sat finishing supper one evening. He dismissed the two servants; it was not a conversation he wished them to hear. Trying to sound as reasonable as possible, he suggested: 'Charlotte, for three years we have been trying for a child, with no success. I am not getting any younger. If you are unable to start a family for us, then maybe we should look to adopt a child in some way. I know it is uncommon, however I believe we can go through some legal process that would make the child ours in the eyes of the law. What do you think?'

Trying to conceal her dislike of the idea, she shot back, 'Husband, I do not know why I have not become with child, but bringing a strange child into the house, whose parents' characters we know nothing of, may cause us problems. We are in danger of inheriting a child who could turn out to be of poor breeding, or unsound mind. I think it is an unwise move. Let us try for a little longer the...normal way?' Deploying her most accommodating smile, she added, 'Maybe we could try again...now?'

Standing up from the table, Henry grunted in pain. 'It was a suggestion to solve our predicament, one I am not inclined to set aside for the moment. I will investigate in more detail what is involved. Ahem, your offer is an attractive one, my darling wife, but I feel I am not up to the task tonight, my legs are giving me some gyp. I doubt I can make it up the stairs unaided, let alone...perform...perhaps tomorrow?'

'Of course, Henry. I am always, as you know, happy to oblige whenever you feel well enough,' said Charlotte, knowing full well time was running out for Henry and his ability to impregnate her.

She looked at her decrepit husband as he hobbled across the room, grateful she didn't have to stomach another hasty, unsatisfying coupling with his flabby body. Enough was enough, she decided, a conversation with Kevin de Bragg was needed, and quickly; this charade must come to an end soon.

Next day she walked with Kevin and the two children in the abbey grounds. 'I cannot continue with this sham any longer. Despite the herbs I am taking and other measures to stop me conceiving, there is always a danger I could become with child. If that happens, we know who he will leave his money and business to and it won't be me, or us.'

'Do you know if he has a will?' asked Kevin.

'Yes, I have seen it, he has not changed it in several years. He is so disorganised with his paperwork that, as it stands, his sister is the one who will inherit almost everything, with a lot of money going to the poorhouse as well. I fear if I push him to change it he may become suspicious; as his wife I should inherit everything, but it will not happen.'

'How...how ill is he, do you think?' asked Kevin.

'He is not a healthy man, though I would not say he is at death's door. Henry's gout causes him pain and makes him shaky on his legs. I, or one of the servants, normally have to help him up or down the stairs. In spite of that he still drinks too much Madeira.'

Does he now? thought Kevin, a plan forming in his mind that might finally see them getting their hands on Henry's wealth, or alternatively, he had to admit, at the end of a hangman's noose. However, with careful thought, and a little luck, after three years of patiently waiting for Henry's windfall maybe they could hasten his demise and make it happen sooner rather than later?

Chapter 28. The sale of Charlotte

Henry knew he was in poor health. He had to do something to produce an heir. It became a fixation, a desperate urge to leave a legacy, a living monument to his success. As the months went by with Charlotte's apparent barrenness making her unable to produce him any children, he was at first upset, then his suspicions arose. The close friendship with Kevin and his two children, with the little girl looking at times remarkably like Charlotte, piqued Henry's interest: Her curly blonde hair, blue eyes, close together over an aquiline nose, were physical coincidences with his wife he found difficult to ignore. He believed she might be the mother of this child and therefore capable of producing him an heir. If that was the case why had she not done so?

Further enquiries among his network of friends and business acquaintances across the county unearthed some worrying information about Charlotte, Kevin and the children. He began to suspect he was the target of some nefarious scheme, but until he discovered more, Henry said nothing, hoping to be proved wrong, and that a baby would quell his doubts about Charlotte's intentions. To avoid arousing their suspicions he played along as he waited for their next move to finally reveal itself. He purposefully told her of his will, with the inheritance going to a distant sister living in London – well away from their influence. Now it was a waiting game.

Charlotte, too, began to feel Henry might be wising up to her duplicity. However, she could do little to ensure he made a new will in her favour and, until he did so, she had to keep him in good health, and acquiesce to his unpalatable bedroom antics as he tried to make her pregnant. Charlotte knew she needed to safeguard their marriage – divorce was extremely expensive and required agreement from Parliament, but Henry's insistence on an heir, and her unwillingness to produce one, might push him to that path of action. He could afford it, she knew.

Which meant Kevin's plan for an 'accident' that could result in Henry's early demise, was discussed at length by them but put on hold – until the will was rewritten in Charlotte's favour, it was a pointless endeavour. His alternative plan was to forge a new will in which Charlotte received all Henry's estate.

'After all, Charlotte, you know his form of words, the way he writes, you could do a passable version of a new will surely,' argued Kevin.

'I could, but his current will was written and witnessed by a local Lawyer. To make it look genuine, we would have to forge something in the lawyer's name too, and that would be a risk I am unwilling to take,' said Charlotte, adding, 'If we are caught in this misdeed, we will be transported or even hung, and these poor children will be in the workhouse. There has to be another way, though as yet the idea has not come to me.'

With both sides becoming frustrated that their respective plans were not coming to fruition, it was only a matter of time before one of them broke the impasse.

Henry, on advice from an old friend, decided to take a course of action rarely seen in Bury, indeed anywhere. His wife, unable (or unwilling) to produce an heir meant, quite simply, she had to be replaced. His plan was unorthodox, and risky, but he saw no other course of action. Divorce was expensive and, for the moment, that was a second option. No, he had checked it out, and his unusual approach to solving the problem could actually make him some money.

One morning, over breakfast he announced to Charlotte he intended to auction her to any other man who could offer him a decent sum of money. If she didn't agree, he would go through with a divorce, no matter how long it took, or the cost. By auctioning her, the matter would be over quickly – and they would be out of each other's lives forever. Conveniently, he would run the auction for her alongside his next big sale taking place in Bury four weeks hence.

Charlotte was aghast at his suggestion. 'You are going to auction me off like an old horse? How can you treat me thus? It is demeaning...what have I done to deserve this belittling treatment?'

'Do I need to spell out your deceitful behaviour, Charlotte?' Henry sighed, calm in the face of his wife's fury and indignation. 'You have deliberately avoided becoming with child by taking some concoction of herbs...ones I discovered some months ago. Is that not the case?' He continued without waiting for her response. 'I have discovered that you are, in fact, Kevin's lover and the children yours out of wedlock – my investigations into the parish records of Haverhill revealed as much. You have been embezzling money from the business, I assume to give to your other family? So you are a harlot and a thief. A crime punishable by a year in gaol, or even transportation to the Americas, I believe. Shall I continue?'

Speechless for some moments, Charlotte spat back, 'And what of your nefarious and underhand business dealings I have discovered while working with you? How would you like those to become public, Henry?'

'Indeed you are right, some of my activities might be regarded as less than honourable. So could the same be said for your lover's thievery and criminal activities. Did you not think I would notice his never-ending stream of items he sends for sale at my auctions? I have kept a separate set of books listing such pieces. I am sure the owners would love to know what happened to the items stolen from them. I am happy to hand this over to the justices, most of whom are very good friends of mine.'

The message was clear to Charlotte: Either concur with his bizarre plan, or risk shame as she was unmasked as a harlot and fraudster. She shuddered at the thought of being publicly humiliated as she was auctioned off like some old heifer. However, years in goal, or transportation overseas, and never seeing her children again was an even worse fate. She said no more, resigned to her fate.

'As you know the next auction is in four weeks' time. I will start publicising you will be one of the lots; to give you credit, I'll list you as the main attraction. I can see this being one of my most popular auctions yet! Henry smiled at the prospect. 'No doubt you wish to tell Kevin of the position you – and he – now find yourselves in. My guess, he will be the main bidder. I hope he has suitable funds at his disposal, I can see other men taking a great interest in buying you.' Henry could barely keep the delight out of his voice.

'I will get the papers prepared for you to sign agreeing to this transaction. Oh, and by the way, you will stay here with your children until the auction. Do not attempt to run away, it will do you no good. If I have to send the constables after you, I will. You may send a note to Kevin informing him of this latest turn of events. That is the only contact you will have with him.'

Her stomach twisted in knots, all Charlotte could do was nod her assent, then climb the stairs to her bedroom. Henry's voice interrupted her progress: 'I think not, Charlotte, you – and your children – will remain in one of the servants' rooms until I say otherwise.'

Charlotte, through tear-filled eyes, stumbled back across the great hall, into the parlour and up to the far from commodious servants' quarters. Her carefully laid plans in tatters, her future out of her control, with the prospect of gaol if she did not go along with Henry's outlandish scheme. She wrote a brief note to Kevin explaining that all their plans had come to nought, and he should bring the children to the house. She then cried herself to sleep.

Henry had previously checked on the legitimacy of selling a wife via auction, and though not a common practice, it was by no means unique. He discovered a woman in Cambridge last year was sold by her husband when he discovered her adultery. Ironically her lover was unable to pay enough to secure her at the sale, and she ended up living with an elderly pig farmer. How appropriate, Henry smiled to himself, if something similar happened to Charlotte.

Courtesy of a large advertisement in the Ipswich Journal, and Bury Post plus flyers distributed throughout the county in the preceding weeks, the auction created the clamour of interest Henry hoped for. Charlotte and Kevin's pleas for him to stop the auction and seek some alternative (even her offer of ceasing to take the herbs that had prevented her from becoming pregnant) fell on deaf ears. Henry's reputation was at stake, as was the potential to make a lot of money; he would not be deterred.

The auction took place just outside of Bury near Sicklesmere, on one of the lots of land up for sale at the same time. Henry deliberately made Charlotte the last lot of the day. By which time a crowd of several hundred people were waiting impatiently to see the outcome of this bizarre affair.

Henry was relishing this moment. He looked across at Charlotte who now sat on a chair next to him, dressed in the finest clothing to make her look polished, attractive and desirable. However, nothing could disguise the fear on her face as she contemplated what the next few minutes would mean to her future.

In the crowd stood Kevin, nervously clutching a small bag of coins. Between them they had scraped together just twenty pounds in the hope it would be enough for a winning bid, and save Charlotte from an uncertain fate with another man.

Henry climbed up onto a cart so that everyone could see him. Then rapped the gavel on his portable desk to get the bidders' attention. Once quiet, he commenced his well-rehearsed speech.

"Ladies and gentlemen, I thank you for your attendance here today, for what is a somewhat unusual auction. We have here, for your consideration, a young woman, now free of all legal matrimonial encumbrances and available to the highest bidder. She is here because of past indiscretions and misdemeanours that have caused me much distress and, yes, embarrassment, I am willing to admit. Her marriage to me has been annulled. This woman, named Charlotte, is 29 years of age and has two children aged eight years and six years. Clearly, therefore, her fecundity is unquestioned, she is capable of providing the winning bidder with more children if he so wishes. She is quick-witted, most capable with figures and words, and with a sound head for business and matters of trade. Except for the aforementioned indiscretions, I believe with a new husband she has excellent wife-making potential.'

Henry paused to let his words settle on the expectant audience, hoping he had done enough to whet their appetites.

'Now, ladies and gentlemen, let us commence the bidding – at shall we say – ten guineas? Anyone?

Silence. Then a hand was raised at the back of the crowd, and a bidding war quickly ensued that took Charlotte's price up to nineteen guineas, then twenty, then twenty-five. Charlotte looked even more distraught as Kevin's hand was raised no more, their funds inadequate to keep up with the bidding.

It took just five minutes before the winning bid of fifty guineas was reached. A man in his forties smiled as he made his way to the front of the crowd to claim his prize. He shook Henry's hand and handed over five £10 notes and fifty shillings in coins. Henry made him sign some paperwork legalising the transaction. He took Charlotte's hand, helped her down from the cart and, to cheers from the crowd, walked away with her to his carriage. Charlotte looked back, trying to see where Kevin and her two children were, wanting to wish them farewell, at least for the time being. She hoped her new husband would take her children as well, however she couldn't be sure that would be the case.

'Please, sir, can I say goodbye to my children?' begged Charlotte.

In a gruff, but friendly, voice he replied, 'Ma'am, my name is Gerald, not sir. There'll be time for all of that. You will get to see them. I am not an unreasonable man. Let us first find a priest to marry us as soon as possible. I have been a widow for five years, and I have certain wants that need satisfying. Once we have consummated our marriage, we can talk about your children.'

Back in Ixworth, they found a local priest willing to marry them the following day. Gerald asked his brother to be witness, and within 24 hours of the auction, Charlotte was a new bride, being led into the bedroom of her husband's small, but comfortable, farmhouse. She knew better than to resist his amorous intentions. To her surprise he proved to be gentle and considerate, as his five years of celibacy was relieved in a series of quick couplings throughout the night.

Over the next few days Charlotte was relieved to discover her new husband was not an ogre, violent or unreasonable. As he had no children of his own he allowed Charlotte's to visit, with a view to their stay becoming permanent.

A chagrined Kevin was last seen heading back towards Haverhill. Once the children were living with Charlotte in Ixworth and his links with Henry swiftly cut after the auction, there was nothing left for him in Bury.

Henry married again a few months later, and his new wife nursed him back to health. She fell pregnant within a few weeks and gave birth to a boy they named Jack, and a year later a girl, Dominique.

The house once again echoed to the sound of children. Both children grew up there, and Dominique stayed until she was married. Jack took over the auction business when Henry died in 1780. His legacy continued into the next generation, just as Henry wished.

Chapter 30
1783/5

I can't breathe, Doctor! Ever since that mist the other morning I have struggled to even get out of bed; do you have something to help me?' The pale middle-aged woman with rheumy eyes and a runny nose hacked another body-shaking cough, holding a filthy rag to her mouth to catch the phlegm.

Doctor Bartholomew Baker sighed. 'I'm sorry, ma'am, all I can suggest is you mix up a potion of horsetail and thyme, boil it, then drink with some honey. I am hopeful your condition is just temporary because of this strange weather. Keep indoors for a few days, take the herbs and it should pass. If you can afford to see the apothecary he may have some other suggestions...now, ma'am, if you'll excuse me I have several other patients waiting.'

He ushered the woman out into Whiting St, to be met by a long queue of people waiting to see him. It had been the same since he opened his doors early that morning – all were suffering with respiratory problems. By late morning the queue had swelled to some twenty people as those from outside Bury made their way to his newly opened doctor's office. The house's great hall was now divided into two, one half a private consultation room, the other his office and library, complete with over 100 medical books he'd collected while practising and studying in London, under Sir John Hunter, the famous Scottish surgeon. Not that the eminent surgeon's famous treatise on *The Natural History of the Human Teeth* would be of much help to him now, he thought.

His wife, Beatrice, daughter of Sir John Cullum, owner of a large estate in Hawstead just outside the town, was the reason for his move from London. It was made clear by Sir John that, if he wished to marry Beatrice, he would have to move to Bury, though as an incentive he would buy a house for Bartholomew to start his own doctor's practice. And so here he was, with a score or more of hacking patients anxious for him to cure their mysterious breathing problems. For which he could offer little to ease their pain.

What intrigued him was the cause of this illness among so many people all at the same time. He, too, saw the low cloud moving slowly across the town a few days ago; even at midday it reduced the sun's strength to that of a full moon, making it cold and miserable. It was unlike any weather he'd seen before, just a continuous slab of grey cloud blotting out the warmth and light from the east to west, north to south. Only after three days, when a breeze appeared, did the odorous haze slowly dissipate.

However, the fog did not just affect people. The weather was more like January than June. The more patients he saw, the more he heard stories of a frost – in their gardens, at this time of year! The farmers who came to see him were complaining their crops were ruined, just a few weeks from harvest, wilting, dead in the field. Some claimed their ponds had frozen over too. It was an unheard of aberration in the weather, and its effects were proving catastrophic, for man and nature.

Over dinner that evening Bartholomew discussed these strange occurrences with Beatrice.

'I don't believe I have ever seen the weather behave in such a strange way. Your father is something of an expert in matters such as this, has he said anything to you?'

'Not so much the weather, Bartholomew, but he does study at great length plants, trees and flowers. He has a whole glass building dedicated to them. I am seeing him tomorrow for tea; I will ask him if he knows more.'

What no one in England knew was that the disruption to the normal weather patterns was experienced around the world after a cataclysmic volcanic eruption 1200 miles away in Iceland spewed countless millions of tons of sulphuric-laced dust into the atmosphere that spread across huge areas of the northern hemisphere. The eruptions started in June 1783 and continued until February of 1784, causing the winter to be one of the coldest on record. Parts of England reported a month of continuous frosts. Elsewhere, widespread crop failure in North America and Europe, and the death of thousands of farm animals, resulted in prices of foodstuffs rising, resulting in the population living close to starvation. Estimates put the loss of life from this cataclysmic eruption at 8000 people in England alone, with another 23,000 dying from the effects of the poisonous gas cloud. In places the gaseous cloud was so thick *'that ships stayed in port, unable to navigate, and the sun was described as "blood coloured,'* so one newspaper reported.

All of this was, of course, unknown to the beleaguered doctor as he struggled to give succour to his stream of suffering patients. Most would survive, but the memory of those strange times would live in their memories as the summer without sun and the winter without end.

Sir John Cullum relayed his observations to Beatrice when she came to see him that dismal June morning. Over tea he enthusiastically explained what he had seen and heard and seen. A keen horticulturist and scientist, he was acutely aware something unusual was taking place. His enquiring mind was fascinated by this quirk of nature.

'I was wondering what the effects this strange miasma would have on people. From what you say, Bartholomew is seeing it firsthand, and it is not a pretty sight by all accounts. I was first made aware of the precipitous change in the weather the other day when I observed the air very much condensed in my chamber window. Soon after I was informed by a tenant that, finding himself cold in bed, about three o'clock in the morning, he looked out his window, and to his great surprise saw the ground covered with a white frost. Yesterday I was told that two men at Barton saw in some shallow tubs, ice the thickness of a crown-piece.'

He went on enthusiastically describing the effect of this 'frost' on trees and crops.

'I spoke to some of the farmers on the estate and they told me the barley, which was coming into ear, was now brown and withered at its extremities, as were the leaves of the oats. The rye had the appearance of being mildewed. Understandably they were alarmed for their crop's prospects. Interestingly, the wheat was not much affected. Walking around the grounds I noticed the larch, Weymouth pine and Scotch fir had the tips of their leaves withered. I am hopeful they will survive. If the crops fail I fear many will go hungry.'

He continued describing the bleak effects of the mysterious cloud and lack of sun. Beatrice, already worried about how she would

326

manage if things took a turn for the worse, politely cut short her father's litany of bad news.

'Thank you, Father dear, that was all most informative. Bartholomew will be interested to hear of your findings, even if it won't help his endless stream of patients who are ill because of this strange phenomenon. Have you any idea what caused it...or how long it will last?'

'Sorry to say, I haven't, Beatrice. If it continues into winter, we could see some very cold days, the sun is not as strong as it should be. Come December it will make for some nasty freezing days. I would get yourself stocked up on wood for the fires if I were you.'

'That is sound advice, Father, I will instruct the servants to get in a large supply of logs. Maybe I'll have the chimney sweep round. Get one of his boys to clean them; we don't want another fire like they had some twenty years ago. What about you and Mother? Will you be warm in this big, draughty house?'

'I shall be fine; thank you for your concern, Beatrice. I shall immerse myself in my work and drink lots of brandy!' He laughed, knowing a scolding was about to follow.

'Father, that is not a proper way to look after yourself. I shall talk to Mama to make sure you stop work often enough to eat and sleep.'

'Yes, of course, my dear, as always you are right.' He smiled, trying not to sound patronising.

'In the meantime, take Bartholomew's advice and stay inside until this foul air has gone. Promise me that at least?'

Sir John stood up and pecked his daughter on the cheek, 'I promise,' he said. 'Now you go back and help Bartholomew, it sounds as though he could do with an extra pair of hands.'

Beatrice returned home to find the queue of patients still straggling down the street; her poor husband she thought, he must be exhausted. She entered the house to find every chair and space on the floor occupied with coughing and wheezing people. She wrinkled her nose at the smell – it would take days for her to ventilate the house, though she vowed to say nothing to her overworked husband.

'What can I do to help, Bartholomew?' asked Beatrice, having weaved her way to him through the throng of people packed into the waiting room.

'Ah! Beatrice, my love, it is good to see you. I am getting overwhelmed here and, in truth, I can do little to help these people. I can only offer them a potion suggested by the apothecary. He brought me a supply of honey, peppermint and thyme, they are in the parlour. If you can, follow these instructions and get the servants to make bottles of the tincture to give to these poor folks.'

Beatrice took the scrap of paper and hurried back to the parlour, quickly organising the two servants to boil water and add in the herbs, then the honey once it had cooled down. Within the hour they were handing out the bottles to the waiting patients, explaining this was, hopefully, a cure for their shortness of breath and coughing. By late afternoon the last of them had left, gratefully clutching their medicine. For the next few weeks every day was the same; then, slowly, the tide of sick people abated.

Nevertheless, for six months the effects of the deadly cloud caused countless deaths across the county. Then winter arrived, the poor harvest and food shortages compounding its effect as everyone froze and for weeks the temperature failed to get above freezing. By the spring of 1784 hundreds in the Bury area had died of its effects. More than died in the plague of 1637.

In August 1785 Sir John Cullum died of consumption. Beatrice was still grieving for the loss of her dear father when in October happier news arrived. There was to be the first ever demonstration of a hot-air balloon taking off from Angel Hill of all places!

Seeing this as an opportunity to divert Beatrice from the malaise of losing her father, Bartholomew suggested they go and see what all the excitement was about. After all, as he explained to Beatrice, only a few such demonstrations of this new mode of travel had been seen in this country. She agreed, finally casting aside her mourning clothes, and venturing out for the first time in many weeks. They took their newly born baby girl, Annette, and were soon enveloped by the crowds streaming to the site of this daring spectacle of a man floating up into the sky (or so he promised on all the posters plastered around the town).

By the time they arrived, Angel Hill was packed with spectators. Every window in the Angel Hotel was open with guests looking down on the proceedings. In fact all the houses surrounding the square sported onlookers leaning out of the windows to see the spectacle. Bartholomew and Beatrice managed to obtain a better view by climbing on one of the crumbling walls of the old abbey. Although only a few feet high, it was enough to see clearly the platform on which a large basket rested with countless ropes curling from it to the ground and a large balloon slowly being inflated. According to the man in charge, one Captain Poole, it wasn't hot air that caused the balloon to rise, but a newly discovered gas called hydrogen: created by using a combination of sulphuric acid and iron filings.

'This looks very dangerous, don't you think?' asked Beatrice. 'Even if he floats up into the clouds...how does he come down safely?'

'Well, from what I have read in the Bury Post, he is not the first person to try this, several Frenchmen have done it already – and they all survived. Mind you, I certainly wouldn't want to do it, though to see the world from up there...' Bartholomew pointed skyward, 'must be an unforgettable experience.'

Beatrice was equally unenthusiastic: 'Rather him than me...I still don't understand why it floats in the first place. What is so special about the air that fills the balloon?'

Bartholomew shook his head. 'That I do not know, or understand, my dear...Oh, look, it now seems to be full enough to lift the basket. Heavens, it is no longer touching the ground! That is truly amazing.'

As he spoke Captain Poole climbed into the basket, momentarily making it touch the ground again, before it strained against some ropes that tethered it to the ground. Three men, on the captain's signal, untied them and, slowly but surely, to huge cheers from the crowd, the balloon and its sole occupant waving from the basket slung beneath it, slowly, silently ascended into the sky.

Captain Poole shouted down on the transfixed spectators, 'I bid you adieu! I shall return and retell my experiences of this journey to you all! God bless the King!'

And then he did something foolhardy: In a gesture designed to foster a sense of history he threw down into the crowd fake threepenny pieces specially minted with his name and a carving of a balloon. To the assembled throng initially the coins looked real. Pandemonium ensued as people scrambled on the ground to snatch up the worthless coins.

Ignorant of the results of his actions Captain Poole wafted off on a gentle breeze that took him over the abbey ruins, Eastgate St, and towards Rougham. Then, as he rose effortlessly without a sound into the clouds, he disappeared from sight.

Back on the ground Bartholomew saw several people in danger of being crushed – all for some valueless token. He ordered Beatrice and Annette to remain where they were, in relative safety from the chaos surrounding them.

'I must go and help those who have been injured. I will be back soon; you must stay here. Don't move until I return.'

Without waiting for a reply he dove into the melee to help an old lady who lay on the ground, gamely waving one of the tokens, despite a nasty gash to her head. 'I got one, I got one! I'm rich!' she crowed, while at the same time trying to stop the blood running down her face. Bartholomew knelt beside her and looked at the coin, realising quickly it was merely a keepsake. He didn't have the heart to tell her the truth. Using his kerchief he pressed it onto her wound to stem the flow. She appeared otherwise unhurt and in full control of her faculties, so he helped her stand up and watch her totter off unsteadily into the rapidly thinning mass of spectators.

He helped a few more people, none of whom were seriously hurt, before returning to where he left his wife and child.

Except they weren't there.

Chapter 30 The kidnapping

For a cutpurse and pickpocket like Stevie Middleton, the crowds jammed into Angel Hill were manna from heaven. His haul by the end of the afternoon was several pocket watches, bracelets, necklaces and the contents of three ladies' purses, the contents of which he had yet to investigate. Then the kerfuffle with the coins dropping from the balloon made his job even easier, until some busybody lady and her child saw him trying to relieve a distracted woman of her purse and shouted at him to stop.

Even in the chaos, as people scrabbled for coins on the ground, her warning was heard by several bystanders who turned round to see what was happening, but to his relief, ignored her cries. The last thing he needed were the constables taking an interest in him. Seeing Beatrice still gesticulating and shouting, he ran a few steps over to her standing on the wall and not so gently pressed his knife into her side.

'Now, lady, let's keep the noise down, shall we, and I'll not hurt you,' he whispered into her ear. 'I'd hate something nasty to happen to your kid, a cut on her sweet face could leave a scar for all her life. Be a shame wouldn't it? Now, not a word now. Quit yer hollering. Let's pretend we are just leaving kinda casual like, along with everyone else. Get me?'

Beatrix nodded in dumb fear, and held onto Annette as tightly as she could. His grip on her arm was vice-like. She thought for a moment of screaming something, anything to gain attention, but the point of his knife now pressed against her daughter's small body quelled her urge to do anything she might regret.

'Please, please just let us go, I will say nothing. I beg you not to hurt my daughter...'

He leant in so closely to her she could smell his beer-laden breath, and the odour of someone who had not bathed in weeks. She tried to pull away, more in disgust than fear, but he was young, and strong, his hold on her unyielding.

'Let's go for a little walk, shall we?' he said. His tone brooked no argument, so Beatrice allowed him to steer her towards the Norman Tower, where the flood of spectators were heading to their homes. She tried to look for Bartholomew in the vain hope she might attract his attention. Even though the crowd was now thinning, no sight of him could she discern. Petrified, she reluctantly let herself be led away from her potential saviour, the sight of her attacker's knife still discreetly poking into her daughter's clothing an incentive to say and do nothing.

As they passed the front of St Mary's Church he pushed her into the graveyard. Quickly the noise and crush of people dissipated behind them, and soon they were alone. With a resolute look on his face he continued to propel her further from the crowds and anyone who might help her. Beatrice tried to pull away. 'Just leave us be, young man. Keep your stolen wares; here...have my necklace, just, please do us no harm and we shall say nothing to anyone about this. You have my word.'

Stevie ignored her pleas, now almost dragging her down into the meadows that abutted the River Lark.

Beatrice suddenly began to think this man might want more than her valuables, or her silence. The prospect of some kind of assault knotted her stomach.

'Where are you taking us...what do you want?' Beatrice tried to keep the fear out of her voice, not wanting to give him the satisfaction of seeing her cry. But it was Annette who now started to wail.

'Just hush that baby, or I'll skewer her like a dead rabbit,' he threatened, waving the knife in front of the baby's face. Doing her best to calm her daughter, for fear of antagonising him further, she held her tightly and caressed her head, rubbing her back, trying to ease her anxiety.

'She is hungry, I need to feed her.' explained Beatrice. Grunting in annoyance, the man stopped, loosening his grip, so she could finally put some space between them.

'Go on then, feed her, but make it quick.'

'Sir, nursing my child is something I only do in private...I cannot, will not, do so with you staring at my naked breast. It is intolerable you should suggest it. Have you no sense of decency?' Beatrice could not keep the anger out of her voice, though knowing it might provoke him to commit some unspeakable act. Here, with no one else to be seen, no hope of rescue, the thought of her exposing herself to him made her shiver.

Suddenly she heard voices coming from the river. Before she could shout for help, two urchins, a young girl and a small boy, both dressed in rags, appeared. 'Father, we were getting a mite worried...Jesus, who's she? What's she doing here? We need money, not prisoners!' demanded the girl on seeing Beatrice.

The man's resolve seemed to wilt in the face of his daughter's censure. He started to explain what happened, but she cut him short... 'So instead of just doin' a runner, even though you are quicker than a woman carrying a baby, you brought her here? What were you planning on doin' to 'er? Knocking 'er off? Good plan, you dolthead, have every constable in the town after us if you did that. This is a real pickle you got us into now.' She paused her tirade, waiting for her father to offer an explanation. Instead he squirmed under her onslaught, lost for words.

Beatrice felt a frisson of hope issuing from this fractious exchange.

'Look, I say again, just let me and my daughter go, I'll say nothing, I promise. I have no interest in telling the constables about what's happened, I just want to go home. Please, I'm begging you, for the sake of my child...'

The girl thought for a moment, then walked over to Beatrice. 'Where do you live, lady?'

Beatrice said nothing, it was information she'd rather the girl didn't have.

'Tell me, lady, or I'll throw your baby in the river...just watch me, I'll do it.'

Beatrice couldn't believe a young girl would be so violent...but...dare she take the risk she was bluffing?

The girl made a move towards her, prompting Beatrice to reply, 'It's the doctor's house on Whiting St, my husband helps sick people. Poor or rich. He is a good man. If you ever get ill, he will always see you. If you can't afford to pay, he will not charge...' She heard herself babbling on in the hope of winning the girl round.

'OK, lady, I get the message, your husband's a saint. So listen; 'ere's what's going to happen. We'll let you go, and you'll say nothing about my father being stupid an' robbing you an' bringing you here. If you do, if we get a sniff the law is coming after us, we know where you live.' She stopped, tickling Annette under the chin. The baby gurgled and smiled. 'Grass on us and we'll come pay you a visit, and it won't be for any medicine, it'll be to slit this kid's throat. Understood?'

Wide-eyed Beatrice was speechless. Here was a girl, probably not even in her teens, threatening the life of a baby? Her baby. Then again, looking at this family, she understood how desperate they were. Living to them was just about surviving. The life of another human being was worthless to them. If they had to take one to subsist in this underworld of poverty, they'd do it.

Beatrice nodded, hope rising in her chest. 'Yes, yes, of course. You have my word I will never reveal anything that has happened today.' In a conciliatory tone, she added, 'I understand you did what was necessary to survive. I forgive you.'

The girl snarled back, 'You stuck-up bitch, I don't want your forgiveness, or pity, I want your money and out of my sight. You're no use to us dead or alive. Just fuck off and, for the sake of your baby's life, tell no one of us.'

She turned to her father and brother, 'Now, because of your stupidity we best leave this town. You're a piece of shit, Father, do us more harm than good most of the time...c'mon, let's go.' Silently he and her brother obediently followed her and within seconds they disappeared into the woods lining the river bank, leaving Beatrice sobbing with relief.

The walk back to her house found Beatrice agitated with indecision. Should she lie to Bartholomew, make up some excuse that she walked around the town before returning? Or some similar untruth? She knew he would ask why she had done so, without first informing him, causing him to worry unnecessarily, he would point out. Or should she tell him the truth? Then persuade him to let matters rest as, in reality, no harm had become to her or Annette? Would he heed her (and the girl's) advice to not inform the authorities? Believing her threats to come back and harm their baby if he did?

'We have to go to the courts...we cannot let a kidnapping go unpunished,' insisted Bartholomew once Beatrice decided to reveal exactly why she disappeared without warning. Just as she feared, his righteous indignation brooked no argument or reasoning from her. Even putting his daughter in possible jeopardy failed to dissuade him from involving the law.

'Please, husband, I know you are angry, but I beg you, let us do nothing until tomorrow when we are calmer. Act in haste and repent at leisure as my father used to say. It is late, let us sleep on it and discuss the matter further tomorrow.' Her reasoning failed to calm him down.

'By tomorrow they will be gone! There'll be little chance of catching them...'

'And you really believe the constables will start searching in the dark by the river now?'

'That's their job; I shall impress upon them the urgency of the matter. Offer to pay them extra if necessary. I will not let this rest, Beatrice. No one threatens my family and gets away with it.'

'Husband, please be realistic, the vagabonds probably have already left the town, who knows in which direction? And aside from giving me a terrible fright, are they going to chase around the countryside for the sake of my necklace? They are desperate people; in a way I am happy for them to keep their ill-gotten gains if it means they leave Bury.'

'Beatrice, why are you being so obdurate?' asked Bartholomew, frustrated she didn't share his desire for justice to be served.

'I am just being realistic. There is little to gain and much to lose if we pursue these people. I beg of you, let this upsetting matter rest, otherwise I will forever be in fear they will make good on their threat and return to hurt our daughter.'

His initial anger abating, he began to see the sense of his wife's arguments. Perhaps it was best to let things go, he reflected. No good would come of chasing these thieves, indeed his faith in the law's ability to find them anyway was questionable.

'Perhaps you are right, my dear; in my haste for justice, the practicalities were forgotten. It pains me to let them get away with their nefarious activities, but it is probably safer for us.'

Beatrice breathed a sigh of relief. 'I'm glad we are agreed. Now, it has been an exhausting day. I will check on Annette then make my way to bed. God bless you for being such an understanding husband.' She kissed him tenderly on the lips, held him tightly for a few moments then left him to finish his glass of port.

A week later Beatrice, while reading a copy of the Bury Post, noticed an advertisement publicising a talk to be given by Captain Poole of his journey from Bury in his balloon. She read it to Bartholomew.

'This could be interesting; would you like to go?' asked Beatrice.

'Possibly, I thought the man was a bit of a buffoon throwing that money down onto the crowd. People were so desperate to get some, injuries resulted. Luckily none serious. And all for nought as they were merely tokens! However, if you really wish to go, of course I shall join you.'

The Assembly Rooms were filled to capacity as the portly Captain Poole ascended the small stage, dressed in his army uniform – even though he was no longer actively serving. He shuffled a few sheets of paper on the lectern, composed himself, then called for everyone's attention. For a man of small stature his voice carried loud and clear across the room. He was, however, not the greatest of orators, as Bartholomew whispered to Beatrice after a few minutes into his speech.

'How can he make something so interesting sound so dull?'

'Hush, husband, give the poor man a chance, you are biased because of that business with the coins. Please just listen in silence!'

The captain, having explained how the balloon was made and what caused it to rise from the ground, began to explain his journey:

'Immediately after my balloon was liberated from the ground, by releasing its ropes, I found myself ascending and heading in an east by northeast direction.

'It was a beautiful clear blue sky and the sensation of the ascent was exceedingly pleasurable and peaceful. On entering the

clouds, I found the mercury in my barometer had fallen four inches and a half which meant my elevation was at some 4000 feet.'

The crowd gasped! Four thousand feet...why, that was as high as a mountain! He allowed the appreciative hubbub to die down before continuing:

'Although my ascent was rapid, the clouds when I reached them were of unequal height but in less than four minutes I found myself parallel with their tops. They wore a snowy whiteness. I could no longer see the ground. I was utterly alone, just me and my Maker in the heavens, at one together.

'I now began to feel cold, though the sunshine with uninterrupted splendour shone down upon me with great intensity.

'My balloon was now considerably expanded and having ascended beyond sight of the ground below, I was struck by the silence which prevailed to such a degree that I heard the watch in my pocket beating.

'Notwithstanding the cold which was considerable, I continued to rise until my barometer fell some 14 inches and a quarter, which I have since found by comparing with my table of altitudes is equal to over three miles or around 16,000 feet. It was then I ascertained my balloon was under such tension I would soon have to start my descent to avoid any damage.

'When there was a gap in the clouds I was astonished to find that looking down onto the earth I could see the fields and farms; the animals were the size of mere toys!'

.

The captain spent several minutes amusing the audience with his descriptions of the buildings, roads and landmarks he saw from his cloud-high perch, comparing the people he saw on the ground to ants, busy at work, oblivious to his spying on them from up in the sky.

'Having been aloft for fifty minutes and made considerable progress to the east I was surprised at not being able to notice the sea. It was a disappointment, but I did not wish the wind to push me too far, so that my landing would be in the ocean.

'I was about to descend when I saw far below a beautiful meandering river, bearing to the southeast and, by tracing its course, I could now perceive the ocean far, far away in the direction to which I was advancing. I thought it rather opaque and luminous in appearance, and judging it not to be very safe, I thought it best to descend quickly.

'I opened my valve, which deflated the balloon in a gradual manner, and by keeping it open began a slow descent. I soon found myself alighted on a small piece of ground at Earl Stonham with no injury to myself or the balloon. I was met by the owner of the land, Mr Reginald Chevely. On enquiring to him exactly where I had landed I discovered my distance from Bury to be eighteen miles, having been in the air one hour and eleven minutes. I am indebted to this kind gentleman for aiding me and bringing me back to Bury late that evening.'

Modestly, he then ended his short speech, by saying he 'did not wish for his talking to become tedious,' and that he was happy to answer any questions about his 'unique and perilous journey.'

There were many questions from the audience, but still underwhelmed with the captain's less than entertaining story,

Bartholomew didn't want to hear them, suggesting instead an 'early night' was in order.

They arrived back at the house as it was getting dark to discover a scribbled note attached to the front door. Puzzled, Beatrice tore it open and, as she read its few words, her face went as pale as the moon.

'Oh, sweet Jesus...Please, God, no...' She thrust the note into Bartholomew's hand and rushed inside, screaming for the housemaid at the top of her voice.

'Angela, Angela, where is Annette? Is she safe?'

The bewildered housemaid rushed down from the upstairs nursery. 'Ma'am, she is here with me, asleep. What is the problem, why are you looking so distraught?'

Beatrice flew past the girl and ran upstairs to find the baby fast asleep in her crib. She came back downstairs cuddling the half-awake infant to her chest, relief plain on her tear-stained face.

'Oh, thank God, that note had me fearing the worst.'

'What note, ma'am?'

'This one,' said Bartholomew, reading it out loud. 'The one that says, "*Keep your silence and keep your baby alive*".'

'Oh, Bartholomew, they have broken their promise to me! They haven't left the town after all, and now they are threatening us, and our baby. I was so stupid to trust them.' Beatrice was angry with herself for being so gullible. 'Maybe we should tell the constables what happened. If they are still in Bury maybe they can find them? What do you think we should do?"

'Nothing for the moment, my dear. I doubt they will break in and try to harm Annette while we are in the house. Let us just keep her with us at all times while we consider what we do next.'

In the end the decision made itself obvious. On the death of her father, her mother inherited the large house in Hawstead - too big for one person and very expensive to maintain. It was decided that they should move in with her. Bartholomew would open a smaller office in the town for his doctor's practice.

They were never troubled by the family of kidnappers again. Their story ended badly with all three being caught in Ipswich a few weeks later attempting to rob, unwisely, the wife of one of the assize judges. Justice was swift and brutal. Transportation for life to the Americas.

Beatrice and Bartholomew, unaware that any threat to their lives was now over 4000 miles away, sold the house.

Chapter 31
(1800)

Here we are, at the dawn of a new century, and still this town does not have room for all the impoverished, starving and homeless. 'Tis a tragedy indeed. We should be ashamed of ourselves!' declared Sir Simon Smith, alderman of the Bury St Edmunds Corporation, while chatting with a few of the members after their regular monthly meeting.

The Corporation, run by 37 men – all fine and noble gentlemen of money and position – controlled almost every aspect of the town's activities. As alderman, a position Sir Simon held for over a decade, he had access, and insight, into every aspect of the Corporation's workings. The power he wielded as a result, made him a man to be reckoned with, and crossed at your peril. He maintained this lofty position by dispensing favours to those of influence, and awarding contracts for work around the town to those prepared to remember his largesse.

As he self-servingly pointed out, 'Patronage is not corruption if everyone benefits,' and, truth be told, he reasoned, the town flourished under his leadership despite the current economic woes brought on by the collapse of the woollen industry. Plus, while the finances remained in profit, no one questioned his running of the Corporation. But as a discussion at the latest meeting revealed, all was not currently well in that department.

It was agreed that a thorough review of the Corporation's budget was required. Sir Simon initially took offence at the implication all was not as it should be, then acquiesced and agreed to have this done by the next meeting. One of the largest expenditures under scrutiny was the expansion of the poorhouse.

'What more can we do?' asked Sir Charles Davers, one of Bury's two MPs. 'We've spent huge sums on a new poorhouse in College St and now we are extending it with the building of the House of Industry. Times are hard for everyone, we cannot keep putting good money after bad. The Corporation's finances won't stand it. Can't some of them be transported?'

'I'm not sure that the courts have the power to do that,' answered John Oakes, local banker and financier to half the aristocrats in the county. 'I believe, gentlemen, we have a duty to look after people in less fortunate circumstances than our own. This new House of Industry will give them a sense of worth and accomplishment, I believe.'

Sir Simon agreed. 'Not to forget – a source of cheap labour for our struggling textile enterprises. My conscience is relieved that we now can help some 200 more unfortunates with some kind of activity to keep them occupied and out of trouble. However, it does little to improve the neighbourhood. But, alas, it is too late to change what has happened.'

'Ha! Simon you are unsuccessful at disguising the real reason for your complaint. Could it be that you have to walk past the poorhouse, on your way to your new house in Whiting St?' John Oakes smiled as he noticed his friend squirm at his gentle jibe.

'No, no, that is not the case at all,' he blustered, 'I am more concerned for the homeowners in Churchgate St that they may find the proximity of these buildings to their homes a cause for concern.'

John ignored the alderman's half-hearted excuse. 'So, how are you settling into your new house? I assume you bought it at a much reduced price? I gather it was in poor condition.' He was well aware, as the town's leading banker, precisely how much the house had cost Sir William. An amount his informal network of sources told him was more than his finances could support.

'The cost was a reasonable one, just over £1500, as you well know, I'm sure, James! I have spent a goodly sum on it since. And between you and me, gentlemen, my wife's demands we furnish it with the latest pieces from people like Chippendale and Sheraton have stretched the finances a little. It is of excellent quality, but damnably expensive.'

John agreed, 'We have some of their pieces too. If you can afford it, ask your wife to acquire some of Hepplewhite's furniture. Exquisitely made, but horrendously priced.' He knew full well Sir Simon couldn't afford such an expense, but a little teasing was all good fun in their close circle.

He knew his wealth originally derived from a number of yarn, wool processing and related trading enterprises. However, in recent years these had collapsed in the face of overseas competition and a change in demand for other cloths. So from where was the Corporation's chairman's income now coming? The banker's casual enquiries amongst Bury's business elite produced little information on this subject, further deepening his suspicions that all was not well with the longstanding chairman's finances. The question of how he could afford the grand house in Whiting St perplexed him. Strangely, as if to keep it a secret from the Bury gossip mill, Sir Simon had not approached him, when seeking money for his new home. A banker in Stowmarket provided that mortgage. He decided to press the matter no further for the moment, as the MP took the conversation in a different direction.

His tongue loosening over a second glass of Madeira, Sir Charles raised another delicate subject with John, 'How are matters with that fellow John Benjafield? I see he continues to oppose practically every motion or proposition you make at these meetings.' He was keen to have the latest gossip on the feud between the two men that at times caused heated debate at the Corporation's meetings.

'The man is a lying rat, an opportunist and a thorn in my side if I am to be truthful, Charles. He is determined to undermine me at every opportunity in his efforts to advance himself in the politics of the town. Now he is using my friends, or at least I thought them so, Dr John Symonds, and John Godbold, to take control of the Guildhall Feoffment and other charitable trusts in the town. This man seems hell-bent on making life difficult for me.' He sighed. 'I am getting too old for the cut and thrust of Bury politics, but I'll be damned if this upstart whippersnapper bests me in such matters.'

Sir Charles nodded, adding conspiratorially, 'I, too, have heard he has a somewhat chequered past when living in London, where he ran some scandal sheet called the Morning Post. Not that I can confirm it but I am given to understand that about fifteen years ago, the government gave him the money to buy the newspaper in return for favourable editorial coverage of their policies. His scruples it seems can be swayed for quite modest sums of money. His name is frequently heard in the corridors of Westminster as a man to keep on your side. I try to avoid him at all costs.'

John added, 'I wish I could do the same, but he and his band of supporters are forever blocking my efforts here on the Corporation, and he has married into an influential family who have connections across the county. I have not spoken to him directly for a couple of years. He is a young buck in a hurry to make a name for himself, at everyone else's expense it would seem.' For a few minutes the men swapped unflattering gossip about Benjafield, agreeing that with his contacts in the upper echelons of Bury society he would be a nuisance for some time to come.

The alderman contributed nothing to the gossipy conversation, absorbed in his thoughts about other matters, the activities of John Benjafield presently of little concern to him.

'Anyway, enough talk of this odious man, he is not worth the effort. I must be on my way,' John announced, finishing off his glass of Madeira. He shook hands with the two men and left for his home in nearby Guildhall St, still idly pondering about Sir Simon's finances – and whether the audit of the Corporation's accounts would reveal anything untoward. He prayed that if it did, the alderman would not be involved; he disliked scandal, especially when it involved one of his oldest friends.

Life in the poorhouse, or workhouse, was exceedingly unpleasant – then again, it was designed to be that way.

Since the 1600s parishes were responsible for the poor, infirm, elderly and those unable to find work. Such places were indeed a last resort; when all hope, all vestige of promise had been crushed out of people by an uncaring society, they ended up in a hellhole, with little chance of escape. So reflected Sir Simon as he walked down Hatter St towards Bury's workhouse.

He knew living in such places could be more perilous than begging on the streets. But that was actively discouraged, and the workhouse became a dumping ground for the human detritus that offended the other residents of the town. Once inside, diseases such as smallpox and measles spread like wildfire. Conditions were cramped with beds squashed together, hardly any room to move and little light or fresh air. Families were separated as soon as they arrived, men, women and children all sent to separate dormitories and different workplace. Often they would not see each other for weeks at a time. Some workhouses did not allow inmates to leave, even for a few hours; if they did so they were punished for stealing their uniforms.

When not in their sleeping quarters, they were expected to work, often mind-numbing and repetitive: men crushing stones, or working in the fields, women doing laundry and children working in local factories – all for no pay, just a bed and food of the most abject quality in return. The workhouse was, in reality, a prison for those whose only crime was that of being unable to work. A receptacle for the jetsam of society to be hidden from those who preferred not to see, hear or think about them.

He arrived at the workhouse and pushed open the huge oak door leading into an imposing vestibule where the warden was waiting for him. As always the stench of unwashed bodies, stale cooking and, if it were possible, hopelessness, abused his senses. However, necessity meant he went there on a weekly basis to meet the warden and settle the financial arrangements between them.

'Good evening, sire, so good to see you again. As always I am grateful for Your Lordship's interest and patronage in our establishment. I hope you are well and flourishing in these difficult times?' He found the warden's obsequiousness odious. Knowing full well it was an act to ingratiate and flatter him, and keep secure his position. One that was moderately well paid with additional benefits provided by the destitute women in his care who would sell their only asset – their bodies – in return for extra food, or visitations to their children. Looking at the corpulent, unwashed, repugnant figure bowing and scraping in front of him, he wondered how desperate those poor women must be to succumb to his advances.

'I am well, thank you, Warden. I have little time on my hands and it is late, can we conclude our business swiftly please?' He hated being here, and having to deal with this loathsome man, but needs must if he were to collect his regular fee from him.

'You have the figures?'

'Yes, sire.' The warden handed over a sheet of paper, showing the money coming in from the various businesses who paid the workhouse for the services of the inmates. And of course the generous donations from many sources, including the Corporation itself. Not that the inmates saw much of it. Ostensibly it was for their food, and other expenses involved in running the establishment. A few of these contracts were with Sir Simon's enterprises at rates well under what he would pay normal workers. It was the other income that interested him, for this was what he shared with the warden, leaving the workhouse barely able to decently look after its occupants.

'My calculations show your share is £19 12s 6d for this week.' said the warden hesitantly, hoping Sir William would not ask for more details.

Knowing full well the warden was embezzling him out of his full share, he chose to accept the amount without comment; it was better than nothing.

'That looks satisfactory. However, a word of warning. The Corporation's finances are being investigated, which will include those of the workhouse. I suggest you destroy as much evidence as you can about our...arrangement. If discovered, you might find yourself an occupant of this, this horrid establishment. I leave you to cover our tracks with the utmost care.'

The warden nodded his understanding, as he handed over the money. 'I will make it as though it never happened. Rest assured, sire, our arrangement will be kept most secret.'

* * * *

For the townsfolk the early months of the new century were consumed by weekly reports in The Bury Post and other newspapers concerning the trial of a young 22-year-old girl called Sarah Lloyd. She was arrested in October 1799 and charged with arson, burglary and attempted murder after letting her lover into the house where she was a servant. The circumstances of the crime and its gory aftermath made the forthcoming trial one that captured the interest of the whole town. Apparently the tryst led to the theft of some items and a fire starting in the house. Its owner, Sara Syer, escaped with only minor injuries but pointed the finger of guilt at Sarah and her lover Joseph Clark.

The trial started in March 1800. Quickly Joseph was cleared of all charges for lack of any real evidence, while Sarah was eventually convicted of theft, to the value of forty shillings. To everyone's horror Sarah was sentenced to death for her part in the crime – a punishment many considered excessive.

The outrage led to a local barrister, Capel Lofft, mounting an appeal against her sentence. In addition petitions were raised and sent to the home secretary, the Duke of Portland, demanding clemency. In court Lofft suggested that Sarah Lloyd was only 19, not 22, and that there were extenuating circumstances to mitigate the death sentence. His defence was long and articulate, and in summary he argued to the judge:

'To sentence such a young girl of previously good character to suffer the ultimate punishment is unjust, unreasonable and undeserved. Sarah was led astray, there can be no doubt, by the violent demands of her lover. In a childish effort to inculcate his affections she let him into the house. Her intentions may have been immoral, my lord, but they did not extend to robbery or violence against her mistress. She is, my lord, an impressionable girl, harmless and eager to please – a desire that has led her to this most terrible of fates. The lack of evidence against her lover, Joseph Clark, should not mitigate his involvement, for which he should take partial blame. I urge you, my lord, to show mercy on this poor girl and lessen her sentence to one of transportation.'

The curmudgeonly old judge, Arthur McConnell, was unswayed by Capel's argument. He believed in setting an example and making those who commit a crime pay severely for their transgressions. A warning to others to stay within the law. He dismissed the barrister's request and ordered the execution should proceed. The spectators in the court vented their fury at the verdict, shouting insults at the judge, even threatening him with violence, so much so that constables quickly surrounded him as he hurriedly left the court.

As a final attempt to thwart the execution, the Duke of Grafton sent another appeal for mercy, alongside the petition, to the Duke of Portland in the hope his influence could be brought to bear. Even John Oakes and other members of the Bury Corporation spoke up in favour of a lesser sentence (a move seen by his enemies as interference in the judicial process).

But it was all to no avail. Sarah Lloyd was to be executed for stealing the paltry sum of forty shillings (or £2 – less than a day's pay for a working man). The judge was intransigent, unmoved by the wave of indignation from the local populace.

On April 23rd, as the cart was taking her to execution, Capel Lofft climbed aboard and harangued the crowd for fifteen minutes about the 'flagrant injustice' soon to take place. Foolishly he criticised the Duke of Portland for denying clemency. As a result he was struck off the roll of magistrates. Finally, with nothing left to say, he watched helpless as Sarah calmly met her end.

Sarah Lloyd was the last person to be executed at Thingoe Hill. Her final words to the large, silent crowd, were simple, but surprisingly eloquent for an uneducated young girl. Through her tears, she claimed her lover had threatened to rape her if she did not steal the money and it was he who set fire to the house in an effort to hide the theft.

'In my few short years on this earth I have received and witnessed much pain and injustice. This is the final time that I shall have to suffer such misery. I go to my God knowing I am at heart a good person, and I am sure my prayers will be answered so that I should be admitted through the gates of heaven as one who has sinned, but asked for, and received, forgiveness.'

With that the executioner gently pulled her long auburn hair away from her neck and slid the noose over her head, tightening the knot. He placed the hood to cover her face, stood back and quickly pulled open the trapdoor for her to fall the few feet to her death. A sharp crack could be heard as her neck broke and her life ended instantly.

* * * *

'I do believe I will finally have that pompous banker, John Oakes, grovelling for an apology. His alliance with Sir Simon, the alderman, will be his downfall,' said John Benjafield to his wife, Mary Ann, as they sat over dinner one evening.

'How so, my dear?'

Mary Ann tried to show an interest in her husband's ambition to become alderman, and in the process crush any dissenters, or those that opposed his progress. However, at times his appetite for power seemed more a question of impressing her father and his aristocratic friends than proving he was better than anyone who crossed his path. No matter, his lust for influence provided her with a pleasant home and more money than she needed. Though she was never quite sure from where he derived his income.

'The investigation into the Corporation's finances is complete. From what little I have heard of the report, some of the members have been less than scrupulous in their financial dealings. Once revealed their reputations will be in tatters. I know from my own enquiries the alderman has been purloining funds from the workhouse, and who knows where else, to fund his expensive new house. To boot he is hand in glove with John Oakes, so it seems likely the crusty old banker will be tarred with the same corrupt brush as his friend!'

'That is indeed wonderful news, John. You deserve success after all your hard work. When is the meeting where you shall make your move?'

'This Friday, once the details of the findings are revealed, John Oakes, Sir Simon and, I believe, three others will have to resign from the Corporation, leaving the way open for my friends and allies to elect me alderman. Finally, we will be the most influential and respected couple in Bury.' Mary Ann smiled and made some encouraging remarks; it wasn't the first time she'd heard his plans to take over the Corporation, and she wouldn't hold her breath that it would happen this time.

Just a few streets away his well-connected opponents, John Oakes, Alderman Sir Simon Smith and Sir Charles Davers MP, quickly foresaw that investigations into the Corporation could be a cause of embarrassment to an unknown number of their friends and decided to undertake some investigations of their own into John Benjafield's murky and largely unknown past. They needed some ammunition to shoot down his high-flying aspirations

The results were as unedifying as they were extraordinary.

It transpired that he frequently used his newspaper in London, the Morning Post, known for its gossip and salacious stories, as a source of illicit income. For those with money he blackmailed them by threatening to publish career or reputation-killing stories, unless they paid him off. Shockingly none other than the prince regent fell under his spell after he and Maria Fitzherbert secretly contracted a marriage that was invalid under English civil law because his father, King George III, had not consented to it. Benjafield, on discovering this, offered not to publish the story for the sum of £350 per year (£10,500 in today's values). And so the litany of his insalubrious activities was revealed, courtesy of some well-connected friends in London.

They were in Sir Simon's house a few days before the next meeting of the Corporation planning the best way to use damning information to silence what they knew would be a painful exposé of the Corporation's unsatisfactory finances.

'This man is simply outrageous. He has no sense of decency. How could he defraud a member of the Crown in such an unsavoury manner? He should be hung for treason! The man is an unscrupulous, misbegotten...words fail me, gentlemen, we must expose him at the meeting.' The MP, almost apoplectic, gulped down his wine in an effort to calm himself.

'I agree with all you say, Charles,' said John. 'But let us plan our move carefully, so we can protect our friends while at the same time revealing this snivelling rat for what he truly is – a vile blackmailer.'

The alderman, well aware the report to be presented to the Corporation might throw an unwelcome light on his illegal financial dealings with the workhouse, trod carefully, suggesting:

'He is indeed a thoroughly disreputable individual. It would be helpful, of course, to gain sight of the report before the meeting to fully ascertain its contents, and plan accordingly.'

'That would be helpful indeed,' agreed John, 'but even with my contacts I have not obtained a copy; the lawyers involved are pledged to confidentiality until the meeting.'

After much discussion they decided that, armed with this information, they would confront John Benjafield about his blackmailing activities before the report on the Corporation was revealed.

John proposed, 'We should, I believe, take the risk of doing so in front of the other members of the Corporation to maximise the damage to his reputation. I hope this will also stop him from using the report's findings to his advantage, and possibly divert attention from any embarrassing revelations in it that could affect us or our allies.'

He knew it was a risky strategy; when publicly humiliated by the news he was a blackmailer, Benjafield might decide that, with nothing left to lose, he would go public with any damaging revelations from the report, and hang the consequences. Then again, John hoped the finances of the Corporation may be in proper order, with no one having a finger of blame pointed at them. That would be ideal – though he wasn't hopeful. All would be revealed in two days' time.

On the last Friday in May, the Corporation members met. Due to the nature of the meeting all but two of the 37 were in attendance. Harold Weatherstone, the lawyer responsible for investigating its finances, stood before the members. One of the top lawyers in Bury, he was a tall, imposing man, with a serious demeanour. Unfazed by the audience of the town's great and good, he stood before them, a sheaf of papers in his hands. He cleared his throat with a loud cough which brought everyone to silence.

'Gentlemen. As you know I was tasked with investigating the finances of the Corporation, with a view to finding any irregularities or fraudulent activities. I should preface my findings by saying that overall they are run in an acceptable, if somewhat chaotic fashion, which in the long term I propose should be addressed and improved. Let me provide you with some more details...'

To the surprise and consternation of the members, John Oakes suddenly stood up before the lawyer could continue, and waved a piece of paper in the air.

'I apologise to the members present for this interruption, but I believe what I have to say is important enough to announce before we proceed further.' He bowed slightly in deference to Harold Weatherstone as if to apologise. The lawyer shrugged his shoulders. 'The floor is yours, Mr Oakes.' And sat down, a frown on his face.

Before anyone could object John launched into his exposé. 'On this piece of paper is the most disturbing news I have ever had the misfortune to read. Based on irrefutable evidence from unimpeachable sources it concerns member John Benjafield...'

Hearing his name he rose quickly from his seat: 'I have no idea what calumny is about to be told here, gentlemen, but I demand that I see it before it is made public, so I can prepare a refutation. I am about to be accused of something that could sully my reputation, with no advance notice. This is reprehensible! I demand Mr Oakes be stopped from further slanderous, baseless lies.'

But John was not to be dissuaded. 'Members of the Corporation, Mr Benjafield exhibits the height of hypocrisy, as you shall see. He is demanding the right to defend himself from public humiliation – a courtesy he failed to offer those he is blackmailing...'

Hearing this inflammatory accusation the room buzzed with anticipation; everyone was agog at what might be revealed next. All except John Benjafield, who sat white-faced, stony silent, awaiting what he now knew would be a devastating, if not terminal, blow to his political ambitions.

'If I may continue?' John paused to see if anyone voiced the wish he should remain silent. None did.

It took only a few minutes for him to read the details of John Benjafield's blackmailing schemes, the most heinous of which involved a member of the royal family – whose name he did not reveal. Gasps of horror could be heard around the table as his litany of corruption was divulged. He shrank back into his chair, avoiding everyone's stare. After a few minutes John sat down, waiting to see the reaction from the members, and John Benjafield himself.

Sir Charles stood up and pointed his finger at the accused. 'So, Mr Dangerfield, what do you say? Are these allegations untrue? From what I have seen and know first hand, I believe you have no grounds to dispute them...but the floor is yours if you wish to do so.'

For a second he said nothing, looking around the room to see if anyone would come to his aid, or offer words of support. None was forthcoming. Furious, embarrassed, he stared round the room, looking at each member of the Corporation, his eyes finally stopping when they reached John. 'You will regret this day, Mr Oakes, and those of you who side with him. I shall see you in court, and sue you for this abominable slander into the workhouse.' With that threat hanging in the air, he turned and strode out of the meeting, his face red with humiliation.

A silence followed. Sir Charles and Sir Simon could barely conceal their glee at their foe's humiliation. Others who had sided in the past with the now disgraced blackmailer silently pondered their futures – and alliances, now he was no longer a person of power or influence. Most couldn't comprehend how someone who they thought was an upstanding, honourable man (if overly ambitious at times) could be such a scoundrel.

Sir Simon let the members quietly discuss the inflammatory news for a few minutes before bringing the meeting back to order.

'I would propose that what we have just heard be the subject of further discussion – and Mr Benjafield's censure and possible expulsion for the Corporation be tabled for consideration at next month's meeting. Now, with my apologies again for the interruption, I invite Mr Weatherstone to continue with his report.'

An hour later, after an excruciatingly dull presentation, Sir Simon, in particular, breathed a sigh of relief. The lawyer had found a long list of errors, miscalculations and downright sloppy accounting, including some questions about the workhouse's finances; 'ones which I would recommend should be subject to closer scrutiny', however, no fingers were pointed, no blame laid at anyone's door. It was more of a call for tighter controls and better financial management.

The alderman thanked the lawyer for his 'detailed and thorough work' then asked the meeting if they wished to discuss the findings. In reality, as Sir Charles said later over drinks, 'I think everyone there was grateful nothing too serious was found, and no one found guilty of any malfeasance. However undeserved, our reputations are intact, except of course, those of Mr Benjafield.' He laughed. 'Though I am sure we have not heard the last of him. I'll wager, he will not go down without a fight.'

John Oakes agreed: 'I fear this is the opening gambit in what will be a long and drawn-out battle. We may have won the opening moves, however that man respects no boundaries, as we have seen.

He will fight dirty and without scruples. We must gird ourselves for his attacks, which will be nasty and underhand for sure.'

The alderman was not part of the celebrations. He knew it was only a matter of time before his dealings with the workhouse would come out into the open if the recommendations made by Weatherstone were followed through. An urgent visit to the warden was in order; it was time to start covering his tracks.

The warden was underwhelmed at Sir Simon's suggestion their 'financial arrangement' should cease, immediately.

'But, sir,' he whined, 'my wage here is not enough for a man to live on, and provide for my family.'

This disgusting specimen has a wife? A family? Or is he just lying to evince some sympathy? No matter, the alderman would not be swayed. Too much was at stake.

'All good things must come to an end, Warden. You have profited handsomely from our arrangement. To continue while we are under such scrutiny would be foolhardy. Enough is enough. You will be sure to destroy any records relating to this?'

'Maybe, my lord, maybe...what is it worth if I don't?' He smirked as he made the veiled threat.

Sir Simon, a good foot taller than the warden, walked over and grabbed him round the throat, pushed him backwards, and slammed him into the wall. Ignoring the warden's disgusting odour he put his face inches from the whimpering man. 'Let me be clear, Warden, if you fail to follow my orders, or if you utter a word to anyone about our arrangement, I have men working for me who will not hesitate to run you through. And then leave you for dead in Thetford Forest, having first emasculated you just to hear you scream for mercy. Do I make myself understood?'

Unable to talk, as Sir Simon's hand slowly throttled him, he nodded in agreement, fear in his bulging, watery eyes.

'Good, a wise choice, you insolent little wretch. Now that our business is concluded, I do not want to hear nor see from you again.'

The warden slumped to the floor as Sir Simon released his grip. Still trembling he watched his former benefactor leave, and with it a highly lucrative gravy train. He quickly decided he wasn't going to give in so easily. If his entitled Lordship thought he would destroy the evidence of their little arrangement, he was much mistaken. Those papers could be worth something, sometime in the future. Indeed, they might just be the insurance he required to one day leave this hellhole. He smiled to himself. Yes, there was always someone wanting to pay good money for such information.

* * * *

The future for both these men did not turn out as either planned.

The warden died within three months of an unspecified disease, but one the doctor suggested he may have contracted from one of the numerous women in the workhouse he consorted with on a regular basis. The trail of paperwork revealing his dealings with the alderman mysteriously vanished when all his belongings were thrown out and burnt. It also became clear he had no family to which his modest nest egg could be given. In a final ironic twist, the Corporation decided it should be given to the workhouse.

The feud between John Benjafield and John Oakes lasted on and off for another twenty years, and could be the subject of a book in itself. During the two decades the men made various truces and agreements, only to regularly break them. Their paths crossed not just at the Corporation but in many other areas of Bury politics. It seemed Benjafield had the knack of annoying as many people as those who sided with him. Events came to a head in 1811 when news of a case in the Court of Chancery ruined his reputation in Suffolk once and for all. The case concerned the trusteeship of Michael Peter Leheup of Hessett and Bury's estate and Benjafield's mismanaging of it. The matter might have died down quickly had John Benjafield not made his position worse by suing one of the papers that carried reports of the case. He lost the libel case, and with it his reputation.

In a paradoxical twist of fate, in 1819 he was appointed Governor of the workhouse – a less than satisfactory position, he felt, for a man of his stature, and retained the office until February 1831 when he was forced to resign: because of anomalies in the accounts! He died in 1832.

John Oakes lived in Bury until his death in 1829.

Sir Simon, despite his diminished circumstances, remained alderman until his death in 1820. Without the income from the workhouse and with his businesses in decline he sold the house three years later to a man who would use it to plumb the depths of depravity in his pursuit of gratification and pleasure.

Chapter 32
(1829)

'You are telling me this pig can spell?'

The man nodded his head vigorously, as if the harder he did so, the more believable his answer.

'Indeed it can, sir. I shall demonstrate if you so wish.'

Stephen Chasteline was sceptical. Who wouldn't be? The boar's owner had brought the animal, at his request, late one evening to his house in Whiting St. He was intrigued to see just what the fuss was all about. The animal's reputation had spread amongst the revellers at the annual Bury Fair; its abilities, by all accounts, were astounding. Everyone who saw the animal performing its tricks were awed at the pig's apparent literary abilities.

Stephen, a louche thirty-year-old son of a wealthy landowner and farmer, was enjoying his newfound wealth. He'd bought the house with the considerable income from his deceased father's estate and was making an excellent career of spending it as quickly as possible. Cloistered around him were his regular band of three sycophants, happy to indulge in any entertainment he provided for them. Normally it was more...primitive in nature, appealing to their baser proclivities; however, this evening's show was an interesting departure from the norm.

Stephen saw no reason to mix with the commoners to view the animal's tricks. He'd requested a private demonstration in his own home. With the money to pay for any indulgence, having the pig in the house was certainly different, to say the least. His entourage were already the worse for drink by the time the animal and its owner arrived. The latter didn't normally go to people's houses, the rough and tumble of the fair was his familiar turf, however the offer of £5 for a private demonstration was too much to ignore. He knocked on the door and was surprised to find Stephen opening it – did a man of this wealth not have servants?

As soon as he entered the room the drunken revellers were assailed by a pungent smell emanating from the pig (or maybe its owner). Keen to see the pig in action and be rid of it and its associated stink, Stephen suggested the porcine entertainer commence his tricks at once.

'Show me what this amazing animal can do, my man. I hear he can spell! I'll give you £1 for every word he completes!'

The owner smiled; this could be a lucrative evening! He emptied from his large sack some 26 blocks of wood, each about six inches square, on which a letter from the alphabet was carved. They were spread out in front of the pig (called Cromwell, his owner informed his now very attentive audience).

Cromwell ambled over and began sniffing the blocks, then stopped as if waiting for a command.

'Cromwell, spell the word 'HELP', as in H.E.L.P.,' commanded the owner. After a moment's deliberation the pig started to move the blocks around with his snout until the letters lined up to spell the requested word. The pig then cast his beady eyes at the momentarily stunned audience, as if to say, 'Next?'

Stephen and his guests clapped and hooted their appreciation. And a one pound coin was dropped into the man's outstretched hand. At his owner's command Cromwell repeated the feat three more times. Earning another three pounds. Sensing his inebriated host was still doubting the pig's abilities, he asked.

'Would you like to choose a word, sir? No more than five letters is all I ask, sir.'

'C.H.E.A.T.E.R' spelled out Stephen, ignoring the owner, now determined to catch the animal out. Convinced he was the subject of some flimflam trick.

The pig appeared to hesitate for a moment. Then, his nose twitching vigorously, he proceeded to arrange the letters in the correct order to spell the requested word. This time silence followed. No round of applause. His friends knew Stephen did not like to be made a fool of, and feared a confrontation might be on the cards. One of the guests broke the awkward hush: 'That animal has God-given abilities, or he is the Devil incarnate. Either way, Stephen, you owe the man another pound.'

Handing over the coin, he said to the owner with a tinge of anger in his voice. 'I know not how you do this, for I cannot believe the animal can spell of its own abilities. Something is amiss here; if I am being swindled I know not how. But enough is enough. Here is your payment, now leave, the entertainment is over.'

Feeling the need to defend himself against accusations of dishonesty, the owner replied. 'There is no trickery here, sir, I have trained this animal for years. He is one of a kind. Pigs are far more intelligent than people think. Cromwell is the cleverest of the lot. I hope you enjoyed his display. He truly can spell! Now if that is all, sir, I must get back to the fair. I thank you for your time.'

As he turned to walk out of the house, the pig stopped for a second. He suddenly seemed to detect a smell from between or beneath the wide oak floorboards. His owner pulled hard on his collar, attempting to lead him to the door. Reluctantly Cromwell stopped his olfactory investigation, lifted his head and proceeded to deposit a large pile of droppings on the expensive rug. Then, with a snort of disapproval, followed his master out to the house.

Theodore, Stephen's younger brother, said, 'Do you think he smelled what we have in the cellar?'

'Maybe', said Stephen, 'but even if he did, I doubt even that pig could spell it out!'

'True,' agreed Theodore, 'but anyway, isn't it time to find some fresh entertainment? Can we see what the fair has to offer? I am in the mood for something different. Please can we go hunting?' he pleaded, his drunken, bloodshot eyes momentarily alight with anticipation.

'Yes, Theo. Let's all go have some fun! Come on, boys, let's be going. It's late and the pickings should be ripe and ready for us. Put those damnable books down, they are giving you too many strange ideas.'

Reluctantly they threw their copies of The 120 Days of Sodom and Philosophy in the Bedroom, onto the floor. The two young men struggled to get up from the chaise longue. They stood up, leaning on each other for support. Both wore more makeup than was customary, their cheeks highlighted in pink powder. Brightly coloured kerchiefs flopped from their coat pockets.

'Come on, Johnny, you dandy, stand up, you're no use to anyone in this state, pull yourself together, we're off to the fair!' announced Theo.

'Stop being such a bossy boots. I am ready and raring to go. Just let me use the piss pot and I'll be all yours,' said Neville, trying his best not to fall over as he walked across the room.

'Not for the first time...' said Johnny sarcastically as he walked to the front door.

The Bury Fair, founded in 1272, came to be known as Bury's St Matthew Fair after a royal visit granted the abbot and Lord of Bury a charter for a fair to be kept annually, three days before and three days after the Feast of St Matthew on the 21st September.

By 1829 it had become a huge, sprawling event spreading way beyond the confines of Angel Hill down towards Eastgate St, up Abbeygate St and even into the Buttermarket. The fair attracted thousands of people from all over the country – it was the biggest such event outside London. Traders and sellers converged by the hundreds to set up stalls selling every conceivable item for the home or personal use. It was a cornucopia of delights, all designed to relieve visitors of their money.

As the British Empire expanded so international trade flourished, and the fair became a shop window for everything from exotic animals to never before seen food, handmade products to weird inventions. These often expensive items attracted buyers from the nobility and gentry who, with their newfound wealth, were eager to buy anything that would elevate their status.

Those less wealthy, who were not able to afford such goods, still found plenty of things to spend their money on. Cheap food, drink and entertainment and just the spectacle and atmosphere.

The fair was a vast stage for showmen and their animals, and those enterprising individuals who offered a dizzying array of entertainment for the curious and gullible. These included puppeteers, actors, musicians, magicians and jugglers. The more outrageous, the more popular. This year there was, for example, a 'Miss Hawtin', an armless female who used her toes to draw and to cut watch papers.

The side shows were often extravagant, bizarre, and at times grotesque. Deformed animals were always popular; one year the fair featured a two-headed cow. Dancing bears, cockfighting, all could be found.

However, like any event that attracted thousands of visitors determined to have a good time with the aid of too much drink and an increasing selection of drugs such as cocaine, laudanum, cannabis and opium, there were those ready to take advantage of the unwary or incapable.

It was the last evening of the Bury Fair and, suitably fortified with a concoction of coca leaves and gin, Stephen and his friends rowdily ventured out, heading for Angel Hill.

'Theo, you double-checked all was secure in the cellar?' asked Stephen as they left the house.

'Yes, brother, all is well...now stop worrying and let us see what the night brings us. I am anticipating some fine specimens will be ready for the taking.'

In the pitch black of the cellar a man and woman lay chained to the walls, their hands bound behind them and mouths gagged. The chains allowed them to move a few feet and reach each other's hands. It was a small comfort, knowing they were alone for a few hours. Unable to talk, they scratched out words on the earth and read them by touch. It was a slow and difficult way to communicate, enabling them only to converse with the most basic questions and answers. By the third day they had little left to say, merely holding hands in a desperate attempt to lift the other's spirits.

For three days they'd been kept prisoner in the cellar, where they were subjected to the most unspeakable atrocities. It was always the same four men who took turns with the hot pokers, and other implements designed to inflict pain in ways the couple endured with decreasing fortitude. Then there were the assaults, the depravations both experienced as the men acted out their most perverted sexual fantasies.

They both knew no one would be looking for them yet. They were just two of the thousands attending the fair from far away, and would not be missed by relatives for another week at least. Though both were now doubting they could survive much more of this harrowing treatment as the violence of the abuse seemed to increase each day. The men seemed unable to achieve whatever pleasure they were seeking unless more pain, more humiliation was employed.

Despair was seeping into their very core, like an icy north wind that cuts through you in winter. Insidious, unstoppable, it was gradually eating at their will to survive, death an inevitable, even preferable, alternative to their ceaseless suffering. The girl, the subject of the most vicious attacks, had a gut-wrenching fear in her stomach, at times more unbearable than her other wounds. She dreaded dying but feared living even more.

* * * *

'Maud, we must do something to help these poor wretches. I cannot bear to see such barbarism in our house! It is sickening, what can be done to stop those evil men?'

'Grace, I have told you before, we cannot become involved, we cannot help. We are merely observers from the other side. Painful and frustrating though it is, there is little we can do. Prayers that their suffering comes to an end are all we can provide. Spirits cannot interfere in earthly matters.'

'Of course they can, just our presence can reassure, or more often, put fear into people. They do not understand who or what we are when they see us. Can we not do something to dissuade those men from their bestial behaviour? Scare them? Please, Maud, you were always willing to help people, why not do something now and save those poor souls?'

'Maybe we have to accept it is their time to join us on the other side, that their suffering will soon cease and they shall be at peace,' said Maud.

'But they are too young to be brought here! They have a fulfilling life before them, with our help. They are obviously in love, they should have the years ahead of them to enjoy their devotion to each other – just as we did,' argued Grace. 'If you are not prepared to do something...I will.'

Chapter 33

Joleyn saw through the gloom a group of men coming down Churchgate St towards them, clearly drunk and behaving in a loud and obnoxious manner. 'Perhaps we should cross over, Robert, those men look like trouble.' The street, lit solely by lamps left in all the houses' windows, provided patchy but adequate light to see where you were going. But not sufficient to feel comfortable passing close to inebriated strangers.

'They are but drunk, my love. If they cause any trouble I shall make short shrift of them. You are quite safe with me.' Robert, a former army captain and well over six feet tall, barrel chested and fit from years of service life, knew how to handle himself and was not going to let four thugs bully him out of the way.

As the men approached within a few feet of the couple, Theodore, in a drunken slur, said, 'Ooh, now she is sooo pretty, let's ask her to come home with us...have, have some fun? How about it, lady?' He ill-advisedly reached out to touch her breast.

Without a word, Robert swung back and landed a punch straight onto the nose of the unsuspecting Theodore. The other men stood in a shocked daze as their friend fell to the ground, blood spurting from his nose through his fingers.

Robert turned, fists raised, to the other men, 'So who's next to insult my wife?'

Their drunken bravado evaporating, Stephen tried his best to save face. 'That was a mistake, sir. Don't you know who I am? I could call you out for assaulting my friend and threatening me, but I shall let the matter rest if you apologise.'

Robert laughed 'Ha! Apologise to you scum? I care not who you are, to me you are a bunch of drunken, loud-mouthed reprobates who deserve to spend the night in gaol. Be off with you all before one of you joins your friend on the pavement.'

Theodore struggled to his feet, and through his bloody nose blubbered, 'Leave it, brothers, let us pass these people and find something to drink. I need one to dull the pain.'

With that, the four stalked off into the darkness, muttering obscenities and threats Robert chose to ignore.

'Didn't you bring your cosh, Johnny?' said Neville. 'You could have knocked that bully out.'

'Sorry, my sweet, the only cosh I have is the one that's hard when you touch it. Not much use against that monster.'

'Johnny, I swear you are of no use to man nor beast,' complained Neville.

'That's not what you said last night, if I remember rightly.' replied Johnny, grabbing his friend's crotch.

'Enough, both of you!' snapped Stephen. "If you want to have fun with some new friends, concentrate and keep your wits about you for a likely couple. The drunker, the better. And beware of those army officers roaming through the fair. Before you know it, you'll be in the barracks ready to go to France or some godforsaken place.'

Stephen's advice was all too true. Army recruitment officers patrolled amongst the throng searching for young men, especially those of lesser means, and the worse for drink, to take back to the barracks and coerce into joining the army with promises of wages, food and shelter. Often by the time they had sobered up, their names signed with a fingerprint on a recruitment form meant the army had secured their services for years to come.

Some of the busiest workers were the hundreds of harlots and mollies selling their services for just a few shillings. As the night wore on practically any doorway, shadowed or secluded corner was claimed by these women to service their clients. Many too drunk to keep their wits about them soon found their pockets picked and any jewellery no longer in their possession.

Even this late at night, Angel Hill was still packed with people enjoying the final evening of the fair. It was an onslaught on the senses: The noises of animals protesting, children squealing with delight, people singing, traders shouting; it was a cacophony of such volume, conversation at times was almost impossible. Musicians added to the raucousness as they walked through the crowd trying to earn a few pennies.

The smells of unwashed bodies, animal dung, food, drink and smoke from the torches, was overwhelming, at times almost choking. A haze hung over the throng across the whole of Angel Hill.

Light came from hundreds of torches and lamps set up on poles across the square. But it did nothing to dissuade the pickpockets, cutpurses and other ne'er-do-wells from their relentless pursuit of those too drunk to know they had been robbed.

The four predators continued drinking and carousing, all the time looking for a couple sober enough to walk, but drunk enough to be persuaded that some free drink - and drugs - was theirs if they returned to Stephen's house.

'And no whores or mollies, I want them clean and as young as possible,' Stephen reminded the others as they cast around for likely victims. After several failed attempts at persuading some young people to join them (one girl - sober enough to have not lost all her wits - kneed Neville between the legs, causing him to accuse her of 'breaking his cosh' as he lurched away clutching his privates). The others roared with laughter at his misfortune. And so the hunt continued.

It was close to midnight, with the crowds thinning, and those the worse for wear wandering in drunken stupors trying to find their way home, that Theo spied a young girl and man sitting by the Assembly Rooms. She was crying, and he was doing his best to console her. It was clear both were inebriated, but not to the point of insensibility.

Theo whistled to get the attention of the others to keep their distance. He didn't want to make the couple feel threatened by a group of four men surrounding them. In his most solicitous manner he approached them and asked if there was a problem, and could he help? Did they need assistance in getting home?

The man, his arm protectively around the young girl's shoulder, looked up at the well-dressed gentleman, who seemed respectable and friendly.

Ancient Hallways

The young man explained their predicament: 'Sir, we have been robbed of all our money. The landlord of our boarding house expects us to pay him this evening. If we don't he threatens to call the law. So we will have to spend the night on the streets and leave tomorrow without our belongings. It is a terrible end to our visit to the fair. I don't know what to do. My wife is pregnant and I worry a night outside may cause her much discomfort. I hate to beg – but do you have some coins to spare, sir?'

In a reassuring voice, Theo suggested, 'I live close by, why don't you come back with me, and stay the night in my guest room? That way your wife will be safe and comfortable. It is the least I can do.' Further embellishing his credentials with the glib lie, 'As a member of the Corporation I am horrified that your visit to my fine town has ended this way.'

'That is most kind of you, sir, but we cannot put you to such an inconvenience.'

'Nonsense! I did the same for another distressed couple a few days ago. The folks of Bury are renowned for their hospitality; I insist you come with me and stay the night. It is of no trouble. My servants will make you a meal before you rest. Here, let me help you up.'

The girl took Stephen's proffered hand and stood up, no longer crying but, he could tell, suspicious of his offer. The man shook Theo's hand. 'My name is Andrew, and this is my wife, Abby. We are from Ipswich. We are both grateful for your kindness.'

Theo immediately realised his choice of victims was not ideal. The man was tall and broad-shouldered. His handshake was vice-like. He looked fit and healthy, except for some bruises and cuts to his face. His wife was a petite blonde, dressed well, but not

376

expensively. As they walked up Churchgate St it was obvious they were far from drunk; in fact, worryingly, thought Stephen, they seemed composed and alert. He noticed Neville, Theo and Johnny were following some distance behind, not wanting to be seen.

Then Andrew casually mentioned he was a professional boxer, but had lost his latest fight that afternoon, leaving him with little money, all of which was subsequently stolen.

Theo suddenly felt unsure of himself. Maybe these were not the easy victims he first assumed they were, ones for whom the threat of violence was enough to be led meekly downstairs into the pleasure cellar. He looked behind him to see where the other men were, but the dark street now obscured their whereabouts.

Stephen couldn't now un-invite this couple to the house. He could concoct some excuse, though none came immediately to mind. Then he wondered what the couple's reaction would be when the others came into the house. Quite possibly put Andrew on his guard, making subduing him and the girl even more difficult.

And let's be honest, he told himself, Neville and Johnny would be useless in a fight, they were effeminate fops who only enjoyed inflicting pain; the possibility of getting hurt would send them cowering into the corner. And he certainly didn't fancy his and Theo's chances at taking down this muscled professional boxer.

'Are we nearly at your house?" asked Abby, interrupting his thoughts.

'Yes, ma'am, down here, it will be just a minute before you are safe and warm,' said Stephen, his facade of concern quickly switched on for the benefit of the girl.

Running out of options, he opened the door and invited them in, leaving it ajar for the others to follow. They did just a few minutes later, and as he anticipated the boxer's battered face immediately registered alarm.

'My apologies, sir, if we are intruding on a gathering of your friends, we will seek alternative accommodation.' He looked at his wife. 'Come, Abby, I think it best we leave these gentlemen to their privacy.' He took her hand and made for the door.

Stephen held up his hand. 'Sir, please stay, I was remiss in not telling you we had other guests. Please stay, it is too late to be wandering the streets with such a lovely lady. Sit down and let us get you some mulled wine to take the chill off you.' He signalled to Neville to fetch a pitcher of drink from the parlour. 'Be generous with the spice, Neville,' said Stephen, a discreet nod of his head telling Neville all he needed to know.

Warily the couple sat down in front of the fire, which Johnny was busily stoking with fresh logs. Within minutes it was warming them through, their anxiety allayed as they relaxed, their cold bodies soothed by the heat. Theo wasted no time in introducing Andrew as a professional boxer, hoping the others would recognise the potential danger he posed if he gained the slightest inkling of their plans for him and his wife. Hopefully, thought Stephen, the drugged wine would dull the big man's senses enough to get him into the cellar without a fight.

Neville appeared with the drinks, the glasses full with a warm red wine, smelling of spices and herbs. The men watched, and hoped the drug would take effect – and quickly. Stephen and Theo were entranced with Abby's looks and buxom figure. Being pregnant only made her more alluring to them. It would be a first for both of them to explore and enjoy a woman in such a condition. Meanwhile Johnny and Neville's attention was on the tightly honed body of the boxer. They were practically salivating over seeing him naked and watching him struggle as they possessed his body for their own perverted pleasures.

Chapter 34

Andrew's head throbbed painfully. He opened his eyes slowly, expecting to see a room, light shining through a window, his wife lying beside him. Instead, he saw nothing, except for some faint slivers of light slanting down from above, barely illuminating the room. Except it wasn't a room, it had bare earth floors and chalk walls. His disappointment increased when he realised the chains on his legs were fastened to a substantial iron bolt in the wall and his wrists shackled tightly together. He was also naked.

'What the fuck..?' he swore, pulling in vain at the restraints which showed no sign of loosening, despite his strength.

Abby's bewildered voice cut through the blackness, 'Andrew? Andrew, is that you? What has happened to us? Why are we down here? I am so cold, they have stripped me of my clothes...Please, Andrew, do something. I am scared what these men will do to us.'

'Abby, don't worry. I am here. I, too, am naked and chained up. When I am free of these shackles I will beat those men to a pulp, I swear I will make them pay for this. But I will get us out of here, I promise; try to remain calm. I know it's difficult.' He paused, dreading the answer to his question, 'Have they...hurt you in any way?'

'No, but I fear they will; why else would I be without clothes?' Andrew heard his wife begin to sob, an uncontrollable keening that wrenched his heart strings. He could do nothing to console her, which added to his anger and frustration.

Suddenly, out of the darkness from the far end of the cellar, a barely audible female voice, laden with despair, whispered.

'God help you both. These men are evil, they take pleasure in hurting you in ways you cannot imagine. Prepare yourself for the worst...'

'Who...who are you?' asked Andrew. 'Are you saying these men have tortured you? What did they do? How long have you been here?'

The unseen girl said nothing, worsening the fear twisting in Andrew's stomach.

Her voice weak, she answered, 'I'm Mildred. I have been here, I don't know, maybe three or four days. My husband is here, too, but I assume he is dead or unconscious. He has said nothing for hours. Two of them seem to like...women, the others spent their energy on him. They are so horrible, so vicious, their depravity knows no bounds. And they made me watch as they enjoyed themselves on my...' Her voice tailed off as she sobbed in the dark.

A brooding, uneasy silence descended. Andrew and Abby digesting the harrowing news Mildred had revealed. They were just too shocked to pass comment. A gut-twisting fear now consumed them both. Though Andrew knew his capacity to withstand pain was greater than most, the thought of seeing his beloved Abby suffer at the hands of these degenerates would be unbearable – a mental torture worse than any physical one they could employ on him.

Everyone was turning over in their minds what desperate straits they were now in. Each wallowing in trepidation at the horrors they were about to face. Both women were crying. Andrew, however, was seething with anger, already planning ways to take on his captors given the slightest opportunity. He quelled his anxiety and composed himself, as he did before each fight. Banishing any doubt about overcoming his opponent. Building his self-belief, his confidence that he would feel no pain, focusing on preparing himself mentally for the fight, and devising the best tactics to overwhelm and crush the other men.

With both hands shackled together and his legs chained to a wall, he was a long way from being able to defend himself, let alone attack, his captors. But the courage he needed every time he stepped into the ring hadn't deserted him. He tested the chains; they were about a foot in length and unbreakable. Though long enough that if he got close enough he could wrap around someone's neck. The chain attaching his leg to a large bolt buried in the chalk wall seemed to offer the best hope of freeing himself. If he could just loosen it, then the fight would be on.

As he started to try and work the bolt loose he heard the clumping of footsteps and muffled conversations from above. It must be morning, he guessed. The men were moving about and he heard broken sentences talking about hangovers, breakfast, and chillingly 'some sport...with our new guests...' It would only be a matter of time before they came into the cellar and their depraved idea of entertainment started. Andrew threw all his strength into loosening the bolt in the chalk wall. He knew if he could pull it out he would be able to take on these four men, hands manacled or not. To his frustration the bolt was proving stubbornly resistant to his frantic efforts. But he continued, knowing if he did nothing, if he couldn't free himself, he and his wife would be subjected to unimaginable horrors.

So intent was Andrew on his efforts to free the bolt he didn't hear the cellar door open and, each carrying a lamp, the four men descended, illuminating the cellar, revealing a room much larger than he thought. He finally saw the poor girl, Mildred. Her body was covered in cuts, burns and bruises. Her breasts had teeth marks all over them, and from what he could see there was blood all over her thighs and stomach.

In between the still unconscious man and Andrew was a large, solid wooden table with manacles bolted to each corner. On the wall hung rows of iron and wooden implements and knives. Abby gasped in panic; it was all too plain to see what these instruments were for. Andrew refused to show any signs of weakness. Instead he just stared at the men, daring them to come near him. He felt revulsion and fear, but he was damned if they would know it.

The one he remembered as Theo stood over Mildred, who started trembling uncontrollably, her eyes averted, shuffling her body against the wall as if it offered some kind of protection. His eyes roamed over her battered, naked body. 'You have been a good sport, young lady. Your body has given me and my brother much pleasure. It seems we will be the first and last men you'll enjoy. For it is time we moved onto pastures new...' He walked over to the wall and plucked a large meat cleaver from a hook, and ran his finger along its edge. 'Good job, Johnny, you have sharpened it to perfection. I think I could shave with this! It will make this so much easier – and quicker for you as well, young lady.' He walked across the cellar and stood above the quaking girl. 'Forgive me, such a display of bad manners. I must ask: Did you enjoy our time together, experimenting with the delights of pain and pleasure as we did?' The girl said nothing, tears falling down her cheeks, eyes closed as she anticipated the fall of the cleaver and the ending of her life. 'I take that as a 'no' then? Oh, well, Stephen we must improve our technique, it seems!'

Theo lifted the girl's arms and deftly ran the razor-sharp cleaver's edge across one wrist, then the other. The girl screamed in pain, looked at the gushing cuts with horror, then mercifully passed out. A steady flow of blood poured from her wounds, collecting in small dark puddles on the earthen floor. Theo stood back as if to admire his handiwork.

'How much do we think this wench weighs? I guess seven stone.' The others agreed. 'Then I think it will be about thirty minutes before she bleeds out and departs this mortal coil. Johnny, why don't you time it?'

Johnny laughed, pulled out his pocket watch and noted the time. 'Half past ten, Theo; she should be dead before eleven o'clock!'

Without a second look Theo turned, replaced the cleaver on the hook and set his eyes on Abby. She curled up into a ball on the damp floor, somehow hoping this would protect her from whatever evil act was about to follow.

'Now, now, young lady, let's get those shackles off and get you onto the table, so we can all see what you have to offer...'

'Touch her and I will kill you. I swear to God you will die if you hurt her in any way!' bellowed Andrew, straining at his chains like a caged lion.

'I think you are in no position to make such threats,' said Stephen. 'And I would be very careful what you say; my friends Neville and Johnny might not be interested in the delights your wife has to offer, but they have been fantasising all night about what they will do to you when you're on this table. I am always impressed at their ingenuity...do you want to see their latest toy?'

He reached across to the array of tools on the wall and took a small metal implement shaped like, and the same size as, a pear. He held it up, for everyone to see. 'This is called the Pear of Anguish. I have not used it yet, only recently has it arrived from France. It is a masterpiece of engineering; I have to hand it to those French, they have a skill for inflicting pain in the most imaginative ways.' Protruding from the tapered end of the 'pear' was a screw head which he proceeded to turn, and gradually the pear opened, four equal sections spreading like wings from a central hinge. Stephen carried on until the sections were fully extended, now looking like petals on a flower stem.

'What I like about this beauty is it can be used on both men and women. When closed it is inserted into their...orifices. Then, when gradually opened, I am told it can administer a level of pain few can withstand. Impressive, don't you think? And such a wonderful piece of engineering.' Stephen paused for a moment to admire the instrument. 'But we will save that for later...we have tamer ways to enjoy ourselves, haven't we, gentlemen?'

The other men agreed with nods and smiles. They wanted to start enjoying their new spoils; Stephen's lectures were a frustrating delay. Theo, anxious to relieve the tension, the urge, building in his groin, moved across to Abby.

'Now, young lady, let the fun begin; your nakedness has been taunting me too long, I need to savour this beautiful body before the others defile it.'

'LEAVE HER ALONE!' Take me first!' howled Andrew. The muscles in his arms and legs bulged as he yet again strained, unsuccessfully, to break his bonds.

'Gentlemen, please silence that man, he is a distraction. I wish to enjoy her in peace. Please see to it, now!'

Neville, Johnny and Stephen approached Andrew. Even chained, they knew he was dangerous. His anger gave him an energy and ferocity that caused them to tread warily towards him. Stephen picked up a small oak beam, the size of a cudgel, and swung it haphazardly at Andrew's head, missing each time.

Then, distracted by a kick from Johnny, Stephen took another swing and caught the boxer on the head, monetarily stunning him, long enough for another blow to connect and render him unconscious.

'Thank the Lord,' said Theo. 'Now I can concentrate on this lady, who after all is deserving of my full attention. Gentlemen, let us put her on the table. Gently now, do not hurt her!'

Within minutes Abby was spreadeagled and tied on the table. She put up little resistance, now almost catatonic in her fear of what was about to happen. Seeing her beloved husband unconscious and unable to help, she lapsed into a semi-comatose state, her body limp, unresisting.

Theo, too, went into almost a dreamlike state, as he studied her body closely, running his hands lovingly over her breasts, face, up her thighs, her stomach, slightly swollen by the baby inside. He leant his face close to her body. He breathed deeply, now trance-like in his euphoria. 'Ah! I can still scent her perfume, she is delectable, an almost perfect specimen,' he whispered to himself.

He buried his head between her breasts, and bit one then the other, causing Abby to yelp in pain.

'And you are with child!' Theo was looking at Abby's belly, mesmerised as he stroked it and then in a sick show of affection placed his ear on her. 'Let me see if I can hear the baby's heartbeat.' With eyes closed he rested his head on her stomach. 'Yes. Yes! I do believe I can detect the tiniest of heartbeats. It is indeed a miracle, a life within a life, and when one dies, so does the other.'

Hearing these threats, Abby tried to take herself out of her body. Imagining she was looking down on someone else suffering this indignity. Trying to make her body numb to his grotesque attentions. This wasn't happening to her, now, but someone else. But it didn't work. All she could do was lie motionless and show no sign of fear or pain.

'I must have her now,' said Theo, breathless in anticipation of his desire soon to be satiated. He undid his trousers and thrust himself between Abby's legs.

As he did so the atmosphere in the cellar changed; the temperature dropped and a sharp wind came from nowhere, snuffing out the candles, plunging the room into absolute darkness. Even the cracks of light through the floorboards above were extinguished. Total blackness enveloped them all. From different parts of the cellar the men cried out in surprise.

'Hell's teeth, what is happening?' asked Stephen, 'How can there be a gust of wind down here? Why has it become so cold? Come on, gentlemen, let us go upstairs; we can continue the games later.' As they approached the steps, everyone stopped.

Standing but a few feet from them were two women, dressed as if from the 1600s. One spoke, though they could not tell which of the women ordered them to 'stop now or this house will be burnt to the ground.'

Johnny and Neville fell backwards against the two other men, panicking at the vision before them. 'Who...who are they?' stammered Johnny.

'I have no idea,' said Stephen, trying to show a calmness he didn't feel, 'But 'tis clear they are warning us to stop what we are doing...'

He walked towards the women, demanding to know who they were, what they were doing in his house. In the darkness their faces were clearly visible. Pale, delicate shades of grey, and white. The one with blonde hair held out her hand as if to stop him approaching closer. Some unseen force halted Stephen mid-stride. Then, as quickly as they appeared, the two women vanished, leaving the men in a bewildered silence.

For a few moments nothing was said, and no one moved, all of them too stunned to react. Finally coming to their senses they scrambled like frightened children up the stairs into the parlour, heading straight for the decanters of whisky and brandy. They all needed something to calm their nerves. The apparition, the strange experience they had just seen and felt rendering them nervous, frightened wrecks. Sometime later, their nerves calming down, Neville asked the obvious:

'What was it we just saw? A ghost? Some kind of spirit? Or were they, God help us, demons? Does anyone have any ideas? It most surely scared the wits out of me. I shall not be going down there again any time soon.'

'And the cold wind that blew through the cellar, how did that happen?' asked Theo; still shivering, he covered his lower body with a rug to hide his nakedness. His ardour now long since deflated, his feelings now were of bafflement and shock, rather than lust.

Stephen's voice quivered slightly as he spoke, 'I...I am at a loss for words, gentlemen, I have no explanation to offer. I have never believed in ghosts but I have to accept that down there, that is what we witnessed. And it seems they have the power to affect the temperature and summon a breeze strong enough to douse our lamps. A most alarming episode, I admit.'

For the rest of the morning they discussed what happened, trying to make sense of it. They all agreed that they had seen the same thing. Something inexplicable, but with a power they could not fully describe. If the two women wanted to stop their perverted cavorting in the cellar, they had achieved their objectives.

Johnny reminded them that four people were still imprisoned in their cellar – and what was to be done with the girl in particular? None of them volunteered to go down there and free her, let alone to carry on where they left off. Seeing a ghost was a guaranteed killer of any lustful appetence.

'But the girl is still chained to the table; should we not at least free her, and shackle her to the wall? They all need some food and water as well too,' said Johnny, the only one to show any concern.

'Unless you want to do it, they can wait until tomorrow. They won't starve. We can plan our course of action over dinner tonight. Now I'm going to get drunk and try to put that girl's divine body out of my mind,' announced Theo as he grabbed a bottle of brandy and headed off to his bedroom. 'We will all be in a better frame of mind to deal with it tomorrow, of that I am confident.'

Theo's confidence was sadly misplaced.

* * * *

'*Grace, that was an unacceptable thing we did, you know that, don't you?' said Maud, but with no tone of censure in her voice.*

'*I do, and I don't care. We cannot always be observers. What was happening in that cellar was pure evil. We did the right thing in scaring them into stopping what they were doing. I only pray they are too terrified to resume those absolutely horrid acts,' replied Grace, not willing to apologise.*

'*I know. I agree, but we must not abuse our place here again. You promise?'*

'*I can't promise, Maud, but I will pray we are never put in this position again.'*

Grace started giggling.

'*What is so funny, Grace?'*

'*Did you see the look of horror on those men's faces? It was just too much fun to scare them like that!'*

Maud smiled. 'Grace, even in the afterlife your sense of humour never ceases to amaze me.'

Chapter 35

In the cellar, later that day, Andrew finally came round to hear Abby frantically calling his name.

'It's alright, Abby, I am here. I was knocked out, but I am back with you. What has happened to you...did they harm you?'

'No, they didn't, though I am still here on the table unable to move. But something really strange happened, Andrew, which I cannot fully explain. Whatever it was, it saved me from being raped and for that I am most grateful. It caused the men to flee the cellar with great haste and in some state of fear.'

'Strange? What do you mean by strange, Abby?'

Abby tried to explain about the chilling wind that blew through the cellar dousing the lamps and some kind of apparition that scared their captors into leaving her alone. Unfortunately, she could not see the ghostly images clearly as they were obscured by the men. Their fearful comments and hasty retreat were her only clues as to how petrified they were by whatever they saw.

'Well, whoever or whatever it was that stopped their dastardly plans, now we must take advantage of it,' said Andrew. 'I am sure they will be back down here soon. I must redouble my efforts to break free.'

Andrew decided the bolt into the wall was the weakest point, and he spent the next few hours twisting, tugging and pushing it from side to side, gradually loosening it a fraction of an inch, then a little more, then enough that it began to pull away from the chalk wall.

Finally, his hands bloodied, his fingers raw with hours of effort, the bolt came free. He could now move about the cellar, albeit in almost total darkness. He stumbled over to the table, found Abby and, by touch alone, undid her bindings. He hugged her tightly as she sat up, her body stiff and cold after so long on the table.

'We must get out of here before they return, but I must free my hands from these shackles first. Then I'll have a fighting chance to give those devils the beating they deserve.'

'I think I saw some keys hanging on the wall...over there by all those horrid instruments.'

As Andrew's sight became used to the darkness, he reached the wall, running his hands along the instruments of torture hanging there in all innocence like some blacksmith's workshop. Fumbling around, he eventually heard the rattle of keys on a large iron ring. Frustratingly it was the last one he tried that unlocked his shackles and with a cry of delight he threw them onto the floor. Stopping for a moment he then went back to the wall and found a large iron bar and, as he picked it up his hand brushed against the Pear of Anguish. Smiling to himself he took it.

'Now I am ready to give those bastards a taste of their own medicine. We must go now!'

'Wait,' said Abby, what about that poor man? We can't leave him here.'

'Once we have dealt with those men upstairs we will come back down for him. I promise. Now let us proceed quietly up the stairs. Surprise will be our best form of attack; you must stay behind me. Here, take this iron bar and hit the first man that comes near you!'

Creeping slowly up the cellar steps, they reached the top and Andrew lifted the trapdoor a few inches. Through the crack he saw the parlour had no one working in it, and he heard no movement close by. He beckoned Abby to follow him. They both stood still, listening for any sign of movement in the house. Next door they could hear two men laughing. Andrew peered around the door into the great hall and saw Neville and Johnny playing cards. Stephen was asleep in the chair, snoring loudly, an empty bottle of brandy resting on his chest.

Andrew motioned to Abby that she should run and hit Stephen over the head with the iron bar, while he dealt with the two card players. She looked horrified at what Andrew suggested.

He put his mouth to her ear and whispered, 'That man tricked us here and was going to rape you; he is the reason you have suffered. Now take your revenge, or I shall, and kill him.'

Wide-eyed, Abby nodded, and held up the iron bar above her head, ready to do as her husband demanded.

Knowing he would be seen as soon as he left the parlour, Andrew gathered his wits, took a deep breath and hurtled into the room and across towards the two men, reaching them before either could even stand up.

Neville managed not a single word of surprise before a piledriving blow to the side of his head from Andrew's massive fist felled him;

he collapsed onto the card table, spilling the cards and coins onto the floor. Johnny, given the extra few seconds, decided to make a run for the front door. To no avail. Adrenaline, anger and revenge pumping through his body, Andrew was onto him before he reached the hallway. He grabbed him round the neck, and squeezed and squeezed until Johnny's breathing faltered, then stopped. He flung the limp body onto the floor like a child's rag doll.

So deep was Stephen's inebriated slumber he was unaware of the fate of his two friends. Despite Andrew's instructions, Abby was just standing over his inert body, iron bar wavering in the air above her. Despite everything this man had done to her, she couldn't bring herself to bring it down on his head.

'I'm sorry, Andrew, I just can't do it...it's just not in me to commit such an act. I am so, so sorry,' Abby said, feeling she had betrayed Andrew's trust.

'Worry not, my dear, hand the bar to me and get that pear-shaped contraption from the parlour, and a bowl of water.'

Moments later Abby returned. By then Andrew had dragged the still half-conscious Stephen into a large chair and was binding his hands to its frame with a torn up blanket from the sofa.

'Throw the water in his face, I want him fully awake for this.' Andrew ordered.

Abby obliged and Stephen spluttered into a semblance of awareness. For a second his face showed surprise and even annoyance; then, when his befuddled brain cleared, it turned to fear.

'What...what is going on?' Stephen looked around, confused. 'What do you want? Money? I have money! Take it all! Please release me. Believe I meant you no harm. It was all Theo's idea to trap you here...he is upstairs, take your anger out on him...I beg you.'

'Shut up, you piece of horseshit. You are all guilty of doing unspeakable things to innocent people. Torturing them and murdering them. You are all animals. Now it is time you suffered the way others have at your hands. Open your mouth.'

Stephen shook his head violently from side to side, trying to break Andrew's grip, his mouth clamped shut. Andrew was not to be deterred; his strong hands made short work of pinching Stephen's cheeks and forcing his jaws open.

'Abby, give me that pear instrument. Time for this shit to feel the kind of pain he's made others endure.'

Stephen frantically tried to shake his head free from Andrew's bone-crunching grasp, to escape what he knew would be unimaginable pain. But he was no match for Andrew's brute strength. He forced the Pear of Anguish between Stephen's teeth. His eyes bulged in panic as Andrew slowly turned the screw and the four metal leaves inexorably unfurled, forcing his mouth open wider and wider.

Both Andrew and Abby, in their frenzy to subdue the men, had forgotten they were still naked. Now, to Abby's horror, she saw through his agony Stephen looking at her body and, to her astonishment, it appeared he was becoming aroused, the bulge in his trousers growing as his eyes roamed up and down her nakedness.

'Please God, I cannot believe this man's perversion!' exclaimed Abby. 'Look, Andrew.' She pointed towards Stephen's privates. 'Does he find pain...enjoyable? It is beyond me how that can be so.'

'I cannot fathom it either,' said Andrew. 'This man is sick, they are all sick. They deserve to die, but I am no murderer. Much as I would like to take revenge for what they have done to us, and who knows how many others, I cannot bring myself to take his life...' He paused, considering his next move. 'We must find Theo and stop him from escaping. Then go and find a constable to take care of matters here, as quickly as we can.

'But first, let us tie up these two, you get dressed, and see if that poor man downstairs is still alive. I will pay a visit to that scoundrel upstairs. I don't think you want to see what I am about to do to him.'

They found some cord in the parlour, with which they tied up Neville and Johnny, putting gags in their mouths to keep them quiet. Andrew went into the parlour and found a long carving knife. I might have a use for that, he told himself. With everyone secured, Abby ran down to the cellar and a still-naked Andrew bounded up the stairs in search of Theo.

He heard him before he found him – the drunken snores led Andrew to a large bedroom, expensively furnished. The room was in darkness, the heavy curtains keeping out the daylight. It stank of sweat, drink and stale smoke. Andrew threw back the curtains and the light flooded in to reveal Theo comatose, an empty bottle of brandy beside him on the bed.

He was also naked. An open copy of Justine, by the Marquis de Sade, lay on his stomach. Andrew looked around and found a silk sash, with which he tied Theo's hands together and then to the bedpost. Still he didn't stir. Unceremoniously, Andrew poked Theo in the ribs with the carving knife. Then threw a jug of water from the wash stand over his head. Cursing and complaining, Theo slowly regained consciousness, opening his eyes to see Andrew holding the carving knife inches from his face.

Theo tried to sit up, found he could barely move and fell back onto the bed, sobering up very quickly.

'You? How...how did you get here? What do you want? Try to harm me and my brother will be here in seconds, as will my friends. Now, untie me, I command you!' Theo snarled, his anger for a moment overcoming his shock at awakening from a very pleasant dream inspired by Justine which, under normal circumstances, would have led him downstairs to satiate his ardour on whichever unfortunate female was captive at the time.

Andrew laughed. 'You are in no position to give orders, and your friends downstairs are, shall we say, otherwise indisposed? It's just you, me and this knife, and you're going to get to know us both a little better. We'll indulge in the kind of perversions you enjoy inflicting on others for a while. Now you'll know how they feel. The fear, the pain, the helplessness. As for me? I'm going to find this most entertaining...I hope you do too...'

'Please...'

Theo's words were cut off as Andrew shoved a piece of cloth roughly into his mouth.

'Let me explain something to you. You were about to rape my wife; you had already molested and abused her. Now, Theo, inside the ring I care for nothing except to knock my opponent out. They feel a moment of pain, then nothing. A quick, merciful conclusion. Here, having seen what you do to people in your cellar, it seems you think the pain should linger, and who am I to disagree with your methods? You were about to rape my wife and your disgusting behaviour was thankfully stopped by some apparition which all you brave men ran from like children. It seems maybe God is on our side.'

As he spoke he dragged the razor-sharp knife down Theo's chest, across his stomach until he was a few inches from Theo's flaccid member, leaving a thin trail of blood behind. He then stopped the knife right at his captive's ball sack.

Theo was writhing in pain, eyes bulging with fear. He tried to move his hips away from the point of the knife, but only succeeded in cutting himself on his hip. He grunted in pain, looked down at the blood flowing from the wound and twisted his whole body across the bed – or at least tried to. It was a futile action, and Theo knew it. He stopped moving, and a look of trepidation crossed his face. He was helpless, unable to control what happened next. A position he found exciting, arousing when he was dominating his victim, but terrifying now.

'Careful, Theo, you will hurt yourself!' said Andrew, enjoying watching this despicable man squirm in fright, just like his countless victims had done in the past.

'Interestingly, your brother seemed to, shall we say, enjoy the attention of that quaint instrument the Pear of Anguish? I thought this knife might be closer to your perverted taste.' Andrew carved a circle on Theo's stomach, and the blood oozed out onto the white sheets. Soundlessly he cried out, tears now running down his cheeks. 'Oh, I see the pain is not so stimulating. Your manhood seems to have taken fright. Well, in that case I may as well, as they say, cut to the chase, or in your case, your balls.'

Theo's eyes for a second showed confusion, then an awful comprehension that the next few seconds would be the most excruciating of his life...

By the time Andrew came back downstairs Abby was waiting for him, now fully dressed, holding his clothes for him. He hurriedly dressed, listening to Abby as she described finding the other man in the cellar dead, alongside the poor girl Mildred.

'That is simply terrible. These men are evil beyond words. I am tempted to kill them all, but it is best we leave them as they are and inform the law, let them deal with this hellhole.'

From across the other side of the great hall, Stephen groaned, the Pear of Anguish still in his mouth rendering speech impossible. 'We won't kill them, but the least I can do for those poor people in the cellar, is this...'

Abby strode across the room, Stephen's eyes following her, wondering what was going to happen next. He knew it wouldn't be pleasant, and he was right. Abby took a lit candle from the mantelpiece, walked back to Stephen. Taking Andrew's knife, she roughly cut a large hole in the top of Stephen's trousers. Tipping the candle over, she poured the hot wax all over his naked privates. As he howled in anguish, she took hold of the screw on the Pear of Anguish and purposefully, slowly, turned it clockwise, opening up the strong metal petals even further until, with a loud crack, Stephen's jaw broke, and he fainted without uttering a further sound.

Andrew watched in silence as Abby wreaked her own personal revenge on a man who violated women as a matter of habit, deciding Stephen was getting what he deserved. She echoed his thoughts as she snarled, 'That is for all the women you have harmed solely for your own pleasure. May you suffer in silence, unable to deceive any more with your lies and promises.'

A quiet descended around them. Abby and Andrew took a moment to compose themselves. The last 24 hours had been hellish beyond words. Now they were safe, and relatively unharmed, at least physically. The memories would take longer to heal, to fade, if ever. They had witnessed the most despicable, cruellest of acts deliberately inflicted upon helpless victims by men of incomprehensible depravity. But what drove them to such despicable acts?

Abby picked up one of the books lying on the floor, just what is this all about?' She read the title: The 120 Days of Sodom. She flicked through the pages. 'Sweet Jesus, Andrew, this book is, is disgusting; if this has been their reading matter no wonder their minds have been corrupted. It is full of the most hideous discourse on matters no normal man would write about. This Marquis de Sade is a degenerate of the worst kind. Ugh! What a vile book.' Abby threw it into the fire, her revulsion of its contents making her want to retch.

Meanwhile, Andrew was looking around the great hall, the fine furnishings and expensive decorations. The stories this house could tell, thought Andrew, though none as barbaric as it has just witnessed.

'This beautiful home has been abused and mistreated by these men. Let us hope once these murderers are in gaol, it will be put to a more blessed use by a new owner. Clearly it has some benevolent presence looking over it, one which saved our lives. I know not who or what it was, but I am eternally grateful for its manifestation. Maybe they were angels...' He paused for a second, then came back to reality.

'Abby, we must leave, and tell the authorities of these people, let them be punished and I hope they are hanged for their crimes. I no longer wish to be in this house.'

He took Abby's hand, leading her out into the bright morning sunshine. It caressed their faces like a refreshing splash of water, lifting their battered spirits. They'd escaped a dreadful fate, and now they needed to make sure their captors paid for their murdering, torturing deeds.

Five weeks later the four men were paraded through the streets of Bury. Slowly the open cart carrying them to the new execution site in the town gaol made its way through the packed streets. News of their atrocities had been widely published in gruesome detail by the local newspapers. As a consequence a raucous crowd lined the route, as normal hurling abuse, stones, rotting vegetables, anything that helped them vent the disgust they felt for the condemned men.

Only Theo said anything on the scaffold, still proclaiming his innocence, and blaming his brother, Stephen, for all the crimes committed in the house. Stephen, his jaw irreparably broken, had said nothing throughout his trial and was still silent as he waited for the noose to be put around his neck. Neville and Johnny, much to the crowd's amusement, cried non-stop, except when pleading for mercy. The crowd expected to see stoicism from those about to be executed, not whimpering. Such displays of weakness just encouraged them to throw more insults and cries for the men to be castrated before they were hung – in the past a common final punishment for such crimes.

They were spared that final, painful indignity. With practised speed, the executioner put the nooses around the four men's necks, quickly followed by black hoods. With the pull of a lever the trapdoors opened and, in a choreographed dance of death, like life-size puppets they fell, their bodies dangling, their legs dancing on a non-existent floor. None died immediately from a broken neck. And no one ran to pull on their legs to quicken their end, instead leaving them to slowly choke to death.

* * * *

The house, its reputation sullied by the activities that took place within its walls, was unsaleable, unrentable for many months. None of Stephen's distant relatives wanted anything to do with it. Soon all its furniture, decorations and the men's possessions were looted. The roof started to leak, causing many of the upper rooms to be damaged. Birds and vermin were the only animals happy to make it their home.

The house slowly became a decaying shadow of its former glory. But its 400-year-old bones were resistant to the elements, even if the fabric was deteriorating. Those massive oak beams, over 100 years old when they were felled in 1485, were now seasoned as hard as iron.

The medieval house would remain standing, patiently awaiting the next owner who would restore it to its former glory. It had survived wars, fires and the elements – a leaky roof was a mere bagatelle, a scratch on the fabric of the house. It had a future, it just needed a new owner (with plenty of money) to restore it to the grand, welcoming family home it once was.

* * * *

'*This is so, so sad,*' said Maud. '*We had such happy times here, and now, because of those disgusting men, our home is in danger of falling down.*'

'*I know, we can only pray that someone will come and rescue it. Fill it with a huge family, let laughter and happiness echo through the house as it did when we lived here,*' agreed Grace, *displaying an optimism she didn't feel inside.*

'*I hope it is soon. I feel our presence here is slowly waning; we are not as tethered to our home as we once were. Maybe ghosts have a lifetime too,*' wondered Maud.

Chapter 36
(1846)

*I*n 1837 a new monarch acceded to the throne following the death of William IV. She would usher in an era of unprecedented change to the lives of her subjects. Victoria was just 18 when she became Queen and would rule for 63 years – the longest reign of any monarch until Queen Elizabeth II. During her tenure, the British Empire would expand until one third of the globe was under its influence. It would be a time of unparalleled industrial, political, scientific, and social change within the country. The town of Bury St Edmunds would feel these tumultuous changes in many ways too. In particular, the momentous arrival of the railway. In just fifteen years since the world's first steam locomotive, Stephenson's Rocket, went into service, the country was already a dense spider web of tracks run by a host of ambitious train operators. At the end of 1830, there were just over 125 miles of railway lines in Britain, yet, by the end of 1871, this figure had jumped to more than 13,000 miles. In 1846 the age of the railway finally came to Bury St Edmunds.

* * * *

'Just another push, Mrs Sydenham, and baby will be out good an' proper.' Midwife Betsey Smithson waited expectantly as the mother, exhausted and covered in sweat, summoned her last few ounces of energy and did as instructed. It had the desired result.

'Wunnerful, ma'am, just wunnerful. Well done, you have another baby gal, said Betsey as she lifted the new born up for Julie Sydenham to see. Quickly completing the post-birth procedures, and then wrapping the already squalling baby in a swaddling blanket she handed her to Julie so the baby could start to nurse.

'Well tha' was nice an' quick. They get a bit easier each time don't they? That makes nine now, dunnit? Quite the brood you have. Two more and you'll ♀'ave your own football team!' Betsey laughed at her own joke. Julie was too tired to join in; the thought of another two births was overwhelming. True, the latest had arrived just a few short hours after her contractions started, but this new Victorian craze for large families was taking a toll on her 35-year-old body. This was her fourteenth confinement though, sadly, five of her children had not seen their third birthday.

There was a knock at the door. 'Julie? Julie, has it happened? Are you feeling well? How is the baby? May I come in?'

In spite of her tiredness Julie couldn't help but smile at her husband's concern and enthusiasm. 'Yes, James, you can come in and say hello to your latest daughter.'

The door flew open and Albert came dashing into the bedroom, two of their eldest children close behind.

He stopped and looked down at his latest child, asleep on Julie's chest. As with all his new born girls, he was smitten the very moment he laid eyes on her for the first time.

'Oh, Lord, she is perfect – and look, I believe she has your cute little nose and blue eyes. My darling, you have done us proud again. May I hold her?'

'Of course. And you two,' she said, looking at Daphne and Rachel, her twin eldest daughters, 'best wash your hands before you pick her up. Or you can look from a distance.' Obediently they both took a step backwards and gazed from afar while their father cooed over his gurgling baby.

'She is beautiful, just perfect, I am the happiest man alive. Thank you, darling.' He leant over, gave the baby back to Julie and kissed his wife gently and longingly on the lips.

'Oh, yuk. Please, Father, that's embarrassing. Mummy's just had a baby and you're getting all...amorous!' said Rachel, chiding her father with a smile.

Albert looked up from the baby to his teenage girls, 'How come girls start off so sweet and harmless, then in just a few years they become.so bossy?'

'That, dear husband, is one of life's certainties, and you have another one who in a few years will also be telling you what to do. Now, if you all don't mind I would like to bathe and rest. Betsey, would you tell the servants to prepare a bath for me? Albert, I am sure you have work to do with the arrival of the railway just a few days away?' Perhaps you could join me for some supper later?'

'Of course, my dear, I shall leave you to your ablutions. Girls, I am sure you have homework to do?'

Rachel and Daphne managed a simultaneous pout of disapproval at their father's question. They passed no comment, however the way they tutted then flounced out of the bedroom made clear they were not impressed with his parental suggestion.

'Those girls get more insolent by the day, Albert; I need you to take them in hand, teach them some manners,' suggested Julie, with a touch of a smile.

'Yes, my dear, you are right.'

'I will not have them talking to us in that manner. You must teach them to respect their parents, indeed anyone older than themselves.'

'Yes, my dear, I will do my best. Now you get some sleep; you have earned it!

Albert knew only too well his efforts at curtailing his headstrong daughters would come to nought. He dared not suggest their wilfulness may be something to do with his wife's Irish ancestry – a trait she was known to show herself when she wanted her own way.

Every time he confronted his daughters about such behaviour, they only had to flutter their eyes, smile beguilingly and the word 'no' vanished from his vocabulary. What is it with daughters and their fathers, he wondered, that makes it almost impossible to chastise them without feeling guilty – and completely useless?

His wife was right on one thing: The arrival of the first train into Bury was imminent and demanded his attention. His recalcitrant daughters would have to wait, thankfully.

Albert walked down the stairs across the newly painted great hall. Awash with investor funds to build the railway, the company also purchased the house for him, spending a fortune on its renovations before Albert and his growing family moved in. The house had turned out just as he and Julie planned. Elegant, but understated. Practical, yet with touches of finery such as the rococo paintings and classic lines of the furniture from Hepplewhite and Chippendale. It was a style that stated loud and clear: upper middle class Victorian values.

Along with four maids and a housekeeper, it was already full. The great hall still was the hub of the house; in the southern gable was the kitchen and parlour, at the back, storage, and upstairs the large rooms were divided between the staff and two of the eldest boys.

Above the great hall were now two bedrooms with windows overlooking the street. Four more children slept there. In the north gable was the nursery and bed for the youngest boy, Paul, only fifteen months old. Albert and Julie's room was there along with a study which, at the rate the family was growing, would inevitably become another bedroom. New privies, with flushing water, were close to all the bedrooms.

The cellar, where sixteen years earlier unspeakable events took place, was now stacked with food and provisions. A cold store of generous proportions for the vast amount the household consumed.

Most impressive of all: throughout the house Albert insisted that the newfangled invention of gas lamps be installed. A novelty in most houses, it provided a hitherto unknown light and airiness to the rooms, prolonging the amount of time people could read, play games and entertain themselves. A benefit enjoyed by his ever-expanding family

Albert left the house, grabbing his coat on the run from the hall stand, in a hurry to get to the station building site, check on its progress, then meet with his managers to finalise plans for the big day.

The new railway station in Northgate St was, due to a variety of factors, lack of material and labour being the main ones, now way behind schedule and unfinished. A temporary station was to be set up not far away to meet the first train. Albert, as an investor and director in the Eastern Union Railway Company, had the responsibility for making sure all was ready for the train's arrival – and the planned celebrations and dinner thereafter. It was unfortunate the formal opening was on December 7th – likely to be a cold or damp day. So some fifty carriages were hired to transport the 300 guests quickly from the train station to the hotel in the centre of the town. This cavalcade would need careful planning to ensure no hold-ups or accidents.

In fact, goods trains were already running on the line, the first only three days ago, and so far the track and trains performed with no problems. After the formal opening and an inspection by the Board of Trade, passenger services would commence just in time for Christmas.

The railway line now linked Bury to Colchester, Ipswich, Stowmarket and then London. As he explained over dinner the previous evening (to a less than enthusiastic audience of bored children), 'A journey that once took eighteen hours by coach would now take just over three hours from Bury to London. And in much more comfort!' enthused Albert.

Playing along, Julie dutifully asked a few questions, 'Is it expensive compared to coaches? How many trains a day will there be to make the journey to these towns?'

'I'm glad you asked that, my darling, as we have just decided on the fares. The trains to London will run five times a day. The fares will be eighteen shillings (*approximately £100 in today's values*) for first class. Compared to fourteen shillings for an uncomfortable coach seat! The cheapest will be just eight shillings for what–'

Julie interrupted what seemed like his rehearsal for the celebration dinner:

'That is wonderful news...I suspect the coachmen and coaching inns along the way are not best pleased about the railways taking all their business?'

Albert waved his hands dismissively, 'They will just have to accept it is progress, the age of the horse carriage is over. There's nothing they can do about it. You can't stop progress, Julie.'

But some were prepared to try.

Chapter 37

Four weeks earlier:

Ned Sherman owned the Kings Arms Inn just outside of Newmarket. He'd called a meeting there of three other inn owners who were likely to be put out of business if the railway line extended from Bury to Newmarket and thence to Cambridge. He not only owned the inn, but also four coaches and six teams of horses. The others in the group were equally dependent on the Bury to London coach network and had invested heavily over the years in horses and equipment. The railways would put them all out of business.

There was a palpable atmosphere of pessimism. For decades the coach routes provided a steady living, Add to that selling food and drink, and overnight accommodation, and all the men present had a lot to lose with the inexorable and frighteningly quick spread of the railway network.

'I hear they're already buying up land 'tween here and Cambridge; those thieving bastards from the Eastern Union Railway are paying stupid money to farmers. I reckon this time next year we'll see those thundering engines rattling through our fields.' Ned's dire predictions evinced nods of agreement from the other men.

'But what can we do 'bout it?' asked Joe Dinwoody, owner of the Racing Arms, west of Newmarket.

'They've got more money than we 'ave, and those crooked MPs just pass bills allowing them to do what they like with the land. Can't really blame the farmers for taking their money – I would!'

The others agreed. Despite several tankards of ale, their mood was downbeat; the prospect of a handsome living disappearing before their eyes in a matter of months had them all worried. There seemed little they could do to stop it.

'My brother near Ipswich owned an inn, he went out of business just two months after the railway opened,' said the third member of the group – Derek Rowbotham, owner of a tavern in the delightfully named Six Mile Bottom, 'People are in such a hurry now'days the train gets them to where they're going in no time. 'Tis pricey but the toffs can afford it.'

Ned banged his tankard down on the table to awaken them from their despairing funk.

'I say we make it as hard as possible for them to build this railway. Make it so expensive they take their money elsewhere – build a railway somewhere else north of here that won't affect our business. I dunno. Anythin' to give us a chance to sell what we have before prices for horses and carriages drop like a stone.'

The men looked at Ned, taken aback by his outburst, nevertheless curious as to what his plan, if any, was.

'So what do you have in mind, Ned?' asked Derek. He took a sup of ale, while he waited for Ned's reply. He was a law-abiding man, married with five children. If Ned was suggesting some kind of protest, he'd go along, no harm in that. Anything more drastic and he couldn't be involved. So he was shocked at Ned's reply.

'Unless we do something that hits their pockets, they'll take no notice. I'm thinking we wait 'til the day the line opens and we blow up some of the line. Mebbe a bridge that will take them months to repair...'

After a shocked silence, Joe Dinwoody stared quizzically at Ned. 'Are you serious? We're innkeepers, not some kinda revolutionaries. Anyways I know nothing about blowing up things. Sounds dangerous to me, let alone against the law. If that's the best plan you can come up with to stop the railways – sorry, count me out, Ned, it's too risky for me.'

Derek nodded his head in agreement. 'It'll get us into serious trouble, Ned, if we're caught. I'm not going to gaol for this. I'll take my chances, find another way to make a living. Sorry, not my cup of tea at all.'

'I'm up for it; we've gotta protect our way of making a living, it's the only way they'll take any notice.'

They turned to look at the youngest member of the group, Arthur Cooper. In his twenties, he'd just inherited his father's inn, The White Hart on the High Street in Newmarket. With his grand plans to expand the business now in jeopardy, he felt he had little to lose.

Ned latched onto the only supporter of his bold plan. 'See, you two lily livers, someone here has the bollocks to take these people on. Good on yer, Arthur, maybe it only needs two of us to stop these shitheads!'

'Yep, count me in, Ned. But I've another idea that might make those railway types think twice. Why don't we threaten the workers; or the bosses, even better?' Make their lives a misery?' Arthur paused to see how his idea would go down.

Ned was all for it.

'Brilliant idea, Arthur! Start with that loudmouth owner who's been in all the papers spouting about how great the railways are for everyone...what's his name? Albert...Albert Sydenham, that's it. Mebbe if we send him a letter saying his children are in danger if his railway comes this way...that'd really scare the shits out of them! Ned was warming to his outrageous plan. 'What d'yer think, fellas?'

'I think yer outta yer ferkin' mind, Ned,' said Derek. He stood up, finished his drink, put on his coat as he made to leave, making it clear. 'I'm wanting nothing more to do with these crazy ideas. Best of luck guys...see you 'round.' There was a blast of cold air as he opened the door, then slammed it shut as he hurriedly left the conspirators to their lethal schemes.

'Jim? Are you in on this?'

'Nope, it's not for me either, sorry. I'm with Derek, it's too dangerous – and could get us in serious trouble. I think I better go before I hear summat I shouldn't.' He stood up, put his coat on and followed Derek out into the cold night, not waiting for the other two to try and persuade him otherwise.

By the end of the evening Arthur and Ned put a rough and ready plan together. Arthur, full of enthusiasm, offered to round up a few friends to help if needed.

'They work for me, they know if this happens they'll be out of a job. They'll be happy to blow up summat. Just need to find some powder now. How we gonna do that?'

'Leave that to me; I know people who can get us some of the stuff, and tell me how to use it. Let's meet agin here in a week to sort out the details. Just you an' me, keep your friends out of it for the time being. Now you keep schtum about this, you hear me?'

It was a busy week for Ned. He eventually ascertained the most effective place to bring the Ipswich-Bury line to a halt would be to blow up the tunnel under Stoke Hill. It was over 350 yards in length, so plenty of places to put the gunpowder without being seen. Luckily, his brother-in-law, who worked at the quarry in Red Lodge, provided two barrels of gunpowder and some very hasty instructions on how to ignite it with the fuses. Ned's eagerness to rush ahead with his plan meant he paid only cursory attention on how best to handle and use the gunpowder. He'd worry about that when he got to the tunnel.

Next was to find out where the man Albert Sydenham lived. A friend who ran a tavern on Churchgate St knew the address. Armed with that information Ned crafted three letters, each threatening ill fortune on Albert and his family if the railway extended westwards to Newmarket. He arranged for the letters to be sent on three different days in the week leading up to the official opening of the line. The final letter also warned of 'unfortunate consequences to railways property' if any plans were announced of a new line heading towards Newmarket. The fact he was going to blow up the tunnel anyway was a duplicity Ned found amusing.

He planned the tunnel explosion early on the day of the celebrations on December 7th. So, he hoped, preventing the first passenger train full of dignitaries reaching Bury. 'Let's royally fuck up their day,' he told Arthur.

He met Arthur and two other men before dawn. There was too much to arrange for just the two of them, so for a small fee two young stable boys had been drafted in to help. They carefully loaded the two barrels of gunpowder onto the carts, resting them on a thick layer of straw, then covering them with even more to stop any movement. No one had any experience dealing with such lethal material, but all knew that if it went off by accident, they would be blown to smithereens.

As a result, Ned was the only one willing to drive the cart. The others wisely followed some distance behind on horseback. It was a two-hour journey to the tunnel, and they arrived just as the sun rose attempting to break through a heavy winter cloud cover. It was cold and damp, and once inside the tunnel, after a few paces they could barely see where they were going. Reluctant to use torches for fear they might set the gunpowder off they stopped only yards from the entrance.

'Right, this'll do. You men, go get the barrels, we'll place them right against the wall here. Be gentle, for chrissake! And keep that fuse taper dry.' It took but a few minutes for the men to get the barrels from the cart and place them where Ned directed. Still petrified they might explode at any minute, everyone except Ned fled back outside the tunnel. The fuse tapers, Ned was told, would take one minute to reach the barrels. Timing was crucial. He wanted the explosion timed so the train would be stranded in the tunnel to create maximum panic and fear. Now he realised he had no way to judge how quickly the train was travelling so the gunpowder went off at the right time; too early and the train could stop before it reached the tunnel, too late and it could be through and on its way to Bury unhindered.

He didn't reveal his dilemma to the other men. He decided to place one at the far end of the tunnel, and another further towards

Ipswich. As soon as one heard the train he would alert the man at the tunnel entrance, who would bellow to Ned to light the fuse. It was pure guesswork, but with only an hour before the train was due to arrive Ned cursed his stupidity at not listening to his brother-in-law more carefully. Whatever happened, he reasoned, the explosion would wreck the tunnel and delay the start of the service between the two towns.

He kept inspecting the long fuses, each around twenty feet long, ensuring they were tightly fitted inside the barrels as his brother-in-law instructed. He kept his tinderbox for lighting them inside his shirt, away from the dampness. On tenterhooks, he paced up and down the tracks, straining to hear a shout from the other end of the tunnel.

It began to rain, heavily. Then the heavens opened, pouring torrents of water onto the track. Ned sheltered inside the tunnel, keeping a close eye on the barrels. To his horror he saw water dripping down the brick walls of the tunnel, forming pools alongside the track. Soon they would rise enough to reach the barrels. To make it worse the fuses were now in danger of becoming too wet to ignite.

Panicking, Ned decided it might be best to detonate the barrels now before the rain made them and the fuses useless. Just as he moved towards them, he heard an echoing shout from the depths of the tunnel. 'The train's coming!'

'Shit, shit, shit,' Ned cursed as he took out his tinderbox and knelt beside the two fuses. Desperately he tried to get them to light. The harder he struck the flint on the fire steel trying to get a spark onto the fuse the more frantic he became as nothing caused them to light. Soon he heard the sound of the train entering the tunnel. Still he couldn't get the fuses to take the sparks. Frustrated, he ran back outside of the tunnel and hid behind a stone wall. Seconds later, in an avalanche of smoke, noise, sparks and clattering of steel on steel, the train emerged from the tunnel. Ned could see inside the carriages people laughing, drinking and celebrating. It sickened him to the core. An opportunity to make those snobs suffer was gone.

Ned was determined to destroy the tunnel anyway, proving to himself he could complete the plan, albeit not as he'd envisaged, and show those money-hungry businessmen they couldn't have it all their own way. He stood up and walked towards the tunnel. Tragically for him, what his tinderbox couldn't do, the deluge of sparks from the train's funnel had accomplished with ease. As Ned entered the gloom, his last vision was two lines of fizzing sparks snaking their way towards the barrels. He turned to run, but it was too late; the explosion, concentrated by the narrowness of the tunnel, exploded like a giant cannon, propelling an eruption of bricks, earth, stone and debris along the track and into the air. Ned's body was flung over 150 feet, the force depositing him in the middle of a field next to the railway line.

Arthur and his two sidekicks heard the explosion and rushed full of excitement to see the result. Initially thrilled at seeing the tunnel entrance blocked, they grew concerned about Ned's whereabouts. It took but a few minutes of searching to find his mangled body in the field, surrounded by some bemused cows warily sniffing his corpse.

'Oh, sweet fucking Jesus!' cried Arthur kneeling down beside Ned. 'He's dead. Musta been too close to the explosion, damn idiot. Wonder if the train's trapped inside?'

'I ain't gonna look, we need to get away from here real quick, before people turn up wonderin' what the noise was,' said one of the young men. And without waiting for any further instructions, he ran to his horse and took off over the fields.

Arthur looked up at the other man. 'C'mon, Jack, give me a hand getting Ned onto my horse. If we leave his body here eventually someone might find out who he is, and we'll get dragged into this mess.'

The two of them lifted Ned's bloodied body onto Arthur's horse and promptly rode off towards Bury, taking a circuitous route to avoid the town. On the way back they concocted a story that they'd been hog hunting, Ned fell off his horse and was attacked by the wild hogs while on the ground. It was a flimsy tale, but it would have to do. They arrived back at the King's Arms, leaving Ned's body with his hysterical wife, and the fabricated cause of his death. The poor woman, who knew nothing of her husband's unlawful escapades, was left to deal with his unexpected and gory death.

No one on the train heard the explosion; it wasn't until some hours later that the news arrived of the incident. Albert was horrified, then annoyed. He quickly connected the event with the strange, threatening letters he'd received over the previous week. Albert didn't know the main perpetrator was dead, so news of the explosion made the content of the letters all the more plausible. But for today he was determined nothing would spoil the celebrations.

The train arrived on time and the guests including the mayor of Bury, local lords and ladies, MPs and any dignitary connected to the railway or the town disgorged onto the fleet of carriages that took them to the Concert Room on Angel Hill for their celebratory dinner.

The room was filled with the great and the good of the county, unaware of how close they had been to disaster. The mood was jubilant, wine flowed, and diamonds glittered in the newly installed gas lamps' unflattering glare. Guests basked in the glow of success. The spirit of Victorian enterprise, invention and determination suffused the room. The lavish festivities lasted until evening with several lengthy, self-congratulatory speeches, including one from Albert, where he repeated his words from earlier that week at home:

'Welcome my lords, ladies, Mr Mayor, honoured guests. Today is a truly historic one for this town. Now for the first time a journey that once took eighteen hours by coach now takes just over three hours by train from Bury to London. And with a level of comfort hitherto many could only dream about! And at cost that anyone can afford: For everyone's convenience our trains will go to London five times a day. The fares will be just eighteen shillings for those in first class. Compared to fourteen shillings for an uncomfortable coach seat – and the delightful aroma of horse dung!'

He waited for the laughter to subside, then continued, 'And the cheapest fare will be just eight shillings for what we are calling the 'Parliamentary Fare' – because it is our earnest wish to encourage the working class to use this new and speedy way to travel. Honoured guests, you are witnessing a revolution in the way we travel. It is the way of the future, a new era, for everyone of every class!' Applause rippled around the room.

Then, as if to spite whomever was behind the bombing and the sinister letters, Albert finished with a pledge to his audience: 'But this is just the start, honoured guests. Within two years we will have built a network of railway lines not just connecting every major town in East Anglia, but the villages as well. England will soon be a country where you can travel from one end to the other speedily, affordably and in comfort. Welcome to the greatest revolution in transport since the invention of the wheel!'

In the weeks that followed the triumphant arrival of the railway to Bury, the threats to Albert and his family never materialised. The damaged tunnel was repaired within a week and the trains ran like clockwork, until a strange accident occurred.

It was early in February when an engine broke down at Bury station. With no spare train immediately available the stationmaster, Gideon Hatchwell, called in four horses. Enterprisingly he hitched them up to the two coaches, controlling them with lengthy reins from the top of the first carriage. He urged them down the track towards Ipswich and off they trotted at a steady pace.

Not wanting to miss such an adventure, the station porter climbed up and sat on top of the second carriage. After an hour they reached Thurston station. There James Walton, the stationmaster, joined in the fun and sat next to Gideon Hatchwell, enjoying the panoramic views of the Suffolk countryside. They negotiated two bridges with just a few inches to spare above their heads. They eventually reached Haughley, where a replacement locomotive awaited them. They decided to continue the fun and stay on the train until it reached Ipswich. Now they were perched on top of the luggage piled high on the first carriage, not realising they were higher up than the top of the funnel of the locomotive.

Fatally, both now chose to ride with their backs to the engine. They passed under one bridge without incident but the next, known as Jennings Bridge, was much lower. Before they could move out of the way, their heads hit the bridge so violently Walton died immediately and Hatchwell soon after. Only the porter lived to explain what had happened – and he was promptly sacked from his job.

Notwithstanding a less than stellar safety record, the Eastern Union Railway continued to expand and prosper, absorbing other less profitable or failing local railway companies along the way. The route to Newmarket was completed within a year and, with a tragic irony, Ned Sherman's widow discovered the inn and the land around it were directly on the proposed path of the new railway's track. She was offered a generous price for her property, which she readily took, and moved to Cheveley to live with her sister. She never knew the real cause of her husband's death and the reason behind it, but being a practical (and financially desperate) woman, even if she had, the EUR's offer was too good to turn down.

Albert stayed with the growing company, becoming a very wealthy man, although he never moved from the house in Whiting St. The family grew by two more children, though by that time the twin girls were married, and in 1860 Rachel gave birth to a boy they called Neil.

* * * *

It was July 21st 1869, Neil's ninth birthday. To celebrate, Albert took the whole family down by train to London's docks to see what at the time was one of the country's greatest inventions: the huge steam-powered ship, the SS Great Eastern, designed and built by the country's most famous engineer, Isambard Kingdom Brunel. It was capable of carrying 4000 passengers from England to Australia without refuelling – the only ship in the world capable of such a feat. Recently repurposed, the SS Great Eastern helped lay the world's first transatlantic telegraph cable. For Albert the ship was the pinnacle of engineering brilliance.

As they watched her steam slowly up the Thames, docking close to Tower Bridge. Neil was wide-eyed with excitement. Awestruck by her size, he asked if he could go aboard.

'I'm sorry, Neil; I tried to arrange it but I was told it wasn't possible, but we can go down to the dock and take a closer look if you like.'

They stayed for an hour, walking up and down the dockside, while Albert pointed out some of the many innovative features of the ship. Eventually the boy grew tired and they made their way back to Liverpool St station. On the way they passed huge long trenches being dug in the ground.

'What are they doing there, Grandfather?' asked the sleepy boy.

'It's another new form of transport; they're calling it, I think, the Underground. Trains just like ours will take passenger carriages in tunnels from one end of London to another. I tell you, Neil, our transport system will be the envy of the world. Who knows what we'll invent next? I believe future decades will show the world just how inventive this Victorian era has been. You are privileged to have lived through such memorable times!'

Neil didn't hear his grandfather's grand vision of the future; he was fast asleep dreaming of becoming captain of a giant steamship.

Epilogue

It's **July 21st 1969**, and a fifteen-year-old boy called Paul is glued to a flickering black and white television set watching, with his father David, the grainy images of a man climbing down a short stepladder onto the surface of the moon.

Holding his breath for fear of some last-minute mishap, he breathed a sigh of relief – as did the rest of the world – when he heard the immortal words uttered by Neil Armstrong...'*That's one small step for man, one giant leap for mankind.*'

'When I was your age, Paul, a car was still a new and novel way to travel; now, in my lifetime, we have achieved a moon landing. Whatever next?' wondered David. Paul shrugged his shoulders. 'Who knows, Father? Who knows? Maybe when I grow up I can go there too!'

Almost sixty years later no such momentous developments in travel have impacted humankind in such a way as the previous hundred. Even by 2069 it seems unlikely we will see such a dramatic leap forward as witnessed since Stephenson's Rocket in 1829 until the dawn of space travel.

In the space of four generations travel had changed from horse-drawn carriages to sending rockets, and their passengers, to another world a quarter of a million miles away. Such a 'giant leap for mankind' is likely never to be repeated.

* * * *

2024: The house in Whiting St still stands. Now divided into three homes, it is a testament to its builders and numerous subsequent owners that it still is as solid and handsome today as when it was built in 1485. Over five centuries it has witnessed history first hand, from wars to pestilence, fire and neglect. The venerable house and its occupants have lived through some of the most turbulent, dangerous and exciting times in English history. It has been entertaining trying to imagine who they were and what they experienced.

Maybe in 2485 someone will write the next instalment of the house's history, as it celebrates its 1000th birthday (it's possible it could still be there: a wooden-framed barn in Essex, England – The Barley Barn – was built in 1220, making it over 800 years old).

What stories will it have to tell?

About the Author

Paul H Rowney has spent most of his working life in magazine publishing.

Born in England, in 1954 he moved to America in 2004 and now lives near Nashville, Tennessee on a farm with his wife Sheri, seven dogs and a menagerie of other two and four legged animals.

This is his sixth book.

A final favour:

You have made your way to the end of the book! Congratulations!

I hope you have enjoyed the reading journey, if so, please leave a review on my Amazon page for 'Ancient Hallways'.

It not only helps other readers make informed decisions before buying, but provides me with helpful feedback on your thoughts about the book.

Thank you.

Printed in Great Britain
by Amazon

54302153R00245